I have edited Clive Gilson's books for over a decade now – he's prolific and can turn his hand to many genres. poetry, short fiction, contemporary novels, folklore, and science fiction – and the common theme is that none of them ever fails to take my breath away. There's something in each story that is either memorably poignant, hauntingly unnerving, or sidesplittingly funny.

Lorna Howarth, *The Write Factor*

Tales From The World's Firesides is a grand project. I've collected "000's of traditional texts as part of other projects, and while many of the original texts are available through channels like Project Gutenberg, some of the narratives can be hard to read by modern readers, & so the Fireside project was born. Put simply, I collect, collate & adapt traditional tales from around the world & publish them as a modern archive. *Part 4* covers a selection of tales from the lands that border the Eastern Mediterranean and its hinterlands. I'm not laying any claim to insight or specialist knowledge, but these collections are born out of my love of storytelling & I hope that you'll share my affection for traditional tales, myths & legends.

Istanbul vector Image by hal1ok from Pixabay

Cover image of Istanbul by Sinan Kızılkaya from Pixabay

Tales from the Meddahs

Traditional tales, fables and sagas

from the Turkish tradition ...

Compiled, Adapted & Edited by Clive Gilson

Tales from the World's Firesides

Book 1 in Part 4 of the series: The Middle East

(al-sharq al-awsat)

Tales from the Meddahs, edited by Clive Gilson, Solitude, Bath, UK

www.clivegilson.com

First print edition © 2023, Clive Gilson

All rights reserved. No portion of this book may be reproduced in any form without permission from the publisher, except as permitted by United Kingdom copyright law.

This is a work of fiction. Names, characters, places, and incidents either are the products of the author's imagination or are used fictitiously. Any resemblance to actual persons, living or dead, businesses, companies, events, or locales is entirely coincidental.

Printed by IngramSpark

ISBN: 978-1-915081-13-1

CONTENTS

Preface

Madschun

The Gardener And His Wife

How The Hodja Saved Allah

The Widow And Her Friend

Better Is The Folly Of Woman Than The Wisdom Of Man

The Old Man And His Son

The Hanoum And The Unjust Cadi

What Happened To Hadji, A Merchant Of The Bezestan

The Lion And The Man

How The Junkman Travelled To Find Treasure In His Own Backyard

The Shark

How Chapkin Halid Became Chief Detective

The Clown Turned First Soldier, Then Merchant

The Ghost Of The Spring And The Shrew

The Boy Who Found Fear At LAst

The River And Its Source

Stone-Patience And Knife-Patience

How Cobbler Ahmet Became The Chief Astrologer

The Lamb And The wolf

The Serpent-Peri And The Magic Mirror

The Wise Son Of Ali Pasha

The Insects, The Bee, And The Ant

The Merciful Khan

The Padishah Of The Forty Peris

The Fox And The Crab

The Prayer Rug And The Dishonest Steward

The World's Most Beauteous Damsel

The Goats And The Wolves

The Goose, The Eye, The Daughter, And The Arm

The Forty Princes And The Seven-Headed Dragon

The Lion, The Wolf, And The Fox

The Forty Wise Men

The Crow-Peri

The Fox And The Sparrow

How The Priest Knew That It Would Snow

The Syrian Priest And The Young Man

The Wind-Demon

Who Was The Thirteenth Son

The Converted Cat

The Magic Turban, The Magic Whip, And The Magic Carpet

Paradise Sold By The Yard

The Horse And His Rider

The Piece Of Liver

The Archer And The Trumpeter

The Metamorphosis

The Wolf, The Fox, And The Shepherd's Dog

The Calif Omar

The Cinder-Youth

Kalaidji Avram Of Balata

How Mehmet Ali Pasha Of Egypt Administered Justice

The Horse-Devil And The Witch

How The Farmer Learned To Cure His Wife—A Turkish Æsop

The Silent Princess

The Golden-Haired Children

The Language Of Birds

The Swallow's Advice

Mad Mehmed

We Know Not What The Dawn May Bring Forth

Old Men Made Young

The Rose-Beauty

The Bribe

The Three Orange-Peris

How The Devil Lost His Wager

The Stag-Prince

The Effects Of Raki

Historical Notes

About The Editor

Tales of the Meddahs: Tales from the Turkish tradition

PREFACE

I've been collecting and telling stories for a couple of decades now, having had several of my own fictional works published in recent years. My particular focus is on short story writing in the realms of magical realities and science fiction fantasies.

I've always drawn heavily on traditional folk and fairy tales, and in so doing have amassed a digital collection of many thousands of these tales from around the world. It has been one of my long-standing ambitions to gather these stories together and to create a library of tales that tell the stories of places and peoples from all corners of our world.

One of the main motivations for me in undertaking the project is to collect and tell stories that otherwise might be lost or, at best, be forgotten by predominantly English-speaking readers. Given that a lot of my sources are from early collectors, particularly covering works produced in the late eighteenth century, throughout the nineteenth century, and in the early years of the twentieth century, I do make every effort to adapt stories for a modern reader. Early collectors had a different world view to many of us today, and often expressed views about race and gender, for example, that we find difficult to reconcile in the early years of the twenty-first century. I try, although with varying degrees of success, to update these stories with sensitivity while trying to stay as true to the original spirit of each story as I can.

I also want to assure readers that I try hard not to comment on or appropriate originating cultures. It is almost certainly true that the early collectors of these tales, with their then prevalent world views, have made assumptions

Tales of the Meddahs: Tales from the Turkish tradition

about the originating cultures that have given us these tales. I hope that you'll accept my mission to preserve these tales, however and wherever I find them, as just that. I have, therefore, made sure that every story has a full attribution, covering both the original collector / writer and the collection title that this version has been adapted from, as well as having notes about publishers and other relevant and, I hope, interesting source data. Wherever possible I have added a cultural or indigenous attribution as well, although for some of the titles, the country-based theme is obvious.

This volume, *Tales from the Meddahs*, is the first in a set of collections covering indigenous tales from what we in Europe know now as The Middle East. *Tales from the Meddahs* covers a wide range of sources and tales that have emerged from the post-Byzantine traditions of the Turkish peoples.

These collections will grow over coming years to tell lost and forgotten tales from every continent, and even then, I'll just be scratching the surface of the world's lore and love. That's the great gift in storytelling. Since the first of our ancestors sat around in a cave, contemplating an ape's place in the world, we have, as a species, continued to tell each other stories of magic and cunning and caution and love. All those years ago, when I began to read through tales from the Celts, tales from Indonesia, tales from Africa and the Far East, tales from everywhere, one of the things that struck me clearly was just how similar are our roots. We share characters and characteristics. The nature of these tales is so similar underneath the local camouflage. Human beings clearly share a storytelling heritage so much deeper than the world that we see superficially as always having been just as it is now.

These tales were originally told by firelight as a way of preserving histories and educating both adult and child. These tales form part of our shared heritage, witches, warts, fantastic beasts, and all. They can be dark and violent. They can be sweet and loving. They are we and we are they in so many ways. I've loved reading and re-reading these stories. I hope that you do too.

Tales of the Meddahs: Tales from the Turkish tradition

Clive

Bath 2023

Tales of the Meddahs: Tales from the Turkish tradition

Tales of the Meddahs: Tales from the Turkish tradition

MADSCHUN

This story has been adapted from Andrew Lang's version of the same tale that originally appeared in The Olive Fairy Book, published in 1907 by Longmans, Green and Co., London and New York. This tale was originally adapted by Andrew Lang from Türkische Volksmärchen aus Stambul, by Dr. Ignácz Kúnos. and published in 1905 by E. J. Brill of Leiden.

Once upon a time there lived, in a small cottage among some hills, a woman with her son, and, to her great grief, the young man, though hardly more than twenty years of age, had not as much hair on his head as a baby. But old as he looked, the youth was very idle, and whatever trade his mother put him to he refused to work, and in a few days always came home again.

On a fine summer morning he was lying as usual half asleep in the little garden in front of the cottage when the sultan's daughter came riding by, followed by a number of gaily dressed ladies. The youth lazily raised himself on his elbow to look at her, and that one glance changed his whole nature.

"I will marry her and nobody else," he thought. And jumping up, he went to find his mother.

"You must go at once to the sultan and tell him that I want his daughter for my wife," he said.

"What?" shouted the old woman, shrinking back into a corner, for nothing but sudden madness could explain such an amazing errand.

"Don't you understand? You must go at once to the sultan and tell him that I want his daughter for my wife," repeated the youth impatiently.

Tales of the Meddahs: Tales from the Turkish tradition

"But - but, do you know what you are saying?" stammered the mother. "You will learn no trade, and have only the five gold pieces left you by your father, and can you really expect that the sultan would give his daughter to a penniless bald-pate like you?"

"That is my affair; do as I bid you." And neither day nor night did her son cease tormenting her, till, in despair, she put on her best clothes, and wrapped her veil about her, and went over the hill to the palace.

It was the day that the sultan set apart for hearing the complaints and petitions of his people, so the woman found no difficulty in gaining admission to his presence.

"Do not think me mad, O Excellency," she began, "though I know I must seem like it. But I have a son who, since his eyes have rested on the veiled face of the princess, has not left me in peace for a day or night till I consented to come to the palace, and to ask your Excellency for your daughter's hand. It was in vain I answered that my head might pay the forfeit of my boldness, but he would listen to nothing. Therefore, am I here; do with me even as you will!"

Now the sultan always loved anything out of the common, and this situation was new indeed. So, instead of ordering the trembling creature to be flogged or cast into prison, as some other sovereigns might have done, he merely said, "Bid your son come here."

The old woman stared in astonishment at such a reply. But when the sultan repeated his words even more gently than before, and did not look in anywise angered, she took courage, and bowing again she hastened homeward.

"Well, how have you sped?" asked her son eagerly as she crossed the threshold.

"You are to go up to the palace without delay, and speak to the sultan himself," replied the mother. And when he heard the good news, his face lightened up so wonderfully that his mother thought what a pity it was that he had no hair, as then he would be quite handsome.

Tales of the Meddahs: Tales from the Turkish tradition

"Ah, the lightning will not fly more swiftly," cried he. And in another instant, he was out of her sight.

When the sultan beheld the bald head of his daughter's wooer, he no longer felt in the mood for joking, and resolved that he must somehow shake himself free of such an unwelcome lover. But as he had summoned the young man to the palace, he could hardly dismiss him without a reason, so he hastily said,

"I hear you wish to marry my daughter. Well and good. But the man who is to be her husband must first collect all the birds in the world and bring them into the gardens of the palace; for hereto no birds have made their homes in the trees."

The young man was filled with despair at the sultan's words. How was he to snare all these birds? Even if he did succeed in catching them it would take years to carry them to the palace! Still, he was too proud to let the sultan think that he had given up the princess without a struggle, so he took a road that led past the palace and walked on, not noticing where he went.

In this manner a week slipped by, and at length he found himself crossing a desert with great rocks scattered here and there. In the shadow cast by one of these was seated a holy man or dervish, as he was called, who motioned to the youth to sit beside him.

"Something is troubling you, my son," said the holy man, "tell me what it is, as I may be able to help you."

"O, my father," answered the youth, "I wish to marry the princess of my country; but the sultan refuses to give her to me unless I can collect all the birds in the world and bring them into his garden. And how can I, or any other man, do that?"

"Do not despair," replied the dervish, "it is not so difficult as it sounds. Two days' journey from here, in the path of the setting sun, there stands a cypress tree, larger than any other cypress that grows upon the earth. Sit down where the shadow is darkest, close to the trunk, and keep very still. By-and-by you will hear a mighty rushing of wings, and all the birds in the world will come

Tales of the Meddahs: Tales from the Turkish tradition

and nestle in the branches. Be careful not to make a sound till everything is quiet again, and then say 'Madschun!' At that the birds will be forced to remain where they are - not one can move from its perch; and you will be able to place them all over your head and arms and body, and in this way you must carry them to the sultan."

With a glad heart the young man thanked the dervish, and paid such close heed to his directions that, a few days later, a strange figure covered with soft feathers walked into the presence of the sultan. The princess's father was filled with surprise, for never had he seen such a sight before. Oh, how lovely were those little bodies, and bright frightened eyes! Soon a gentle stirring was heard, and what a multitude of wings unfolded themselves: blue wings, yellow wings, red wings, green wings. And when the young man whispered, "Go," they first flew in circles round the sultan's head, and then disappeared through the open window, to choose homes in the garden.

"I have done your bidding, O Sultan, and now give me the princess," said the youth. And the sultan answered hurriedly:

"Yes! Oh, yes! You have pleased me well! Only one thing remains to turn you into a husband that any girl might desire. That head of yours, you know - it is so very bald! Get it covered with nice thick curly hair, and then I will give my daughter to you. You are so clever that I am sure this will give you no trouble at all."

Silently the young man listened to the sultan's words, and silently he sat in his mother's kitchen for many days to come, till, one morning, the news reached him that the sultan had betrothed his daughter to the son of the vizir, and that the wedding was to be celebrated without delay in the palace. With that he arose in wrath and made his way quickly and secretly to a side door, used only by the workmen who kept the building in repair, and unseen by anyone, he made his way into the mosque, and then entered the palace by a gallery which opened straight into the great hall. Here the bride and bridegroom and two or three friends were assembled, waiting for the appearance of the sultan for the contract to be signed.

Tales of the Meddahs: Tales from the Turkish tradition

"Madschun!" whispered the youth from above. And instantly everyone remained rooted to the ground; and some messengers whom the sultan had sent to see that all was ready shared the same fate.

At length, angry and impatient, the sultan went down to behold with his own eyes what had happened, but as nobody could give him any explanation, he bade one of his attendants to fetch a magician, who dwelt near one of the city gates, to remove the spell which had been cast by some evil genius.

"It is your own fault," said the magician, when he had heard the sultan's story. "If you had not broken your promise to the young man, your daughter would not have had this ill befall her. Now there is only one remedy, and the bridegroom you have chosen must yield his place to the bald-headed youth."

Sore though he was in his heart, the sultan knew that the magician was wiser than he and so, he despatched his most trusted servants to seek out the young man without a moment's delay and bring him to the palace. The youth, who all this time had been hiding behind a pillar, smiled to himself when he heard these words, and, hastening home, he said to his mother, "If messengers from the sultan should come here and ask for me, be sure you answer that it is a long while since I went away, and that you cannot tell where I may be, but that if they will give you money enough for your journey, as you are very poor, you will do your best to find me." Then he hid himself in the loft above, so that he could listen to all that passed.

The next minute someone knocked loudly at the door, and the old woman jumped up and opened it.

"Is your bald-headed son here?" asked the man outside. "If so, let him come with me, as the sultan wishes to speak with him directly."

"Alas, sir," replied the woman, putting a corner of her veil to her eyes, "he left me long since, and since that day no news of him has reached me."

"Oh, good lady, can you not guess where he may be? The sultan intends to bestow on him the hand of his daughter, and he is certain to give a large reward to the man who brings him back."

Tales of the Meddahs: Tales from the Turkish tradition

"He never told me where he was going," answered the crone, shaking her head. "But it is a great honour that the sultan does him, and well worth some trouble. There are places where, perhaps, he may be found, but they are known to me only, and I am a poor woman and have no money for the journey."

"Oh, that will not stand in the way," cried the man. "In this purse are a thousand gold pieces; spend them freely. Tell me where I can find him, and you shall have as many more."

"Very well," said she, "it is a bargain; and now farewell, for I must make some preparations; but in a few days at furthest you shall hear from me."

For nearly a week both the old woman and her son were careful not to leave the house till it was dark, lest they should be seen by any of the neighbours, and as they did not even kindle a fire or light a lantern, everyone supposed that the cottage was deserted. At length one fine morning, the young man got up early and dressed himself, and put on his best turban, and after a hasty breakfast took the road to the palace.

The huge guard before the door evidently expected him, for without a word he let him pass, and another attendant who was waiting inside conducted him straight into the presence of the sultan, who welcomed him gladly.

"Ah, my son! Where have you hidden yourself all this time?" said he. And the bald-headed man answered, "Oh, Sultan! Fairly I won your daughter, but you broke your word, and would not give her to me. Then my home grew hateful to me, and I set out to wander through the world! But now that you have repented of your ill-faith, I have come to claim the wife who is mine of right. Therefore, bid your vizir prepare the contract."

So, a fresh contract was prepared, and at the wish of the new bridegroom was signed by the sultan and the vizir in the chamber where they met. After this was done, the youth begged the sultan to lead him to the princess, and together they entered the big hall, where everyone was standing exactly as they were when the young man had uttered the fatal word.

"Can you remove the spell?" asked the sultan anxiously.

Tales of the Meddahs: Tales from the Turkish tradition

"I think so," replied the young man (who, to say the truth, was a little anxious himself), and stepping forward, he cried, "Let the victims of Madschun be free!"

No sooner were the words uttered than the statues returned to life, and the bride placed her hand joyfully in that of her new bridegroom. As for the old one, he vanished completely, and no one ever knew what became of him.

Tales of the Meddahs: Tales from the Turkish tradition

Tales of the Meddahs: Tales from the Turkish tradition

THE GARDENER AND HIS WIFE

This story has been adapted from Turkish Literature by Epiphanius Wilson, A.M., published in 1901 by P. F. Collier & Son, New York.

A certain Gardener had a young and pretty woman for his wife. One day, when, according to her habit, she had gone to wash her linen in the river, the Gardener, entering his house, said to himself, "I do not know, really, whether my wife loves me. I must put it to the test."

On saying this, he stretched himself full length upon the ground, in the middle of the room, as if dead. Soon, his wife returned, carrying her linen, and perceived her husband's condition.

"Tired and hungry as I am," she said to herself, "is it necessary that I should begin at once to mourn and lament? Would it not be better to begin by eating a morsel of something?"

She accordingly cut off a piece of dried, smoked meat, and set it to roast on the coals. Then she hurriedly went upstairs to the garret, took a pot of milk, drank some of it, and put the rest on the fire. At this moment, an old woman, her neighbour, entered, with an earthen vessel in her hand, and asked for some burning coals.

"Keep your eye on this pot," she said to the old woman, rising to her feet. Then she burst into sobs and lamentations. "Alas!" she cried, "my poor husband is dead!"

Tales of the Meddahs: Tales from the Turkish tradition

The neighbours, who heard her voice, rushed in, and the deceitful hussy kept on repeating, "Alas! What a wretched fate has my husband met with," and tears flowed afresh.

At that instant the dead man opened his eyes. "What are you doing?" he said to her. "First finish the roasting of the pasterma, then quench your dry throat with milk, and boil the remainder of it. Afterward you will find time to weep for me."

First myself, and then those I love, says a proverb.

Tales of the Meddahs: Tales from the Turkish tradition

HOW THE HODJA SAVED ALLAH

This story has been adapted from Told in the Coffee House by Cyrus Adler and Allan Ramsay, published in 1898 by MacMillan and Company, London. Allan Ramsay was a Scottish poet, playwright, publisher, librarian, and wig-maker active in the early and mid-eighteenth century. Cyrus Adler adapted Ramsay's work in the nineteenth century, being an American educator, Jewish religious leader, and scholar.

Not far from the famous Mosque Bayezid an old Hodja kept a school, and very skilfully he taught the rising generation the everlasting lesson from the Book of Books. Such knowledge had he of human nature that by a glance at his pupil he could at once tell how long it would take him to learn a quarter of the Koran. He was known over the whole Empire as the best reciter and imparter of the Sacred Writings of the Prophet. For many years this Hodja, famed far and wide as the Hodja of Hodjas, had taught in this little school. The number of times he had recited the Book with his pupils is beyond counting; and should we attempt to consider how often he must have corrected them for some misplaced word, our beards would grow grey in the endeavour.

Swaying to and fro one day as fast as his old age would let him, and reciting to his pupils the latter part of one of the chapters, Bakara, divine inspiration opened his inward eye and led him to pause at the following sentence, "And he that spends his money in the ways of Allah is likened to a grain of wheat that brings forth seven sheaves, and in each sheaf a hundred grains; and Allah gives twofold to whom He pleases." As his pupils, one after the other,

Tales of the Meddahs: Tales from the Turkish tradition

recited this verse to him, he wondered why he had overlooked its meaning for so many years. Fully convinced that anything either given to Allah, or in the way that He proposes, was an investment that brought a percentage undreamed of in known commerce, he dismissed his pupils, and putting his hand into his bosom drew forth from the many folds of his dress a bag and proceeded to count his worldly possessions. Carefully and attentively, he counted and then recounted his money, and found that if invested in the ways of Allah it would bring a return of no less than one thousand piasters.

"Think of it," said the Hodja to himself. "One thousand piasters! One thousand piasters! Mashallah! A fortune."

So, having dismissed his school, he sallied forth, his bag of money in his hand, and began distributing its contents to the needy that he met in the highways. Before many hours had passed the whole of his savings was gone. The Hodja was very happy, for now he was the creditor in Allah's books for one thousand piasters. He returned to his house and ate his evening meal of bread and olives and was content.

The next day came. The thousand piasters had not yet arrived. He ate his bread, he imagined he had olives, and was content.

The third day came. The old Hodja had no bread, and he had no olives. He suffered the pangs of hunger. So, when the end of the day had come, and his pupils had departed to their homes, the Hodja, with a full heart and an empty stomach, walked out of the town, and soon got beyond the city walls. There, where no one could hear him, he lamented his sad fate, and the great calamity that had befallen him in his old age. What sin had he committed? What great wrong had his ancestors done, that the wrath of the Almighty had thus fallen on him, when his earthly course was well-nigh run?

"Ya! Allah! Allah!" he cried and beat his breast.

As if in answer to his cry, the howl of the dreaded Fakir Dervish came over across the plain. In those days the Fakir Dervish was a terror in the land. He knocked at the door, and it was opened. He asked and received food. If refused, life often paid the penalty. The Hodja's lamentations were now

Tales of the Meddahs: Tales from the Turkish tradition

greater than ever; for should the Dervish ask him for food and the Hodja have nothing to give, he would certainly be killed.

"Allah! Allah! Allah! Guide me now. Protect one of your faithful followers," cried the frightened Hodja, and he looked around to see if there was anyone to rescue him from his perilous position. But not a soul was to be seen, and the walls of the city were five miles distant. Just then the howl of the Dervish again reached his ear, and in terror he flew, he knew not where. As luck would have it, he came upon a tree, up which, although stiff from age and weak from want, the Hodja, with wonderful agility, scrambled and, trembling like a leaf, awaited his fate.

Nearer and nearer came the howling Dervish, till at last his long hair could be seen floating in the air, as with rapid strides he preceded the wind upon his endless journey. On and on he came, his wild yell sending the blood from very fear to unknown parts of the poor Hodja's body and leaving his face as yellow as a melon. To his utter dismay, the Hodja saw the Dervish approach the tree and sit down under its shade.

Sighing deeply, the Dervish said in a loud voice, "Why have I come into this world? Why were my forefathers born? Why was anybody born? Oh, Allah! Oh, Allah! What have you done! Misery! Misery! Nothing but misery to mankind and everything living. Shall I not be avenged for all the misery my father and my father's fathers have suffered? I shall be avenged."

Striking his chest a loud blow, as if to emphasise the decision he had come to, the Dervish took a small bag that lay by his side, and slowly proceeded to untie the leather strings that bound it. Bringing forth from it a small image, he gazed at it a moment and then addressed it in the following terms, "You, Job! You bore much. You have written a book in which your history is recorded. You have earned the reputation of being the most patient man that ever lived, yet I have read your history and found that when real affliction oppressed you, you cursed God. You have made men believe, too, that there is a reward in this life for all the afflictions they suffer. You have misled mankind. For these sins no one has ever punished you. Now I will punish you," and taking his long, curved sword in his hand he cut off the head of the figure.

The Dervish bent forward, took another image and gazing upon it with a contemptuous smile, thus addressed it, "David, David, singer of songs of peace in this world and in the world to come, I have read your sayings in which you counsel men to lead a righteous life for the sake of the reward which they are to receive. I have learned that you have misled your fellow-mortals with your songs of peace and joy. I have read your history, and I find that you have committed many sins. For these sins and for misleading your fellow men you have never been punished. Now I will punish you," and taking his sword in his hand he cut off David's head.

Again, the Dervish bent forward and brought forth an image which he addressed as follows, "You, Solomon, are reputed to have been the wisest man that ever lived. You had command over the host of the Genii and could control the legion of the demons. They came at the bidding of your signet ring, and they trembled at the mysterious names to which you gave utterance. You understood every living thing. The speech of the beasts of the field, of the birds of the air, of the insects of the earth, and of the fishes of the sea, was known to you. Yet when I read your history, I found that in spite of the vast knowledge that was vouchsafed to you, you committed many wrongs and did many foolish things, which in the end brought misery into the world and destruction to your people; and for all these no one has ever punished you. Now I will punish you," and taking his sword he cut off Solomon's head.

Again, the Dervish bent forward and brought forth from the bag another figure, which he addressed thus, "Jesus, Jesus, prophet of God, you came into this world to atone, by giving your blood, for the sins of mankind and to bring to them a religion of peace. You founded a church, whose history I have studied, and I see that it set fathers against their children and brethren against one another; that it brought strife into the world, that the lives of men and women and children were sacrificed so that the rivers ran red with blood to the seas. Truly you were a great prophet, but the misery you caused must

Tales of the Meddahs: Tales from the Turkish tradition

be avenged. For it no one has yet punished you. Now I will punish you," and he took his sword and cut off Jesus' head.

With a sorrowful face the Dervish bent forward and brought forth another image from the bag. "Mohammed," he said, "I have slain Job, David, Solomon, and Jesus. What shall I do with you? After the followers of Jesus had shed much blood, their religion spread over the world, was acceptable to man, and the nations were at peace. Then you came into the world, and you brought a new religion, and father rose against father, and brother rose against brother. Hatred was sown between your followers and the followers of Jesus, and again the rivers ran red with blood to the seas; and you have not been punished. For this I will punish you. By the beard of my forefathers, whose blood was made to flow in your cause, you too must die," and with a blow the head of Mohammed fell to the ground.

Then the Dervish prostrated himself to the earth, and after a silent prayer rose and brought forth from the bag the last figure. Reverently he bowed to it, and then he addressed it as follows, "Oh, Allah! The Allah of Allahs. There is but one Allah, and you are He. I have slain Job, David, Solomon, Jesus, and Mohammed for the folly that they have brought into the world. You, God, are all powerful. All men are your children, you create them and bring them into the world. The thoughts that they think are your thoughts. If all these men have brought all this evil into the world, it is your fault. Shall I punish them and allow you to go unhurt? No. I must punish you also," and he raised his sword to strike.

As the sword circled in the air the Hodja, secreted in the tree, forgot the fear in which he stood of the Dervish. In the excitement of the moment, he cried out in a loud tone of voice, "Stop! Stop! He owes me one thousand piasters."

The Dervish reeled and fell senseless to the ground. The Hodja was overcome at his own words and trembled with fear, convinced that his last hour had arrived. The Dervish lay stretched upon his back on the grass as if he were dead. At last, the Hodja took courage. Breaking a twig from off the tree, he threw it down upon the Dervish's face, but the Dervish made no sign. The Hodja took more courage, removed one of his heavy outer shoes and

Tales of the Meddahs: Tales from the Turkish tradition

threw it on the outstretched figure of the Dervish, but still the Dervish lay motionless. The Hodja carefully climbed down the tree, gave the body of the Dervish a kick, and climbed back again, and still the Dervish did not stir. At length the Hodja descended from the tree and placed his ear to the Dervish's heart. It did not beat. The Dervish was dead.

"Ah, well," said the Hodja, "at least I shall not starve. I will take his garments and sell them and buy me some bread."

The Hodja commenced to remove the Dervish's garments. As he took off his belt, he found that it was heavy. He opened it and saw that it contained gold. He counted the gold and found that it was exactly one thousand piasters.

The Hodja turned his face toward Mecca and raising his eyes to heaven said, "Oh God, you have kept your promise, but," he added, "not before I saved your life."

Tales of the Meddahs: Tales from the Turkish tradition

THE WIDOW AND HER FRIEND

This story has been adapted from Turkish Literature by Epiphanius Wilson, A.M., published in 1901 by P. F. Collier & Son, New York.

A Widow, tired of single blessedness, wanted to marry again, but feared to draw down upon herself the remarks of the public.

A Friend of hers, to show her how the tongues of neighbours discussed everything, decided to paint the Widow's ass green. Then leading the beast, she traversed all the streets of the town.

At first not only the children, but also their elders, who had never seen anything like it before, came to see the sight, and followed behind the ass.

After a few days, when the Widow's ass went out in the town people simply remarked, "What a very singular animal!"

Soon, however, the people ceased to pay any more attention to the spectacle.

The Friend of the Widow who wished to marry again returned to her and said, "You have seen what has just happened. It will be the same in your case. For some days you will be on the tongues of the people and have to endure their gossip and remarks, but at the last they will leave off talking about you."

There is nothing so extraordinary in this world that cannot become familiar in time.

Tales of the Meddahs: Tales from the Turkish tradition

Tales of the Meddahs: Tales from the Turkish tradition

BETTER IS THE FOLLY OF WOMAN THAN THE WISDOM OF MAN

This story has been adapted from Told in the Coffee House by Cyrus Adler and Allan Ramsay, published in 1898 by MacMillan and Company, London. Allan Ramsay was a Scottish poet, playwright, publisher, librarian, and wig-maker active in the early and mid-eighteenth century. Cyrus Adler adapted Ramsay's work in the nineteenth century, being an American educator, Jewish religious leader, and scholar.

There lived in Constantinople an old Hodja, a learned man, who had a son. The boy followed in his father's footsteps, went every day to the Mosque Aya Sofia, seated himself in a secluded spot, to the left of the pillar bearing the impress of the Conqueror's hand, and engaged in the study of the Koran. Daily he might be seen seated, swaying his body to and fro, and reciting to himself the verses of the Holy Book.

The dearest wish of a theological student is to be able to recite the entire Koran by heart. Many years are spent in memorising the Holy Book, which must be recited with a prescribed cantillation, and in acquiring a rhythmical movement of the body which accompanies the chant.

When Abdul, for that was the young man's name, had reached his nineteenth year, he had, by the most assiduous study, finally succeeded in mastering three-quarters of the Koran. At this achievement his pride rose, his ambition was fired, and he determined to become a great man.

Tales of the Meddahs: Tales from the Turkish tradition

The day that he reached this decision he did not go to the Mosque, but stopped at home, in his father's house, and sat staring at the fire burning in the grate. Several times the father asked, "My son, what do you see in the fire?"

And each time the son answered, "Nothing, father."

He was very young, and he could not see his way. Finally, the young man picked up courage and gave expression to his thoughts. "Father," he said, "I wish to become a great man."

"That is very easy," said the father.

"And to be a great man," continued the son, "I must first go to Mecca." For no Islamic holy man or theologian, or even layman, has fulfilled all of the cardinal precepts of his faith unless he has made the pilgrimage to the Holy City.

To his son's last observation, the father blandly replied, "It is very easy to go to Mecca."

"How, easy?" asked the son. "On the contrary," he continued. "It is very difficult, for the journey is costly, and I have no money."

"Listen, my son," said the father. "You must become a scribe, the writer of the thoughts of your brethren, and your fortune is made."

"But I have not even the implements necessary for a scribe," said the son.

"All that can be easily arranged," said the father. "Your grandfather had an inkhorn. I will give it to you. I will buy you some writing-paper, and we will get you a box to sit in. All that you need to do is to sit still, look wise and your fortune is made."

And indeed, the advice was good, for letter-writing is an art which only a few possess. The ability to write by no means carries with it the ability to compose, though. Epistolary genius is rare.

Tales of the Meddahs: Tales from the Turkish tradition

Abdul was very happy with the counsel that had been given him, and he lost no time in carrying out the plan. He took his grandfather's inkhorn, the paper his father bought, got himself a box and began his career as a scribe.

Abdul was a child, he knew nothing, but thought he was wise, and he sought to surpass the counsel of his father.

"To look wise," he said, "is not sufficient. I must have some other attraction."

And after much thought he hit upon the following idea. Over his box he painted a legend, "The wisdom of man is greater than the wisdom of woman." People thought the sign very clever, customers came, the young Hodja took in many piasters, and he was correspondingly happy.

This sign one day attracted the eyes and mind of a Hanoum, a Turkish lady. Seeing that Abdul was a manly youth, she went to him and said, "Hodja, I have a difficult letter to write. I have heard that you are very wise, so I have come to you. To write the letter you will need all your wit. Moreover, the letter is a long one, and I cannot stand here while it is being written. Come to my Konak, to my house, at three this afternoon, and we will write the letter."

The Hodja was overcome with admiration for his fair client and surprised at the invitation. He was enchanted, his heartbeat wildly, and so great was his agitation that his reply of acquiescence was scarcely audible.

The invitation had more than the charm of novelty to make it attractive. He had never talked with a woman outside of his own family circle. To be admitted to a lady's house was in itself an adventure.

Long before the appointed time, the young Hodja, an impetuous youth, gathered together his reeds, ink, and sand. With feverish steps he went on his way to the house. Lattices covered the windows, a high wall surrounded the garden, and a ponderous gate barred the entrance. Three times he raised the massive knocker.

"Who is there?" called a voice from within.

"The scribe," was the reply.

Tales of the Meddahs: Tales from the Turkish tradition

"It is good," said the porter. The gate was unbarred, and the Hodja was permitted to enter. Directly he was ushered into the apartment of his fair client.

The lady welcomed him cordially. "Ah! Hodja Effendi, I am glad to see you, pray sit down."

The Hodja nervously pulled out his writing-implements.

"Do not be in such a hurry," said the lady. "Refresh yourself, and take a cup of coffee, smoke a cigarette, and we will write the letter afterwards."

So he lit a cigarette, drank a cup of coffee, and they fell to talking. Time flew and the minutes seemed like seconds, and the hours were as minutes. While they were thus enjoying themselves there suddenly came a heavy knock at the gate.

"It is my husband, the Pasha," cried the lady. "What shall I do? If he finds you here, he will kill you! I am so frightened."

The Hodja was frightened too. Again, there came a knock at the gate.

"I have it," and taking Abdul by the arm, she said, "you must get into the box," indicating a large chest in the room. "Quick, quick, if you prize your life utter not a word, and, Inshallah, I will save you."

Abdul now, too late, saw his folly. It was his lack of experience, but driven by the sense of danger, he climbed into the chest, and the lady locked it and took the key.

A moment afterwards the Pasha came in. "I am very tired," he said. "Bring me coffee and a chibouk."

"Good evening, Pasha Effendi," said the lady. "Sit down. I have something to tell you."

"Bah!" said the Pasha. "I want none of your woman's talk. 'A woman's hair is long, and her wits are short,' says the proverb. Bring me my pipe."

"But, Pasha Effendi," said the lady, "I have had an adventure today."

Tales of the Meddahs: Tales from the Turkish tradition

"Bah!" said the Pasha. "What adventure can a woman have? Did you forget to paint your eyebrows or colour your nails?"

"No, Pasha Effendi. Be patient, and I will tell you. I went out today to write a letter."

"A letter?" said the Pasha. "To whom would you write a letter?"

"Be patient," she said, "and I will tell you my story. So, I came to the box of a young scribe with beautiful eyes."

"A young man with beautiful eyes," shouted the Pasha. "Where is he? I'll kill him!" and he drew his sword.

The Hodja in the chest heard every word and trembled in every limb.

"Be patient, Pasha Effendi. I said I had an adventure, and you did not believe me. I told the young man that the letter was long, and I could not stand in the street to write it. So, I asked him to come and see me this afternoon."

"Here? To this house?" thundered the Pasha.

"Yes, Pasha Effendi," said the lady. "So, the Hodja came here, and I gave him coffee and a cigarette, and we talked, and the minutes seemed like seconds, and the hours were as minutes. All at once came your knock at the gate, and I said to the Hodja, 'That is the Pasha, and if he finds you here, he will kill you.'"

"And I will kill him," screamed the Pasha, "where is he?"

"Be patient, Pasha Effendi," said the lady, "and I will tell you. When you knocked a second time, I suddenly thought of the chest, and I put the Hodja in."

"Let me at him!" screamed the Pasha. "I'll cut off his head!"

"O Pasha," she said, "what a hurry you are in to slay this comely youth. He is your prey. He cannot escape you. The youth is not only in the box, but it is locked, and the key is in my pocket. Here it is."

Tales of the Meddahs: Tales from the Turkish tradition

The lady walked over to the Pasha, stretched out her hand and gave him the key. As he took it, she said, "Philopena!"

"Bah!" said the Pasha, in disgust. He threw the key on the floor and left the harem, slamming the door behind him.

After he had gone, the lady took up the key, unlocked the box, and let out the trembling Hodja.

"Go now, Hodja, to your writing box," she said. "Take down your sign and write instead, 'The wit of woman is twice the wit of man,' for I am a woman, and in one day I have fooled two men."

Tales of the Meddahs: Tales from the Turkish tradition

THE OLD MAN AND HIS SON

This story has been adapted from Turkish Literature by Epiphanius Wilson, A.M., published in 1901 by P. F. Collier & Son, New York.

A feeble old man had given his home to his son. Soon the hapless father found himself driven from his home and forced to take refuge in a hospital. Sometime afterward, he saw his son one day passing by, and called out to him, "For the love of God, my son," he said in a supplicating tone, 'send me a simple pair of sheets from all that I have earned with the sweat of my brow."

The son promised his unfortunate father to do so. "I will send them at once," he answered him.

When he arrived at home he said to his own son, "Take this pair of sheets, and carry them to your grandfather at the hospital."

The young man left one of the sheets at home and carried the other to his grandfather. Sometime afterward his father happened to count his sheets. "Why didn't you do as I told you and carry the two sheets to your grandfather?" he asked his son.

"When my father becomes old and goes to the hospital, I said to myself, I shall need this sheet to send to him."

Your child will behave toward you as you behaved toward your parents

Tales of the Meddahs: Tales from the Turkish tradition

Tales of the Meddahs: Tales from the Turkish tradition

THE HANOUM AND THE UNJUST CADI

This story has been adapted from Told in the Coffee House by Cyrus Adler and Allan Ramsay, published in 1898 by MacMillan and Company, London. Allan Ramsay was a Scottish poet, playwright, publisher, librarian, and wigmaker active in the early and mid-eighteenth century. Cyrus Adler adapted Ramsay's work in the nineteenth century, being an American educator, Jewish religious leader, and scholar.

It was once, in some parts of Constantinople, the custom of the refuse-gatherer to go about the streets with a basket on his back, and a wooden shovel in his hand, calling out 'refuse removed.'

A certain Chepdji, plying this trade, had, in the course of five years of assiduous labour, amassed, the important sum of five hundred piasters. He was afraid to keep this money by him, so hearing that the Cadi of Istanbul was highly and reverently spoken of, he decided to entrust his hard-earned savings to the Cadi's keeping.

Going to the Cadi, he said, "Oh learned and righteous man, for five long years have I laboured, carrying the dregs and dross of rich and poor alike, and I have saved a sum of five hundred piasters. With the help of our Lord, in another two years I shall have saved a further sum of at least one hundred piasters, when, Inshallah, I shall return to my country and clasp my wife and children again. In the meantime, you will be granting a favour to your slave, if you will consent to keep this money for me until the time for departure has come."

Tales of the Meddahs: Tales from the Turkish tradition

The Cadi replied, "You have done well, my son. The money will be kept and given to you when required."

The poor Chepdji, well satisfied, departed. But after a very short time he learned that several of his friends were about to return to their Memleket province, and he decided to join them, thinking that his five hundred piasters were ample for the time being. "Besides," said he, "who knows what may or may not happen in the next two years?" So, he decided to depart with his friends at once.

He went to the Cadi, explained that he had changed his mind, that he was going to leave for his country immediately, and asked for his money. The Cadi called him a dog and ordered him to be whipped out of the place by his servants. Alas! What could the poor Chepdji do? He wept in impotent despair, as he counted the number of years he must yet work before beholding his loved ones.

One day, while moving the dirt from the Konak of a wealthy Pasha, his soul uttered a sigh which reached the ears of the Hanoum, and from the window she asked him why he sighed so deeply. He replied that he sighed for something that could in no way interest her. The Hanoum's sympathy was excited, and after much persuasion, he finally, with tears in his eyes, related to her his great misfortune. The Hanoum thought for a few minutes and then told him to go the following day to the Cadi at a certain hour and again ask for the money as if nothing had happened.

The Hanoum in the meantime gathered together a quantity of jewellery, to the value of several hundred pounds, and instructed her favourite and confidential slave to come with her to the Cadi and remain outside whilst she went in, directing her slave that when she saw the Chepdji come out and learned that he had gotten his money, she was to come in the Cadi's room hurriedly and say to her mistress, the Hanoum, "your husband has arrived from Egypt, and is waiting for you at the Konak."

The Hanoum then went to the Cadi, carrying in her hand a bag containing the jewellery. With a profound salaam she said, "Oh Cadi, my husband, who

Tales of the Meddahs: Tales from the Turkish tradition

is in Egypt and who has been there for several years, has at last asked me to come and join him there. These jewels are of great value, and I hesitate to take them with me on so long and dangerous a journey. If you would kindly consent to keep them for me until my return, or if I never return to keep them as a token of my esteem, I will think of you with lifelong gratitude."

The Hanoum then began displaying the rich jewellery. Just then the Chepdji entered, and bending low, said, "Oh master, your slave has come for his savings in order to proceed to his country."

"Ah, welcome," said the Cadi. "So, you are going already!" He immediately ordered the treasurer to pay the five hundred piasters to the Chepdji.

"You see," said the Cadi to the Hanoum, "what confidence the people have in me. This money I have held for some time without receipt or acknowledgment; but directly it is asked for it is paid."

No sooner had the Chepdji gone out of the door, than the Hanoum's slave came rushing in, crying, "Hanoum Effendi! Hanoum Effendi! Your husband has arrived from Egypt and is anxiously awaiting you at the Konak."

The Hanoum, in well-feigned excitement, gathered up her jewellery and, wishing the Cadi a thousand years of happiness, departed.

The Cadi was thunderstruck, and caressing his beard with grave affection thoughtfully said, "Allah! Allah! For forty years have I been judge, but never was a cause pleaded in this fashion before."

Tales of the Meddahs: Tales from the Turkish tradition

Tales of the Meddahs: Tales from the Turkish tradition

WHAT HAPPENED TO HADJI, A MERCHANT OF THE BEZESTAN

This story has been adapted from Told in the Coffee House by Cyrus Adler and Allan Ramsay, published in 1898 by MacMillan and Company, London. Allan Ramsay was a Scottish poet, playwright, publisher, librarian, and wig-maker active in the early and mid-eighteenth century. Cyrus Adler adapted Ramsay's work in the nineteenth century, being an American educator, Jewish religious leader, and scholar.

Hadji was a married man, but even Turkish married men are not invulnerable to the charms of other women. It happened one day, when possibly the engrossing power of his lawful wife's influence was feeble upon him, that a charming Hanoum came to his shop to purchase some spices. After the departure of his fair visitor Hadji, do what he might, could not drive from his mind's eye, either her image, or her attractive power. He was further greatly puzzled by a tiny black bag containing twelve grains of wheat, which the Hanoum had evidently forgotten.

Hadji stayed on in his shop until a late hour that night, in the hope that either the Hanoum or one of her servants would come for the bag, and thus give him the means of seeing her again or at least of learning where she lived. But Hadji was doomed to disappointment, and, much preoccupied, he returned to his home. There he sat, unresponsive to his wife's conversation, thinking, and no doubt making mental comparisons between her and his visitor.

Tales of the Meddahs: Tales from the Turkish tradition

Hadji remained downcast day after day, and at last, giving way to his wife's entreaties to share his troubles, he frankly told her what had happened, and that ever since that day his soul was in his visitor's bondage.

"Oh husband," replied his wife, "and do you not understand what that black bag containing the twelve grains of wheat means?"

"Alas, no," replied Hadji.

"Why, my husband, it is plain, plain as if it had been told. She lives in the Wheat Market, at house No. 12, with a black door."

Much excited, Hadji rushed off and found that there was a No. 12 in the Wheat Market, with a black door, so he promptly knocked. The door opened, and who should he behold but the lady in question? She, however, instead of speaking to him, threw a basin of water out into the street and then shut the door. Hadji, with mingled feelings of gratitude to his wife for having so accurately directed him, but none the less surprised at his reception, lingered about the doorway for a time and then returned home. He greeted his wife more pleasantly than he had for many days and told her of his strange reception.

"Why," said his wife, "don't you understand what the basin of water thrown out of the door means?"

"Alas, no," said Hadji.

"Veyh! Veyh! Oh, such pity. It means that at the back of the house there is a running stream, and that you must go to her that way."

Off rushed Hadji and found that his wife was right, for there was a running stream at the back of the house, so he knocked at the back door. The Hanoum, however, instead of opening it, came to the window, showed a mirror, reversed it and then disappeared. Hadji lingered at the back of the house for a long time, but seeing no further sign of life, he returned to his home much dejected.

On entering the house, his wife greeted him with, "Well, was it not as I told you?"

Tales of the Meddahs: Tales from the Turkish tradition

"Yes," said Hadji. "You are truly a wonderful woman, Mashallah! But I do not know why she came to the window and showed me a mirror both in front and back, instead of opening the door."

"Oh," said his wife, "that is very simple. She means that you must go when the face of the moon has reversed itself, about ten o'clock."

The hour arrived, Hadji hurried off, and so did his wife, the one to see his love, and the other to inform the police. Whilst Hadji and his charmer were talking in the garden the police seized them and carried them both off to prison, and Hadji's wife, having accomplished her mission, returned home.

The next morning, she baked a quantity of lokum cakes, also known as Turkish Delight, and taking them to the prison, begged entrance of the guards and permission to distribute these cakes to the prisoners, for the repose of the souls of her dead. This being a request which could not be denied, she was allowed to enter. Finding the cell in which the lady who had infatuated her husband was confined, she offered to save her the disgrace of the exposure, provided she would consent never again to look upon Hadji, the merchant, with envious or loving eyes. The conditions were gratefully accepted, and Hadji's wife changed places with the prisoner.

When they were brought before the judge, Hadji was thunderstruck to see his wife, but being a wise man, he held his peace, and left her to do the talking, which she did most vigorously, vehemently protesting against the insult inflicted on both her and her husband in bringing them to prison, because they chose to converse in a garden, being lawfully wedded people. As witnesses, she called upon the Bekdji, the local watchman, and the Imam of the district and several of her neighbours.

Poor Hadji was dumfounded, and, accompanied by his better half, left the prison, where he had expected to stay at least a year or two, saying, "Truly you are a wonderful woman, Mashallah."

Tales of the Meddahs: Tales from the Turkish tradition

Tales of the Meddahs: Tales from the Turkish tradition

THE LION AND THE MAN

This story has been adapted from Turkish Literature by Epiphanius Wilson, A.M., published in 1901 by P. F. Collier & Son, New York.

A Lion and a Man were journeying together as friends; they took turns in boasting each of his own merits. As they advanced on their way, they saw a mausoleum on which was carved in marble a man trampling a lion under his feet.

The Man called the attention of the Lion to this sculpture.

"I need say no more," he remarked, "this is sufficient to show that man surpasses the Lion in strength and vigour."

"The chisel is in the hands of men," replied the beast, 'so they represent in sculpture however they like. If we Lions could handle a chisel as you do, you would see very different subjects in our works."

Artists do not base their creations upon the realities of life but follow the ideas which pass through their heads.

Tales of the Meddahs: Tales from the Turkish tradition

Tales of the Meddahs: Tales from the Turkish tradition

HOW THE JUNKMAN TRAVELLED TO FIND TREASURE IN HIS OWN BACKYARD

This story has been adapted from Told in the Coffee House by Cyrus Adler and Allan Ramsay, published in 1898 by MacMillan and Company, London. Allan Ramsay was a Scottish poet, playwright, publisher, librarian, and wigmaker active in the early and mid-eighteenth century. Cyrus Adler adapted Ramsay's work in the nineteenth century, being an American educator, Jewish religious leader, and scholar.

In one of the towers overlooking the Sea of Marmora and skirting the ancient city of Istanbul, there lived an old junkman, who earned a precarious livelihood in gathering cinders and useless pieces of iron and selling them to smiths.

Often, he would moralise on the sad Kismet that had reduced him to the task of daily labouring for his bread to make a shoe, perhaps for an ass. Surely, he, a true Muslim, might at least be permitted to ride the ass. His eternal longing often found satisfaction in passing his hours of sleep in dreams of wealth and luxury. But with the dawning of the day came reality and increased longing.

He often called on the spirit of sleep to reverse matters, but in vain, for with the rising of the sun the gathering of the cinders and iron began all over again.

One night he dreamt that he begged this nocturnal visitor to change his night into day, and the spirit of sleep said to him, "Go to Egypt, and it shall be so."

Tales of the Meddahs: Tales from the Turkish tradition

This encouraging phrase haunted him by day and inspired him by night. So persecuted was he with the thought that when his wife said to him, from the door, "Have you brought home any bread?" he would reply, "No, I have not gone out today. I will go tomorrow," thinking she had asked him, "Have you gone to Egypt?"

At last, when friends and neighbours began to pity poor Ahmet, for that was his name, as a man on whom the hand of Allah was heavily laid, removing his intelligence, he left his house one morning, saying, "I go! I go! I go to the land of wealth!" And he left his wife wringing her hands in despair, while the neighbours tried to comfort her. Poor Ahmet went straight on board a boat which he had been told was bound for Alexandria, and assured the captain that he was summoned there, and that he was bound to take him. Half-witted and mad persons being more holy than others, Ahmet was conveyed to Alexandria.

Arriving in Alexandria, Hadji Ahmet roamed far and wide, proceeding as far as Cairo, in search of the luxuries he had enjoyed at Constantinople when in the land of Morpheus, which he had been promised that he would enjoy in the sunshine, if he came to Egypt. Alas for Hadji Ahmet. The only bread he had to eat was that which was given him by sympathising humanity. Time sped on, sympathy was growing tired of expending itself on Hadji Ahmet, and his crusts of bread were few and far between.

Wearied of life and suffering, he decided to ask Allah to let him die, and wandering out to the Pyramids he solicited the stones to have pity and fall on him. It happened that a Turk heard this prayer, and said to him, "Why so miserable, father? Has your soul been so strangled that you prefer its being dashed out of your body, and to it remaining the prescribed time in bondage?"

"Yes, my son," said Hadji Ahmet. "Far away in Istanbul, with the help of God, I managed as a junkman to feed my wife and myself; but here am I, in Egypt, a stranger, alone and starving, with possibly my wife already dead of starvation, and all this through a dream."

Tales of the Meddahs: Tales from the Turkish tradition

"Alas, alas, my father, that you at your age should be tempted to wander so far from home and friends, because of a dream. Why, were I to obey my dreams, I would at this present moment be in Istanbul, digging for a treasure that lies buried under a tree. I can even now, although I have never been there, describe where it is. In my mind's eye I see a wall, a great wall, that must have been built many years ago, and supporting or seeming to support this wall are towers with many corners, towers that are round, towers that are square, and others that have smaller towers within them. In one of these towers, a square one, there live an old man and woman, and close by the tower is a large tree, and every night when I dream of the place, the old man tells me to dig and disclose the treasure. But, father, I am not such a fool as to go to Istanbul and seek to verify this. It is an oft-repeated dream and nothing more. See what you have been reduced to by coming so far."

"Yes," said Hadji Ahmet, "it is a dream and nothing more, but you have interpreted it. Allah be praised, you have encouraged me. I will return to my home."

And Hadji Ahmet and the young stranger parted, the one grateful that it had pleased Allah to give him the power to revive and encourage a drooping spirit, and the other grateful to Allah that when he had despaired of life a stranger should come and give him the interpretation of his dream. He certainly had wandered far and long to learn that the treasure was in his own garden.

Hadji Ahmet in due course, much to the astonishment of both wife and neighbours, again appeared upon the scene and was not much changed as a man. In fact, he was the cinder and iron gatherer of old. To all questions as to where he was and what he had been doing, he would answer, "A dream sent me away, and a dream brought me back."

And the neighbours would say, "Truly he must be blessed."

One night Hadji Ahmet went to the tree, carrying a spade and a pick that he had secured from an obliging neighbour. After digging for a short time, a heavy case was brought to view, in which he found gold, silver, and precious

Tales of the Meddahs: Tales from the Turkish tradition

jewels of great value. Hadji Ahmet replaced the case and earth and returned to bed, much lamenting that it had pleased God to furnish women, more especially his wife, with a long tongue, long hair, and very short wits. Alas, he thought, if I tell my wife, I may be hung as a robber, for it is against the laws of nature for a woman to keep a secret. Yet, becoming more generous when thinking of the years of toil and hardship she had shared with him, he decided to try and see if, by chance, his wife was not an exception to other women. Who knows, she might keep the secret. To test her, at no risk to himself and the treasure, he conceived a plan.

Crawling from his bed, he sallied forth and bought, found, or stole an egg. This egg on the following morning he showed to his wife, and said to her, "Alas, I fear I am not as other men, for evidently in the night I laid this egg, and, wife of mine, if the neighbours hear of this, your husband, the long-suffering Hadji Ahmet, will be bastinadoed, bowstrung, and burned to death. Ah, truly, my soul is strangled."

And without another word Hadji Ahmet, with a sack on his shoulder, went forth to gather the cast-off shoes of horse, ox, or ass, wondering if his wife would prove an exception in this, as she had in many other ways, to other women.

In the evening he returned, heavily laden with his finds, and as he neared home he heard rumours, ominous rumours, that a certain Hadji Ahmet, who had been considered a holy man, had done something that was unknown in the history of man, even in the history of hens - that he had laid a dozen eggs.

Needless to add that Hadji Ahmet did not tell his wife of the treasure, but daily went forth with his sack to gather iron and cinders, and invariably found, when separating his finds of the day, in company with his wife, at first one, and then more gold and silver pieces, and now and then a precious stone.

Tales of the Meddahs: Tales from the Turkish tradition

THE SHARK

This story has been adapted from Turkish Literature by Epiphanius Wilson, A.M., published in 1901 by P. F. Collier & Son, New York.

A Shark, taking up his station at the mouth of a river, ruled over all the inhabitants of the waters. As he conducted himself with extreme violence toward them, they showed every sign of submissiveness. He had, in fact, become their King, and they treated him as such.

The Shark was unduly elated by his situation. "Why," he said to himself, 'should I not extend my dominion still farther?"

Taking advantage of a favourable opportunity, he left the river and went out to sea, with a view of expanding his kingdom. "I must now subjugate the fishes who dwell here," he remarked.

He was thus dreaming of ocean conquest, when he met the whale. Seized with alarm, and frozen with terror, the would-be conqueror fled back to the mouth of the river, feeling quite dejected. Henceforth he was very careful not to leave his lurking-place.

Let us beware of giving up a satisfactory position, in pursuit of vainglory, and for the sake of increasing our power. In all cases let us limit our desires.

Tales of the Meddahs: Tales from the Turkish tradition

Tales of the Meddahs: Tales from the Turkish tradition

HOW CHAPKIN HALID BECAME CHIEF DETECTIVE

This story has been adapted from Told in the Coffee House by Cyrus Adler and Allan Ramsay, published in 1898 by MacMillan and Company, London. Allan Ramsay was a Scottish poet, playwright, publisher, librarian, and wig-maker active in the early and mid-eighteenth century. Cyrus Adler adapted Ramsay's work in the nineteenth century, being an American educator, Jewish religious leader, and scholar.

In Balata there lived, some years ago, two scapegraces, called Chapkin Halid and Pitch Osman. These two young rascals lived by their wits and at the expense of their neighbours. But they often had to lament the ever-increasing difficulties they encountered in procuring the few piasters they needed daily for bread and the tavern. They had tried several schemes in their own neighbourhood, with exceptionally poor results, and were almost disheartened when Chapkin Halid conceived an idea that seemed to offer every chance of success. He explained to his chum Osman that Balata was 'played out', at least for a time, and that they must go elsewhere to satisfy their needs. Halid's plan was to go to Istanbul, and feign death in the principal street, while Osman was to follow and collect the usual funeral expenses for his friend, Halid.

Arriving in Istanbul, Halid stretched himself on his back on the pavement and covered his face with an old sack, while Osman sat himself down beside the supposed corpse, and every now and then bewailed the hard fate of the stranger who had met with death on the first day of his arrival. The corpse

Tales of the Meddahs: Tales from the Turkish tradition

prompted Osman whenever the coast was clear, and the touching tale told by Osman soon brought contributions for the burial of the stranger. Osman had collected about thirty piasters, and Halid was seriously thinking of a resurrection, but was prevented by the passing of the Grand Vizier, who, upon inquiring why the man lay on the ground in that fashion, was told that he was a stranger who had died in the street. The Grand Vizier thereupon gave instructions to an Imam, who happened to be at hand, to bury the stranger and come for the money to the Sublime Porte.

Halid was reverently carried off to the Mosque, and Osman thought that it was time to leave the corpse to take care of itself. The Imam laid Halid on the marble floor and prepared to wash him prior to interment. He had taken off his turban and long cloak and got ready the water; when he remembered that he had no soap, and immediately went out to purchase some. No sooner had the Imam disappeared than Halid jumped up, and, donning the Imam's turban and long cloak, repaired to the Sublime Porte. Here he asked admittance to the Grand Vizier, but this request was not granted until he told the nature of his business. Halid said he was the Imam who, in compliance with the verbal instructions received from his Highness, had buried a stranger and that he had come for payment. The Grand Vizier sent five gold pieces (twenty piasters each) to the supposed Imam, and Halid made off as fast as possible.

No sooner had Halid departed than the cloak-less Imam arrived in breathless haste and explained that he was the Imam who had received instructions from the Grand Vizier to bury a stranger, but that the supposed corpse had disappeared, and so had his cloak and turban. Witnesses proved this man to be the bona-fide Imam of the quarter, and the Grand Vizier gave orders to his Chief Detective to capture, within three days, on pain of death, and bring to the Sublime Porte, this fearless evildoer.

The Chief Detective was soon on the track of Halid, but the latter was on the keen lookout. With the aid of the money he had received from the Grand Vizier to defray his burial expenses, he successfully evaded the clutches of the Chief Detective, who was greatly put about at being thus frustrated. On

Tales of the Meddahs: Tales from the Turkish tradition

the second day he again got scent of Halid and determined to follow him till an opportunity offered for his capture. Halid knew that he was followed and divined the intentions of his pursuer. As he was passing a pharmacy he noticed there several young men, so he entered and explained in Jewish-Spanish to the Jew druggist, as he handed him one of the gold pieces he had received from the Grand Vizier, that his uncle, who would come in presently, was not right in his mind; but that if the druggist could manage to douche his head and back with cold water, he would be all right for a week or two. No sooner did the Chief Detective enter the shop than, at a word from the apothecary, the young men seized him and, by means of a large squirt, they did their utmost to effectively give him the salutary and cooling douche. The more the detective protested, the more the apothecary consolingly explained that the operation would soon be over and that he would feel much better and told of the numerous similar cases he had cured in a like manner. The detective saw that it was useless to struggle, so he abandoned himself to the treatment; and in the meantime, Halid made off. The Chief Detective was so disheartened that he went to the Grand Vizier and asked him to behead him, as death was preferable to the annoyance he had received and might still receive at the hands of Chapkin Halid. The Grand Vizier was both furious and amused, so he spared the Chief Detective and gave orders that guards be placed at the twenty-four gates of the city, and that Halid be seized at the first opportunity. A reward was further promised to the person who would bring him to the Sublime Porte.

Halid was finally caught one night as he was going out of the Top-Kapou, the Cannon Gate, and the guards, rejoicing in their capture, after considerable consultation decided to bind Halid to a large tree close to the Guard house, and thus both avoid the loss of sleep and the anxiety incident to watching over so desperate a character. This was done, and Halid now thought that his case was hopeless. Towards dawn, Halid perceived a man with a lantern walking toward the Armenian Church, and rightly concluded that it was the Beadle going to make ready for the early morning service. So, he called out in a loud voice, "Beadle! Brother! Beadle! Brother! Come here quickly."

Tales of the Meddahs: Tales from the Turkish tradition

Now it happened that the Beadle was a poor hunchback, and no sooner did Halid perceive this than he said, "Quick! Quick! Beadle, look at my back and see if it has gone!"

"See if what has gone?" asked the Beadle, carefully looking behind the tree.

"Why, my hump, of course," answered Halid.

The Beadle made a close inspection and declared that he could see no hump.

"A thousand thanks!" fervently exclaimed Halid, "then please undo the rope."

The Beadle set about liberating Halid, and at the same time earnestly begged to be told how he had got rid of the hump, so that he also might free himself of his deformity. Halid agreed to tell him the cure, provided the Beadle had not yet broken fast, and also that he was prepared to pay a certain small sum of money for the secret. The Beadle satisfied Halid on both of these points, and the latter immediately set about binding the hunchback to the tree, and further told him, on pain of breaking the spell, to repeat sixty-one times the words, "Esserti! Pesserti! Sersepeti!" If he did this, the hump would of a certainty disappear. Halid left the poor beadle religiously and earnestly repeating the words.

The guards were furious when they found, bound to the tree, a madman, as they thought, repeating incoherent words, instead of Halid. They began to unbind the captive, but the only answer they could get to their host of questions was 'Esserti, Pesserti, Sersepeti.' As the knots were loosened, the louder did the Beadle in despair call out the charmed words in the hopes of arresting them. No sooner was the Beadle freed than he asked God to bring down calamity on the destroyers of the charm that was to remove his hunch. On hearing the Beadle's tale, the guards understood how their prisoner had secured his liberty and sent word to the Chief Detective. This gentleman told the Grand Vizier of the unheard-of cunning of the escaped prisoner. The Grand Vizier was amused and also very anxious to see this Chapkin Halid, so he sent criers all over the city, giving full pardon to Halid on condition that he would come to the Sublime Porte and confess in person to the Grand

Vizier. Halid obeyed the summons and came to kiss the hem of the Grand Vizier's garment, who was so favourably impressed by him that he then and there appointed him to be his Chief Detective.

Tales of the Meddahs: Tales from the Turkish tradition

Tales of the Meddahs: Tales from the Turkish tradition

THE CLOWN TURNED FIRST SOLDIER, THEN MERCHANT

This story has been adapted from Turkish Literature by Epiphanius Wilson, A.M., published in 1901 by P. F. Collier & Son, New York.

A certain Clown, occupied in cultivating his field, guided the plough now this way, now that, and in the midst of his task felt sorry that he had not been more favoured by fortune.

A number of volunteers, who formed part of a brigade, which had just come back victorious from war, happened at this moment to pass by, loaded with rich and abundant booty, and plentifully supplied with provisions. Moved by the sight of them, the labourer set to work to sell his sheep, goats, and oxen. With the money received for these he collected horses, weapons, and ammunition, with a view to joining the army on campaign. Just on his arrival, this army was beaten by the enemy, and utterly routed. The baggage of the newcomer was seized, and he himself returned home, crippled with wounds.

"I am disgusted with the military profession," he said, "and I am going to be a businessman. In spite of my slender income, I shall be able to realise great profits in trade."

He accordingly sold his remaining arms and ammunition and employed the proceeds in the purchase of goods which he put on board a ship and embarked himself as passenger. As soon as they had put to sea, a tempest fell upon the ship, which went down with the Merchant on board.

Tales of the Meddahs: Tales from the Turkish tradition

He who seeks for a better position in life, finds a worse one and falls at last into misery. Do not try to learn by experience the disadvantages of each several condition.

Tales of the Meddahs: Tales from the Turkish tradition

THE GHOST OF THE SPRING AND THE SHREW

This story has been adapted from Turkish Fairy Tales and Folk Tales by Dr. Ignácz Kúnos, published in 1901 by A. H. Bullen, London.

Once upon a time which was no time if it was a time, in the days when my mother was my mother and I was my mother's daughter, when my mother was my daughter and I was my mother's mother, in those days, I say, it happened that we once went along the road, and we went on and on and on. We went for a little way, and we went for a long way, we went over mountains and over valleys, we went for a month continually, and when we looked behind us, we had not gone a step. So, we set out again, and we went on and on and on till we came to the garden of the Chin-i-Machin Pasha. We went in, and there was a miller grinding grain, and a cat was by his side. And the cat had woe in its eye, and the cat had woe on its nose, and the cat had woe in its mouth, and the cat had woe in its fore paw, and the cat had woe in its hind paw, and the cat had woe in its throat, and the cat had woe in its ear, and the cat had woe in its face, and the cat had woe in its fur, and the cat had woe in its tail.

Hard by this realm lived a poor woodcutter, who had nothing in the world but his poverty and a horrid shrew of a wife. What little money the poor man made his wife always took away, so that he had not a single piaster left. If his supper was over-salted, and so it was many a time, and her husband chanced to say to her, "Mother, you have put too much salt in the food," so venomous was she that next day she would cook the supper without one single grain of salt, so that there was no savoury in it at all. But if he dared

Tales of the Meddahs: Tales from the Turkish tradition

to say, "There is no savour in the food, mother!" she would put so much salt in it next day that her husband could not eat anything at all.

Now what was it that befell this poor man one day? This is what befell. He put by a couple of pence from his earnings to buy a rope to hang himself with. But his wife found the coins in her husband's pocket. "Ho, ho!" she cried. "So, you hide your money in corners to give it to your comrades, eh?"

In vain the poor man swore by his head that it was not so, but his wife would not believe him. "My dear," said her husband, "I wanted to buy me a rope with the money."

"To hang yourself with, eh?" inquired his affectionate spouse.

"Well, you know what a hideous racket you make sometimes," replied her husband, meaning to pacify her.

"What I have done so far is little enough for a blockhead like you," she replied, and with that she gave her husband such a blow that it seemed to him as if the red dawn was flashing before him.

The next morning the woodcutter rose early, saddled his ass, and went towards the mountains. All that he said to his wife before starting was to beg her not to follow him into the forest. This was quite enough for the wife. Immediately he was gone she saddled her ass, and after her husband she went without more ado. "Who knows," murmured she to herself, "what he may be up to in the mountains, if I am not there to look after him!"

The man saw that his wife was coming after him, but he made as if he did not see, never spoke a word, and as soon as he got to the foot of the mountain, he set about cutting wood. His wife, however, for she was a restless soul, went up and down and all about the mountain, poked her nose into everything, till at last her attention was fixed by a deserted well, and she made straight for it.

Then her husband cried to her, "Take care, there's a well right before you!"

Tales of the Meddahs: Tales from the Turkish tradition

The only effect this warning had upon the wife was to make her draw still nearer. Again, he cried to her, "Can you not hear me? Do not go further on, for there's a well in front of you."

"What do I care what he says?" thought she. Then she took another step forward, but before she could take another the earth gave way beneath her, and into the well she plumped. As for the husband, he was thinking of something else, for he always minded his own business, so, his work over, he took his ass and never stopped till he got home.

The next day, at dawn, he again arose, saddled the ass, and went to the mountains, when the thought of his wife suddenly came into his mind. "I'll see what has become of the poor woman!" said he.

So, he went to the opening of the well and looked into it, but nothing was to be seen or heard of his wife. His heart was sore, for anyhow was she not his wife? He began to think whether he could get her out of the well. So, he took a rope, let it down into the well, and cried into the great depth, "Catch hold of the rope, Mother, and I'll draw you up!"

Presently the man felt that the rope had become very heavy. He pulled away at it with all his might. He tugged and tugged, all the while wondering what creature of Allah's it could be that he was pulling out of the well? And lo! It was none other than a hideous ghost! The poor woodcutter was very afraid.

"Rise up, poor man, and fear not," said the ghost. "The mighty Allah rather bless you for your deed. You have saved me from so great a danger, that to the very day of judgment I will not forget your good deed."

Then the poor man began to wonder what this great danger might be.

"How many many years I lived peaceably in this well I know not," continued the ghost, "but up to this very day I knew no trouble. But yesterday, and from where she came, I know not, but an old woman suddenly plumped down on my shoulders, and caught me so tightly by both my ears, that I could not get loose from her for a moment. By a thousand good fortunes you came to the spot, let down your rope, and called to her to seize hold of it. In trying to get hold of it she let me go, and I at once seized the rope myself,

Tales of the Meddahs: Tales from the Turkish tradition

and, the merciful Allah be praised for it, here I am on dry land again. Good awaits you for your good deed, so listen now to what I say to you!"

With that the ghost drew forth three wooden tablets, gave them to the woodcutter, and said to him, "I now go to take possession of the daughter of the Sultan. Up to this day the princess has been hale and well, but now she will have leeches and wise men without number, but all in vain, for not one of them will be able to cure her. You will hear of the matter, you will hasten to the Padishah, moisten these three wooden tablets with water, lay them on the face of the damsel, and I will come out of her, and a rich reward will be yours."

With that the woodcutter took the three tablets, put them in his pocket, and the ghost went to the right and he went to the left, and neither of them thought any more of the old woman in the well. But let us first follow the ghost.

Scarcely had this son of a devil quitted the woodcutter than he stood in the Serai of the Padishah and entered into the poor daughter of the Sultan. The poor girl immediately fell to the ground in great pain. "O my head! O my head!" she cried continually. They sent word to the Padishah, and he, hastening there, found his daughter lying on the ground and groaning. Straightway he sent for leeches, wise men, drugs, and incense, but none of them assuaged her pain. They sent for them a second time, they sent for them a third time, but all their labour was in vain. At last, they had ten doctors and ten wise men trying everything that they could do, and all the time the poor girl kept moaning, "My head, my head!"

"O my sweet child," groaned the Padishah, "if your head aches, believe me my head, and my heart also, ache a thousand times as much to hear you. What shall I do for you? I know what I will do. I will go call the astrologers, and perhaps they will know more than I do." And with that he called together all the most famous astrologers in his kingdom. One of them had one plan, another had another, but not one of them could cure the complaint of the poor damsel.

Tales of the Meddahs: Tales from the Turkish tradition

But now let us see what became of the poor woodcutter.

He lived on in the world without his wife, and gradually he forgot all about her, and about the ghost and the three wooden tablets, and the ghost's advice and promise. But one day, when he had not thought at all of these things, a herald from the city of the Padishah came to where he was with a firman in his hand and read this out of it in a loud voice, "The damsel, the Sultan's daughter, is very sick. The leeches, the wise men, the astrologers, all have seen her, and not one of them can cure her complaint. Whoever is a master of mysteries, let him come forward and doctor her. If he be a Muslim, and cure her, my daughter now and my realm after my death shall be his reward, and if he be a Giaour, a follower of another religion, and cure her, all the treasures in my realm shall be his."

The woodcutter needed no more to remind him of the ghost, the three tablets, and his wife. He arose and went up to the herald. "By the mercy of Allah, I will cure the Sultan's daughter, if she be still alive," said he. At these words the servant of the Padishah caught hold of the woodcutter and led him into the Serai.

Word was sent at once of his arrival to the Padishah, and in an instant, everything was made ready for him to enter the sick chamber. There before him lay the poor damsel, and all she did was to cry continually, "My head, my head!" The woodcutter brought forth the wooden tablets, moistened them, and scarcely had he spread them on the Sultan's daughter than immediately she became as well again as if she had never been ill. At this there was great joy and gladness in the Serai, and they gave the daughter of the Sultan to the woodcutter, and so the poor man became the son-in-law of the Padishah.

Now this Padishah had a brother who was also a Padishah, and his kingdom was the neighbouring kingdom. He also had a daughter, and it occurred to the ghost of the well to possess her likewise.

So, she also began to be tormented in the same way, and nobody could find a cure for her complaint. They searched and searched for assistance high and

Tales of the Meddahs: Tales from the Turkish tradition

low, till at last they heard how the daughter of the neighbouring Padishah had been cured of a like sickness. So that other Padishah sent many men into the neighbouring kingdom, and begged the first Padishah, for the love of Allah, to send there his son-in-law to cure the other damsel also. If he cured her, he was to have the damsel for his second wife.

So, the Padishah sent his son-in-law that he might cure the damsel. "It would be nothing to such a master of mysteries as he," they all said. All that the former woodcutter could say was in vain, and the poor fellow had to set out, and as soon as he arrived, they led him at once into the sick chamber. But now the ghost of the well had a word to say in the matter.

For that evil spirit was furious with his poor comrade. "You did a good deed for me, it is true," began the ghost, "but you cannot say that I remained in your debt. I left the beautiful daughter of the Sultan for your sake, and then I chose another for myself, and you would now take her from me also? Well, wait a while, and you shall see that for this deed of yours I will take them both away from you."

At this the poor man was deeply troubled.

"I did not come here for the damsel," said he, 'she is your property, and, if such be your desire, you may take mine away also."

"Then what's your errand here?" roared the ghost.

"Alas! It's my wife, the old woman of the well," sighed the former woodcutter, "and I only left her in the well that I might be rid of her."

On hearing this the ghost was terribly frightened, and it was with a small voice that he now inquired whether by chance she had come to light again.

"Yes, indeed, she's outside," sighed the man. "Wherever I go I am saddled with her. I haven't the heart to free myself from her. Listen! She's at the door now. She'll be in the room in a moment."

The ghost needed no more. He immediately left the Sultan's daughter, and the Serai, and the whole city, and the whole kingdom, so that not even the rumour of him remained. And not a child of man has ever seen him since.

Tales of the Meddahs: Tales from the Turkish tradition

But the daughter of the Sultan recovered instantly, and they gave her to the former woodcutter, and he took her home as his second wife.

Tales of the Meddahs: Tales from the Turkish tradition

Tales of the Meddahs: Tales from the Turkish tradition

THE BOY WHO FOUND FEAR AT LAST

This story has been adapted from Andrew Lang's version of the same tale that originally appeared in The Olive Fairy Book, published in 1907 by Longmans, Green and Co., London and New York. This tale was originally adapted by Andrew Lang from Türkische Volksmärchen aus Stambul, by Dr. Ignácz Kúnos. and published in 1905 by E. J. Brill of Leiden.

Once upon a time there lived a woman who had one son whom she loved dearly. The little cottage in which they dwelt was built on the outskirts of a forest, and as they had no neighbours, the place was very lonely, and the boy was kept at home by his mother to bear her company.

They were sitting together on a winter's evening, when a storm suddenly sprang up, and the wind blew the door open. The woman started and shivered and glanced over her shoulder as if she half expected to see some horrible thing behind her. "Go and shut the door," she said hastily to her son, "I feel frightened."

"Frightened?" repeated the boy. "What does it feel like to be frightened?"

"Well - just frightened," answered the mother. "A fear of something, you hardly know what, takes hold of you."

"It must be very odd to feel like that," replied the boy. "I will go through the world and seek fear till I find it." And the next morning, before his mother was out of bed, he had left the forest behind him.

After walking for some hours, he reached a mountain, which he began to climb. Near the top, in a wild and rocky spot, he came upon a band of fierce

Tales of the Meddahs: Tales from the Turkish tradition

robbers, sitting round a fire. The boy, who was cold and tired, was delighted to see the bright flames, so he went up to them and said, "Good greeting to you, sirs," and wriggled himself in between the men, till his feet almost touched the burning logs.

The robbers stopped drinking and eyed him curiously, and at last the captain spoke.

"No caravan of armed men would dare to come here, even the very birds shun our camp, and who are you to venture in so boldly?"

"Oh, I have left my mother's house in search of fear. Perhaps you can show it to me?"

"Fear is wherever we are," answered the captain.

"But where?" asked the boy, looking round. "I see nothing."

"Take this pot and some flour and butter and sugar over to the churchyard which lies down there, and bake us a cake for supper," replied the robber. And the boy, who was by this time quite warm, jumped up cheerfully, and slinging the pot over his arm, ran down the hill.

When he got to the churchyard, he collected some sticks and made a fire. Then he filled the pot with water from a little stream close by, and mixing the flour and butter and sugar together, he set the cake on to cook. It was not long before it grew crisp and brown, and then the boy lifted it from the pot and placed it on a stone, while he put out the fire. At that moment a hand was stretched from a grave, and a voice said, "Is that cake for me?"

"Do you think I am going to give to the dead the food of the living?" replied the boy, with a laugh. And giving the hand a tap with his spoon, and picking up the cake, he went up the mountain side, whistling merrily.

"Well, have you found fear?" asked the robbers when he held out the cake to the captain.

"No, was it there?" answered the boy. "I saw nothing but a hand which came from a grave, and belonged to someone who wanted my cake, but I just

Tales of the Meddahs: Tales from the Turkish tradition

rapped the fingers with my spoon, and said it was not for him, and then the hand vanished. Oh, how nice the fire is!" And he flung himself on his knees before it, and so did not notice the glances of surprise cast by the robbers at each other.

"There is another chance for you," said one at length. "On the other side of the mountain lies a deep pool. Go to that, and perhaps you may meet fear on the way."

"I hope so, indeed," answered the boy. And he set out at once.

He soon beheld the waters of the pool gleaming in the moonlight, and as he drew near, he saw a tall swing standing just over it, and in the swing a child was seated, weeping bitterly.

"That is a strange place for a swing," thought the boy, "but I wonder what he is crying about." And he was hurrying on towards the child, when a maiden ran up and spoke to him.

"I want to lift my little brother from the swing," cried she, "but it is so high above me, that I cannot reach. If you will get closer to the edge of the pool, and let me mount on your shoulder, I think I can reach him."

"Willingly," replied the boy, and in an instant the girl had climbed to his shoulders. But instead of lifting the child from the swing, as she could easily have done, she pressed her feet so firmly on either side of the youth's neck, that he felt that in another minute he would be choked, or else fall into the water beneath him. So, gathering up all his strength, he gave a mighty heave, and threw the girl backwards. As she touched the ground a bracelet fell from her arm, and this the youth picked up.

"I may as well keep it as a remembrance of all the queer things that have happened to me since I left home," he said to himself, and turning to look for the child, he saw that both it and the swing had vanished, and that the first streaks of dawn were in the sky.

With the bracelet on his arm, the youth started for a little town which was situated in the plain on the further side of the mountain, and as, hungry and

Tales of the Meddahs: Tales from the Turkish tradition

thirsty, he entered its principal street, a Jew stopped him. "Where did you get that bracelet?" asked the Jew. "It belongs to me."

"No, it is mine," replied the boy.

"It is not. Give it to me at once, or it will be the worse for you!" cried the Jew.

"Let us go before a judge, and tell him our stories," said the boy. "If he decides in your favour, you shall have it. If in mine, I will keep it!"

To this the Jew agreed, and the two went together to the great hall, in which the Cadi was administering justice. He listened very carefully to what each had to say, and then pronounced his verdict. Neither of the two claimants had proved his right to the bracelet, therefore it must remain in the possession of the judge till its fellow was brought before him.

When they heard this, the Jew and the boy looked at each other, and their eyes said, "Where are we to go to find the other one?" But as they knew there was no use in disputing the decision, they bowed low and left the hall of audience.

Wandering he knew not where, the youth found himself on the seashore. At a little distance was a ship which had struck on a hidden rock, and was rapidly sinking, while on deck the crew were gathered, with faces white as death, shrieking and wringing their hands.

"Have you met with fear?" shouted the boy. And the answer came above the noise of the waves.

"Oh, help! Help! We are drowning!"

Then the boy flung off his clothes, and swam to the ship, where many hands were held out to draw him on board.

"The ship is tossed here and there, and will soon be sucked down," cried the crew again. "Death is very near, and we are frightened!"

Tales of the Meddahs: Tales from the Turkish tradition

"Give me a rope," said the boy in reply, and he took it, and made it safe round his body at one end, and to the mast at the other, and sprang into the sea. Down he went, down, down, down, till at last his feet touched the bottom, and he stood up and looked about him. There, sure enough, a sea-maiden with a wicked face was tugging hard at a chain which she had fastened to the ship with a grappling iron and was dragging it bit by bit beneath the waves. Seizing her arms in both his hands, he forced her to drop the chain, and the ship above remaining steady, the sailors were able gently to float her off the rock. Then taking a rusty knife from a heap of seaweed at his feet, he cut the rope round his waist and fastened the sea-maiden firmly to a stone, so that she could do no more mischief, and bidding her farewell, he swam back to the beach, where his clothes were still lying.

The youth dressed himself quickly and walked on till he came to a beautiful shady garden filled with flowers, and with a clear little stream running through. The day was hot, and he was tired, so he entered the gate, and seated himself under a clump of bushes covered with sweet-smelling red blossoms, and it was not long before he fell asleep. Suddenly a rush of wings and a cool breeze awakened him, and raising his head cautiously, he saw three doves plunging into the stream. They splashed joyfully about, and shook themselves, and then dived to the bottom of a deep pool. When they appeared again, they were no longer three doves, but three beautiful damsels, bearing between them a table made of mother of pearl. On this they placed drinking cups fashioned from pink and green shells, and one of the maidens filled a cup from a crystal goblet, and was raising it to her mouth, when her sister stopped her.

"To whose health do you drink?" asked she.

"To the youth who prepared the cake, and rapped my hand with the spoon when I stretched it out of the earth," answered the maiden, "and was never afraid as other men were! But to whose health do you drink?"

"To the youth on whose shoulders I climbed at the edge of the pool, and who threw me off with such a jerk, that I lay unconscious on the ground for

Tales of the Meddahs: Tales from the Turkish tradition

hours," replied the second. "But you, my sister," added she, turning to the third girl, "to whom do you drink?"

"Down in the sea I took hold of a ship and shook it and pulled it till it would soon have been lost," said she. And as she spoke, she looked quite different from what she had done with the chain in her hands, seeking to work mischief. "But a youth came and freed the ship and bound me to a rock. To his health I drink," and they all three lifted their cups and drank silently.

As they put their cups down, the youth appeared before them.

"Here am I, the youth whose health you have drunk, and now give me the bracelet that matches a jewelled band which of a surety fell from the arm of one of you. A Jew tried to take it from me, but I would not let him have it, and he dragged me before the Cadi, who kept my bracelet till I could show him its fellow. And I have been wandering here and there in search of it, and that is how I have found myself in such strange places."

"Come with us, then," said the maidens, and they led him down a passage into a hall, out of which opened many chambers, each one of greater splendour than the last. From a shelf heaped up with gold and jewels the eldest sister took a bracelet, which in every way was exactly like the one which was in the judge's keeping and fastened it to the youth's arm.

"Go at once and show this to the Cadi," said she, "and he will give you the fellow to it."

"I shall never forget you," answered the youth, "but it may be long before we meet again, for I shall never rest till I have found fear." Then he went his way and won the bracelet from the Cadi. After this, he again set forth in his quest of fear.

On and on walked the youth, but fear never crossed his path, and one day he entered a large town, where all the streets and squares were so full of people, he could hardly pass between them.

"Why are all these crowds gathered together?" he asked of a man who stood next to him.

Tales of the Meddahs: Tales from the Turkish tradition

"The ruler of this country is dead," was the reply, "and as he had no children, it is needful to choose a successor. Therefore, each morning one of the sacred pigeons is let loose from the tower yonder, and on whomsoever the bird shall perch, that man is our king. In a few minutes the pigeon will fly. Wait and see what happens."

Every eye was fixed on the tall tower which stood in the centre of the chief square, and the moment that the sun was seen to stand straight over it, a door was opened and a beautiful pigeon, gleaming with pink and grey, blue and green, came rushing through the air. Onward it flew, onward, onward, till at length it rested on the head of the boy. Then a great shout arose, "The king! the king!" but as he listened to the cries, a vision, swifter than lightning, flashed across his brain. He saw himself seated on a throne, spending his life trying, and never succeeding, to make poor people rich, miserable people happy, bad people good, and never doing anything he wished to do, not able even to marry the girl that he loved.

"No! No!" he shrieked, hiding his face in his hands, but the crowds who heard him thought he was overcome by the grandeur that awaited him, and paid no heed.

"Well, to make quite sure, let fly more pigeons," said they, but each pigeon followed where the first had led, and the cries arose louder than ever, "The king! the king!" And as the young man heard them, a cold shiver, that he knew not the meaning of, ran through him.

"This is fear whom you have so long sought," whispered a voice, which seemed to reach his ears alone. And the youth bowed his head as the vision once more flashed before his eyes, and he accepted his doom, and made ready to pass his life with fear beside him.

Tales of the Meddahs: Tales from the Turkish tradition

Tales of the Meddahs: Tales from the Turkish tradition

THE RIVER AND ITS SOURCE

This story has been adapted from Turkish Literature by Epiphanius Wilson, A.M., published in 1901 by P. F. Collier & Son, New York.

A river one day said to its source, "How idle and good-for-nothing you are! In spite of your incessant movement, you do not contain the slightest quantity of fish! In me, on the contrary, are seen more choice fishes swimming than in any other watercourse. That means I produce joy and happiness in all the plains and their inhabitants, through which I pass! You seem to me to be a corpse, from which life has completely vanished."

The source, indignant at these insulting words, made no reply, but began to diminish the quantity of water which she furnished to the river. Soon she entirely ceased to feed it. By this means the height of the flood sank gradually, until, at the last, water failed entirely, and river and fish disappeared together.

This fable is addressed to those who treat their friends in a similar manner and imagine that their prosperity is specially and directly due to the munificence of God.

An ungrateful man, says the poet, is one who addresses no thanks to Divine Providence for the innumerable gifts showered upon him. He is a blasphemer, as well as an ingrate, who is grateful toward no one excepting the giver of them all.

Tales of the Meddahs: Tales from the Turkish tradition

Tales of the Meddahs: Tales from the Turkish tradition

STONE-PATIENCE AND KNIFE-PATIENCE

This story has been adapted from Turkish Fairy Tales and Folk Tales by Dr. Ignácz Kúnos, published in 1901 by A. H. Bullen, London.

There was once a poor woman who had one daughter, and this poor woman used to go out and wash linen, while her daughter remained at home at her working-table. One day she was sitting by the window as was her wont, when a little bird flew on to the sewing-table and said to the damsel, "Oh, little damsel, poor little damsel! Death is your Kismet!" The little bird promptly flew away again. From that hour the damsel's peace of mind was gone, and in the evening, she told her mother what the bird had said to her. "Close the door and the window," said her mother, "and sit at your work as usual."

So, the next morning she closed the door and the window and sat down at her work. But all at once there came a "Whirr-r-r-r" and there was the little bird again on the worktable. "Oh, little damsel, poor little damsel! Death is your Kismet," and with that it flew away again. The damsel was more and more terrified than ever at these words, but her mother comforted her again, "Tomorrow," said she, "close fast the door and the window, and get into the cupboard. There light a candle and go on with your work!"

Scarcely had her mother departed with the dawn than the girl closed up everything, lit a candle, and locked herself in the cupboard with her worktable. But scarcely had she stitched two stitches when the bird stood before her again, and said, "Oh, little damsel, poor little damsel! Death is your Kismet," and whirr-r-r-r, it flew away again. The damsel was in such

Tales of the Meddahs: Tales from the Turkish tradition

distress that she scarce knew where she was. She threw her work aside and began tormenting herself as to what this saying might mean. Her mother, too, could not get to the bottom of the matter, so she remained at home the next day, that she also might see the bird, but the bird did not come again.

So, their sorrow was perpetual, and all the joy of their life was gone. They never stirred from the house but watched and waited continually, if perhaps the bird might come again. One day the damsels of their neighbour came to them and asked the woman to let her daughter go with them. "If she went for a little outing," said they, 'she might forget her trouble." The woman did not like to let her go, but they promised to take great care of her and not to lose sight of her, so at last she let her go.

So, the damsels went into the fields and danced and played till the day was on the decline. On the way home the neighbour's daughters sat down by a well and began to drink out of it. The poor woman's daughter also went to drink the water, but a wall rose up between her and the other damsels, but such a wall as never the eye of man yet beheld. A voice could not get beyond it, it was so high, and a man could not get through it, it was so hard. Oh, how terrified was the poor woman's daughter, and what weeping and wailing and despair there was among her comrades. What would become of the poor girl, and what would become of her poor mother!

"I will not tell," said one of them, "for she will not believe us!"

"But what shall we say to her mother," cried another, "now that she has disappeared from before our eyes?"

"It is your fault; it is your fault! It was you that asked her!"

"No, it was you."

So, they fell to blaming each other, looking all the time at the great wall.

Meanwhile the mother was awaiting her daughter. She stood at the door of the house and watched the damsels coming. The damsels came weeping, and scarce dared to tell the poor woman what had befallen her daughter. When they admitted what had happened, the woman rushed to the great wall, but

Tales of the Meddahs: Tales from the Turkish tradition

her daughter was inside it and she herself was outside, and so they wept and wailed so long as either of them had a tear to flow.

In the midst of this great weeping the damsel fell asleep, and when she woke up next morning, she saw a great door beside the wall. "Happen to me what may, if I am to perish, let me perish, but open this door I will!" So, she opened it.

Beyond the door was a beautiful palace, the like of which is not to be seen even in dreams. This palace had a vast hall, and on the wall of this hall hung forty keys. The damsel took the keys and began opening the doors of all the rooms around her, and the first set of rooms was full of silver, and the second set full of gold, and the third set full of diamonds, and the fourth set full of emeralds. Each set of rooms was full of stones more precious than the precious things of the rooms before it, so that the eyes of the damsel were almost blinded by their splendour.

She entered the fortieth room, and there, extended on the floor, was a beautiful Bey, with a fan of pearls beside him, and on his breast a piece of paper with these words written on it, "Whoever fans me for forty days and prays all that time by my side will find her Kismet!"

Then the damsel thought of the little bird. So, it was by the side of this sleeper that she was to meet her fate! She made her ablutions, and, taking the fan in her hand, she sat down beside the Bey. Day and night she kept on fanning him, praying continually till the fortieth day was at hand. And on the morning of the last day, she peeped out of the window and beheld a girl in front of the palace. Then she thought she would call this girl for a moment and ask her to pray beside the Bey, while she herself made her ablutions and took a little repose. She called the girl and set her beside the Bey, that she might pray beside him and fan his face. But the damsel hastened away and made her ablutions and adorned herself, so that the Bey, when he awoke, might see his life's Kismet at her best and rejoice at the sight.

Meanwhile the girl read the piece of paper, and while the lost damsel tarried the youth awoke. He looked about him, and scarcely did he see the girl than

Tales of the Meddahs: Tales from the Turkish tradition

he embraced her and called her his wife. The poor lost damsel could scarce believe her own eyes when she entered the room.

The new girl, who was jealous of her, said to the Bey, "I, a Sultan's daughter, am not ashamed to go about just as I am, and this chit of a serving-maid dares to appear before me arrayed so finely!" Then she chased her out of the room and sent her to the kitchen to finish her work and boil and fry. The Bey was surprised, but he would not say a word, for the new girl was his bride, while the other damsel was only a kitchen-wench.

Now the Feast of Bairam fell about this time, and as is the custom at such times, the Bey wished to give gifts to the members of his household. So, he went to his wife and asked her what she would like on the Feast of Bairam. And his wife asked for a garment that never a needle had sewn and never scissors had cut. Then he went down into the kitchen and asked the damsel what she would like. "The stone-of-patience has a yellow colour, and the knife-of-patience has a brown handle, bring them both to me," said the damsel. The Bey went on his way, and got his wife her garment, but the stone-of-patience and the knife-of-patience he could find nowhere. What was he to do? He could not return home without the gifts, so he got on board his ship.

The ship had only got half-way when suddenly it stopped short and could neither go backwards nor forwards. The captain was terrified and told his passengers that there was someone on board who had not kept his word, and that was why they could not get on. Then the Bey came forward and said that he it was who had not kept his word. So, they put the Bey ashore, that he might keep his promise and then return back to the ship. Then the Bey walked along the seashore, and from the seashore he came to a great valley, and he went wandering on and on till he stood beside a large spring. And he had scarce trodden on the stones around it when suddenly a huge man stood before him and asked him what he wanted.

"The stone-of-patience is of a yellow colour and the knife-of-patience has a brown sheath, bring them both to me!" said the Bey to the man. And the next moment both the stone and the knife were in his hand, and he came back to

76

Tales of the Meddahs: Tales from the Turkish tradition

the ship, went on board, and returned home. He gave the garment to his wife, but the stone and the knife he put in the kitchen. But the Bey was curious to know what the damsel would do with them, so one evening he crept down into the kitchen and watched her.

When night approached, she took the knife in her hand and placed the stone in front of her and began telling them her story. She told them what the little bird had thrice told her, and in what great terror both her mother and she had fallen into. And while she was looking at the stone it suddenly began to swell, and its yellow hue hissed and bubbled as if there were life in it.

Then the damsel went on to say how she had wandered into the palace of the Bey, how she had prayed forty days beside him, and how she had entrusted the other girl with the praying while she went to wash and dress herself. And the yellow stone swelled again, and hissed and foamed as if it were about to burst.

Then the damsel told how the other girl had deceived her, and how instead of her the Bey had taken the interloper to wife. And all this time the yellow stone went on swelling and hissing and foaming as if there were a real living heart inside it, till suddenly it burst and turned to ashes.

Then the damsel took the little knife by the handle and said, "Oh, you, yellow patience-stone, you were but a stone, and yet you could not endure that I, a tender little damsel, a poor little damsel, should thus be thrust out." And with that she would have buried the knife in her breast, but the Bey rushed forward and snatched away the knife.

"You are my real true Kismet," cried the youth, as he took her into the upper chamber in the place of his current wife. But the treacherous girl they slew, and they sent for the damsel's mother, and all lived together with great joy.

And the little bird came sometimes and perched in the window of the palace and sang his joyful lay. And this is what he sang, "Oh, little damsel, happy little damsel, that have found your Kismet!"

Tales of the Meddahs: Tales from the Turkish tradition

Tales of the Meddahs: Tales from the Turkish tradition

HOW COBBLER AHMET BECAME THE CHIEF ASTROLOGER

This story has been adapted from Told in the Coffee House by Cyrus Adler and Allan Ramsay, published in 1898 by MacMillan and Company, London. Allan Ramsay was a Scottish poet, playwright, publisher, librarian, and wig-maker active in the early and mid-eighteenth century. Cyrus Adler adapted Ramsay's work in the nineteenth century, being an American educator, Jewish religious leader, and scholar.

Each day cobbler Ahmet, year in and year out, measured the breadth of his tiny cabin with his arms as he stitched old shoes. To do this was his Kismet, his decreed fate, and he was content, and why not? His business brought him quite sufficient to provide the necessaries of life for both him and his wife. Had it not been for a coincidence that occurred, in all probability he would have mended old boots and shoes to the end of his days.

One day cobbler Ahmet's wife went to the Hamam, the bath house, and while there she was much annoyed at being obliged to give up her compartment, owing to the arrival of the Harem and retinue of the Chief Astrologer to the Sultan. Much hurt, she returned home and vented her pique upon her innocent husband.

"Why are you not the Chief Astrologer to the Sultan?" she said. "I will never call or think of you as my husband until you have been appointed Chief Astrologer to his Majesty."

Tales of the Meddahs: Tales from the Turkish tradition

Ahmet thought that this was another phase in the eccentricity of womankind, which in all probability would disappear before morning, so he took small notice of what his wife said. But Ahmet was wrong. His wife persisted so much in his giving up his present means of earning a livelihood and becoming an astrologer, that finally, for the sake of peace, he complied with her desire. He sold his tools and collection of sundry old boots and shoes, and, with the proceeds purchased an inkwell and reeds. But this, alas, did not constitute him an astrologer, and he explained to his wife that this mad idea of hers would bring him to an unhappy end. She, however, could not be moved, and insisted on his going to the highway, there to wisely practise the art, and thus ultimately become the Chief Astrologer.

In obedience to his wife's instructions, Ahmet sat down on the highroad, and his oppressed spirit sought comfort in looking at the heavens and sighing deeply. While in this condition a Hanoum in great excitement came and asked him if he communicated with the stars. Poor Ahmet sighed, saying that he was compelled to converse with them.

"Then please tell me where my diamond ring is, and I will both bless and handsomely reward you."

With this, the Hanoum immediately squatted on the ground, and began to tell Ahmet that she had gone to the bath that morning and that she was positive that she then had the ring, but every corner of the Hamam had been searched, and the ring was not to be found.

"Oh, astrologer, for the love of Allah, exert your eye to see the unseen."

"Hanoum Effendi," replied Ahmet, the instant her excited flow of language had ceased, "I perceive a rent," referring to a tear he had noticed in her shalvars or baggy trousers. Up jumped the Hanoum, exclaiming, "A thousand holy thanks! You are right! Now I remember! I put the ring in a crevice of the cold-water fountain." And in her gratitude, she handed Ahmet several gold pieces.

In the evening he returned to his home, and giving the gold to his wife, said, "Take this money, wife. May it satisfy you, and in return all I ask is that you

Tales of the Meddahs: Tales from the Turkish tradition

allow me to go back to the trade of my father, and not expose me to the danger and suffering of trudging the road shoeless."

But her purpose was unmoved. Until he became the Chief Astrologer, she would neither call him nor think of him as her husband.

In the meantime, owing to the discovery of the ring, the fame of Ahmet the cobbler spread far and wide. The tongue of the Hanoum never ceased to sound his praise.

It happened that the wife of a certain Pasha had appropriated a valuable diamond necklace, and as a last resource, the Pasha determined, seeing that all the astrologers, Hodjas, and diviners had failed to discover the article, to consult Ahmet the cobbler, whose praises were in every mouth.

The Pasha went to Ahmet, and, in fear and trembling, the wife who had appropriated the necklace sent her confidential slave to overhear what the astrologer would say. The Pasha told Ahmet all he knew about the necklace, but this gave no clue, and in despair Ahmet asked how many diamonds the necklace contained. On being told that there were twenty-four, Ahmet, to put off the evil hour, said it would take an hour to discover each diamond. Consequently, would the Pasha come on the morrow at the same hour when, Inshallah, he would perhaps be able to give him some news.

The Pasha departed, and no sooner was he out of earshot, than the troubled Ahmet exclaimed in a loud voice, "Oh woman! Oh woman! What evil influence impelled you to go the wrong path and drag others with you! When the twenty-four hours are up, you will perhaps repent! Alas! Too late. Your husband will be gone from you forever, without a hope even of being united in paradise."

Ahmet was referring to himself and his wife, for he fully expected to be cast into prison on the following day as an impostor. But the slave who had been listening gave another interpretation to his words, and hurrying off, told her mistress that the astrologer knew all about the theft. The good man had even bewailed the separation that would inevitably take place. The Pasha's wife was distracted and hurried off to plead her cause in person with the

Tales of the Meddahs: Tales from the Turkish tradition

astrologer. On approaching Ahmet, the first words she said, in her excitement, were, "Oh learned Hodja, you are a great and good man. Have compassion on my weakness and do not expose me to the wrath of my husband! I will do such penance as you may order and bless you five times daily as long as I live."

"How can I save you?" asked Ahmet innocently. "What is decreed is decreed!" Then Ahmet sat in silence, for he instinctively knew that words unuttered were arrows still in the quiver.

"If you won't pity me," continued the Hanoum, in despair, "I will go and confess to my Pasha, and perhaps he will forgive me."

To this appeal Ahmet said he must ask the stars for their views on the subject. The Hanoum inquired if the answer would come before the twenty-four hours were up. Ahmet's reply to this was a long and concentrated gaze at the heavens.

"Oh Hodja Effendi, I must go now, or the Pasha will miss me. Shall I give you the necklace to restore to the Pasha without explanation, when he comes tomorrow for the answer?"

Ahmet now realized what all the trouble was about, and in consideration of a fee, he promised not to reveal her theft on the condition that she would at once return home and place the necklace between the mattresses of her Pasha's bed. This the grateful woman agreed to do, and departed invoking blessings on Ahmet, who in return promised to exercise his influence in her behalf for astral intervention.

When the Pasha came to the astrologer at the appointed time, he explained to him, that if he wanted both the necklace and the thief or thieves, it would take a long time, as it was impossible to hurry the stars, but if he would be content with the necklace alone, the horoscope indicated that the stars would oblige him at once. The Pasha said that he would be quite satisfied if he could get his diamonds again, and Ahmet at once told him where to find them. The Pasha returned to his home not a little sceptical, and immediately searched for the necklace where Ahmet had told him it was to be found. His

Tales of the Meddahs: Tales from the Turkish tradition

joy and astonishment on discovering the long-lost article knew no bounds, and the fame of Ahmet the cobbler was the theme of every tongue.

Having received handsome payment from both the Pasha and the Hanoum, Ahmet earnestly begged his wife to desist and not bring down sorrow and calamity upon his head. But his pleadings were in vain. Satan had closed his wife's ear to reason with envy. Resigned to his fate, all he could do was to consult the stars, and after mature thought give their communication, or assert that the stars had, for some reason best known to the applicant, refused to commune on the subject.

It happened that forty cases of gold were stolen from the Imperial Treasury, and every astrologer had failed to get even a clue as to where the money was or how it had disappeared. Ahmet was approached. Poor man, his case now looked hopeless! Even the Chief Astrologer was in disgrace. What might be his punishment he did not know, but most probably death. Ahmet had no idea of the numerical importance of forty but concluding that it must be large he asked for a delay of forty days to discover the forty cases of gold. Ahmet gathered up the implements of his occult art, and before returning to his home, went to a shop and asked for forty beans, neither one more nor one less. When he got home and laid them down, he appreciated the number of cases of gold that had been stolen, and also the number of days he had to live. He knew it would be useless to explain to his wife the seriousness of the case, so that evening he took from his pocket the forty beans and mournfully said, "Forty cases of gold, forty thieves, forty days; and here is one of them," handing a bean to his wife. "The rest remain in their place until the time comes to give them up."

While Ahmet was saying this to his wife one of the thieves was listening at the window. The thief was sure he had been discovered when he heard Ahmet say, "And here is one of them," and hurried off to tell his companions.

The thieves were greatly distressed, but decided to wait till the next evening to see what would happen then. Another of the number was sent to listen and see if the report would be verified. The listener had not long been stationed at his post when he heard Ahmet say to his wife, "And here is

83

Tales of the Meddahs: Tales from the Turkish tradition

another of them," meaning another of the forty days of his life. But the thief understood the words otherwise, and hurried off to tell his chief that the astrologer knew all about it and knew that he had been there. The thieves consequently decided to send a delegation to Ahmet, confessing their guilt and offering to return the forty cases of gold intact. Ahmet received them, and on hearing their confession, accompanied with their condition to return the gold, boldly told them that he did not require their aid, and that it was in his power to take possession of the forty cases of gold whenever he wished, but that he had no special desire to see them all executed, and he would plead their cause if they would go and put the gold in a place he indicated. This was agreed to, and Ahmet continued to give his wife a bean daily, but now with another purpose. He no longer feared the loss of his head but discounted by degrees the great reward he hoped to receive. At last, the final bean was given to his wife, and Ahmet was summoned to the Palace. He went and explained to his Majesty that the stars refused both to reveal the thieves and the gold, but whichever of the two his Majesty wished would be immediately granted. The Treasury being low, it was decided that, provided the cases were returned with the gold intact, his Majesty would be satisfied. Ahmet conducted them to the place where the gold was buried, and amidst great rejoicing it was taken back to the Palace. The Sultan was so pleased with Ahmet, that he appointed him to the office of Chief Astrologer, and his wife attained her desire.

The Sultan was one day walking in his Palace grounds accompanied by his Chief Astrologer. Wishing to test Ahmet's powers he caught a grasshopper, and holding his closed hand out to the astrologer asked him what it contained. Ahmet, in a pained and reproachful tone, answered the Sultan by a much-quoted proverb, "Alas! Your Majesty! The grasshopper never knows where its third leap will land it," figuratively alluding to himself and the dangerous hazard of guessing what was in the clenched hand of his Majesty. The Sultan was so struck by the reply that Ahmet was never again troubled to demonstrate his powers.

Tales of the Meddahs: Tales from the Turkish tradition

THE LAMB AND THE WOLF

This story has been adapted from Turkish Literature by Epiphanius Wilson, A.M., published in 1901 by P. F. Collier & Son, New York.

A tender lamb was in the fold, when suddenly a wolf entered intent on devouring her. Throwing herself at the feet of the wolf, she said, weeping, "God has put me in your power. Sound your horn in order to grant me one moment's delight. Then my desires will be perfectly satisfied, for my parents have told me that the race of wolves are the best players on the horn."

The wolf heard this silly proposal and set himself to cry out with all his might and main. Lo and behold, the dogs woke up and attacked him. He took to flight, and did not stop until he reached a hill, where he said, lamenting, "I certainly deserve this mishap, for who has made me a musician, when I have never been anything but a butcher?"

This fable proves that many good people are deceived by attending to silly proposals, and afterward, like the wolf, are sorry for it, and that many others undertake, either in word or deed, things for which they are not adapted, and consequently fall into misfortune.

Tales of the Meddahs: Tales from the Turkish tradition

Tales of the Meddahs: Tales from the Turkish tradition

THE SERPENT-PERI AND THE MAGIC MIRROR

This story has been adapted from Turkish Fairy Tales and Folk Tales by Dr. Ignácz Kúnos, published in 1901 by A. H. Bullen, London.

There was once upon a time a poor woodcutter who had an only son. One day this poor man fell sick and said to his son, "If I should die follow my handicraft, and go every day into the wood. You may cut down whatever trees you find there, but at the edge of the wood is a cypress-tree, and that you must leave standing." Two days afterwards the man died and was buried.

But the son went into the wood and cut down the trees, only the cypress-tree he left alone. One day the youth stood close to this tree and thought to himself, "What can be the matter with this tree, seeing that I am not allowed to lay a hand upon it?"

So, he looked at it, and considered it curiously, till at last he took his axe and went with evil intent towards the tree. But he had scarcely lifted his foot when the cypress-tree drew away from him. The woodcutter mounted his ass and pursued the tree but could not overtake it, and in the meantime, eventide came upon them. Then he dismounted from his ass and tied it to a tree, but he himself climbed to the top of the tree to await the dawn.

Next morning, when the sky grew red, he descended from the tree, and there at the foot of it lay only the bones of his ass. "Never mind, I'll go on foot," said the woodcutter, and he continued his pursuit of the cypress, the tree going on before and he following on after. All that day he pursued but could

Tales of the Meddahs: Tales from the Turkish tradition

not catch up with it. The third day he also shouldered his axe and pursued the tree, but this time he suddenly came upon an elephant and a serpent fighting with each other. Believe the truth or not as you will, but the truth is this, that the serpent was swallowing the elephant, but the elephant's great tusk stuck in the serpent's throat, and both beasts, seeing the youth staring at them, begged him to help them.

What didn't the elephant promise him if only he would slay the serpent! "Nay, but all I would have you do," said the serpent, "is to break his tusk off. The work is lighter, and the reward will be greater."

At these words the youth seized his axe and chopped the elephant's tusk right off. The serpent then swallowed the elephant, thanked the youth, and promised to keep his word and give him his reward.

While they were on the road the serpent stopped at a spring and said to the youth, "Wait while I bathe in this water, and whatever may happen, fear not!"

With that the serpent plunged into the water, and immediately there arose such a terrible storm, such a tempest, such a hurricane, with lightning-flash upon lightning-flash, and thunderbolt upon thunderbolt, that the Day of Judgment could not well be worse. Presently the serpent came out of the bath, and then all was quiet again.

They went a long way, and they went a little way, they took coffee, and they smoked their chibouks. They even gathered violets on the road, till at last they drew near to a house, and then the serpent said, "In a short time we shall arrive at my mother's house. When she opens the door, say you are my kinsman, and she will invite you into the house. She will offer you coffee but do not drink it. She will offer you meat but do not eat it. But there's a little bit of a mirror hanging up in the corner of the door, ask my mother for that!"

So, they came to the house, and no sooner had the Peri knocked at the door than his mother came and opened it. "Come, my brother!" said the serpent to the youth behind him.

Tales of the Meddahs: Tales from the Turkish tradition

"Who is your brother?" asked his mother.

"He saved my life," replied her son, and with that he told her the whole story. So they went into the house, and the woman brought the youth coffee and a chibouk, but he would not take them. "My journey is a hasty one," said he, "I cannot remain very long."

"Rest awhile at least," said the woman. "We cannot let our guests depart without anything."

"I want nothing, but if you will give me that bit of mirror in the corner of the door I will take it," said the youth. The woman did not want to give it, but the youth insisted that perhaps his life might depend upon that very piece of mirror, so at last she gave it to him, though very unwillingly.

The youth went on his way with the bit of mirror, and as he looked into it he turned over in his mind what use he should make of it. As he was still turning it over and looking at it, suddenly there stood before him a great spirit. The poor youth was so frightened, that if the spirit had not said, "What are your commands, my Sultan?" he would have run away for ever and ever. As it was, it was as much as he could do to ask for something to eat, and immediately there stood before him a rich and rare banquet, the like of which he had never seen at his father's table.

Then the youth felt very curious about the mirror, and looked into it again, and immediately the spirit stood before him again and said, "What do you command, my Sultan?" He could think of nothing at first, but at last his lips murmured the word "Palace," and immediately there stood before him a palace so beautiful that the Padishah himself could not have a finer one. "Open!" cried the youth, and immediately the gates of the palace flew open before him.

The youth rejoiced greatly in his bit of mirror, and his one thought was what he should ask it to get him next. He thought of the beautiful Sultana-damsel, the Padishah's daughter, and the next moment his eye sought his mirror and he desired from the spirit a palace in which the world-renowned daughter of the Padishah should be sitting beside him, and he had scarce time to look

Tales of the Meddahs: Tales from the Turkish tradition

around him when he found himself sitting in the palace with the Sultan's daughter by his side. Then they kissed and embraced each other and lived a whole world of joy.

Meanwhile the Sultan learnt that his daughter had disappeared from her own palace. He searched for her the whole realm through. He sent heralds in every direction, but in vain were all his labours, for the girl could not be discovered. At last, an old woman came to the Padishah and told him to make a large casket, line it well with zinc, put her inside it, and cast it into the sea She would find the daughter of the Sultan, she said, for if she was not here, she must be beyond the sea So, they made ready the great casket, put the old woman inside it, put food for nine days beside her, and cast it into the sea. The casket was tossed from wave to wave, till at last it came to that city where the Sultan's daughter dwelt with the youth.

Now the fishermen were just then on the shore and saw the huge casket floating in the sea. They drew it ashore with ropes and hooks, and when they opened it, an old woman crept out of it. They asked her how she had got inside it.

"Oh, that my enemy might lose the sight of his little eye that is so dear to him!" lamented the old woman. "I have not deserved this of him!" and with that she fell a-weeping and wailing till the men believed every word she said. "Where is the Bey of your city?" cried she, "perhaps he will have compassion upon me and receive me into his house," she said to the men. Then they showed her the palace, and exhorted her to go there, as perhaps she might get alms.

The old woman went to the palace, and when she knocked at the door, the Sultan's daughter came down to see who it was. The old woman immediately recognized the damsel and begged her to take her into her service.

"My lord comes home tonight, I will ask him," replied the damsel. "Meanwhile rest in this corner!" And the damsel's lord allowed her to

Tales of the Meddahs: Tales from the Turkish tradition

receive the old woman into the house, and the next day she waited upon them.

There the old woman stayed for one day and for two days, for a week, for two weeks, and there was no cook to cook the food, and no servant to keep the place clean, and yet every day there was a costly banquet, and everything was as clean as clean could be. Then the old woman went to the damsel and asked her whether she did not feel dull at being alone all day. "If I were allowed to help you pass the time away," added she, "perhaps it might be better."

"I must first ask my lord," replied the damsel.

The youth did not mind the old woman helping his wife to pass away the time, and so she went up to the damsel's rooms and stayed with her for days together.

One day the old woman asked the damsel where all the rare meats came from, and who did the service of the house. But the damsel did not know about the piece of mirror, so she could tell the old woman nothing. "Find out from your lord," said the old woman, and scarcely had the youth come home, scarce had he had time to eat, than the damsel wheedled him so that he showed her the mirror.

That was all the old woman wanted. A couple of days she let go by, but on the third and the fourth days she bade the damsel beg her lord for the piece of mirror so that she might amuse herself with it, and make the time pass more easily. And indeed, she had only to ask her lord for it, for he, not suspecting her falseness, gave it to her.

In the meantime, the old woman was not asleep. She knew where the damsel had put the mirror, stole it, and when she looked into it the spirit appeared. "What is your command?" inquired he of the old woman.

"Take me with this damsel to her father's palace," was her first command. Her second command turned the youth's palace into a heap of ashes, so that when the young woodcutter returned home he found nought but the cat

Tales of the Meddahs: Tales from the Turkish tradition

meowing among the ashes. There was also a small piece of meat there that the Sultan's daughter had thrown down for the cat.

The youth took up the fragment of meat and set out to seek his consort. Find her he would, though he roamed the whole world over. He went on and on. He searched and searched till he came to the city where his wife now lived. He went up to the palace, and there he begged the cook to take him into the kitchen as a servant out of pure compassion. In a couple of days, he had learnt from his fellow-servants in the kitchen that the Sultan's daughter had returned home.

One day the cook fell sick and there was no heart in him to attend to the cooking. The youth, seeing this, bade him rest, and said he would cook the food in his stead. The cook agreed, and told him what to cook, and how to season it. So, the youth set to work, roasting and stewing, and when he sent up the dishes, he also sent up the scrap of food that he had found on the ashes. He put it on the damsel's plate. Scarcely had the damsel cast eyes on this little scrap than she knew within herself that her lord was near her. She called the cook and asked whom he had with him in the kitchen. At first, he denied that he had anyone, but at last he confessed that he had taken a poor lad in to assist him.

Then the damsel went to her father and said to him that there was a young lad in the kitchen who prepared coffee so well that she should like some coffee from his hands. The lad was ordered up, and from then onwards he prepared the coffee and took it to the Sultan's daughter. Through this they came together again, and she told her lord how the matter had gone. Then they took some time to think about how they should await their turn and get the mirror back again.

Scarcely had the youth gone into the damsel than the old woman appeared. Although she had not seen him for long, she recognized him, and, looking into the mirror, caused the poor lad to be sent back again to the ashes of his old palace. There he found the cat still squatting. When she felt hungry, she caught mice, and such ravages did she make upon them that at last the Padishah of the mice had scarce a soldier left.

Tales of the Meddahs: Tales from the Turkish tradition

The poor Padishah of the mice was very angry, but he dared not tackle the cat. One day, however, he observed the youth, went up to him, and begged his assistance in his dire distress, for if he waited till the morrow his whole realm would be ruined.

"I'll help you," said the youth, "though, indeed, I have enough troubles of my own to carry already."

"What is your trouble?" asked the Padishah of the mice. The youth told him about the history of the piece of looking glass, and how it had been stolen from him, and into whose hands it had fallen.

"Then I can help you," cried the Padishah, whereupon he called together all the mice in the world. And he asked which of them had access to this palace, and which knew of such-and-such an old woman, and the piece of looking-glass. At these words a lame mouse hobbled forth, kissed the ground at the feet of the Padishah, and said that it was his habit to steal food from the old woman's box. He had seen through the keyhole how she took out a little bit of looking glass every evening and hid it under a cushion.

Then the Padishah commanded him to go and steal this bit of mirror. The mouse, however, begged that he might have two comrades. He sat on the back of one of them, and so went on to the old woman. It was evening when they arrived there, and the old woman was just eating her supper.

"We have come at the right time," said the lame mouse. "We shall get something to eat." And with that they scampered into the room, satisfied their hunger, and waited for the night. They arranged between them what they should do, and when the old woman lay down, they waited till she was asleep. Scarcely had she fallen asleep than the lame mouse leaped into her bed, made for her face, and began tickling her nose with the end of its tail.

"P-chi! P-chi!" the old woman sneezed, so that her head nearly leaped from her shoulders. "P-chi! P-chi!" she sneezed again, and meanwhile the two other little mice rushed out, picked up the piece of looking-glass from underneath the cushion, took the lame mouse on their backs, and hurried home again.

Tales of the Meddahs: Tales from the Turkish tradition

The youth rejoiced greatly at the sight of the mirror. Then he took the cat with him so that it should do no more harm to the mice and went into other parts. There he took out the bit of mirror, looked into it, and lo, the spirit stood before him and said, "What is your command, my Sultan?"

The youth asked for a raiment of cloth of gold and a whole army of soldiers, and before he had time to look round, in front of him stood costly raiment, and he put it on; and a beautiful horse, and he sat on its back. He also had a large army which marched behind him into the city. When he arrived there, he stood before the palace, and surrounded it with his soldiers. Oh, how terrified the Padishah was at the sight of that vast army!

The youth went into the palace and demanded the damsel from her father. In his terror the Padishah gave him not only his daughter but his realm. The old woman was given into the hands of the mirror spirit, but the bride and bridegroom lived happily in the midst of their glorious kingdom. And close beside them stood the magic mirror that made all their woes vanish.

Tales of the Meddahs: Tales from the Turkish tradition

THE WISE SON OF ALI PASHA

This story has been adapted from Told in the Coffee House by Cyrus Adler and Allan Ramsay, published in 1898 by MacMillan and Company, London. Allan Ramsay was a Scottish poet, playwright, publisher, librarian, and wig-maker active in the early and mid-eighteenth century. Cyrus Adler adapted Ramsay's work in the nineteenth century, being an American educator, Jewish religious leader, and scholar.

A servant of his Majesty Sultan Ahmet, who had been employed for twenty-five years in the Palace, begged leave of the Sultan to allow him to retire to his native home, and at the same time solicited a pension to enable him to live. The Sultan asked him if he had not saved any money. The man replied that owing to his having to support a large family, he had been unable to do so. The Sultan was very angry that any of his servants, especially in the immediate employ of his household, should, after so many years' service, say that he was penniless. Disbelieving the statement, and in order to make an example, the Sultan gave orders that Hassan should quit the Palace in the identical state he had entered it twenty-five years before. Hassan was accordingly disrobed of all his splendour, and his various effects, the accumulation of a quarter of a century, were confiscated, and distributed amongst the legion of Palace servants. Poor Hassan, without a piaster in his pocket, and dressed in the rude costume of his native province, began his weary journey homeward on foot.

In time he reached the suburbs of a town, and seeing some boys playing, he approached them, sat on the ground, and watched their play. The boys were

Tales of the Meddahs: Tales from the Turkish tradition

playing at state affairs. One was a Sultan, another his Vizier, who had his cabinet of Ministers, while close by were a number of boys bound hand and foot, representing political and other prisoners, awaiting judgment for their imaginary misdeeds. The Sultan, who was sitting with worthy dignity on a throne made of branches and stones, decorated with many-coloured centrepieces, beckoned to Hassan to draw near, and asked him where he had come from. Hassan replied that he had come from Istanbul, from the Palace of the Sultan.

"That's a lie," said the mock Sultan. "No one ever came from Istanbul dressed in that fashion, much less from the Palace. You are from the far interior, and if you do not confess that what I say is true, you will be tried by my Ministers, and punished accordingly."

Hassan, partly to participate in their boyish amusement, and partly to unburden his aching heart, related his sad fate to his youthful audience. When he had finished, the boy Sultan, Ali by name, asked him if he had received his twenty-five years. Hassan, not fully grasping what the boy said, replied, "Nothing! Nothing!"

"That is unjust," continued Ali, "and you shall go back to the Sultan and ask that your twenty-five years be returned to you so that you may plough and till your ground, and thus make provision for the period of want in your old age."

Hassan was struck by the sound advice the boy had given him, thanked him, and said he would follow it to the letter. The boys then in thoughtless mirth separated, to return to their homes, never dreaming that the seeds of destiny of one of their number had been sown in play. Hassan, retracing his steps, reappeared in time at the gates of the Palace and begged admittance, stating that he had forgotten to communicate something of importance to his Majesty. His request being granted, he humbly solicited, that, inasmuch as his Majesty had been dissatisfied with his long service, the twenty-five years he had devoted to him should be returned, so that he might labour and put by something to provide for the inevitable day when he could no longer work.

Tales of the Meddahs: Tales from the Turkish tradition

The Sultan answered, "That is well said and just. As it is not in my power to give you the twenty-five years, the best equivalent I can grant you is the means of sustenance for a period of that duration should you live so long. But tell me, who advised you to make this request?"

Hassan then related his adventure with the boys while on his journey home, and his Majesty was so pleased with the judgment and advice of the lad that he sent for him and had him educated. The boy studied medicine and distinguishing himself in the profession ultimately rose to be Hekim Ali Pasha.

He had one son who was known as Doctor Ali Pasha's son. He studied calligraphy, and became so proficient in this art, now almost lost, that his imitations of the Imperial Iradés, or decrees, were perfect facsimiles of the originals. One day he took it into his head to write an Iradé appointing himself Grand Vizier, in place of the reigning one, a protégé of the Imperial Palace, which Iradé he took to the Sublime Porte and there and then installed himself. By chance the Sultan happened to drive through Istanbul that day, in disguise, and noticing considerable excitement and cries of "Padishahim chok yasha" (long live my Sultan) amongst the people, made inquiries as to the cause of this unusual occurrence. His Majesty's informers brought him the word that the people rejoiced in the fall of the old Grand Vizier, and the appointment of the new one, Doctor Ali Pasha's son. The Sultan returned to the Palace and immediately sent one of his eunuchs to the Sublime Porte to see the Grand Vizier and find out the meaning of these strange proceedings.

The eunuch was announced, and the Grand Vizier ordered him to be brought into his presence. Directly he appeared in the doorway, he was greeted with, "What do you want, you black dog?"

Then turning to the numerous attendants, he said, "Take this man to the slave market, and see what price he will bring."

The eunuch was taken to the slave market, and the highest price bid for him was fifty piasters. On hearing this, the Grand Vizier turned to the eunuch

Tales of the Meddahs: Tales from the Turkish tradition

and said, "Go and tell your master what you are worth and tell him that I think it too much by far."

The eunuch was glad to get off and communicated to his Majesty the story of his strange treatment. The Sultan then ordered his Chief Eunuch, a not unimportant personage in the Ottoman Empire, to call on the Grand Vizier for an explanation. At the Sublime Porte, however, no respect was paid to this high dignitary. Ali Pasha received him in precisely the same manner as he had received his subordinate. The chief was taken to the slave market, and the highest sum bid for him was five hundred piasters. The self-appointed Grand Vizier ordered him to go and tell his master the amount some foolish people were willing to pay for him.

When the Sultan heard of these strange proceedings he sent an autograph letter to Ali Pasha, commanding him to come to the Palace. The Grand Vizier immediately set out for the Palace and was received in audience, when he explained to his Majesty that the affairs of State could not be managed by men not worth more than from fifty to five hundred piasters, and that if radical changes were not made, certain ruin would be the outcome. The Sultan appreciated this earnest communication, and ratified the appointment, as Grand Vizier, of Ali Pasha, the son of the boy who had played at state affairs in a village of Asia Minor.

Tales of the Meddahs: Tales from the Turkish tradition

THE INSECTS, THE BEE, AND THE ANT

This story has been adapted from Turkish Literature by Epiphanius Wilson, A.M., published in 1901 by P. F. Collier & Son, New York.

A great number of insects took themselves one winter to the dwellings of the bee and the ant.

"Give us some food," they said, "for we are dying of hunger."

The bee and the ant answered, "What do you do in summertime?"

"We rest on the spreading trees," they replied, "and we cheer the traveller with our pleasant songs."

"If that be so," was the reply, "it is no wonder that you are dying of hunger, and you are, therefore, no proper objects of charity."

This fable shows that the foolish virgins ask charity, and those who are wise refuse to give it, because there comes a time when not charity, but justice is to be rendered.

During the time of this life, which is our summer, we must gather, by wisdom and industry, the spiritual food, without which, we shall be made, at the day of judgment, to die of hunger in hell.

Tales of the Meddahs: Tales from the Turkish tradition

Tales of the Meddahs: Tales from the Turkish tradition

THE MERCIFUL KHAN

This story has been adapted from Told in the Coffee House by Cyrus Adler and Allan Ramsay, published in 1898 by MacMillan and Company, London. Allan Ramsay was a Scottish poet, playwright, publisher, librarian, and wig-maker active in the early and mid-eighteenth century. Cyrus Adler adapted Ramsay's work in the nineteenth century, being an American educator, Jewish religious leader, and scholar.

There lived once near Isfahan a tailor, a hard-working man, who was very poor. So poor was he that his workshop and house together consisted of a wooden cottage of but one room.

But poverty is no protection against thieves, and so it happened that one night a thief entered the tailor's hut. The tailor had driven nails in various places in the walls on which to hang the garments that were brought to him to mend. It chanced that in groping about for plunder, the thief struck one of these nails and put out his eye.

The next morning the thief appeared before the Khan and demanded justice. The Khan accordingly sent for the tailor, stated the thief's complaint, and said that in accordance with the law, 'an eye for an eye,' it would be necessary to put out one of the tailor's eyes. As usual, however, the tailor was allowed to plead in his own defence, whereupon he thus addressed the court, saying, "Oh great and mighty Khan, it is true that the law says an eye for an eye, but it does not say my eye. Now I am a poor man, and a tailor. If the Khan puts out one of my eyes, I will not be able to carry on my trade, and so I shall starve. Now it happens that there lives near me a gunsmith. He

Tales of the Meddahs: Tales from the Turkish tradition

uses but one eye with which he squints along the barrel of his guns. Take his other eye, oh Khan, and let the law be satisfied."

The Khan was favourably impressed with this idea, and accordingly sent for the gunsmith. He recited to the gunsmith the thief's complaint and the tailor's statement, whereupon the gunsmith said, "Oh great and mighty Khan, this tailor knows not whereof he talks. I need both of my eyes, for while it is true that I squint one eye along one side of the barrel of the gun, to see if it is straight, I must use the other eye for the other side. If, therefore, you put out one of my eyes you will take away from me the means of livelihood. It happens, however, that a flute player lives not far from me. Now I have noticed that whenever he plays the flute, he closes both of his eyes. Take out one of his eyes, oh Khan, and let the law be satisfied."

Accordingly, the Khan sent for the flute-player, and after reciting to him the complaint of the thief, and the words of the gunsmith, he ordered him to play upon his flute. This the flute-player did, and though he endeavoured to control himself, he did not succeed, and as the result of long habit, closed both of his eyes. When the Khan saw this, he ordered that one of the flute-player's eyes be put out, which being done, the Khan said, "Oh flute-player, I saw that when playing upon your flute you closed both of your eyes. It was thus clear to me that neither was necessary for your livelihood, and I had intended to have them both put out, but I have decided to put out only one in order that you may tell men how merciful the Khans are."

Tales of the Meddahs: Tales from the Turkish tradition

THE PADISHAH OF THE FORTY PERIS

This story has been adapted from Turkish Fairy Tales and Folk Tales by Dr. Ignácz Kúnos, published in 1901 by A. H. Bullen, London.

In the old, old time, in the age of fairy tales, there was once the daughter of a Padishah who was as fair as the full moon, as slim as a cypress-tree, with eyes like coals, and hair like the night, and her eyebrows were like bows, and her eyeballs like the darts of archers. In the palace of the Padishah was a garden, and in the midst of the garden a fountain of water, and there the maid sat the livelong day sewing and stitching.

One day she put her ring upon her sewing-table, but scarcely had she laid it down when a little dove came and stole the ring and flew away with it. Now the little dove was so lovely that the damsel at once fell in love with it. The next day the damsel took off her bracelet, and immediately the dove was there and flew off with that too. Then the damsel was so consumed with love that she neither ate nor drank and could scarce wait till the next day for the dove to come forth again. And on the third day she brought her sewing-table, put upon it her lace handkerchief, and placed herself close beside it. She waited for the dove, and waited and waited, and lo, all at once there he was right before her, and he caught up the handkerchief and away he flew. Then the damsel had scarce strength enough to rise up, and weeping bitterly she went into the palace, and there she threw herself on the ground in a passion of grief.

Her old waiting-woman came running towards her. "O Sultana!" cried she, "Why do you weep so sorely? What ails you?"

Tales of the Meddahs: Tales from the Turkish tradition

"I am sick, my heart is sick!" replied the daughter of the Sultan, and with that she fell a-weeping and a-wailing worse than ever.

The old waiting-woman feared to tell of this new thing, for the damsel was the only daughter of the Padishah, but when she perceived how pale the damsel was growing, and how she wept and sobbed, the waiting-woman took her courage in both hands, went to the Padishah, and told him of his daughter's woe. Then the Padishah was afraid, and went to see his daughter, and after him came many wise men and many cunning leeches, but not one of them could cure her sickness.

But on the next day the Padishah's Vizier said to him, "The wise men and the leeches cannot help the damsel, the only medicine that can cure her lies hidden elsewhere." Then he advised the Padishah to make a great bath of water which should cure all sick people. That same water would also make whoever bathed therein to tell the story of his life. So, the Padishah caused the bath to be made, and proclaimed throughout the city that the water of this bath would give back his hair to the bald, and his hearing to the deaf, and his sight to the blind, and the use of his legs to the lame. Then all the people flocked in crowds to have a bath for nothing, and each one of them had to tell the story of his life and his ailment before he returned home again.

Now in that same city dwelt the bald-headed son of a bed-ridden mother, and the fame of the wonder-working bath reached their ears also. "Let us go too," said the son. "Perhaps the pair of us shall be cured."

"How can I go when I can't stand on my legs?" groaned the old woman.

"Oh, we shall be able to manage that," replied bald-pate, and taking his mother on his shoulders he set out for the bath. They went on and on and on, through the level plains by the flowing river, till at last the son was tired and put his mother down upon the ground. At that same instant a cock flew down beside them with a big pitcher of water on its back and then quickly flew off with it. Then the young man became very curious to know why and where this cock was carrying water, so, after the bird he went. The cock went on till it came to a great castle, and at the foot of this castle was a little hole

104

Tales of the Meddahs: Tales from the Turkish tradition

through which water was gurgling. Still the youth followed the cock, squeezed himself with the utmost difficulty through the hole, and no sooner had he begun to look about him than he saw before him a palace so magnificent that his eyes and mouth stood wide open with astonishment. No other human being had ever stood in the path that led up to this palace. He went all over the place, through all the rooms, from vestibule to attic, admiring their splendour without ceasing, till weariness overcame him. "If only I could find a living being here!" he said to himself, and with that he hid himself in a large armoury, from where he could easily pounce upon anyone who came by.

He had not waited very long when three doves flew on to the windowsill, and after shivering there a little while turned into three damsels, all so beautiful that the young man did not know which to look at first.

"Alas, alas!" cried the three damsels, "We are late, we are late! Our Padishah will be here presently, and nothing is ready!" Then one seized a broom and brushed everything clean, the second spread the table, and the third fetched all manner of meats. Then they all three began to shiver once more, and three doves flew out of the window.

Meanwhile the bald-pate had grown very hungry, and he thought to himself, "Nobody sees me, so, why should I not take a morsel or two from that table?" He stretched his hand out from his hiding-place and was just about to touch the food with it when he got such a blow on the fingers that they swelled right up. He stretched out the other hand and got a still greater blow on that. The youth was very frightened at this, and he had scarcely drawn back his hand when a white dove flew into the room. It fell a-shivering and immediately turned into a beautiful youth.

And now he went to a cupboard, opened it, and took out a ring, a bracelet, and a lace handkerchief. "Oh, lucky ring that you are," cried he, "to be allowed to sit on a beautiful finger; and oh, lucky bracelet, to be allowed to lie on a beautiful arm." Then the beautiful youth fell to sobbing and dried his tears one by one on the lace handkerchief. Then he put them into the cupboard again, tasted one or two of the dishes, and laid down to sleep.

Tales of the Meddahs: Tales from the Turkish tradition

It was as much as the bald-pate could do to await the dawn of the day. But then the beautiful youth arose, shivered, and flew away as a white dove. Bald-pate too came out of his hiding-place, went down into the courtyard, and crept once more through the hole at the foot of the tower.

Outside he found his poor old mother weeping all alone, but the youth pacified her with the assurance that their troubles were nearly at an end. He took her on his back again and went to the bath. There they bathed, and immediately the old woman was able to stand on her legs, and the bald-pate got his hair back again. Then they began to tell their stories, and when the Sultan's daughter heard what the youth had seen and heard at midnight, it was as though a stream of fresh health instantly poured into her. She rose from her bed and promised the youth a great treasure if he would bring her to that tower. So, the youth went with the princess, showed her the walls of the palace, helped her through the little hole, brought her into the chamber of the doves, and pointed out to her the armoury where he had been able to hide himself. After that the youth returned home with great treasure and perfect health and lived all his days with his old mother.

At eventide the three doves flew into the room. They scoured and cleaned, brought the meats for the table, and flew away again. Soon afterwards the white dove came flying in, and how did that damsel feel when she saw her darling little dove once more? But when the dove had turned into a youth again, and stood there like a glorious full moon, the damsel scarcely knew where she was, but gazed continuously on his dazzling face.

Then the youth went to the cupboard, opened it, and took out the ring, the bracelet, and the lace handkerchief that belonged to the daughter of the Sultan. "Oh, you ring! How happy should you be to sit on a beauteous finger! Oh, you bracelet! How happy you should be to lie on a beauteous arm!" he cried. Then he took the lace handkerchief and dried his tears, and at the sight of it the heart of the damsel was nigh to breaking. Then she tapped with her fingers on the door of the armoury. The youth approached it, opened the door, and there stood his heart's darling. Then the youth's joy was so great that it was almost woe.

Tales of the Meddahs: Tales from the Turkish tradition

He asked the damsel how she had come there to the palace of the Peris. Then she told him of her journey, and how sick for love she had been.

The youth told her that he also was the son of a mortal mother, but when he was only three days old the Peris had stolen him and carried him to this palace and made him their Padishah. He was with them the whole day and had only two hours to himself in the twenty-four. The damsel, he said, might stay with him, and walk about here the whole day, but towards evening she must hide herself, for if the forty Peri came and saw her with him, they would not leave her alive. Tomorrow, he said, he would show her his mother's palace, where they would live in peace, and he would be with her for two hours out of the twenty-four.

The next day the Padishah of the Peris took the damsel and showed her his mother's palace. "When you go there," said the Padishah, "bid them have compassion, and receive you in memory of Bahtiyar Bey, and when my mother hears my name, she will not refuse your request."

The damsel went up to the house and knocked at the door. An old woman came and opened it, and when she saw the damsel and heard her son's name, she burst into tears and took her in. There the damsel stayed a long time, and every day the little bird came to visit her, until a son was born to the daughter of the Sultan. But the old woman never knew that her son came to the house, nor that the damsel had been brought to bed.

One day the little bird came, flew upon the windowsill, and said, "Oh, my Sultana, what is my little seedling doing?"

"No harm has come to our little seedling," replied she, "but he awaits the coming of Bahtiyar."

"Oh, if only my mother knew," sighed the youth, 'she would open her best room." With that he flew into the room, turned into a man, and fondled in his arms his wife and his little child. But when two hours had passed, he shivered a little, and a little dove flew out of the window.

But the mother had heard her son's speech and could scarce contain herself for joy. She hastened to her daughter-in-law, fondled and caressed her, led

Tales of the Meddahs: Tales from the Turkish tradition

her into her most beautiful room, and put everything in order against her son's arrival. She knew that the forty Peris had robbed her of him, and she thought long and hard about how she might steal him back again.

"When my son comes tomorrow," said the old woman, "contrive so that he stays beyond his time, and leave the rest to me."

The next day the bird flew into the window, and the damsel was nowhere to be seen in the room. Then he flew into the more beautiful room, and cried, "Oh, my Sultana, what is our little seedling doing?"

And the damsel replied, "No harm has come to our little seedling, but he awaits the coming of Bahtiyar."

Then the bird flew into the room and changed into a man and was so taken up with talking to his wife, so filled with the joy of playing with his child and seeing it play, that he took no count of time at all.

But what was the old woman doing all this time?

There was a large cypress-tree in front of the house, and there the forty doves sometimes settled. The old woman went and hung this tree full of venomous needles. Towards evening, when the Padishah's two hours had run out, the doves who were the forty Peris came to seek their Padishah, and alighted on the cypress-tree, but scarcely had their feet touched the needles than they fell down to the ground poisoned.

Meanwhile, however, the youth suddenly remembered the time, and great his terror was great when he came out of the palace so late. He looked to the right of him, and he looked to the left, and when he looked towards the cypress-tree there were the forty doves. And now his joy was as great as his terror had been before. First, he kissed the neck of his consort, and then he ran to his mother and embraced her, so great was his joy that he had escaped from the hands of the Peris.

Then they made such a banquet that even after forty days they had not got to the end of it. So, they had their hearts' desires, and ate and drank and

Tales of the Meddahs: Tales from the Turkish tradition

rejoiced with a great joy. May we too get the desires of our hearts, with good eating and drinking to comfort us!

Tales of the Meddahs: Tales from the Turkish tradition

Tales of the Meddahs: Tales from the Turkish tradition

THE FOX AND THE CRAB

This story has been adapted from Turkish Literature by Epiphanius Wilson, A.M., published in 1901 by P. F. Collier & Son, New York.

The Fox and the Crab lived together like brothers. They sowed their land together, reaped the harvest, thrashed the grain, and garnered it.

The Fox said one day, "Let's go to the hill-top, and whoever reaches it first shall carry off the grain for his own."

While they were mounting the steep the Crab said, "Do me a favour. Before you set off running, touch me with your tail, so that I shall know it and be able to follow you."

The Crab opened his claws, and when the Fox touched him with his tail, he leaped forward and seized it, so that when the Fox reached the goal and turned round to see where the Crab was, the latter fell upon the heap of grain and said, "These three bushels and a half are all mine."

The Fox was thunderstruck and exclaimed, "How did you get here, you rascal?"

This fable shows that deceitful men devise many methods for getting things their own way, but they are often defeated by the feeble.

Tales of the Meddahs: Tales from the Turkish tradition

Tales of the Meddahs: Tales from the Turkish tradition

THE PRAYER RUG AND THE DISHONEST STEWARD

This story has been adapted from Told in the Coffee House by Cyrus Adler and Allan Ramsay, published in 1898 by MacMillan and Company, London. Allan Ramsay was a Scottish poet, playwright, publisher, librarian, and wig-maker active in the early and mid-eighteenth century. Cyrus Adler adapted Ramsay's work in the nineteenth century, being an American educator, Jewish religious leader, and scholar.

A poor Hamal, a porter, brought to the Pasha of Istanbul his savings, consisting of a small canvas bag of medjidies (Turkish silver dollars), to be kept for him, while he was absent on a visit to his home. The Pasha, being a kind-hearted man, consented, and after sealing the bag, called his steward, instructing him to keep it till the owner called for it. The steward gave the man a receipt, to the effect that he had received a sealed bag containing money.

When the poor man returned, he went to the Pasha and received his bag of money. On reaching his room he opened the bag, and to his horror found that it contained, instead of the medjidies he had put in it, copper piasters, which are about the same size as medjidies. The poor Hamal was miserable, for his hard-earned savings were gone.

He at last gathered courage to go and put his case before the Pasha. He took the bag of piasters, and with trembling voice and faltering heart he assured the Pasha that though he had received his bag apparently intact, on opening it he found that it contained copper piasters and not the medjidies he had put

Tales of the Meddahs: Tales from the Turkish tradition

in it. The Pasha took the bag, examined it closely, and after some time noticed a part that had apparently been darned by a master-hand. The Pasha told the Hamal to go away and come back in a week, and in the meantime, he would see what he could do for him. The grateful man departed, uttering prayers for the life and prosperity of his Excellency.

The next morning after the Pasha had said his prayers kneeling on a most magnificent and expensive rug, he took a knife and cut a long rent in it. He then left his Konak (his official residence) without saying a word to anyone. In the evening when he returned, he found that the rent had been so well repaired that it was with difficulty that he discovered where it had been. Calling his steward, he demanded who had repaired his prayer rug. The steward told the Pasha that he thought the rug had been cut by accident by some of the servants, so he had sent to the Bazaar for the darner, Mustapha, and had it mended, the steward, by way of apology, adding that it was very well done.

"Send for Mustapha immediately," said the Pasha, "and when he comes bring him to my room."

When Mustapha arrived, the Pasha asked him if he had repaired the rug. Mustapha at once replied that he had mended it that very morning. "It is indeed well done," said the Pasha. "Much better than the darn you made in that canvas bag."

Mustapha agreed, saying that it was very difficult to mend the bag as it was full of copper piasters. On hearing this, the Pasha gave him a backsheesh and told him to retire. The Pasha then called his steward, and not only compelled him to pay the Hamal his money, but discharged him from his service, in which he had been engaged for many years.

Tales of the Meddahs: Tales from the Turkish tradition

THE WORLD'S MOST BEAUTEOUS DAMSEL

This story has been adapted from Turkish Fairy Tales and Folk Tales by Dr. Ignácz Kúnos, published in 1901 by A. H. Bullen, London.

There was once upon a time a Padishah who had an only son. His father guarded him as the apple of his eye, and there was not a desire of his heart that was not instantly gratified.

One night a dervish appeared to the King's son in a dream, and showed him the world's most beauteous damsel, and there he drained with her the cup of love. After that the prince became another man. He could neither eat nor drink. Sleep brought him neither pleasure nor refreshment, and he all at once grew sallow and withered. They sent for doctor after doctor, they sent for wizard after wizard, but they could not tell the nature of the malady or find a cure for it.

Then the sick prince said to his father, "My lord Padishah and father, no leech, no wise man can help me, why weary them in vain? The world's most beauteous damsel is the cause of my complaint, and she will be either the life or the death of me."

The Padishah was frightened at the words of his son, and his chief care was to drive the damsel out of the lad's head. "It's dangerous to even think of such a thing," said he, "for her love will be your death."

But his son continued to pine away daily, and life had no joy for him. Again, and again the father begged his son to tell him his heart's desire and it should

Tales of the Meddahs: Tales from the Turkish tradition

be instantly fulfilled, and the eternal reply of the son was, "Let me seek the world's most beauteous damsel."

Then the Padishah thought to himself, "If I do not let him go, he will only perish, and he cannot, therefore, be worse off if he goes." Then said he, "Go, my son, after your love, and may the righteous Allah be merciful to you."

The next day the prince set out on his journey. He went up hill and down dale, he crossed vast deserts, and he traversed rugged wildernesses in search of his beloved, the world's most beauteous damsel. On and on he went, till he came at last to the seashore, and there he saw a poor little fish writhing in the sand, and the fish begged him to throw it back into the sea again. The youth felt compassion for the fish and threw it back into the sea again. Then the little fish gave him three scales, and said to him, "If ever you get into any trouble, burn these scales."

Again, the youth went on his way till he came to a vast desert, and there on the ground in front of him he saw a lame ant. The little creature told him that he was going to a wedding but could not overtake his comrades because they hastened so quickly. Then the youth took up the ant and carried him to his comrades. As they parted the ant gave him a little piece of its wing and said, "If ever you should get into any trouble, burn this bit of wing."

Again, the youth followed his road, full of weary woefulness, and reaching the borders of a large forest he there saw a little bird struggling with a large serpent. The little bird asked help of the youth, and with one blow he cut the serpent in two. The bird then gave him three feathers. "If ever you should get into trouble," it said, "burn these little feathers."

Again, he took up his pilgrim's staff and went beyond the mountains, beyond the sea, till he came to a large city. It was the realm of the father of the world's most beauteous damsel. He went straight into the palace to the Padishah and begged the hand of his daughter in the name of Allah.

"Nay," said the Padishah, "you must first of all accomplish three tasks for me. Only after that can you make known your wishes to my daughter."

Tales of the Meddahs: Tales from the Turkish tradition

With that he took a ring, cast it into the sea, and said to the King's son, "If you cannot find it for me in three days, you are a dead man."

Then the King's son fell to thinking till he remembered the three scales, and he had no sooner burnt them than the little fish stood before him and said, "What do you command, O my Sultan?"

"The ring of the world's most beauteous damsel has been cast into the sea, and I want it back again," said the prince.

Then the fish searched for the ring but couldn't find it. It dived down a second time and still it couldn't find it. A third time it descended right down into the seventh ocean, drew up a fish, cut it open, and there was the ring. So, the youth gave the ring to the Padishah, and the Padishah gave it to his daughter.

Now there was a cave near the palace full of gravel and grain. "My second task," said the Padishah, "is that you separate the grain from the gravel."

Then the youth entered the cave, took out the ant's wing and burned it, whereupon the whole cave was swarming with ants, and they set to work upon the grain in hot haste. The day was now nearly over, and the same evening the youth sent word to the Padishah that the second task also was accomplished.

"The third task still remains," said the Padishah, "and then you may have my daughter." With that he sent for a maidservant, had her head cut off straightway, and then said to the youth, "This shall be done to your head also if you don't restore this damsel to life again."

The youth quitted the palace in deep thought, and at last he remembered that the bird's feathers might help him. He took them out and burned them, and lo, the bird stood before him before his lips had commanded it to appear. And the youth complained bitterly to the bird of the task that was set him.

Now the bird had friends among the Peris, and, flying up into the air, in no very long time was back again with a cruse of water in its beak. "I have

Tales of the Meddahs: Tales from the Turkish tradition

brought you heavenly water which can give life even to the dead," said the bird.

The prince entered the palace, and no sooner had he sprinkled the damsel with the water than she sprang up as if she had never been dead at all.

Now the rumour of all these things reached the ears of the world's most beauteous damsel, and she ordered the prince to be brought before her. The damsel dwelt in a little marble palace, and before the palace was a golden basin which was fed by the water of four streams. The courtyard of this palace also was a vast garden wherein were many great trees and fragrant flowers and singing birds, and to the youth it seemed like the gate of Paradise.

Suddenly the door of the palace was opened, and the garden was so flooded with light that the eyes of the youth were dazzled even to blindness. It was the world's most beauteous damsel who had appeared in the door of the palace, and the great light was the rosiness of her two radiant cheeks. She approached the prince and spoke to him, but scarcely did the youth perceive her than he fainted away before her eyes. When he came to himself again, they brought him into the damsel's palace, and there he rejoiced exceedingly in the world's most beauteous damsel, for her face was as the face of a Houri, and her presence was as a vision of Peris.

"Oh, prince," began the damsel, "you are the son of Shah Suleiman, and you can aid me in my deep distress. In the vast garden of the Demon of Autumn there is a bunch of singing-pomegranates. If you can get them for me, I will be yours for ever and ever."

Then the youth gave her his hand upon it, the hand of loyal friendship, and departed far, far away. He went on and on without stopping. He went on, and for months and months. He crossed deserts where man had never trod, and mountains over which there was no path. "Oh, my Creator," he sighed, "will you not show me the right way?"

He rose up again each morning from the place where he had sunk down exhausted the night before, and so he went on and on from day to day till the

118

Tales of the Meddahs: Tales from the Turkish tradition

path led him right down to the roots of the mountains. There it seemed to him as if it were the Day of Judgment. Such a noise, such a hubbub, such a hurly-burly of sounds arose that all the hills and rocks around him trembled. The youth did not know whether it was friend or foe, man, or spirit, and as he went on further, trembling with fear, the noise grew louder, and the dust rose up round about him like smoke. He still did not know where he was going, but he might have understood from what he heard that the smaller garden of the Demon of Autumn was now only six-months' journey off, and all this great hubbub and clamour was made by the talisman of the gate of the garden.

Eventually he drew close and could see the gate of the smaller garden and could hear the roaring of the talismans in the gate and could also see the guardian of the gate. Then he went up to the guardian and told him of his trouble.

"But aren't you afraid of this great commotion?" asked the guardian of the gate. "Is it not because of you that all the talismans are so impatient? Even I am afraid of them!"

But the youth did nothing but inquire continually about the cluster of singing-pomegranates.

"It's a hard task to reach that," said the guardian, "yet if you are not afraid, perhaps you may get it after all. Three-months' journey from here you will come to another place full of talismans, and there is also a garden, and the guardian of that garden is my own mother. But whatever you do, take care not to draw close to her, nor let her draw close to you. Give her my salaams but tell her nothing of your trouble unless she asks you."

The youth went on towards the second garden, and after a three-months' journey a monstrous din and racket arose around him that was so much louder than before. This was the greater garden of the Demon of Autumn, and the great din came from the talismans of the garden. The youth lay down beside a rock, and when he had waited a little, he saw something like a man approaching him, but as it came nearer, he saw that it was an old woman, a

Tales of the Meddahs: Tales from the Turkish tradition

little beldame of ninety winters. The hairs of her head were as white as snow, red circles were round her eyes, her eyebrows were like pointed darts, the fire of hell was in her eyes, her nails were two ells long, her teeth were like faggots, her two lips had only one jaw, she shuffled along leaning on a stick, drew in her breath through her nose, and coughed and sneezed at every step she took.

"Oh-oh, oh-oh!" she groaned, shuffling painfully along in her large slippers, till it seemed as if she would never be able to reach the new-comer. This was the mother of the guardian of the lesser garden, and she herself was the guardian of the larger one.

At last, she got up to the youth, and asked him what he was doing in those parts? The prince gave her the compliments of her son.

"Ah, the vagabond!" said the old woman, "Where did you meet with him? That wicked lad of mine knew that I would have compassion on you, so he sent you here. Very well, let us make an end of you." With that she seized hold of him, and cried, "Hi, Earless!" and something came running up to him, and before he knew where he was, the youth found himself seated on its back. He looked down upon it and saw beneath him a creature like a shrunken huddled toad, that had neither eyes nor ears. This was Earless, and away it went with him. When he first saw it, it was as small as a worm, but the moment he was on its back it took such leaps that every three of them covered as much space as a vast ocean. Suddenly Earless stopped short and said to him, "Whatever you may see, whatever you may hear, take care not to speak, or it will be all up with you," and with that it vanished.

There in the rippling water in front of the prince, like a dream-shape, lay a large garden. This garden had neither beginning nor end, and within it were such trees and flowers and sweet fruit as the eye of man has never seen. Wherever one turned nothing was to be heard but the rustling of soft wings and the songs of nightingales, so that the whole atmosphere of that garden seemed to be an eternal song. The youth looked about him, his reason died away within him, and he entered the garden. But then he heard quite near to him such a woeful wailing that his heart was like to break, and h thought of

Tales of the Meddahs: Tales from the Turkish tradition

the cluster of pomegranates. His eyes sought for them in every direction but in vain, till he came to the centre of the garden, where there was a fountain and a little palace made of flowers, and the pomegranates hung down from the flowery palace like so many shining lamps. The youth plucked a branch, but no sooner had he done so than there was a horrible cry, and a warning voice exclaimed, "A son of man has taken us. We are slain by a son of man!"

The youth scarce had time to escape from the garden. "Hurry! Fly!" cried Earless, who was waiting again at the gate. The youth jumped on its back, and in a couple of leaps they were beyond the ocean. Only then did the youth think of looking at the cluster of pomegranates. There were fifty pomegranates, and each one had a different voice, and each voice had a different song. It was just as if all the music in the wide world was gathered together in one place. By this time, they had reached the old grandmother, the old old beldame of three times thirty winters.

"Guard your pomegranate cluster well," said the old woman. "Never leave it out of your sight. If on the first night of your wedding you and your bride are able to listen to their music all night without going to sleep once, these pomegranates will love you, and after that you will have nothing more to fear, for they will deliver you from every ill."

Then they went from the old mother to the son, and he also bade them take to heart his mother's words, and then the youth went on his way to his sole-beloved, the world's most beauteous damsel. The girl was awaiting him with the greatest impatience, for she also dearly loved the prince, and her days were passed in anxiety lest some mischief should befall the youth.

All at once she heard the sound of music, the fifty pomegranates were singing fifty different songs with fifty different voices, and she opened her heart to the beautiful music. The damsel rushed forth to meet the youth, and at their joyous embrace the pomegranates rang out with a melody so sweet that the like of it is not to be found in this world, but only in Allah's world beyond the grave. The wedding feast lasted for forty days and forty nights, and on the fortieth day the King's son went to his bride, and they lay down and listened to the pomegranates. Then when the day was born again, they

Tales of the Meddahs: Tales from the Turkish tradition

arose, and the pomegranate cluster rejoiced again in their love, and so they went on their way to the prince's own kingdom. There all the feasting began again, and in his joy the old Padishah resigned his kingdom to his son, who was forever known as the Padishah of the Cluster of Pomegranates.

Tales of the Meddahs: Tales from the Turkish tradition

THE GOATS AND THE WOLVES

This story has been adapted from Turkish Literature by Epiphanius Wilson, A.M., published in 1901 by P. F. Collier & Son, New York.

All the Goats gathered together and sent a message to the nation of the Wolves. They said, "Why do you make this ceaseless war upon us? We beseech you, make peace with us, as the kings of nations are wont to do."

The Wolves assembled in great joy and sent a long letter and many presents to the nation of the Goats. And they said to them, "We have learned by your excellent resolution, and we have rendered thanks to God for it. The news of this peace will occasion great joy in the world. But we beg to inform your wisdom that the shepherd and his dog are the causes of all our differences and quarrels. If you make an end of them, tranquillity will soon return."

On learning this, the Goats drove away the shepherds and their dogs, and ratified a treaty of peace and friendship with the Wolves. The Goats then went out and scattered themselves without fear among the hills and valleys and began to feed and render thanks to God. The Wolves waited for ten days, then they gathered themselves together against the Goats, and strangled them every one of them.

This fable shows that hatred and aversion between nations and families, or between individuals, is deeply rooted in the heart of man, and that peace and friendship are not established among them, excepting with the greatest difficulty.

Tales of the Meddahs: Tales from the Turkish tradition

Tales of the Meddahs: Tales from the Turkish tradition

THE GOOSE, THE EYE, THE DAUGHTER, AND THE ARM

This story has been adapted from Told in the Coffee House by Cyrus Adler and Allan Ramsay, published in 1898 by MacMillan and Company, London. Allan Ramsay was a Scottish poet, playwright, publisher, librarian, and wig-maker active in the early and mid-eighteenth century. Cyrus Adler adapted Ramsay's work in the nineteenth century, being an American educator, Jewish religious leader, and scholar.

A Turk decided to have a feast, so he killed and stuffed a goose and took it to the baker to be roasted. The Cadi of the village happened to pass by the oven as the baker was basting the goose and was attracted by the pleasant and appetising odour. Approaching the baker, the Cadi said it was a fine goose; that the smell of it made him quite hungry and suggested that he had better send it to his house. The baker expostulated, saying, "I cannot, for it does not belong to me."

The Cadi assured him that was no difficulty. "You tell Ahmet, the owner of the goose, that it flew away."

"Impossible!" said the baker. "How can a roasted goose fly away? Ahmet will only laugh at me, your Worship, and I will be cast into prison."

"Am I not a Judge?" said the Cadi, "Fear nothing."

At this the baker consented to send the goose to the Cadi's house. When Ahmet came for his goose the baker said, "Friend, your goose has flown."

Tales of the Meddahs: Tales from the Turkish tradition

"Flown?" said Ahmet, "What lies! Am I your grandfather's grandchild that you should laugh in my beard?"

Seizing one of the baker's large shovels, he lifted it to strike him, but, as fate would have it, the handle put out the eye of the baker's boy, and Ahmet, frightened at what he had done, ran off, closely followed by the baker and his boy, the latter crying, "My eye!"

In his hurry Ahmet knocked over a child, killing it, and the father of the child joined in the chase, calling out, "My daughter!"

Ahmet, well-nigh distracted, rushed into a mosque and up a minaret. To escape his pursuers, he leaped from the parapet, and fell upon a vender who was passing by, breaking his arm. The vender also began pursuing him, calling out, "My arm!"

Ahmet was finally caught and brought before the Cadi, who no doubt was feeling contented with the world, having just enjoyed the delicious goose. The Cadi heard each of the cases brought against Ahmet, who in turn told his case truthfully as it had happened.

"A complicated matter," said the Cadi. "All these misfortunes come from the flight of the goose, and I must refer to the book of the law to give just judgment."

Taking down a ponderous manuscript volume, the Cadi turned to Ahmet and asked him what number egg the goose had been hatched from. Ahmet said he did not know.

"Then," replied the Cadi, "the book writes that such a phenomenon was possible. If this goose was hatched from the seventh egg, and the hatcher also from the seventh egg, the book writes that it is possible for a roasted goose, under those conditions, to fly away."

"With reference to your eye," continued the Cadi, addressing the baker's lad, "the book provides punishment for the removal of two eyes, but not of one, so if you will consent to your other eye being taken out, I will condemn Ahmet to have both of his removed."

Tales of the Meddahs: Tales from the Turkish tradition

The baker's lad, not appreciating the force of this argument, withdrew his claim.

Then turning to the father of the dead child, the Cadi explained that the only provision for a case like this in the book of the law, was that he take Ahmet's child in its place, or if Ahmet had not a child, to wait till he got one. The bereaved parent not taking any interest in Ahmet's present or prospective children, also withdrew his case.

These cases settled, there remained but the vender's, who was angry at having his arm broken. The Cadi expatiated on the justice of the law and its far-seeing provisions, that the vender at least could claim ample compensation for having his arm broken. The book of the law provided that he should go to the very same minaret, and that Ahmet must station himself at the very same place where he had stood when his arm was broken, and that he might jump down and break Ahmet's arm.

"But be it understood," concluded the Cadi, "if you break his leg instead of his arm, Ahmet will have the right to delegate someone to jump down on you to break your leg."

The vender not seeing the force of the Cadi's proposal, also withdrew his claim. Thus ended the cases of the goose, the eye, the daughter, and the arm.

Tales of the Meddahs: Tales from the Turkish tradition

Tales of the Meddahs: Tales from the Turkish tradition

THE FORTY PRINCES AND THE SEVEN-HEADED DRAGON

This story has been adapted from Turkish Fairy Tales and Folk Tales by Dr. Ignácz Kúnos, published in 1901 by A. H. Bullen, London.

There was once upon a time a Padishah, and this Padishah had forty sons. All day long they played themselves in the forest, snaring birds, and hunting beasts, but when the youngest of them was fourteen years old their father wished to marry them. So, he sent for them all and told them his desire. "We will marry," said the forty brothers, "but only when we find forty sisters who are the daughters of the same father and the same mother." Then the Padishah searched the whole realm through to find forty such sisters, but though he found families of thirty-nine sisters, he could never find families of forty sisters.

"Let the fortieth of you take another wife," said the Padishah to his sons. But the forty brothers would not agree to this, and they begged their father to allow them to go and search to see if they might find what they wanted in another empire. What could the Padishah do? He could not refuse them their request, so he gave them his permission. But before they departed, he summoned them into his presence, and this is what their father the Padishah said to them, "I have three things to say to you, which you should bear well in mind. When you come in your journey to a large spring, take heed not to pass the night near it. Beyond the spring is a caravanserai, and there also you must not abide. Beyond the caravanserai is a vast desert; and there also you must not take a moment's rest." The sons promised their father that they

Tales of the Meddahs: Tales from the Turkish tradition

would keep his words, and with baggage light of weight but exceedingly precious, they took horse and set out on their journey.

They went on and on, they smoked their chibouks and drank forty cups of coffee, and when evening descended the large spring was right before them. "Truly," began the elder brothers, "we will not go another step further. We are weary, and the night is upon us, and what need forty men fear?" And with that they dismounted from their horses, ate their suppers, and laid down to rest. Only the youngest brother, who was fourteen years of age, remained awake.

It might have been near midnight when the youth heard a strange noise. He caught up his arms and turning in the direction of the sound saw before him a seven-headed dragon. They rushed towards each other, and three times the dragon fell upon the prince, but could do him no harm. "Well, now it is my turn," cried the youth, "will you be converted to the true faith?" and with these words he struck the monster such a blow that six of his seven heads came flying down.

"Strike me once more," groaned the dragon.

"Not I," replied the youth, "I myself only came into the world once."

Immediately the dragon fell to pieces, but his one remaining head began to roll and roll and roll till it stood on the brink of the well. "Whoever can take my soul out of this well," it said, "shall have my treasure also," and with these words the head bounded into the well.

The youth took a rope, fastened one end of it to a rock, and seizing the other end himself, lowered himself into the well. At the bottom of the well he found an iron door. He opened it, passed through, and there right before him stood a palace compared with which his father's palace was a hovel. Into this palace he went, and in it were forty rooms, and in each room was a damsel sitting by her embroidery frame with enormous treasures behind her. "Are you a man or a spirit?" cried the terrified damsels.

"I am a man, and the son of a man," replied the prince. "I have just slain a seven-headed dragon and have followed its rolling head here."

Tales of the Meddahs: Tales from the Turkish tradition

Oh, how the forty damsels rejoiced at hearing these words. They embraced the youth, and begged and prayed him not to leave them there. They were the children of one father and one mother they said. The dragon had killed their parents and carried them off, and they had nobody to look to in the whole wide world.

"We also are forty," said the youth, "and we are seeking forty damsels." Then he told them that he would first of all ascend to his brethren, and then he would come for them again. So, he ascended out of the well, went to the spring, lay down beside it and fell asleep.

Early in the morning the forty brothers arose and laughed at their father for trying to frighten them with the well. Again, they set out on their way, and went on and on till evening overtook them, when they perceived a caravanserai before them.

"Not a step further will we go," said the elder brothers. The youngest brother indeed insisted that it would be well to remember their father's words, for his speech could surely not have been in vain. But they laughed at their youngest brother, ate and drank, said their prayers, and lay down to sleep. Only the youngest brother remained wide awake.

About midnight he again heard a noise. The youth snatched up his arms, and again he saw before him a seven-headed dragon, but much larger than the former one. The dragon rushed at him first of all but could not overcome him. Then the youth dealt him one blow and off went six of the dragon's heads. Then the dragon wished him to take one more blow, but he would not. The head rolled into a well, the youth went after it, and came upon a palace larger than the former one, and with ever so much more treasures and precious things in it. He marked the well so that he should know it again, returned to his brothers, and wearied out with his great combat slept so soundly that his brothers had to wake him up with blows next morning.

Again, they arose, took horse, went up hill and down dale, and just as the sun was setting, a vast desert stood before them. They fell to eating straightway, drank their fill, and were just going to lie down to sleep when

Tales of the Meddahs: Tales from the Turkish tradition

all at once such a roaring, such a bellowing arose that the very mountains fell down from their places.

The princes were horribly afraid, especially when they saw coming against them a gigantic seven-headed dragon. He vomited forth venomous fire in his wrath, and roared furiously, "Who killed my two brothers? Here with him! I'll conclude this business with him now!"

The youngest brother saw that his brethren were more dead than alive from fear, so he gave them the keys of the two wells, in one of which was the vast heap of treasure, and in the other the forty damsels. Let them take everything home, he said. As for himself he must first slay the dragon and then he would follow after them. The thirty-nine brothers lost no time in mounting their horses and galloping off. They drew the treasure out of one well and the forty damsels out of the other, and so returned home to their father. But now we will see what happened to the youngest brother.

He fought the dragon, and the dragon fought him, but neither could get the better of the other. The dragon perceived that it was vain to try and vanquish the youth, so he said to him, "If you will go to the Empire of Chin-i-Machin and fetch me from there the Padishah's daughter, I will not worry the life out of you." To this the prince readily agreed, for he could not have sustained the conflict much longer.

Then Champalak, for that was the dragon's name, gave the prince a bridle and said to him, "A good steed comes here to feed every day, seize him, put this bridle in his mouth, and bid him take you to the Empire of Chin-i-Machin!"

So, the youth took the bridle and waited for the good charger. Presently a golden-maned charger came flying through the air, and the moment the prince had put the bridle in its mouth, the charger said, "What do you command, little Sultan?" and before you could wink your eyes, the Empire of Chin-i-Machin stood before him.

Tales of the Meddahs: Tales from the Turkish tradition

Then he dismounted from his horse, took off the bridle, and went into the town. There he entered into an old woman's hut and asked her whether she received guests.

"Willingly," answered the old woman. Then she made ready a place for him, and while he was sipping his coffee, he asked her all about the talk of the town. "Well," said the old woman, "a seven-headed dragon is very much in love with our Sultan's daughter. A war has been raging between them on that account these many years, and the monster presses us so hardly that not even a bird can fly into our realm."

"Then where is the Sultan's daughter?" asked the youth.

"In a little palace in the Padishah's garden," replied the old woman, "and the poor thing dare not put her foot outside it."

The next day the youth went to the Padishah's garden and asked the gardener to take him as a servant, and he begged and prayed till the gardener had not the heart to refuse him. "Very well, I will take you," said he, "and you will have nothing to do but water the flowers of the garden."

Now the Sultan's daughter saw the youth, called him to her window, and asked him how he had managed to reach that realm. Then the youth told her that his father was a Padishah, that he had fought with the dragon Champalak on his travels and had promised to bring the Sultan's daughter to his father. "Yet fear nothing," added the youth, "for my love is stronger than the love of the serpent, and if you will only have the courage to come with me, then trust me to find a way of disposing of him."

The damsel was so much in love with the prince, and so eager to escape from her captivity, that she consented to trust herself to him, and one night they escaped from her palace and went straight towards the desert where the dragon Champalak lived. They agreed on the way that the girl should find out what the dragon's talisman was, so that they might destroy him that way if they could do it no other.

Imagine the joy of Champalak when he saw the princess! "What joy, what rapture, that you have come!" cried Champalak, but fondle and caress her as

133

Tales of the Meddahs: Tales from the Turkish tradition

he might, the damsel did nothing but weep. Days passed by, then weeks passed by, and yet the tears never left the damsel's eyes.

"Tell me at least what your talisman is," said the damsel to him one day, "if you would see me happy and not wretched with you all your days."

"Alas, my soul!" said the dragon, "my talisman is guarded in a place where it is impossible ever to come. It is in a large palace in a neighbouring realm, and though one may venture there for it, no one has ever been able to get back again."

The prince needed no more information. That was quite good enough for him. He took his bridle, went with it to the seashore, and summoned his golden-maned steed.

"What do you command me, little Sultan?" said the steed.

"I want you to convey me to the neighbouring realm, to the palace of the talisman of the dragon Champalak," cried the youth, and in no more time than it takes to wink an eye, the palace stood before him.

Then the steed said to the youth, "When we reach the palace you will tie the bridle to two iron gates, and when I neigh once and strike my iron hoofs together, a door will open. In this open door you will see a lion's throat, and if you cannot kill that lion at one stroke, flee, or you are a dead man."

With that they went up to the palace, the youth tied the horse to the two iron gates by his bridle, and when the horse neighed the door flew open. The youth struck with all his might at the gaping throat of the lion in the doorway and split it right in two. Then he cut open the lion's belly and drew out of it a little gold cage with three doves in it, so beautiful that the like of them is not to be found in the wide world. He took one of them and began softly stroking and caressing it, when all at once, pr-r-r-r, away it flew out of his hand. The steed galloped swiftly after it, and if he had not caught it and wrung its neck it would have gone badly for the good youth.

Then the youth mounted his steed again, and in the twinkling of an eye he stood once more before Champalak's palace. In the gateway of the palace,

134

Tales of the Meddahs: Tales from the Turkish tradition

he killed the second dove, so that when the youth entered the dragon's room, there the monster lay quite helpless, and there was no more spirit in him at all. When he saw the dove in the youth's hand, he implored him to let him stroke it for the last time before he died. The youth's heart felt for him, and he was just about to hand the bird to him when the princess rushed out, snatched the dove from his hand, and killed it, whereupon the dragon expired before their very eyes.

"It was well for you," said the steed, "that you did not give him the dove, for if he had got it, fresh life would have flowed into him." And with that the steed disappeared, bridle and all.

Then they got together the dragon's treasures and went with them to the Empire of Chin-i-Machin. The Padishah was sick for grief at the loss of the damsel, and after searching for her in all parts of the kingdom in vain, was persuaded that she had fallen into the hands of the dragon. But there she stood before him now, hand in hand with the King's son. Then there was such a marriage-feast in that city that it seemed as if there was no end to it. After the marriage they set out on their journey again and travelled with a great escort of soldiers to the prince's father. There they had long held the King's son to be dead and would not believe that it was he even now till he had told them the tale of the three seven-headed dragons and the forty damsels.

The fortieth damsel was waiting patiently for him there, and the prince said to his wife, "Behold now my second bride!"

"You saved my life from the dragon," replied the Princess of Chin-i-Machin, "I therefore give her to you, do as you will with her!"

So, they made a marriage-feast for the second bride also, and they spent half their days in the Empire of the prince's father, and the other half in the Empire of Chin-i-Machin, and their lives flowed away in happiness.

Tales of the Meddahs: Tales from the Turkish tradition

Tales of the Meddahs: Tales from the Turkish tradition

THE LION, THE WOLF, AND THE FOX

This story has been adapted from Turkish Literature by Epiphanius Wilson, A.M., published in 1901 by P. F. Collier & Son, New York.

The Lion, the Wolf, and the Fox, having made an alliance, went forth to hunt, and captured a ram, a sheep, and a lamb.

When dinner time came the Lion said to the Wolf, "Divide the prey among us."

The Wolf replied, "O King, God apportions them like this - the ram is for you, the sheep for me, and the lamb for the Fox."

The Lion flew into a violent rage at this and gave the Wolf a blow upon the cheek that made his eyes bulge out. He retired in bitter tears.

Then the Lion addressed the Fox, bidding him apportion the prey.

"O King," he answered, "God has already apportioned it. The ram is for your dinner, we will join you in eating the sheep, and you shall sup upon the lamb."

"Little rogue of a Fox," said the Lion, "who taught you to apportion things with such equity?"

"The starting eyes of the Wolf taught me that," replied the Fox.

This fable shows that many wicked men see the error of their ways, and amend, so soon as kings and princes cause robbers and malefactors to be hanged.

Tales of the Meddahs: Tales from the Turkish tradition

Tales of the Meddahs: Tales from the Turkish tradition

THE FORTY WISE MEN

This story has been adapted from Told in the Coffee House by Cyrus Adler and Allan Ramsay, published in 1898 by MacMillan and Company, London. Allan Ramsay was a Scottish poet, playwright, publisher, librarian and wig-maker active in the early and mid-eighteenth century. Cyrus Adler adapted Ramsay's work in the nineteenth century, being an American educator, Jewish religious leader and scholar.

Once upon a time there lived and laboured for the welfare of our people an organized body of men. At whose suggestion this society was formed I know not. All that we know of them today, through our fathers, is that their forefathers chose from among them the most wise, sincere, and experienced forty brethren. These forty were named the Forty Wise Men. When one of the forty was called away from his labours here, perhaps to continue them in higher spheres, or to receive his ultimate reward, the remaining thirty-nine consulted and chose from the community a man whom they thought capable, and worthy of guiding and of being guided, to add to their number. They lived and held their meetings in a mosque of which little remains now, the destructive hand of time having left it but a battered dome, with cheerless walls and great square holes, where once were iron bars and stained glass. It has gone and so have the wise men. But its foundations are solid, and they may in time come to support an edifice dedicated to noble work, and, Inshallah, the seed of the Forty Wise Men will also bear fruit in days that are yet to come.

Tales of the Meddahs: Tales from the Turkish tradition

What was the good of this body of men? Great, great, my friends. Not only did they administer justice to the oppressed and give to the needy substantial aid; but their very existence had the most beneficial effect on the community. Each man vied with his peers to be worthy of being nominated for the vacancy when it occurred. No station in life was too low to be admitted, no station was too high for one of the faithful to become one of the 'Forty.' Here all were equal. As Allah himself considers mankind by deeds, so also mankind was considered by the Forty Wise Men, who presided over the welfare and smoothed the destiny of the children of Allah. With their years, their wisdom grew, and they were blessed by Allah.

In the town of Scutari, over the way, there lived and laboured a Dervish. His counsel to the rash was ever ready, and his sole object, apparently, in life was to become one of the Forty Wise Men, who presided over the people and protected them from all ills.

The years went on, and still without a reward he patiently laboured, no doubt contenting himself with the idea that the day would come when the merit of his actions would be recognized by Allah. That was a mistake, my friends. True faith expects nothing. However, the day did come, and the Dervish's great desire had every appearance of being realized. One of the Forty Wise Men having accomplished his mission on earth, departed this life. The remaining thirty-nine, who still had duties to fulfil, consulted as to whom they should call to aid them in their work. A eulogy was pronounced in favour of the Dervish. They not unjustly considered how he had laboured among the poor in Scutari, ever ready to help the needy, ever ready to counsel the rash, ever ready to comfort and encourage the despairing. It was decided that he should be nominated. A deputation consisting of three, two to listen, one to speak, was named, and with the blessing of their brethren they entered a caique and were rowed to Scutari. Arriving at the Dervish's gate, the spokesman thus addressed the would-be member of the Forty Wise Men, "Brother in the flesh, your actions have been noted, and we come to put a proposition to you, which, after consideration, you will either accept

Tales of the Meddahs: Tales from the Turkish tradition

or reject as you think best for all interested therein. We would ask you to become one of us. We are sent here by, and are the representatives of, the sages who preside over the people. Brother, we number in all one hundred and thirty-eight in spirit. Ninety-nine, having accomplished their task in the flesh, and have departed. Thirty-nine, still in the flesh, endeavour to fulfil their duty. And it is the desire of the one hundred and thirty-eight souls to add you to our number in order to complete our number of labourers in the flesh. Brother, your duties, which will be everlasting, you will learn when with us. Do consider our offer, and we will return at the setting of the sun of the third day, to receive your answer."

And they turned to depart. But the Dervish stopped them, saying, "Brothers, I have no need to consider the subject for three days, seeing that my inmost desire for thirty years, and my sole object in life has been to become worthy of being one of you. In spirit I have long been your brother, in the flesh it is easy to comply, seeing that it has been the spirit's desire."

Then answered the spokesman, "Brother, you have spoken well. Allah, you are with us in our choice, and we praise You. Brother, one word! Our ways are different to all men's ways, and you must have faith, and all is well."

"Brethren, faith! I have had faith. My faith is now even stronger. I do your bidding."

"Brother, first of all your worldly goods must be disposed of and rendered into gold. Every earthly possession you have must be represented by a piece of gold. Therefore, see to that. We have other duties to fulfil but will return before the sun sets in the west."

The Dervish set about selling all his goods, and when the colouring of the sky in the west harbingered the closing of the day, he had disposed of everything and stood waiting with nothing but a sack of gold.

The three wise men returned, and, on seeing the Dervish, said, "Brother, you have done well. Let's go."

A caique was in waiting, and the four entered. Silently the caique glided over the smooth surface of the Bosphorus, and the occupants sat there in silence.

Tales of the Meddahs: Tales from the Turkish tradition

When they were just beyond Maidens' Tower, the spokesman, turning to the Dervish, said, "Brother, with your inmost blessing give me that sack, representing everything you possess in this world."

The Dervish handed the sack as he was bidden, and the wise man solemnly rose, and holding it on high, said, "With the blessing of our brother Mustapha," and dropped it where the current is strongest. Then, sitting down, resumed his silence. The deed was done, and nothing outward told the story. The Caique oarsman dipped his oars, and the waves rippled as soft as before. Nothing broke the stillness except for but the distant, soothing cry of the Muezzin, calling the faithful to prayer, now waxing, now waning, now completely dying away as they moved around the minarets.

Before long the boat was brought to the shore, the four men wended their way up the steep hill, and the horizon, wrapped in the mantle of night, hid them from the boatman's sight. A few minutes' walk brought them to the mosque of the Forty Wise Men. The spokesman turned to the Dervish, and said, "Brother, faithfully follow," and then passed through the doorway. They entered a large, vaulted chamber, the ceiling of which was artistically inlaid with mosaics, and the floor covered with tiles of the ceramic art of bygone ages. From the centre hung a large chandelier holding a number of little oil cups, each shedding its tiny light, as if to show that union was strength. Round this chandelier were seven brass filagreed, hemispherical-shaped lanterns, holding several oil burners. These many tiny burners gave a soothing, contented, though undefined light, which, together with the silence, added to the impressiveness of the place. Round this hall were forty boxes of the same shape and size.

Our friend stood in the centre of the hall and under the influence of the scene, he was afraid to breathe. He did not know whether to be happy or sad, for having come so far.

As he stood thus thinking, dreaming, one of the curtains was raised, and there came forth a very old man, his venerable white beard all but touching his girdle. Solemnly and slowly, he walked over to the opposite side, and

Tales of the Meddahs: Tales from the Turkish tradition

following in his train came thirty-eight more, the last apparently being the youngest.

Chill after chill went coursing down the spinal cord of the astonished would-be brother, whilst these men moved about in the unbroken silence, as if talking to invisible beings, now embracing, now clasping hands, now bidding farewell.

The Dervish closed his eyes, and then opened them. Were these things so? Yes, it was no dream, no hallucination. Yet he could not understand why he heard he no sound.

Each of the brethren now took his place beside a box, but there was one vacancy. No one stood at the side of the box to the left of the youngest brother. Making a profound salaam, which all answered, the old man silently turned, raised the curtain, and passed into the darkness, each in his order following. As one in a trance, the Dervish watched one after another disappear. The last now raised the curtain, but before vanishing, turned (it was the spokesman), and whispered, "Brother, faith, follow!" and stepped into the darkness.

These words acted upon the Dervish like a spell, and he followed.

Up, up, the winding stairway of a minaret they went. At last, they arrived, and to the horror of the Dervish, what did he see? One, two, three, disappear over the parapet, and his friend the spokesman, with, "Brother, faith, follow!" also vanished into the inky darkness.

Again, at the eleventh hour the cheering words of the brother spokesman acted upon the Dervish like magic. He raised his foot to the parapet, and, in faltering decision, jumped up two or three times. But man's guardian does not lead him over the rugged paths of life. He gives the impulse, and you must go. So, it was with the Dervish. He jumped once, twice, thrice, but each time fell backward instead of forward. My friends, he hesitated again. At the eleventh hour he was encouraged but remained undecided. He was not equal to the test. So, with a great weight on his heart, he descended the winding

Tales of the Meddahs: Tales from the Turkish tradition

stairs of the minaret. He had reached his zenith only in desire and was now on his decline.

Lamenting, like the weak mortal that he was, for not having followed, he again entered the hall he had just left, with the intention, no doubt, of departing.

But the charm of the place was on him again, and as he stood the curtain moved, and the old man advanced and as before, the silence was unbroken. Again, each man took his place beside a box, and again the old man said, "Salaam", with the simultaneous response of the others. Again, they gestured as if talking to invisible beings of some calamity which had befallen them which they all regretted.

The old man went and opened the box that stood alone. From this he took the identical bag of gold that had been dropped into the Bosphorus some hours ago. The spokesman came forward and took it from the hand of the old man. The Dervish now no longer believed that he was in the real world, and that these things were truly taking place. He understood not, he knew not.

Coming forward, the spokesman thus addressed the spell-bound Dervish, his voice giving a strange echo, as if his words were emphasized by a hundred invisible mouths, "Friend and brother in the flesh, but weak of the spirit, you have proved yourself unworthy to impart that which you have not yourself - Faith! Your previous actions, of seeming conviction, have not been done for the eye of the Almighty, the All-seeing, the All-powerful alone, but for the approbation of mankind. To get this approbation you have soared out of your element. The atmosphere is too rarified, you cannot live, you must return! Get back into the world, back to your brothers. You cannot be one of us. One hundred and thirty-nine in the spirit have regretfully judged you as lacking in faith, and not having a sheltered apartment within yourself, you cannot shelter others. No man can bequeath that which he has not. Go your way, and in secret build a wall, brick by brick, action by action, and let no one see your place except the eye that sees all, lest a side, when all but completed, fall, and you are again exposed to the four winds. Take your

Tales of the Meddahs: Tales from the Turkish tradition

money, your everything, and when hesitation interrupts, offer a prayer in your heart, and then faithfully follow! Farewell!"

And the Dervish was led out into the street, a lone and solitary man. In his hand he had everything, that being a bag of gold.

Tales of the Meddahs: Tales from the Turkish tradition

Tales of the Meddahs: Tales from the Turkish tradition

THE CROW-PERI

This story has been adapted from Turkish Fairy Tales and Folk Tales by Dr. Ignácz Kúnos, published in 1901 by A. H. Bullen, London.

Once upon a time that was no time there was a man who had one son. This man used to go out into the forest all day and catch birds for sale to the first comer. At last, however, the father died, and the son was left all alone. Now he did not know what his father's profession had been, but while he was searching all about the floor he came upon the fowling-snare. So, he took it, went out into the forest, and set the snare on a tree. At that moment a crow flew down upon the tree, but as the snare was cunningly laid the poor bird was caught. The youth climbed up after it, but when he had got hold of the bird, the crow began begging him to let her go, promising to give him in exchange something more beautiful and more precious than herself. The crow begged and prayed till at last he let her go free, and again he set the snare in the tree and sat down at the foot of it to wait. Presently another bird came flying up and flew right into the snare. The youth climbed up the tree again to bring it down, but when he saw it, he was full of amazement, for such a beautiful thing he had never seen in the forest before.

While he was still gazing at it and chuckling, the crow again appeared to him and said, "Take that bird to the Padishah, and he will buy it from you."

So, the youth took away the bird, put it in a cage, and carried it to the palace. When the Padishah saw the beautiful little creature, he was filled with joy, and gave the youth so much money for it that he did not know what to do with it all. But the bird they placed in a golden cage, and the Padishah had his joy of it day and night.

Now the Padishah had a favourite who was grievously jealous of the good fortune of the youth who had brought the bird and kept cudgelling his brains as to how he could get him beneath his feet. At last, he hit upon a plan, and going to the Padishah one day he said, "How happy that bird would be if only he had an ivory palace to dwell in!"

"Yes," replied the Padishah, "but where could I get enough ivory to make him a palace?"

"He who brought the bird here," said the favourite, "will certainly be able to find the ivory."

The Padishah sent for the little fowler and ordered him to make an ivory palace for the bird there and then. "I know you can get the ivory," said the Padishah.

"Alas, my lord Padishah!" lamented the youth, "Where am I to get all this ivory from?"

"That is your business," replied the Padishah. "You may search for it for forty days, but if it is not here by that time your head shall be where your feet are now."

The youth was sorely troubled, and while he was still pondering in his mind which road he should take, the crow came flying up to him, and asked him what he was grieving about so much. Then the youth told her what a great trouble that one little bird had brought down upon his head.

"Why this is nothing at all to fret about," said the crow, "but go to the Padishah, and ask him for forty wagon loads of wine!"

The youth returned to the palace, got all that quantity of wine, and as he was coming back with the cars, the crow flew up and said, "Nearby is a forest, on the border of which are forty large trenches, and as many elephants as there are in the wide world come to drink out of these trenches. Go now and fill them with wine instead of water. The elephants will get drunk and tumble

Tales of the Meddahs: Tales from the Turkish tradition

down, and you will be able to pull out their teeth and take them to the Padishah."

The youth did as the bird said, crammed his ears full of elephants" tusks instead of wine, and returned with them to the palace. The Padishah rejoiced greatly at the sight of all the ivory, had the palace built, rewarded the little fowler with rich gifts, and sent him home.

So, there was the sparkling bird in his ivory palace, and right merrily did he hop about from perch to perch, but he could never be got to sing.

"Ah!" said the evil counsellor, "if only his master were here, he would sing of his own accord."

"Who knows who his master is, or where he is to be found?" asked the Padishah sadly.

"He who fetched the elephants' tusks could fetch the bird's master also," replied the evil counsellor.

The Padishah sent for the little fowler once more and commanded him to bring the bird's master before him.

"How can I tell who his master is, when I caught him by chance in the forest?" asked the fowler.

"That is your look-out," said the Padishah, "but if you don't find him I will slay you. I give you forty days for your quest and let that be enough."

The youth went home, and sobbed aloud in his despair, when suddenly the crow came flying up and asked him what he was crying for.

"Why should I not cry?" said the poor youth, and with that he began to tell the crow of his new trouble.

"Nay, but 'tis a shame to weep for such a trifle," said the crow. "Go quickly now to the King and ask him for a large ship, but it must be large enough to hold forty maidservants, a beautiful garden also, and a bath house."

The youth returned to the King and told him what he wanted for his journey. The ship was prepared as he had desired it, the youth embarked, and was

Tales of the Meddahs: Tales from the Turkish tradition

just thinking whether he should go to the left or the right, when the crow came flying up, and said to him, "Steer your ship always to the right, and go straight on until you perceive a huge mountain. At the foot of this mountain dwell forty Peris, and when they perceive your ship, they will feel a strong desire to look at everything on board. But you must allow only their Queen to come on board, for she is the owner of the bird, and while you are showing her the ship, set sail and never stop till you reach home."

The youth went on board the ship, steered steadily to the right, and never stopped once till he came to the mountain. There the forty Peris were walking on the seashore, and when they saw the ship, they all came rushing up wanting to examine the beautiful thing. The Queen of the Peris asked the little fowler whether he would show her the ship, especially the inside of it, and he took her off in a little skiff and brought her to the vessel.

The Peri was monstrously delighted with the beautiful ship. She walked in the garden with the damsels on board the ship, and when she saw the bath house she said to the waiting-maids, "If I have come so far, I may as well have a bath into the bargain." With that she stepped into the bath house, and while she was bathing the ship went off.

They had gone a good distance across the sea before the Peri had finished her bathing. The Peri made haste, for it was now growing late, but when she stepped upon the deck, she saw nothing but the sea around her. At this she fell to weeping bitterly.

"What will become of me?" she asked. "Where are you taking me? Into whose hands am I about to fall?" But the youth comforted her with the assurance that she was going to a King's palace and would be among good people.

Not very long afterwards they arrived in the city and sent word to the King that the ship had come back. Then he brought the Peri to the palace, and as she passed by the little bird's ivory palace, it began to sing so beautifully that all who heard it were beside themselves for joy. The Peri was a little comforted when she heard it, but the King was filled with rapture, and he

Tales of the Meddahs: Tales from the Turkish tradition

loved the beautiful Peri so fondly that he could not be a single moment without her. The wedding-banquet quickly followed, and with the beauteous Peri on his right hand, and the sparkling bird on his left, there was not a happier man in the world than that Padishah. But the poison of envy devoured the soul of the evil counsellor.

One day, however, the Sultana suddenly fell ill, and took to her bed. Every remedy was tried in vain, but the sages said that nothing could cure her but the drug which she had left behind in her own fairy palace. Then, by the advice of the evil counsellor, the young fowler was again sent for and commanded to go and seek the drug.

The good youth embarked on his ship again and was just about to sail when the crow came to him and asked him where he was going. The youth told her that the Sultana was ill, and he had been sent to fetch the drug from the fairy palace.

"Well then, go!" said the crow. "You will find the palace behind a mountain. Two lions stand in the gates but take this feather and touch their mouths with it, and they will not lift so much as a claw against you."

The youth took the feather, arrived in front of the mountain, disembarked, and quickly beheld the palace. He went straight up to the gates, and there stood the two lions. He took out his feather, and no sooner had he touched their mouths than they lay down one on each side and let him go into the palace. The Peris about the palace also saw the youth, and immediately guessed that their Queen was ill. They gave him the drug, and immediately he took ship again, and returned to the palace of the Padishah. Just as he entered the Peri's chamber with the drug in his hand, the crow alighted on his shoulder, and thus they went together to the sick Sultana's bed.

The Sultana was already in the throes of death, but no sooner had she tasted of the healing drug than she seemed to return to life again at a single bound. She opened her eyes, gazed upon the little fowler, and perceiving the crow upon his shoulder addressed her directly, saying, "Oh, you sooty slave! Are you not sorry for all the things you've made this good youth suffer for my

Tales of the Meddahs: Tales from the Turkish tradition

sake?" Then the Sultana told her lord that this same crow was her serving-maid, whom, for negligence in her service, she had changed into a crow. "Nevertheless," she added, "I now forgive her, for I see that her intentions towards me were good."

At these words the crow trembled all over, and immediately a lovely damsel stood before the young fowler, and to be sure there was really very little difference between her and the Queen of the Peris. At the petition of the Sultana, the Sultan married the youth to the Crow-Peri, and the evil-minded counsellor was banished. The fowler became Vizier in his stead, and he and his bride's happiness lasted till death.

Tales of the Meddahs: Tales from the Turkish tradition

THE FOX AND THE SPARROW

This story has been adapted from Turkish Literature by Epiphanius Wilson, A.M., published in 1901 by P. F. Collier & Son, New York.

The Fox held a Sparrow in his mouth and was on the point of eating it, when the latter said, "You ought first to give thanks to God, and then you can eat me, for at this moment I am on the point of laying an egg, big as that of an ostrich. It is a priceless egg, but let me go, that I may lay it, and afterward you may eat me. I swear that I will put myself at your disposal."

As soon as the Fox dropped him, he flew off and lighted on the branch of a very high tree. Then the Fox said to him, "Come, now, do as you have decided, and return when I ask you."

"Do you think I am as senseless as you are?" asked the Sparrow, "that I should return at your pleasure? How could you possibly believe me, or imagine that such a little body could lay such a disproportionately large egg? Listen to the advice I give you. Don't credit extravagant statements or go to sleep under a tottering wall."

The Fox answered, "God will judge you for the trick you have played me."

"Some falsehoods," answered the Sparrow, "are praiseworthy; God highly rewards the lie that delivers one from death or danger, and which saves another's life."

The Fox then concealed himself nearby and began to plot and plan for the capture of the Sparrow, but the latter dropped dung into his eyes, saying, "O fool, listen to another piece of advice. Do not strive after that which you

Tales of the Meddahs: Tales from the Turkish tradition

cannot attain, and in the quarrels of husband and wife, or of brothers, say not a single indiscreet word of which you may afterward repent."

Tales of the Meddahs: Tales from the Turkish tradition

HOW THE PRIEST KNEW THAT IT WOULD SNOW

This story has been adapted from Told in the Coffee House by Cyrus Adler and Allan Ramsay, published in 1898 by MacMillan and Company, London. Allan Ramsay was a Scottish poet, playwright, publisher, librarian, and wig-maker active in the early and mid-eighteenth century. Cyrus Adler adapted Ramsay's work in the nineteenth century, being an American educator, Jewish religious leader, and scholar.

A Turk travelling in Asia Minor came to a Christian village. He journeyed on horseback, was accompanied by a slave, and seeming a man of consequence, the priest of the village offered him hospitality for the night. The first thing to be done was to conduct the traveller to the stable, that he might see his horse attended to and comfortably stalled for the night. In the stable was a magnificent Arab horse, belonging to the priest, and the Turk gazed upon it with covetous eyes, but nevertheless, in order that no ill should befall the beautiful creature and to counteract the influence of the evil eye with certainty, he spat at the animal. After they had dined, the priest took his guest for a walk in the garden, and in the course of a very pleasant conversation he informed the Turk that on the morrow there would be snow on the ground.

"Never! Impossible!" said the Turk.

"Well, tomorrow you will see that I am right," said the priest.

Tales of the Meddahs: Tales from the Turkish tradition

"I am willing to stake my horse against yours, that you are wrong," answered the Turk, who was delighted at this opportunity which gave him a chance of securing the horse, without committing the breach in Oriental etiquette of asking his host if he would sell it. After some persuasion the priest accepted his wager, and they separated for the night.

Later that night, the Turk said to his slave, "Go, Sali, go and see what the weather says, for truly my life is in want of our good host's horse."

Sali went out to make an observation, and on returning said to his master, "Master, the heavens are like your face, without a frown and many kindly sparkling eyes, and the earth is like to that of your slave."

"It's well, Sali, 'tis well. What a beautiful animal that is!"

Later on, before retiring to rest, he sent his slave on another inspection, and was gratified to receive the same answer. Early in the morning he awoke, and calling his slave, who had slept at his door, he sent him forth again to see if any change had taken place.

"Oh master!" reported Sali, in trembling tones, "Nature has reversed herself, for the heavens are now like the scowling face of your slave, and the earth is like yours, white, entirely white."

"Chok shai! Wonderful thing. Then I have lost not only that beautiful animal but my own horse as well. Oh pity! Oh pity!"

He gave up his horse, but before parting he begged the priest to tell him how he knew it would snow.

"My pig told me as we were walking in the garden yesterday. I saw it put its nose in the heap of manure you see in that corner, and I knew that to be a sure sign that it would snow on the morrow," replied the priest.

Deeply mystified, the Turk and his slave proceeded on foot. Reaching a Turkish village before nightfall, he sought and obtained shelter for the night from the Imam. While partaking of the evening meal he asked the Imam when the feast of the Bairam would be.

Tales of the Meddahs: Tales from the Turkish tradition

"Truly, I do not know! When the cannons fire, I will know it is Bairam," said his host.

"What!" said the traveller, becoming angry, "You an Imam, a learned Hodja, and you don't know when it will be Bairam, and the pig of the Greek priest knew when it would snow? Shame! Shame!"

And becoming much angered, he declined the hospitality of the Imam and went elsewhere.

Tales of the Meddahs: Tales from the Turkish tradition

Tales of the Meddahs: Tales from the Turkish tradition

THE SYRIAN PRIEST AND THE YOUNG MAN

This story has been adapted from Turkish Literature by Epiphanius Wilson, A.M., published in 1901 by P. F. Collier & Son, New York.

A Syrian priest, good and wise, and an Armenian were engaged in a dispute. The young man, at last enraged, said to the priest, "I will drive this stone down your throat, in order that your thirty-two teeth may choke you."

The priest returned hastily to his house, lost in astonishment, and said to his wife, "In the name of God, wife, light a candle, and count how many teeth I have."

She counted them and said, "They are just thirty-two in number."

The Priest at once returned to the Young Man and said, "How did you learn the number of my teeth? And who told you?"

"Sir," replied the other, "I learned the number of your teeth from the number of my own."

This fable shows that from my own bad qualities I am able to guess yours, for all faults are common.

Tales of the Meddahs: Tales from the Turkish tradition

Tales of the Meddahs: Tales from the Turkish tradition

THE WIND-DEMON

This story has been adapted from Turkish Fairy Tales and Folk Tales by Dr. Ignácz Kúnos, published in 1901 by A. H. Bullen, London.

There was once upon a time an old Padishah who had three sons and three daughters. One day the old man fell ill, and though they called all the leeches together to help him, his disease would not take a turn for the better. "I already belong to Death," he thought, and calling to him his sons and daughters, he thus addressed them, "If I die, he among you shall be Padishah who watches three nights at my tomb. As for my daughters, I give them to him who first comes to woo them." And with that he died and was buried as became a Padishah.

Now as the realm could have a Padishah in no other way, the eldest son went to his father's tomb and sat there for half the night, said his prayers upon his carpet, and awaited the dawn. But all at once a horrible din arose in the midst of the darkness, and so frightened was he that he snatched up his slippers and never stopped till he got home. The next night the middling son also went out to the tomb, and he also sat there for half the night, but no sooner did he hear the great din than he too caught up his slippers and hurried off homewards. Now came to the turn of the third and youngest son.

The third son took his sword, stuck it in his girdle, and went off to the tomb. Sure enough, when he had sat there till midnight, he heard the horrible din, and so horrible was it that the very earth trembled. The youth pulled himself together, went straight towards the spot from where the noise came loudest, and right in front of him stood a huge dragon. Drawing his sword, the youth

Tales of the Meddahs: Tales from the Turkish tradition

fell upon the dragon so furiously that at last the monster had scarcely strength enough left to say, "If you are a man, put your heel upon me and strike me with your sword but once more!"

"Not I," cried the King's son. "My mother only bore me into the world once," whereupon the dragon yielded up its filthy soul. The King's son would have cut off the beast's ears and nose, but he could not see very well in the dark, and began groping about for them, when all at once he saw far off a little shining light. He went straight towards it, and there in the midst of the brightness he saw an old man. Two globes were in his hand, one black and the other white. The black globe he was turning round and round, and from the white globe proceeded the light.

"What are you doing, old father?" asked the King's son.

"Alas, my son," replied the old man, "my business is my bane, I hold fast the nights and let go the days."

"Alas, my father," replied the King's son, "my task is even greater than yours."

With that he tied together the old man's arms, so that he might not let go the days, and went on still further to seek the light. He went on and on till he came to the foot of a castle wall, and forty men were taking counsel together beneath it.

"What's the matter?" inquired the King's son.

"We should like to go into the castle to steal the treasure," said the forty men, "but we don't know how."

"I would very soon help you if you only gave me a little light," said the King's son. This the robbers readily promised to do, and after that he took a packet of nails, knocked them into the castle wall, row after row, right up to the top, clambered up himself, and then shouted down to them, "Now you come up one by one, just as I have done."

The robbers caught hold of the nails and began to clamber up, one after another, the whole forty of them. But the youth was not idle. He drew his

162

Tales of the Meddahs: Tales from the Turkish tradition

sword, and the moment each one of them reached the top, he chopped off his head and pitched his body into the courtyard, and so he did just that to the whole forty. Then he leaped down into the courtyard himself, and there right before him was a beautiful palace.

No sooner had he opened the door than a serpent glided past him and crawled up a column close by the staircase. The youth drew his sword to strike the serpent. He struck and cut the serpent in two, but his sword remained in the stone wall, and he forgot to draw it out again. Then he mounted the staircase and went into a room, and there lay a lovely damsel fast asleep. He went out again, closed the door very softly behind him, and ascended to the second flight, and went into a room there, and before him lay a still lovelier damsel on a bed. This door he also closed, and went up to the third and topmost flight, and opened a door there as well. The whole room was piled up with nothing but steel, and such a splendid damsel lay asleep there that if the King's son had had a thousand hearts, he would have loved her with them all. This door he also closed, remounted the castle wall, descended on the other side by means of the nails, which he took out as he descended, and so reached the ground again. Then he went straight up to the old man whose arms he had tied together.

"Oh, my son!" cried he from afar, "You have remained away a long time. Everybody's side will be aching from so much lying down."

Then the youth untied his arms, the old man let the white globes of day move round again, and the youth went up to the dragon, cut off its ears and nose, and put them in his knapsack. Then he went back to his home at the old palace, and when he drew near to it, he found that they had made his eldest brother Padishah. However, he let it be and said nothing.

Not very long afterwards a lion came to the palace and went straight up to the Padishah. "What do you want?" asked the Padishah.

"I want your eldest sister to wife," replied the lion.

"I'll not give my sister to a brute beast," said the Padishah, and forthwith they began chasing the lion away.

163

Tales of the Meddahs: Tales from the Turkish tradition

Then the King's youngest son appeared and said, 'Such was not our father's will, for he said we were to give her to whomsoever asked for her." With that they brought the damsel and gave her to the lion, and he took her and was gone.

The next day a tiger came and demanded the middling daughter from the Padishah. The two elder brethren would by no means give her up, but again the youngest brother insisted that they should do so, as it was their father's wish. So, they sent for the damsel and gave her to the tiger.

On the third day a bird alighted in the palace and said that he must have the youngest of the Sultan's daughters. The Padishah and the second brother were again unwilling to agree to it, but the youngest brother persuaded them that the bird ought to be allowed to fly back with his sister. Now this bird was the Padishah of the Peris, the emerald Anka.

But now let us see what happened in that castle of which we have before spoken. In this castle there dwelt just about this time a Padishah and his three daughters. Rising one morning and going out, he saw a man walking in the palace. He went out into the courtyard, and saw a serpent cut in two on the staircase, and a sword sticking in the stone column, and going on still further, and searching in all directions, he perceived the bodies of the forty robbers in his castle moat. "Only the hand of a friend could have done this," thought he, "and he has saved me from the robbers and the serpent. The sword belongs to my good friend, but where is the sword's master?" And he took counsel with his Vizier.

"Oh, we'll soon get to the bottom of that," said the Vizier. "Let us make a great bath and invite everyone to come and bathe in it for nothing. We will watch each single man carefully, and whosoever has a sheath without a sword will be the man who has saved us." And the Padishah did so. He made ready a big bath, and the whole realm came and bathed in it.

Next day the Vizier said to him, "Everyone has been here to bathe save only the King's three sons, they still remain behind."

Tales of the Meddahs: Tales from the Turkish tradition

Then the Padishah sent word to the King's three sons to come and bathe, and looking closely at their garments, he perceived that the youngest of the three wore a sheath without a sword. Then the Padishah called the King's son to him and said, "Great is the good you have done to me, so ask me what you will for it!"

"I ask nothing of you," replied the King's son, "but your youngest daughter."

"Alas, my son, ask me anything but that," sighed the Padishah. "Ask for my crown, and my kingdom, and I'll give them to you, but my daughter I cannot give."

"If you give me your daughter I will take her," replied the King's son, "but I want nothing else from your hand."

"My son," groaned the Padishah, "I will give you my eldest daughter. I'll give you my second daughter, nay, I'll give you the pair of them if you will, but my youngest daughter has a deadly enemy, the Wind-Demon. Because I would not give her to him, I have fenced her room with walls of steel, lest any of the devil race draw near to her. For the Wind-Demon is such a terrible monster that eye cannot see, nor dart overtake him. He flies like the tempest, and his coming is like the coming of a whirlwind."

But whatever the Padishah might say to turn him from wanting the damsel fell on deaf ears. He begged and pleaded so hard for the damsel that the Padishah was wearied by his speaking and promised him the damsel. Soon they held the bridal banquet. The two elder brothers received the two elder damsels, and returned to their kingdom, but the youngest brother remained behind to guard his wife against the Wind-Demon.

Time came and went, and the King's son avoided the light of day for the sake of his lovely Sultana. One day, however, the King's son said to his wife, "Behold now, my Sultana, all this time I have never moved from your side. I think I will go hunting, though it only be for a little hour or so."

"Alas, my King," replied his wife, "if you depart from me, I know that you will never see me again."

Tales of the Meddahs: Tales from the Turkish tradition

But as he begged her for leave again and again, and promised to be back again immediately, his wife consented. Then he took his weapons and went into the forest.

Now the Wind-Demon had been awaiting this chance all along. He feared the famous prince and dared not snatch his wife from his arms, but as soon as the King's son had put his foot out of doors, the Wind-Demon came in and vanished with the young man's wife.

Not very long afterwards the King's son came back and could find his wife nowhere. He went to the Padishah to seek her, and came back again, for it was certain that the Demon must have taken her, for no other living soul could have got near her. He wept bitterly, and he dashed himself against the floor fiercely, but then he quickly rose up again, took horse, and galloped away into the wide world, determined to find either death or his consort.

He went on for days, he went on for weeks, and in his trouble and anguish he gave himself no rest. All at once a palace sprang up before him, but it seemed to him like a mirage, which baffles the eye that looks upon it. It was the palace of his eldest sister. The damsel was just then looking out of the window, and she caught sight of a man wandering there where never a bird had flown and never a caravan had travelled. Then she recognized him as her brother, and so great was their mutual joy that they could not come to words for hugging and kissing.

Towards evening the damsel said to the King's son, "The lion will be here shortly, and although he is very good to me, he is only a brute beast for all that, and may do you a mischief." And she took her brother and hid him.

In the evening the lion came home sure enough, and when they had sat down together and begun to talk, the girl asked him what he would do if any of her brothers should chance to come there.

"If the eldest were to come," said the lion, "I would strike him dead with one blow. If the second came I would slay him also, but if the youngest came, I would let him go to sleep on my paws if he liked."

"Then he has come," said his wife.

166

Tales of the Meddahs: Tales from the Turkish tradition

"Where is he, where is he? Bring him out, let me see him!" cried the lion.

When the King's son appeared, the lion did not know what to do with himself for joy. Then they began to talk, and the lion asked him why he had come there, and where he was going. The youth told him what had happened, and said he was going to seek the Wind-Demon.

"I know but the rumour of him," said the lion, "but take my word for it, you had better have nothing to do with him, for there is none that can cope with the Wind-Demon."

But the King's son would not listen to reason. He remained there that night, and next morning mounted his horse again. The lion accompanied him to show him the right way, and then they parted, one going to the right and the other to the left.

Again, he went on and on, till he saw another palace, and this was the palace of his middling sister. The damsel saw from the window that a man was on the road, and no sooner did she recognize him than she rushed out to meet him and led him into the palace. Full of joy, they conversed together till the evening, and then the damsel said to the youth, "In a short time my tiger-husband will be here, I'll hide you from him, lest a mischief befall you," and she took her brother and hid him.

In the evening the tiger came home, and while they talked together his wife asked him what he would do if any of her brothers should chance to look in upon them.

"If the elder were to come," said the tiger, "I would strike them dead, but if the youngest came, I would go down on my knees before him."

The damsel called to her youngest brother, the King's son, to come forth. The tiger was overjoyed to see him, welcomed him as a brother, and asked him where he came from and where he was going. Then the King's son told the tiger of all his trouble and asked him whether he knew the Wind-Demon.

"Only by hearsay," replied the tiger, and then he tried to persuade the King's son not to go, for the danger was great. But the red dawn had no sooner

Tales of the Meddahs: Tales from the Turkish tradition

appeared than the King's son was ready to set out again. The tiger showed him the way, and the one went back and the other went forward.

He pursued his way, and it was endlessly long, but time passes quickly in a fairy tale, and at last a dark object stood out against him. "What can it be?" thought he, but when he drew nearer, he saw that it was a palace. It was the abode of his youngest sister. The damsel was just then looking out of the window. "Alas, my brother!" cried she, and very nearly fell out of the window for pure joy. Then she led him into the house. The youth rejoiced that he had found all his sisters so well, but the lack of his wife was still a weight upon his heart.

Now when evening was drawing nigh the girl said to her brother, "My bird-husband will be here anon, so conceal yourself from him, for if he sees you, he will tear your heart out," and with that she took her brother and hid him.

And now there was a great clapping of wings, and the Anka had scarce rested a while when his wife asked him what he would do if any of her brothers came to see them.

"As to the two elder ones," said the bird, "I would take them in my mouth, fly up to the sky with them, and cast them down from there, but if the youngest were to come, I would let him sit down on my wings and go to sleep there if he liked." Then the girl called forth her youngest brother.

"Alas, my dear little child," cried the bird, "how did you find your way here? Were you not afraid of the long journey?"

The youth told the Anka what had happened to him, and asked the Anka whether he could help him to get to the Wind-Demon.

"It is no easy matter," said the bird, "but even if you could get to him, I would counsel you to let it alone and stay rather among us."

"Not I," replied the resolute youth, "I will either release my wife or perish there!"

Then the Anka saw that he could not turn him from his purpose and began to explain to him all about the palace of the Wind-Demon. "He is now

Tales of the Meddahs: Tales from the Turkish tradition

asleep," said the Anka, "and you may be able to carry off your wife, but if he should awake and see you, he will without doubt grind you to atoms. Guard against him you cannot, for eye cannot see and fire cannot harm him, so look well to yourself!"

Next day the youth set out on his journey, and when he had gone on and on for a long, long time, he saw before him a vast palace that had neither door nor chimney, nor length nor breadth. It was the palace of the Wind-Demon. His wife chanced just then to be sitting at the window, and when she saw her husband, she leaped clean out of the window to him. The King's son caught his wife in his arms, and there were no bounds to their joy and their tears, till at last the girl remembered the terrible demon.

"This is now the third day that he has slept," cried she, "let us hurry away before the fourth day is spent also."

So, they mounted, whipped up their horses, and were already well on their way when the Wind-Demon awoke on the fourth day. Then he went to the girl's door and ordered her to open the door, that he might at least see her face for a brief moment. He waited, but he got no answer. Then, guessing at some evil, he beat in the door, and the place where the damsel should have lain was cold.

'So, Prince Mehmed!" cried he, "You have come here, eh, and stolen away my Sultana? Well, wait a while! Go your way, whip up your fleet steed! I'll catch you up in the long run." And with that he sat down at his ease, drank his coffee, smoked his chibouk, and then rose up and went after them.

Meanwhile the King's son was galloping off with the girl with all his might, when all at once the girl felt the demon's breath, and cried out in her terror, "Alas, my King, the Wind-Demon is here!"

Like a whirlwind the invisible monster was upon them, caught up the youth, tore off his arms and legs, and smashed his skull and all his bones till there was not a bit of him left.

Tales of the Meddahs: Tales from the Turkish tradition

The damsel began to weep bitterly. "Even if you have killed him," sobbed she, "let me at least gather together his bones and pile them up somewhere, for if you will allow it, I would like to bury him."

"I care not what you do with his bones!" cried the Demon.

The damsel took the bones of the King's son and piled them up together, kissed the horse between the eyes, placed the bones on his saddle, and whispered in his ear, "Take these bones, my good steed, take them to the proper place."

Then the Demon took the girl and led her back to the palace, for the power of her beauty was so great that it always kept the Demon close to her. Into her presence, indeed, she never suffered the monster to come. At the door of her chamber, he had to stop, but he was allowed to show himself to her now and then.

Meanwhile the good steed galloped away with the youth's bones till he stopped at the door of the palace of the youngest sister, and then he neighed and neighed till the damsel heard him. She rushed out to the horse, and when she perceived the knapsack, and in the knapsack the bones of her brother, she began to weep bitterly, and dashed herself against the ground as if she would have dashed herself to pieces. She could hardly wait for her lord the Anka to come home. At last, there was a sound of mighty wings, and the Padishah of the Birds, the emerald Anka, came home, and when he saw the scattered bones of the King's son in the basket, he called together all the birds of the air and asked them, saying, "Which of you goes to the Garden of Paradise?"

"An old owl is the only one that goes there," said the birds, "and he has now grown so old that he has no more strength left for such a journey."

Then the Anka sent a bird to bring the owl on his back. The bird flew away, and in a very short time was back again, with the aged owl on his back.

"Well, my father," said the Bird-Padishah, "have you ever been in the Garden of Paradise?"

Tales of the Meddahs: Tales from the Turkish tradition

"Yes, my little son," croaked the aged owl, "a long, long time ago, twelve years or more, and I haven't been there since."

"Well, if you have been there," said the Anka, "go again now, and bring me from there a little glass of water." The old owl kept on saying that it was a long, long way for him to go, and that he would never be able to hold out the whole way. The Anka would not listen to him, but perched him upon a bird's back, and the two flew into the Garden of Paradise, drew a glass of water, and returned to the Anka's palace.

Then the Anka took the youth's bones and began to put them together. The arms, the legs, the head, the thighs, everything he put in its proper place, and when he had sprinkled it all with the water, the youth fell to yawning, as if he had been asleep and was just coming to himself again. The youth looked about him, and asked the Anka where he was, and how he came there.

"Didn't I say that the Wind-Demon would twist you round his little finger?" replied the Anka. "He ground all your bones and sinews to dust, and we have only just now picked them all out of the basket. But now you had better leave the matter alone, for if you get once more into the clutches of this demon, I know that we shall never be able to put you together again."

But the youth was not content to do this and said he would go seek his consort a second time.

"Well, if you are bent on going at any price," counselled the Anka, "go first to your wife and ask her if she knows the Demon's talisman. If only you can get hold of that, even the Wind-Demon will be in your power."

The King's son took horse, and again he went right up to the Demon's palace, and as the Demon was dreaming dreams just then, the youth was able to find and converse with his wife. After they had rejoiced with a great joy at the sight of each other, the youth told the lady to discover the secret of the Demon's talisman and win it by wheedling words and soft caresses if she could get at it no other way. Meanwhile the youth hid himself in the neighbouring mountain, and there awaited the good news.

Tales of the Meddahs: Tales from the Turkish tradition

When the Wind-Demon awoke from his forty days' sleep he again presented himself at the damsel's door. "Depart from before my eyes," cried the girl. "Here have you been doing nothing but sleep these forty days, so that life has been a loathsome thing to me all the while."

The Demon rejoiced that he was allowed to be in the room along with the damsel, and in his happiness asked her what he should give her to help her to while away the time.

"What can you give me," said the girl, 'seeing that you are but wind? Now if, at the least, you had a talisman, that, at any rate, would be something to while away the time with."

"Alas, my Sultana," replied the Demon, "my talisman is far away, in the uttermost ends of the earth, and one cannot fetch it here in a little instant. If only we had some such brave man as your Mehmed was, he perhaps might be able to go for it."

The damsel was now more curious than ever about the talisman, and she coaxed and coaxed till at last she persuaded the Demon to tell her about the talisman, but not till she had granted his request that he might sit down quite close to her. The damsel could not refuse him that happiness, so he sat down beside her, and breathed into her ear the secret of the talisman.

"On the surface of the seventh layer of sea," began the Demon, "there is an island, and on that island an ox is grazing. In the belly of that ox there is a golden cage, and in that cage, there is a white dove. That little dove is my talisman."

"But how can one get to that island?" inquired the Sultana.

"I'll tell you," said the Demon. "Opposite to the palace of the emerald Anka is a huge mountain, and on the top of that mountain is a spring. Every morning forty seahorses come to drink at that spring. If anyone can be found to catch one of these horses by the leg (but only while he is drinking the water), bridle him, saddle him, and then leap on his back, he will be able to go wherever he likes. The seahorse will say to him, 'What do you command, my sweet master?' and will carry him wherever he bids him."

Tales of the Meddahs: Tales from the Turkish tradition

"What good will the talisman be to me if I cannot get near it?" said the girl. With that she drove the Demon from the room, and when the time of his slumber arrived, she hastened with the news to her lord. Then the King's son made great haste, leaped on his horse, hastened to the palace of his youngest sister, and told the matter to the Anka.

Early next morning the Anka arose, called five birds, and said to them, "Lead the King's son to the spring on the mountain beyond, and wait there till the seahorses come up. Forty steeds will appear by the running water, and when they begin to drink, seize one of them, bridle and saddle it, and put the King's son on its back."

The birds took the King's son, carried him up to the mountain close by the spring, and as soon as the horses came up, they did to one of them what the Anka had said. The King's son sat on the horse's back forthwith, and the first thing the good steed said was, "What do you command, my sweet master?"

"There is an island on the surface of the seventh ocean," cried the King's son, "and there should I like to be!" And the King's son had flown away before you could shut your eyes; and before you could open them again, there he was on the shore of that island.

He dismounted from his horse, took off the bridle, stuck it in his pocket, and went off to seek the ox. As he was walking up and down the shore a Jew met him and asked him what had brought him there.

"I have suffered shipwreck," replied the youth. "My ship and everything I possess have perished, and only with difficulty did I swim ashore."

"As for me," said the Jew, "I am in the service of the Wind-Demon. You must know that there is an ox on this island, and I must watch it night and day. Would you like to enter the service? You will have nothing else to do all day but watch this beast."

The King's son took advantage of the opportunity and could scarce await the moment when he was to see the ox. At watering-time the Jew brought it along, and no sooner did he find himself alone with the beast than he cut

Tales of the Meddahs: Tales from the Turkish tradition

open its belly, took out the golden cage, and hastened with it to the seashore. Then he drew the bridle from his pocket, and when he had struck the sea with it, the steed immediately appeared and cried, "What do you command, sweet master?"

"I desire to be taken to the palace of the Wind-Demon," cried the youth.

Shut your eyes, open your eyes - and there they were before the palace. Then he took his wife, made her sit down beside him, and when the steed said, "What do you command, sweet master?" he bade it fly straight to the emerald Anka.

Away with them flew the steed. It flew right up to the very clouds, and as they were approaching the Anka's palace the Demon awoke from his sleep. He saw that his wife had again disappeared, and immediately set off in pursuit. Already the Sultana felt the breath of the Demon, and he had all but overtaken them when the steed hastily bade them twist the neck of the white dove in the cage. They had barely time to do so, when the Wind died away and the Demon was destroyed.

With great joy they arrived at the Anka's palace, let the horse go his way, and rested themselves awhile. On the next day they went to their second brother, and on the third day to their third brother, and it was only then that the King's son discovered that his lion brother-in-law was the King of the Lions, and his tiger brother-in-law the King of the Tigers. At last, they reached the damsel's old home and here they made a great banquet and rejoiced their hearts for forty days and forty nights, after which they arose and went to the prince's own empire. There he showed them the tongue of the dragon and its nose, and as he had thus fulfilled the wishes of his father, they chose him to be their Padishah, and their lives were full of joy till the day of their death, and their end was a happy one.

Tales of the Meddahs: Tales from the Turkish tradition

WHO WAS THE THIRTEENTH SON

This story has been adapted from Told in the Coffee House by Cyrus Adler and Allan Ramsay, published in 1898 by MacMillan and Company, London. Allan Ramsay was a Scottish poet, playwright, publisher, librarian, and wig-maker active in the early and mid-eighteenth century. Cyrus Adler adapted Ramsay's work in the nineteenth century, being an American educator, Jewish religious leader, and scholar.

In the town of Adrianople there lived an Armenian Patriarch, Munadi Hagop by name, respected and loved alike by Muslim and Christian. He was a man of wide reading and profound judgment. The Ottoman Governor of the same place, Usref Pasha, happened also to be a man of considerable acquirements and education. The Armenian and the Turk associated much together. In fact, they were always either walking out together or visiting, one at the residence of the other. This went on for some time, and the twelve wise men who were judges in the city thought that their Governor was doing wrong in associating so much with a dog of a Christian, so they resolved to call him to account.

This resolution taken, the entire twelve proceeded to the house of the Governor and told him that he was setting a bad example to his subjects. They feared, too, that the salvation of his own soul and of his posterity was in danger, should this Armenian in any way influence his mind.

"My friends," answered the Governor, "this man is very learned, and the only reason why we come together so often is because a great sympathy exists between us, and much mutual pleasure is derived from this friendship.

Tales of the Meddahs: Tales from the Turkish tradition

I ask his advice, and he gives me a clear explanation. He is my friend, and I would gladly see him your friend."

"Oh," said the spokesman of the judges, "is it his wise answers that act as magic upon you? We will give him a question to answer, and if he solves this to our satisfaction, he will then in reality be a great man."

"I am sure you will not be disappointed!" said the Pasha. "He has never failed me, and I have sometimes put questions to him which appeared unanswerable. He will surely call tomorrow. Shall I send him to you or bring him myself?"

"We wish to see him alone," said the judges.

"I shall not fail to send him to you tomorrow, after which I am sure you will often seek his company."

On the following day the Pasha told the Patriarch how matters stood and begged him to call on the gentlemen who took so lively an interest in their friendly association.

The Patriarch, never dreaming of what would happen, called on the twelve wise men and introduced himself. They were holding the Divan, and the entrance of the Patriarch gave considerable pleasure to them. On the table lay a turban and a drawn sword.

The customary salutations having been duly exchanged, the Patriarch seated himself, and at once told them that his friend the Governor had asked him to call, and he took much pleasure in making their acquaintance, adding that he would be happy to do anything in his power that they might wish.

The spokesman of the Divan rose and said, "Effendi, our friend the Governor has told us of your great learning, and we have decided to put a question to you. The reason for our taking this liberty is because the Governor told us that he had never put a question to you which had remained unanswered."

And as he spoke, he moved toward the table.

"Effendi, our question will consist of only a few words."

Tales of the Meddahs: Tales from the Turkish tradition

Laying his right hand on the turban and his left hand on the sword, he asked, "Is this the right, or is this the right?"

The Patriarch paused aghast at the terrible feature of the interrogation. He saw destruction staring him in the face. Nevertheless, he said to them with great composure, "Gentlemen, you have put an exceedingly difficult question to me, the most difficult that could be put to man. However, it is a question put, and now, according to your laws, cannot be recalled."

"No," answered the twelve wise men, rubbing their hands, "it cannot be recalled."

"I will say that it grieves me much to have to reply to this," the Patriarch continued, "and I cannot do so without continued prayers for guidance. Therefore, I beg to request a week's time before giving my answer."

To this no objection was made, and the Patriarch prepared to go. Respectfully bowing to all present, as if nothing out of the common had happened, he slowly moved toward the door apparently in deep thought.

Just as he reached the door he turned back and addressing the judges, said, "Gentlemen, one of the reasons I had great pleasure in meeting you today was because I wished to have your advice on a difficult legal problem which has been presented to me by some members of my community. Knowing your great wisdom, I thought you might assist me, and as you are now sitting in lawful council I shall, if agreeable to you, put the case before you and be greatly pleased to learn your opinion."

The judges, whose curiosity was aroused, and who were flattered that a man of such reputation for wisdom should submit a matter to them for their opinion, signalled to him to proceed.

"Gentlemen and wise men," began the Patriarch, "there was once a father, and this father had thirteen sons, who were esteemed by all who knew them. As time with its sure hand marked its progress on the issue of this good man, and the children grew into youth, they one by one went into the world, spreading to the four known quarters of the globe, and carrying with them the good influence given by their father. Through them the name of the

177

Tales of the Meddahs: Tales from the Turkish tradition

father spread, causing a great moral and mental revolution throughout the world. The father in his native home, however, saw that his days were few, that he had well-nigh turned the leaves of the book of life, and yearned to see his sons once more. He accordingly sent messengers all over the world, saying, 'Come, my sons, and receive your father's blessing, for he is about to depart this life, come and get each one your portion of the worldly possessions I have, together with my blessing, and again go forth, doing each your duty to God and man.'

"One by one the sons of the aged father came, and once more were united in the ancient home of their childhood, with the exception of one son. The remaining days of the old man were spent with his twelve sons, and the brothers found that all of them had retained the teachings of infancy, and the pleasure was great. The reuniting of the family, though of comparatively short duration, was happier by far than the years of childhood and youth which they had spent together. Still the thirteenth son was not found. The messengers returned one after the other, bearing no tidings of him. The old father saw that he could wait no longer, that he must dispose of his worldly possessions, give his blessing to his twelve sons, and re-join his Father. So, he called them to his side and said, 'My sons, as you have done may it be done to you. You have cheered my last steps to the grave, and I bless you.' And the father's blessing was bestowed on each.

"'Of all I possess I give to each of you an equal share with my blessing. You are my offspring and the representatives of your father on earth. It is my will that you should continue as you have begun. You are my twelve sons, and I have no other. Your brother who was, is no longer. We have waited long, that he should take his portion and my blessing; but he has tarried elsewhere, and now the hand of my Father is on me, and as you have come to me, so I must go to show Him my work.'

"So, the father ordained that the twelve should be his heirs and declared that anyone coming after claiming to be his son, was an impostor. He also confirmed in the existing and competent courts that these alone were his

Tales of the Meddahs: Tales from the Turkish tradition

representatives on earth. This was duly registered in conformity with the law, and the old father passed away to rejoin his forefathers.

"The twelve sons again went forth into the world and carried with them the blessings and teachings of their father, and these teachings and ideas developed and grew, and the memory of their father was cherished and blessed.

"Many years after, a person turned up claiming to be the missing son and sought to obtain the part due to him. Not only did he wish his share, but he claimed the whole worldly possessions of his father, that he was the son blessed by his father, and exhorted all to follow his teachings. By those who knew the circumstances, he was not believed, but many were ignorant of the father, and also ignorant of the registering in the courts of law and were inclined to believe in the impostor.

"Now, gentlemen, this is the case that has troubled me much. As you are sitting in lawful council, it would give me much pleasure if you could cast light on the case. Your statement will help me, and I will be ever grateful to you. Had this son, the late returned person, any right to all the worldly possessions of the father, or, in fact, even any right to an equal share?"

Having spoken he turned to the Hodjas with an inquiring look. They one and all, unanimously, and in a breath said, that all the legal formalities having been carried out, the will of the father was law, and the law he passed should be respected, therefore the thirteenth son was an impostor. On returning he should have gone to his brothers, and no doubt he would have been received as a brother, but he acted otherwise. He should receive nothing.

"I am glad to see that you look at it in that light, and I will now say that that has always been my opinion, but your statement now adds strength to the conviction, and had there been any doubt on my part, your unanimous declaration would have dispelled it. I would further esteem it a great kindness and a favour if, as a reference and as a proof of my authority, or rather as a corroboration of many proofs, you would, as you are sitting in lawful Divan, give your signatures to the effect that the decision of the

Tales of the Meddahs: Tales from the Turkish tradition

learned council was unanimous, and to this said effect, that the thirteenth son was an impostor, and had no right to any of the possessions he claimed."

Flattered that their opinion had such weight, the judges also consented to do this, and the Patriarch set about drawing up the case. This he read to them, and each put his hand and seal to the document. The Patriarch thanked them and departed.

A week had passed, and the judges had entirely forgotten the case that had been put to them, but they had not forgotten the Patriarch, and eagerly awaited his answer to their question which left no alternative, and which would cause his head to be separated from his body by the executioner's blow. But the Patriarch did not make his appearance, and as the prescribed time had passed, the judges went to the Governor to see what steps should be taken.

The Governor was deeply grieved when the judges told him of the terrible question that they had put to the Patriarch. He remembered leaving the Patriarch earlier that morning and who seemed in no way anxious. He said that he was convinced that either a satisfactory answer had been given or would be forthcoming. He questioned the Hodjas as to what had taken place, and they answered that nothing had been said beyond the question that had been put to him and his request for a week's time in which to answer.

"Did he say nothing at all," asked the Pasha, "before he left?"

"Nothing," said the spokesman of the judges, "except that he put to us a case which he had been called on to decide and asked our opinion."

"What was this case?" asked the Pasha. And the judges recited it to him, told what opinion they had given, and stated that they had, at the Patriarch's request and for his use, placed their seal to this opinion.

"Go home, you heads of asses," said the Governor, "and thank Allah that it is to a noble and a great man who would make no unworthy use of it that you have delivered a document testifying that Mohammed is an impostor. In future, venture not to enter into judgment with men whom it has pleased God to give more wit than to yourselves."

Tales of the Meddahs: Tales from the Turkish tradition

THE CONVERTED CAT

This story has been adapted from Turkish Literature by Epiphanius Wilson, A.M., published in 1901 by P. F. Collier & Son, New York.

The Cat, having put on the cowl and become a monk, sent word to the mice, and said, "It is an abominable thing to shed blood. As for me, I will shed no more, for I am become religious."

Then the mice replied, "Although we saw in you the whole Order of St. Anthony, or of our holy Father St. Mark, we could have no confidence in your hypocrisy."

The Cat covered herself with a dust rag and smeared herself with flour. The mice approached her, saying, "Wretch, we see through your dust rag!"

Then she pretended to be dead, and lay in the path of the mice, who approached her and said, "Miserable cheat, although your skin be made into a purse, we could not believe that you had given up your habitual knavery."

This fable shows that when you have once found out a person of dishonest, treacherous, and evil character, you should not trust him, even if he tries to do right, for he cannot change his nature.

Tales of the Meddahs: Tales from the Turkish tradition

Tales of the Meddahs: Tales from the Turkish tradition

THE MAGIC TURBAN, THE MAGIC WHIP, AND THE MAGIC CARPET

This story has been adapted from Turkish Fairy Tales and Folk Tales by Dr. Ignácz Kúnos, published in 1901 by A. H. Bullen, London.

Once upon a time that was no time there were two brothers. Their father and mother had died and divided all their property between them. The elder brother opened a shop, but the younger brother, who was a featherbrain, idled about and did nothing, so that at last, what with eating and drinking and gadding abroad, the day came when he had no more money left. Then he went to his elder brother and begged a copper or two of him, and when that all was spent, he came to him again, and so he continued to live upon him.

At last, the elder brother began to grow tired of this waste but seeing that he could not be quit of his younger brother, he turned all his possessions into sequins, and embarked on a ship in order to go into another kingdom. The younger brother, however, had got wind of it, and before the ship started, he managed to creep on board and conceal himself without anyone observing him. The elder brother suspected that if the younger one heard of his departure, he would be sure to follow, so he took good care not to show himself on deck. But scarcely had they unfurled the sails when the two brothers came face to face, and the elder brother found himself saddled with his younger brother again.

The elder brother was very angry, but what was the use of that, for the ship did not stop till it came to Egypt. There the elder brother said to the younger

Tales of the Meddahs: Tales from the Turkish tradition

brother, "You stay here, and I will go and get two mules that we may go on further."

The youth sat down on the shore and waited for his brother, and waited, but waited in vain. "I think I had better look for him," thought he, and up he got and went after his elder brother.

He went on and on and on, he went a short distance, and he went a long distance, and he took six months to cross a single field, but when he looked over his shoulder, he saw that for all his walking he had walked no further than a barley-stalk reaches. Then he strode still more, he strode still further, he strode for half a year continuously, and he kept plucking violets as he went along, and as he went striding, striding, his feet struck upon a hill, and there he saw three youths quarrelling with one another about something. He joined them and asked them what they were tussling about.

"We are the children of one father," said the youngest of them, "and our father has just died and left us, by way of inheritance, a turban, a whip, and a carpet. Whoever puts the turban on his head is hidden from mortal eyes. Whoever lays on the carpet and strikes it once with the whip can fly far away, after the manner of birds, and we are eternally quarrelling among ourselves as to whose shall be the turban, whose the whip, and whose the carpet."

"All three of them must belong to one of us," they cried.

"They are mine, because I am the biggest," said one.

"They are mine by right, because I am the middling-sized brother," cried the second.

"They are mine, because I am the smallest," cried the third.

From words they speedily came to blows, so that it was as much as the youth could do to keep them apart.

"You can't settle it like that," said he, "I'll tell you what we'll do. I'll make an arrow from this little piece of wood and shoot it off. You run after it, and whoever brings it to me here soonest shall have all three things."

184

Tales of the Meddahs: Tales from the Turkish tradition

Away flew the dart, and the three brothers pelted after it, helter-skelter, but the wise youth knew a trick worth two of that, for he stuck the turban on his head, sat down on the carpet, tapped it once with the whip, and cried, "Hip-hop! Let me be where my elder brother is!" and when he awoke a large city lay before him.

He had scarce taken more than a couple of steps through the street, when the Padishah's herald came along, and proclaimed to the inhabitants of the town that the Sultan's daughter disappeared every night from the palace. Whoever could find out what became of her should receive the damsel and half the kingdom.

"Here am I!" cried the youth, "lead me to the Padishah, and if I don't find out, let them take my head!"

So, they brought the fool into the palace, and in the evening, there lay the Sultan's daughter watching, with her eyes half-closed, all that was going on. The damsel was only waiting for him to go to sleep, and presently she stuck a needle into her heel, took the candle with her, lest the youth should awake, and went out by a side door.

The youth had his turban on his head in a trice, and no sooner had he popped out of the same door than he saw a spirit efrit standing there with a golden buckler on his head, and on the buckler sat the Sultan's daughter, and they were just on the point of starting off. The lad was not such a fool as to fancy that he could keep up with them by himself, so he also leaped on to the buckler, and very nearly upset the pair of them in consequence. The efrit was alarmed, and asked the damsel in Allah's name what she was about, as they were within a hair's-breadth of falling.

"I never moved," said the damsel, "I am sitting on the buckler just as you put me there."

The efrit had scarcely taken a couple of steps, when he felt that the buckler was unusually heavy. The youth's turban naturally made him invisible, so the efrit turned to the damsel and said, "My Sultana, you are so heavy todday that I all but break down beneath you!"

Tales of the Meddahs: Tales from the Turkish tradition

"Darling Lala!" replied the girl, "You are very odd tonight, for I am neither bigger nor smaller than I was yesterday."

Shaking his head, the efrit went his way, and they went on and on till they came to a wondrously beautiful garden, where the trees were made of nothing but silver and diamonds. The youth broke off a twig and put it in his pocket. Then, straight away the trees began to sigh and weep and say, "There's a child of man here who tortures us! There's a child of man here who tortures us!"

The efrit and the damsel looked at each other. "They sent a youth in to me today," said the damsel, "maybe his soul is pursuing us."

Then they went on still further, till they came to another garden, where every tree was sparkling with gold and precious stones. Here too the youth broke off a twig and shoved it into his pocket, and immediately the earth and the sky shook, and the rustling of the trees said, "There's a child of man here torturing us, there's a child of man here torturing us," so that both he and the damsel very nearly fell from the buckler in their fright. Not even the efrit knew what to make of it.

After that they came to a bridge, and beyond the bridge was a fairy palace, and there an army of slaves awaited the damsel, and with their hands straight down by their sides they bowed down before her till their foreheads touched the ground. The Sultan's daughter dismounted from the efrit's head, and the youth also leaped down. When they brought the princess a pair of slippers covered with diamonds and precious stones, the youth snatched one of them away, and put it in his pocket. The girl put on one of the slippers, but being unable to find the other, sent for another pair. Again, one of these also disappeared. At this the damsel was so annoyed that she walked on without slippers, but the youth, with the turban on his head and the whip and the carpet in his hand, followed her everywhere like her shadow.

The damsel went on before, and he followed her into a room, and there he saw the Peri, one of whose lips touched the sky, while the other lip swept the ground. He angrily asked the damsel where she had been all the time,

Tales of the Meddahs: Tales from the Turkish tradition

and why she hadn't come sooner. The damsel told him about the youth who had arrived the evening before, and about what had happened on the way, but the Peri comforted her by saying that the whole thing was fancy, and she was not to trouble herself about it anymore. After that he sat down with the damsel and ordered a slave to bring them sherbet. A slave brought the noble drink in a lovely diamond cup, but just as he was handing it to the Sultan's daughter the invisible youth gave the hand of the slave such a wrench that he dropped and broke the cup to pieces. The youth also then concealed a piece of the cup in his pocket.

"Now didn't I say that something was wrong?" cried the Sultan's daughter. "I want no sherbet nor anything else, and I think I had better get back again as soon as possible."

"Tush, tush!" said the efrit, and he ordered other slaves to bring them something to eat. So, they brought a little table covered with many dishes, and they began to eat together; whereupon the hungry youth also set to work, and the viands disappeared as if three were eating instead of two.

And the Peri himself began to be a little impatient, when not only the food but also the forks and spoons began to disappear, and he said to his sweetheart, the Sultan's daughter, that perhaps it would be as well if she did make haste home again. First of all, the efrit wanted to kiss the girl, but the youth slipped in between them, pulled them apart, and one of them fell to the right and the other to the left. They both turned pale and called the Lala with his buckler, The damsel sat upon it, and away they went. But the youth took down a sword from the wall, bared his arm, and with one blow he chopped off the head of the Peri. No sooner had his head rolled from his shoulders than the heavens roared terribly, and the earth groaned horribly, and a voice cried mightily, "Woe to us, a child of man has slain our king!" The terrified youth knew not whether he stood on his head or his heels.

He seized his carpet, sat upon it, gave it one blow with his whip, and when the Sultan's daughter returned to the palace, there she found the youth snoring in his room.

187

Tales of the Meddahs: Tales from the Turkish tradition

"Oh, you wretched bald-pate," cried the damsel viciously, "what a night I've had of it. So much the worse for you!"

Then she took out a needle and pricked the youth in the heel, and because he never stirred, she fancied he was asleep, and lay down to sleep herself also.

Next morning when she awoke, she made the youth prepare for death, as his last hour had come. "Nay," replied he, "I don't have to justify myself to you. Let us both go before the Padishah."

Then they led him before the father of the damsel, but he said he would only tell them what had happened in the night if they called all the people of the town together. "In that way I shall find my brother, perhaps," thought he.

So, the town-crier called all the people together, and the youth stood on a high daïs beside the Padishah and the Sultana, and began to tell them the whole story, from the efrit's buckler to the Peri king.

"Do not believe him, my lord Padishah and father, for he lies, my lord father and Padishah!" stammered the damsel, whereupon the youth drew from his pocket the diamond twig, the twig of gems, the golden slipper, the precious spoons, and the golden forks. Then he went on to tell them of the death of the Peri, when all at once he caught sight of his elder brother, whom he had been searching for so long. He had now neither eyes nor ears for anything else, but leaping off the daïs, he forced his way on and on through the crowd to his brother, till they both came together.

Then the elder brother told their story, while the younger brother begged the Padishah to give his daughter and half the kingdom to his elder brother. He was quite content, he said, with the magic turban and the magic whip and carpet to the day of his death, if only he might live close to his elder brother.

But the Sultan's daughter rejoiced most of all when she heard of the death of the Peri king. He had carried her off by force from her room one day, and so enchanted her with his power that she had been unable to set herself free. In her joy she agreed that the youth's elder brother should be her lord, and they made a great banquet, at which they feasted forty days and forty nights

188

Tales of the Meddahs: Tales from the Turkish tradition

with one another. I also was there, and I begged so much pilaw from the cook, and I got so much in the palm of my hand, that I limp to this day.

Tales of the Meddahs: Tales from the Turkish tradition

Tales of the Meddahs: Tales from the Turkish tradition

PARADISE SOLD BY THE YARD

This story has been adapted from Told in the Coffee House by Cyrus Adler and Allan Ramsay, published in 1898 by MacMillan and Company, London. Allan Ramsay was a Scottish poet, playwright, publisher, librarian, and wig-maker active in the early and mid-eighteenth century. Cyrus Adler adapted Ramsay's work in the nineteenth century, being an American educator, Jewish religious leader, and scholar.

The chief Imam of the Vilayet of Broussa owed to a moneylender the sum of two hundred piasters. The moneylender wanted his money and would give no rest to the Imam. Daily he came to ask for it, but without success. The moneylender was becoming very anxious and determined to make a great effort. Not being able to take the Imam to court, he decided to try and shame him into paying the sum due, and to make this happen, he came, sat on his debtor's doorstep, and bewailed his sad fate in having fallen into the hands of a tyrant. The Imam saw that if this continued, his reputation as a man of justice would be considerably impaired, so he thought of a plan by which to pay off his creditor. Calling the moneylender into his house, he said, "Friend, what will you do with the money if I pay you?"

"Get food, clothe my children, and advance in my business," answered the moneylender.

"My friend," said the Imam, "your pitiful position awakens my compassion. You are gathering wealth in this world at the cost of your soul and peace in the world to come, and I wish I could help you. I will tell you what I will do

Tales of the Meddahs: Tales from the Turkish tradition

for you. I would not do the same thing for any other moneylender in the world, but you have awakened my commiseration. For the debt I owe you, I will sell you two hundred yards of Paradise, and being owner of this incomparable possession in the world to come, you can fearlessly go forth and earn as much as possible in this world, having already made ample provision for the next."

What could the moneylender do but take what the Imam was willing to give him? So, he accepted the deed for the two hundred yards of Paradise. A happy thought now struck the moneylender. He set off and found the tithe-collector of the revenues of the mosque and made friends with him. He then explained to him, when the intimacy had developed, how he was the possessor of a deed entitling him to two hundred yards of Paradise, and offered the collector a handsome commission if he would help him in disposing of it. When the money had been gathered for the quarter, the collector came and discounted the Imam's document, returning it to him as two hundred piasters of the tithes collected, with the statement that this document had been given to him by a peasant, and that bearing his holy seal, he dared not refuse it.

The Imam was completely deceived and thought that the moneylender had sold the deed at a discount to some of his subjects who were in arrears, and of course had to receive it as being as good as gold. Nevertheless, the moneylender was not forgotten, and the Imam determined to have him taken into court and sentenced if possible. His charge against the moneylender was that he, the chief priest of the province, had taken pity on this man, thinking what a terrible thing it was to know no future. As the man hereto had an irreproachable character, in consideration of a small debt he had against the faith, which it was desirable to balance, he thought he would give this moneylender two hundred yards of Paradise, which he did.

"Now, gentlemen, this ungrateful dog sold this valuable document, and it was brought back to me as payment of taxes in arrears due to the faith. Therefore, I say that this moneylender has committed a great sin and ought to be punished accordingly."

Tales of the Meddahs: Tales from the Turkish tradition

The Cadis now turned to hear the moneylender, who, the personification of meekness, stood as if awaiting his death sentence. With the most innocent look possible, the moneylender replied, when the Cadis asked him what he had to say for himself, "Effendim, it is needless to say how I appreciate the kindness of our Imam, but the reason that I disposed of that valuable document was this: When I went to Paradise I found a seat, and measured out my two hundred yards, and took possession of it. I had not been there long when a Turk came and sat beside me. I showed him my document and protested against his taking part of my place, but, gentlemen, I assure you it was altogether useless. The Turks came and came, one after the other, till, to make a long story short, I had no place in Paradise, and here I am. The Turks in Paradise will take no heed of your document, and either will not recognize the authority of the Imam or will not let the moneylenders enter therein. Effendim, what could I do but come back and sell the document to men who could enter Paradise, and this I did."

The Cadis, after consulting, gave judgment as follows, "We note that you could not have done anything else but sell the two hundred yards of Paradise, and the fact that you cannot enter there is ample punishment for the wrong committed. But there is still a grievous charge against you, which, if you can clear to our satisfaction, you will at once be dismissed. How much did the document cost you and what did you sell it for?"

"Effendim, it cost me two hundred piasters, and I sold it for two hundred piasters."

This statement having been proved by producing the deed in question, and the tithe-collector who had given it to the Imam for two hundred piasters, the moneylender was acquitted.

Tales of the Meddahs: Tales from the Turkish tradition

Tales of the Meddahs: Tales from the Turkish tradition

THE HORSE AND HIS RIDER

This story has been adapted from Turkish Literature by Epiphanius Wilson, A.M., published in 1901 by P. F. Collier & Son, New York.

The Horse complained to his rider, saying that it was unjust that a fair and powerful creature, such as he was, should be a slave and carry so weak a thing as man.

His rider replied, "I feed you, I shelter you with a roof, and I show you where water and grass are to be found."

"But you take away my liberty and put a hard bit in my mouth. You weary me with long journeys, and sometimes expose me to the dangers of battle," answered the Horse.

"Take, then, your liberty," said his master, removing the bridle from his head and the saddle from his back.

The Horse bounded off into the mountains, where grass and water abounded. For many weeks he enjoyed ease and plenty. But a pack of wolves, seeing him in good condition, pursued him. At first, he easily outstripped them, but he was now heavy with much nourishment, and his breath began to fail. The wolves overtook and threw him to the ground.

When he found his last hour had come, he exclaimed mournfully, "How happy and safe I was with my master, and how much lighter and easier were his bridle and spur than the fangs of these blood-thirsty enemies!"

Tales of the Meddahs: Tales from the Turkish tradition

This fable shows that many people do not estimate duly the blessings of their condition, and complain about those duties, the performance of which is the sole condition of their life and safety.

Tales of the Meddahs: Tales from the Turkish tradition

THE PIECE OF LIVER

This story has been adapted from Turkish Fairy Tales and Folk Tales by Dr. Ignácz Kúnos, published in 1901 by A. H. Bullen, London.

Once upon a time there was an old woman who felt she would very much like to have a piece of liver, so she gave a girl two or three pence, and bade her buy the liver in the marketplace, wash it clean in the pond, and then bring it home. The girl went to the marketplace, bought the liver, and took it to the pond to wash it, and while she was washing it a stork popped down, snatched the liver out of her hand, and flew away with it.

The girl cried, "Stork, stork! Give me back my liver, that I may take it to my mammy, lest my mammy beat me!"

"If you will fetch me a barley-ear instead of it, I'll give you back your liver," said the stork.

The girl went to the straw-stalk, and said: "Straw-stalk, straw-stalk! Give me a barley-ear, that I may give the barley-ear to the stork, that the stork may give me back my liver, that I may give the liver to my mammy."

"If you will pray Allah for rain, you shall have a little barley-ear," said the straw-stalk.

But while she was beginning her prayer, saying, "Oh, Allah, give me rain, that I may give the rain to the straw-stalk, that the straw-stalk may give me a barley-ear, that I may give the barley-ear to the stork, that the stork may give me back my liver, that I may give the liver to my mammy," up came a man to her and said that without a censer no prayers could ever get to heaven, so she must go to the bazaar-keeper for a censer.

She went to the bazaar-keeper, and cried, "Bazaar-keeper, bazaar-keeper! Give me a censer, that I may burn incense before Allah, that Allah may give me rain, that I may give rain to the straw-stalk, that the straw-stalk may give me a barley-ear, that I may give the barley-ear to the stork, that the stork may give me back my liver, that I may give my liver to my mammy!"

"I'll give it you," said the bazaar-keeper, "if you will bring me a boot from the cobbler."

So, the girl went to the cobbler, and said to him, "Cobbler, cobbler! Give me a boot, that I may give the boot to the bazaar-keeper, that the bazaar-keeper may give me a censer, that I may burn incense before Allah, that Allah may give me rain, that I may give rain to the straw-stalk, that the straw-stalk may give me a barley-ear, that I may give the barley-ear to the stork, that the stork may give me back the liver, that I may give the liver to my mammy."

But the cobbler said, "If you fetch me a hide you shall have a boot for it."

So, the girl went to the tanner, and said, "Tanner, tanner! Give me a hide, that I may give the hide to the cobbler, that the cobbler may give me a boot, that I may give the boot to the bazaar-keeper, that the bazaar-keeper may give me a censer, that I may burn incense before Allah, that Allah may give me rain, that I may give the rain to the straw-stalk, that the straw-stalk may give me a barley-ear, that I may give the barley-ear to the stork, that the stork may give me back my liver, that I may give the liver to my mammy."

"If you get a hide from the ox, you will get a hide fit for making a boot," said the tanner.

So, the girl went to the ox, and said to it, "Ox, ox! Give me a hide, that I may give the hide to the tanner, that the tanner may give me boot-leather, that I may give the boot-leather to the cobbler, that the cobbler may give me a boot, that I may give the boot to the bazaar-keeper, that the bazaar-keeper may give me a censer, that I may burn incense before Allah, that Allah may give me rain, that I may give the rain to the straw-stalk, that the straw-stalk

Tales of the Meddahs: Tales from the Turkish tradition

may give me a barley-ear, that I may give the barley-ear to the stork, that the stork may give me back my liver, that I may give the liver to my mammy."

The ox said, "If you get me straw, I'll give you a hide for it!"

So, the girl went to the farmer, and said to him, "Farmer, farmer! Give me straw, that I may give the straw to the ox, that the ox may give me a hide, that I may give the hide to the tanner, that the tanner may give me shoe-leather, that I may give the shoe-leather to the cobbler, that the cobbler may give me a shoe, that I may give the shoe to the bazaar-keeper, that the bazaar-keeper may give me a censer, that I may burn incense before Allah, that Allah may give me rain, that I may give rain to the straw-stalk, that the straw-stalk may give me a barley-ear, that I may give the barley-ear to the stork, that the stork may give me back my liver, that I may give the liver to my mammy."

The farmer said to the girl, "I'll give you the straw if you give me a kiss."

"Well," thought the girl to herself, "a kiss is but a little matter if it free me from all this bother." So, she went up to the farmer and kissed him, and the farmer gave her straw for the kiss. She took the straw to the ox, and the ox gave her a hide for the straw. She took the hide to the tanner, and the tanner gave her shoe-leather. She took the shoe-leather to the cobbler, and the cobbler gave her a shoe for it. She took the shoe to the bazaar-keeper, and the bazaar-keeper gave her a censer. She lit the censer and cried, "Oh, Allah! Give me rain, that I may give the rain to the straw-stalk, that the straw-stalk may give me a barley-ear, that I may give the barley-ear to the stork, that the stork may give me back my liver, that I may give the liver to my mammy."

Then Allah gave her rain, and she gave the rain to the straw-stalk, and the straw-stalk gave her a barley-ear, and she gave the barley-ear to the stork, and the stork gave her back her liver, and she gave the liver to her mammy, and her mammy cooked the liver and ate it.

Tales of the Meddahs: Tales from the Turkish tradition

Tales of the Meddahs: Tales from the Turkish tradition

THE ARCHER AND THE TRUMPETER

This story has been adapted from Turkish Literature by Epiphanius Wilson, A.M., published in 1901 by P. F. Collier & Son, New York.

The Archer and the Trumpeter were travelling together in a lonely place. The Archer boasted of his skill as a warrior and asked the Trumpeter if he bore arms.

"No," replied the Trumpeter, "I cannot fight. I can only blow my horn and make music for those who are at war."

"But I can hit a mark at a hundred paces," said the Archer. As he spoke an eagle appeared, hovering over the treetops. He drew out an arrow, fitted it on the string, and shot at the bird, which straightway fell to the ground, transfixed to the heart.

"I am not afraid of any foe, for that bird might just as well have been a man," said the Archer proudly. "But you would be quite helpless if anyone attacked you."

They saw at that moment a band of robbers approaching them with drawn swords. The Archer immediately discharged a sharp arrow, which laid low the foremost of the wicked men. But the rest soon overpowered him and bound his hands.

"As for this Trumpeter, he can do us no harm, for he has neither sword nor bow," they said, and did not bind him, but took away his purse and wallet.

Tales of the Meddahs: Tales from the Turkish tradition

Then the Trumpeter said, "You are welcome, friends, but let me play you a tune on my horn."

With their consent he blew loud and long on his trumpet, and in a short space of time the King's guards came running up at the sound, and surrounded the robbers and carried them off to prison.

When they unbound the hands of the Archer he said to the Trumpeter, "Friend, I have learned today that a trumpet is better than a bow, for you have saved our lives without doing harm to anyone."

This fable shows that one man ought not to despise the trade of another. It also shows that it is better to be able to gain the help of others than to trust to our own strength.

Tales of the Meddahs: Tales from the Turkish tradition

THE METAMORPHOSIS

This story has been adapted from Told in the Coffee House by Cyrus Adler and Allan Ramsay, published in 1898 by MacMillan and Company, London. Allan Ramsay was a Scottish poet, playwright, publisher, librarian, and wigmaker active in the early and mid-eighteenth century. Cyrus Adler adapted Ramsay's work in the nineteenth century, being an American educator, Jewish religious leader, and scholar.

Hussein Agha was much troubled in spirit and mind. He had saved a large sum of money in order that he might make the pilgrimage to Mecca. What troubled him was, that after having carefully provided for all the expenses of this long journey he still had a few hundred piasters left over. What was he to do with these? True, they could be distributed amongst the poor, but then, might not he, on his return, require the money for a more meritorious purpose?

After much consideration, he decided that it was not Allah's wish that he should at once give this money in charity. On the other hand, he felt convinced that he should not give it to a brother for safe keeping, as he might be inspired, during Hussein's pilgrimage, to spend it on some charitable purpose. After a time, he thought of a kindly trader who was his neighbour and decided to leave his savings in the hands of this man, to whom Allah had been good, seeing that his possessions were great. After a period of mature thought, he decided not to put temptation in the way of his neighbour. He secured a jar, at the bottom of which he placed a small bag containing his surplus of wealth, and then he filled the jar with olives. This he carried

Tales of the Meddahs: Tales from the Turkish tradition

to his neighbour and begged him to take care of it for him. The trader of course consented, and Hussein Agha departed on his pilgrimage, contented.

On his return from the Holy Land, Hussein, now a Hadji, repaired to the trader's house and asked for his jar of olives, and at the same time presented the man with a rosary of Yemen stones, in recognition of the service rendered him in the safe keeping of the olives, which, he said, were exceptionally palatable. His friend thanked him, and Hadji Hussein departed with his jar, well satisfied.

During the absence of Hussein Agha, it happened that the trader had some distinguished visitors, to whom, as is the Eastern custom, he served raki. Unfortunately, however, he had no mézé to offer, as is also the custom in the East. He remembered the olives and immediately went to the cellar, opened the jar, and extracted some of them, saying, "Olives are not rare. Hussein will never know the difference if I replace them."

The olives were excellent, and the trader helped his friends to them again and again. Great was his surprise when he found that instead of olives, he brought forth a bag containing a quantity of gold. The trader could not understand this phenomenon but took the gold and held his peace.

Arriving home, poor Hussein Agha was distracted to find that his jar contained nothing but olives. He protested to his friend in vain.

"My friend," he would reply, "you gave me the jar, saying it contained olives. I believed you and kept the jar safe for you. Now you say that in the jar you had put some money together with the olives. Perhaps you did, but is not that the jar you gave me? If, as you say, there was gold in the jar and it is now gone, all I can say is, the stronger has overcome the weaker, and that in this case the gold has either been converted into olives or into oil. What can I do? The jar you gave me I returned to you."

Hadji Hussein admitted this, and fully appreciated that he had no case against the man, so saying, "Chok shai!" he returned to his home.

That night Hussein mingled in his prayers a vow to recover his gold at no matter what cost or trouble.

Tales of the Meddahs: Tales from the Turkish tradition

In his younger days Hadji Hussein had been a pipe-maker, and many were the chibouks of exceptional beauty that he had made. Go to the potters' lane at Tophane, and the works of art displayed by the majority of them have been fashioned by the hands of Hussein. The art that had fed him for years was now to be the means of recovering his money.

Hadji Hussein daily met his trader friend, but he never again referred to the money, and further, Hussein's sons were always in company with his friend's only son, a lad of ten.

Time passed, and the trader entirely forgot about the jar, olives, and gold, but not so Hadji Hussein. He had been working. First, he had made an effigy of his friend. When he had completed this image to his satisfaction, he dressed it in the identical manner and costume that the man habitually wore. He then purchased a monkey. This monkey was kept in a cage opposite the effigy. Twice a day regularly the monkey's food was placed on the shoulders of the effigy, and Hussein would open the cage, saying, "Babai git" (go to your father). At a bound the monkey would plant himself on the shoulders of the effigy and would not be dislodged until its hunger had been satisfied.

In the meantime, Hadji Hussein and the trader remained greater friends than ever, and their children were likewise playmates. One day Hussein took the man's son to his Harem and told him, much to the lad's joy, that he was to be their guest for a week. Later on, the trader called on Hadji Hussein to know the reason why his son had not returned as usual at sundown.

"Ah, my friend," said Hussein, "a great calamity has befallen you! Your son, alas, has been converted into a monkey, a furious monkey! So furious that I was compelled to put him into a cage. Come and see for yourself."

No sooner did the man enter the room in which the caged monkey was, than it set up a howl, not having had any food that day. The poor trader was thunderstruck, and Hadji Hussein begged him to take the monkey away.

Next day Hussein was summoned to the court, and the case of the poor trader was heard, and the Hadji was ordered to return the child at once. This he vowed he could not do, and to convince the judges he offered to bring the

Tales of the Meddahs: Tales from the Turkish tradition

monkey caged as it was to the court, and, Inshallah, they would see for themselves that the child of the trader had been converted into a monkey. This was ultimately agreed to, and the monkey was brought. Hadji Hussein took special care to place the cage opposite his old friend, and no sooner did the monkey catch sight of him than it set up a scream, and the judges said, 'Chok shai!'

Hussein Agha then opened the cage door, saying, "Go to your father," and the monkey with a bound and a yell embraced the poor trader, putting his head, in search of food, first on one shoulder and then on the other. The judges were thunderstruck and declared their incompetency to give judgment in such a case. The trader protested, saying that it was against the laws of nature for such a metamorphosis to take place, whereupon Hadji Hussein told the judges of an analogous instance of some gold pieces turning into olives, and called upon his old friend to witness the veracity of his statement. The judges, much perplexed, dismissed the case, declaring that provision had not been made in the law for it, and there being no precedent to their knowledge they were incompetent to give judgment.

Leaving the court, Hadji Hussein informed his old friend that there would still be pleasure and happiness in this world for him, provided he could reconvert the olives into gold. Needless to add that the trader handed the money to Hadji Hussein, and the man's son returned to his home none the worse for his transformation.

Tales of the Meddahs: Tales from the Turkish tradition

THE WOLF, THE FOX, AND THE SHEPHERD'S DOG

This story has been adapted from Turkish Literature by Epiphanius Wilson, A.M., published in 1901 by P. F. Collier & Son, New York.

A Fox was once carrying home to his young a leveret which he had caught by stealth. On his way he met a Wolf, who said to him, "I am very hungry, and I hope you will not refuse me a taste of your prey."

"In the name of God," cried the Fox, "eat your fill, but leave me a fragment for the supper of my little ones."

The Wolf, however, swallowed the dainty morsel at a mouthful. Although the Fox was very angry, he said in a humble voice, "I am glad that your appetite is so good. Farewell. Perhaps someday I will gain for you another meal of equal sweetness."

When they parted the Fox began to plot how he might revenge himself upon his enemy the Wolf. Now it happened that a Shepherd's Dog came to the Fox for advice. He asked him how he should destroy the Wolf, who every night kept robbing his master's folds.

"That is an easy matter," replied the Fox. "You must put on a wolf's skin, so that when the Wolf sees you, he will walk up to you without fear, and then you can seize him by the throat and strangle him."

The Wolf also came to the Fox for counsel. "The Shepherd's Dog," he complained, "barks when I approach the fold, and the sticks and stones of

Tales of the Meddahs: Tales from the Turkish tradition

the shepherds often give me a severe mauling. How shall I be able to kill him?"

"That is easy," said the Fox, "put on a sheep's skin, enter the fold with the flock, and lie down with them. At midnight you can strangle the Dog unawares, afterward feast as much as you like."

Then the Fox went back to the Dog and told him to look out for the Wolf disguised as a sheep.

When night came the Wolf entered the fold dressed like a sheep, and had no fear, for he saw no dog, but only a wolf at the door. But the Dog saw the fierce eyes of the Wolf and flew at his throat. Meanwhile the shepherds heard the noise, and as they saw a wolf mangling a sheep, they laid on the Dog's back with their heavy staves until he died, but not before he had strangled the Wolf.

This fable shows how unwise it is to seek help from people without principle.

Tales of the Meddahs: Tales from the Turkish tradition

THE CALIF OMAR

This story has been adapted from Told in the Coffee House by Cyrus Adler and Allan Ramsay, published in 1898 by MacMillan and Company, London. Allan Ramsay was a Scottish poet, playwright, publisher, librarian and wig-maker active in the early and mid-eighteenth century. Cyrus Adler adapted Ramsay's work in the nineteenth century, being an American educator, Jewish religious leader and scholar.

The Calif Omar, one of the first Califs after the Prophet, is deeply venerated to this day, and is continually quoted as a lover of truth and justice. Often in the face of appalling evidence he refrained from judgment, thus liberating the innocent and punishing the guilty. The following is given as an example of his perseverance in fathoming a murder.

At the feast of the Passover, a certain Jew of Bagdad had sacrificed his sheep and was offering up his prayers, when suddenly a dog came in, and snatching up the sheep's head ran off with it. The Jew pursued in hot haste, in his excitement still carrying the bloody knife and wearing his besmeared apron. The dog, carrying the sheep's head, rushed into an open doorway, followed closely by the Jew. The Jew in his hurried pursuit fell over the body of what proved to be a murdered man. The murder was laid against the Jew, and witnesses swore that they had seen him coming out of the house covered with blood, and in his hand a bloody dagger. The Jew was arrested and tried, but with covered head he swore by his forefathers and children that he was innocent. Omar would not condemn him as none of the witnesses had seen the Jew do the deed, and until further evidence had been given to prove his

Tales of the Meddahs: Tales from the Turkish tradition

guilt the case was adjourned. Spies and detectives, unknown to anybody, were put to track the murderers. After a time, they were discovered, condemned, put to death, and the Jew liberated.

Tales of the Meddahs: Tales from the Turkish tradition

THE CINDER-YOUTH

This story has been adapted from Turkish Fairy Tales and Folk Tales by Dr. Ignácz Kúnos, published in 1901 by A. H. Bullen, London.

Once upon a time that was no time, in the days when the servants of Allah were many and the misery of man was great, there lived a poor woman who had three sons and one daughter. The youngest son was half-witted and used to roll about all day in the warm ashes.

One day the two elder brothers went out to plough, and said to their mother, "Boil us something, and send our sister out with it into the field."

Now the three-faced devil had pitched his tent close to this field, and in order that the girl might not come near them he determined to persuade her to go all round about instead of straight to them.

The mother cooked the dinner, and the girl went into the field with it, but the devil contrived to make her lose her road, so that she wandered further and further away from the place where she wanted to go. At last, when her poor head was quite confused, the devil's wife appeared before her and asked the terrified girl what she meant by trespassing there. Then she talked her over and persuaded her to come home with her, that she might hide her from the vengeance of the devil, her husband.

But the three-faced devil had got home before them, and when they arrived the old woman told the girl to make haste and get something ready to eat while her maidservant stirred up the fire. But scarcely had she begun to get

Tales of the Meddahs: Tales from the Turkish tradition

the dish ready than the devil crept stealthily up behind her, opened his mouth wide, and swallowed the girl whole, clothes and all.

Meanwhile her brothers were waiting in the field for their dinner, but neither the damsel nor the victuals appeared. Afternoon came and went and evening too, and then the lads went home, and when they heard from their mother that their sister had gone to seek them early in the morning, they suspected what had happened, sensing that their little sister must have fallen into the hands of the devil. The two elder brothers did not think twice about it, and the elder of them set off at once to seek his sister.

He went on and on, puffing at his chibouk, sniffing the perfume of flowers and drinking coffee, till he came to an oven by the wayside. By the oven sat an old man, who asked the youth on what errand he was bent. The youth told him of his sister's case, and said he was going in search of the three-faced devil and would not be content till he had killed him.

"You will never be able to slay the devil," said the man, "till you have eaten bread that has been baked in this oven."

The youth thought this no very difficult matter, took the loaves out of the oven, but scarcely had he bitten a piece out of one of them than the oven, the man, and the loaves all disappeared before his eyes, and the bit he had taken swelled within him so that he nearly burst.

The youth hadn't gone two steps further on when he saw on the highway a large cauldron, and the cauldron was full of wine. A man was sitting in front of the cauldron, and the youth asked him the way, and told him the tale of the devil.

"You will never be able to cope with the devil," said the man, "if you do not drink this wine."

The youth drank, but shrieked, "Woe betide my stomach, woe betide my bowels!", for so plagued was he that he could not have stood upright if he had not seen two bridges before him. One of these bridges was of wood and the other was of iron, and beyond the two bridges were two apple-trees, and one bore unripe bitter apples and the other sweet ripe ones.

Tales of the Meddahs: Tales from the Turkish tradition

The three-faced devil was waiting on the road to see which bridge he would choose, the wooden or the iron one, and which apples he would eat, the sour or the sweet ones. The youth went along the iron bridge, lest the wooden one might break down, and plucked the sweet apples, because the green ones were bitter. That was just what the devil wanted him to do, and he at once sent his mother to meet the youth and entice him into his house as he had done his sister, and it was not long before he also found his way into the devil's belly.

And next in order, the middling brother, not wishing to be behind hand, also went in search of his kinsmen. He also could not eat the bread and his inside also was plagued by the wine. He went across the iron bridge and ate the sweet apples, and so he also found his way into the devil's belly.

Only the youngest brother who lay among the ashes remained. His mother begged him not to forsake her in her old age. If the others had gone, he at least could remain and comfort her, she said. But the youth would not listen.

"I will not rest," said Cinderer, "till I have found the three lost ones, my two brothers and my sister, and slain the devil."

Then he rose from his chimney corner, and no sooner had he shaken the ashes off him than such a tempest arose that all the labourers at work in the fields left their ploughs where they stood and ran off as far as their eyes could see. Then the youngest son gathered together the ploughshares and bade a blacksmith make a lance of them, but a lance of such a kind as would fly into the air and come back again to the hand that hurled it without breaking its iron point. The smith made the lance, and the youth hurled it. Up into the air flew the lance, but when it came down again on to the tip of his little finger it broke to pieces. Then the youth shook himself still more violently in the ashes, and again the labourers in the field fled away before the terrible tempest which immediately arose, and the youth gathered together a still greater multitude of ploughshares and took them to the smith. The smith made a second lance, and that also flew up into the air and broke to pieces when it came down again. Then the youth shook himself in the ashes a third time, and such a hurricane arose that there was scarce a

Tales of the Meddahs: Tales from the Turkish tradition

ploughshare in the whole countryside that was not carried away. It was only with great difficulty that the smith could make the third lance, but when that came down on the youth's finger it did not break in pieces like the others.

"This will do pretty well," said the youth, and catching up the lance he went forth into the wide world.

He went on and on and on till he also came to the oven and the cauldron. The men who guarded the oven and the cauldron stopped him and asked him his business, and on finding out that he was going to kill the devil, they told the youth that he must first eat the bread of the oven and then drink the wine in the cauldron if he could. The son of the cinders wished for nothing better. He ate the loaves that were baked in the oven, drank all the wine, and further on he saw the wooden bridge and the iron bridge, and beyond the bridges the apple-trees.

The devil had observed the youth from afar, and his courage began to ooze out of him when he saw the deeds of the son of the ashes. "Any fool can go across the iron bridge," thought the youth, "I'll go across the wooden one," and as it was no very great feat to eat the sweet apples, he ate the sour ones.

"There will be no joking with this one," said the devil, "I see I must get ready my lance and measure my strength with him."

The son of the ashes saw the devil from afar, and full of the knowledge of his own valour went straight up to him.

"If you don't pay homage to me, I'll swallow you straight off," cried the devil.

"And if you don't pay homage to me, I'll knock you to pieces with my lance," replied the youth.

"Oh ho, if we're so brave as all that," cried the three-faced monster, "let us fight with our lances without losing any more time."

The devil picked up his lance, whirled it round his head, and aimed it with all his might at the youth, who gave but one little twist with his finger, and crick-crack, the devil's lance broke all to bits.

214

Tales of the Meddahs: Tales from the Turkish tradition

"Now it's my turn," cried the son of the cinders. He hurled his lance at the devil with such force that the devil's first soul flew out of his nose.

"Try it it again, if you are a man!" yelled the devil, with a great effort.

"Not I," cried the youth, "for my mother only bore me once," whereupon the devil breathed forth his last soul also. Then the youth went on to seek the devil's wife. Her also he chased down the road after her husband, and when he had cut them both in two, all three of his kinsfolks stood before him, so he turned back home and took them with him. Now his brothers and sister had grown very thirsty in the devil's belly, and when they saw a large well by the wayside, they asked their brother Cinder-son to draw them a little water. Then the youths took off their girdles, tied them together, and let down the biggest brother, but he had scarcely descended more than half-way down when he began to shriek unmercifully, "Oh, oh, draw me up, I have had enough," so that they had to pull him up and let the second brother try. And with him it went the same way.

"Now 'tis my turn," cried Cinder-son, "but mind you do not pull me up, however loudly I holler."

So, they let down the youngest brother, and he too began to holler and bawl, but they paid no heed to it, and let him down till he stood on the dry bottom of the well. A door stood before him, he opened it, and there were three lovely damsels sitting in a room together, and each of them shone like the moon when she is only fourteen days old. The three damsels were amazed at the sight of the youth.

"How dare you come into the devil's cavern?" they asked, and they begged him to escape if he valued dear life. But the youth would not budge at any price, till he had got the better of this devil also. The end of the matter was that he slew the devil and released the three damsels, who were Sultan's daughters, and had been stolen from their fathers and kept here for the last seven years. The two elder princesses he intended for his two brothers, but the youngest, who was also the loveliest, he chose for himself, and filling

Tales of the Meddahs: Tales from the Turkish tradition

the pitcher with water he brought the damsels to the bottom of the well, right below the mouth of it.

First of all, he let them draw up the eldest princess for his eldest brother, then he made them pull up the middling princess for his middling brother, and then it came to the youngest damsel's turn. But she desired that the youth should be drawn up at all hazards and herself afterwards. "Your brethren," she explained, "will be angry with you for keeping the loveliest damsel for yourself and will not draw you out of the well for sheer jealousy."

"I'll find my way out even then," answered the youth, and though she begged him till there was no more soul in her, he would not listen to her. Then the damsel drew from her breast a casket and said to the youth, "If any mischief befalls you, open this casket. Inside it is a piece of flint, and if you strike it once an efrit will appear before you and fulfil all your desires. If your brethren leave you in the well, go to the palace of the devil and stand by the well. Two rams come there every day, a black one and a white one. If you cling fast to the white one, you will come to the surface of the earth, but if you cling on to the black one you will sink down into the seventh world."

Then he let them draw up the youngest damsel, and no sooner did his brethren see their brother's bride and perceive that she was the loveliest of all, than jealousy overtook them, and in their anger, they left him in the well and went home with the damsels.

What else could the poor youth at the bottom of the well do than go back to the devil's palace, stand by the well, and wait for the two rams? Not very long afterwards a white ram came bounding along before him, and after that a black ram, and the youth, instead of catching hold of the white ram, seized the black one and immediately perceived that he was at the bottom of the seventh world. He went on and on, he went for a long time, and he went for a short time, he went by day, and he went by night, he went up hill and down dale till he could do no more and stopped short by a large tree to take a little rest. But what was that he saw before him? A large serpent was gliding up the trunk of the tree and would have devoured all the young birds on the tree

Tales of the Meddahs: Tales from the Turkish tradition

if Cinder-son had let him. But the youth quickly drew forth his lance and cut the serpent in two with a single blow. Then, like one who has done his work well, he lay down at the foot of the tree, and inasmuch as he was tired, and it was warm, he fell asleep at once.

Now while he slept the emerald Anka, who is the mother of the birds and the Padishah of the Peris, passed by that way, and when she saw the sleeping youth, she fancied him to be her enemy, who was wont to destroy her children year by year. She was about to cut him to pieces, when the birds whispered to her not to hurt the youth, because he had killed their enemy the serpent. It was only then that the Anka saw the two halves of the serpent. And now, lest anything should harm the sleeping youth, she hopped round and round him, and touched him softly and sheltered him with both her wings lest the sun should scorch him, and when he awoke from his sleep the wing of the bird was spread over him like a tent. And now the Anka approached him and said she would like to reward him for his good deed, and he might make a request of her. Then the youth replied, "I would like to get to the surface of the earth again."

"Be it so," said the emerald bird, "but first you must get forty tons of ox-flesh and forty pitchers of water and sit on my back with them, so that when I say 'Gik!' you may give them to me to eat, and when I say 'Gak!' you may give me drink."

Then the youth remembered his casket, took the flint-stone out of it, and struck it once, and immediately an efrit with a mouth as big as the world stood before him and said, "What do you command, my Sultan?"

"Forty tons of ox-flesh, and forty pitchers of water," said the youth.

In a short time, the efrit brought the flesh and the water, and the youth packed it all up together and mounted on the wing of the bird. Off they went, and whenever the Anka cried "Gik!" he gave her flesh, and whenever she cried "Gak!" he gave her water. They flew from one layer of worlds to the next, till in a short time they got above the surface of the earth again, and he

Tales of the Meddahs: Tales from the Turkish tradition

dismounted from the bird's back and said to her, "Wait here a while, and in a short time I shall be back."

Then the youth took out his coffer, struck the flint-stone, and bade the bounding efrit get him tidings of the three sisters. In a short time, the efrit re-appeared with the three damsels, who were preparing a banquet for the brothers. He made them all sit on the bird's back, took with him again forty tons of ox-flesh and forty pitchers of water, and away they all went to the land of the three damsels. Every time the Anka said "Gik!" he gave her flesh to eat, and every time she said "Gak!" he gave her water to drink. But as the youth now had three with him besides himself, it came to pass that the flesh ran short, so that when the Anka said "Gik!" once more he had nothing to give her. Then the youth drew his knife, cut a piece of flesh out of his thigh, and stuffed it into the bird's mouth. The Anka saw that it was human flesh and did not eat it, but kept it in her mouth, and when they had reached the realm of the three damsels, the bird told him that he might now go in peace.

But the poor youth could not move a step because of the smart in his leg. "You go on first," he said to the bird, "but I will first rest here a while."

"No, but you are a droll rogue," said the bird, and with that it spit out of its mouth the piece of human flesh and put it back in its proper place just as if it had never been cut out.

The whole city was amazed at the sight of the return of the Sultan's daughters. The old Padishah could scarce believe his own eyes. He looked and looked and then he embraced the first princess. He looked and looked and then he kissed the second princess, and when they had told him the story, he gave his whole kingdom and his three daughters to Cinder-son. Then the youth sent for his mother and his sister, and they all sat down to the banquet together. Moreover, he found his sister a husband who was the son of the Vizier, and for forty days and forty nights they were full of joyfulness.

Tales of the Meddahs: Tales from the Turkish tradition

KALAIDJI AVRAM OF BALATA

This story has been adapted from Told in the Coffee House by Cyrus Adler and Allan Ramsay, published in 1898 by MacMillan and Company, London. Allan Ramsay was a Scottish poet, playwright, publisher, librarian and wigmaker active in the early and mid-eighteenth century. Cyrus Adler adapted Ramsay's work in the nineteenth century, being an American educator, Jewish religious leader and scholar.

Balata, situated on the Golden Horn, is mostly inhabited by folks of the poorer classes, who make their livelihood as tinsmiths, tinkers, and hawkers.

Here, in the early days when the Janissaries flourished, there lived a certain tinsmith called Kalaidji Avram. Having rather an extensive business, his neighbours, especially those who lived nearest, were always complaining of the annoying smoke and disagreeable odour of ammonia which he used in tinning his pots and pans.

Opposite Avram's place the village guardhouse was situated, and the chief, a Janissary, often had disputes with Avram about the smoke. Avram would invariably reply, "I have my children to feed, and I must work, and without smoke I cannot earn their daily bread."

The Janissary, much annoyed, cultivated a dislike for Avram and a thirst for revenge.

It happened that one day a man came to the Janissary and said to him, "Do you want to make a fortune? If so, you have the means of doing this, provided you will agree to halve with me whatever is made."

219

Tales of the Meddahs: Tales from the Turkish tradition

The Janissary, on being assured that he had but to say a word or two to a person he would designate, and the money would be forthcoming, accepted the conditions. The man then said, "All you have to do is to go up to a funeral procession that will pass by here tomorrow on its way to the necropolis outside the city and order it to stop. It is against the religion of the Jews for such a thing to happen, and the Chacham, their Rabbi, will offer you first ten, then twenty, and finally one hundred and ten thousand piasters to allow the funeral to proceed. The half will be for you to compensate you for your trouble and the other fifty-five thousand piasters are for me."

This, as the man had told him, seemed very simple to the Janissary. The next day, true enough, he beheld a funeral, and immediately went out and ordered it to stop. The Chacham protested, offering first small bribes, then larger and larger, till ultimately, he promised to bring to the worthy captain one hundred and ten thousand piasters for allowing the funeral to proceed.

That evening, as agreed, the Chacham came and handed the money to the captain of the Janissaries. Then taking another bag containing a second one hundred and ten thousand piasters, he said, "If you will tell me who informed you that we would pay so much money rather than have a funeral stopped, you can have this further sum."

The Janissary immediately thought of Avram, the tinsmith, and accused him as his informant, and the Chacham, satisfied, paid the sum and departed.

Avram disappeared, and nobody knew where. The Chacham said that death had taken him for his own as a punishment for stopping him while on a journey.

The Janissary's accomplice came a few days later for his share of the money. The Janissary handed him the fifty-five thousand piasters, and at the same time said, "Of these fifty-five thousand piasters, thirty thousand must be given to the widow and children of Avram, and I advise you to give it willingly, for Avram has taken your place."

Tales of the Meddahs: Tales from the Turkish tradition

HOW MEHMET ALI PASHA OF EGYPT ADMINISTERED JUSTICE

This story has been adapted from Told in the Coffee House by Cyrus Adler and Allan Ramsay, published in 1898 by MacMillan and Company, London. Allan Ramsay was a Scottish poet, playwright, publisher, librarian and wig-maker active in the early and mid-eighteenth century. Cyrus Adler adapted Ramsay's work in the nineteenth century, being an American educator, Jewish religious leader and scholar.

A merchant was in the habit of borrowing, and sometimes of lending money to an Armenian merchant of Cairo. Receipts were never exchanged, but at the closing of an old account or the opening of a new one they would simply say to each other, I have debited or credited you in my books, as the case might be, with so much.

On one occasion the Armenian lent the merchant the sum of twenty-five thousand piasters, and after the usual verbal acknowledgment the Armenian made his entry. A reasonable time having elapsed, the Armenian sent his greetings to the merchant. This, in Eastern etiquette, meant, 'Kindly pay me what you owe.' The merchant, however, did not take the hint but returned complimentary greetings to the Armenian. This was repeated several times. Finally, the Armenian sent a message requesting the merchant to call upon him. The merchant, however, told the messenger to inform the Armenian, that if he wished to see him, he must come to his house. The Armenian called upon the merchant and requested payment of the loan. The merchant brought out his books and showed the Armenian that he was both credited and

Tales of the Meddahs: Tales from the Turkish tradition

debited with the sum of twenty-five thousand piasters. The Armenian protested, but in vain, and the merchant maintained that the debt had been paid.

In the hope of recovering his money, the Armenian had the case brought before Mehmet Ali Pasha of Egypt, a clever and learned judge. No witnesses, however, could be cited to prove that the money had either been borrowed or repaid. The entries were verified, and it was thought that perhaps the Armenian had forgotten. Before dismissing the case, however, Mehmet Ali Pasha called in the Public Weigher and ordered that both of the merchants be weighed. This done, Mehmet Ali Pasha took note of their respective weights. The merchant weighed fifty okes and the Armenian sixty okes. He then discharged them, saying that he would send for them later on.

The Armenian waited patiently for a month or two, but no summons came from the Pasha. Every Friday he endeavoured to meet the Pasha so as to bring the case to his mind, but without avail, for the Pasha, seeing him from a distance, would turn away his head or otherwise purposely avoid catching his eye. At last, after about eight months of anxious waiting, the Armenian and his fellow merchant were summoned to appear before the court. Mehmet Ali Pasha, in opening the case, called in the Public Weigher and had them weighed again. On this occasion it was found that the Armenian had decreased, now only weighing fifty okes, for worry makes a man grow thin, but the Jew, on the contrary, had put on several okes. These facts were gravely considered, and the Pasha accused the merchant of having received the money and at once ordered the brass pot to be heated and placed on his head to force confession. The merchant did not care to submit to this fearful ordeal, so he confessed that he had not repaid the debt and had to do so then and there.

Tales of the Meddahs: Tales from the Turkish tradition

THE HORSE-DEVIL AND THE WITCH

This story has been adapted from Turkish Fairy Tales and Folk Tales by Dr. Ignácz Kúnos, published in 1901 by A. H. Bullen, London.

There was once upon a time a Padishah who had three daughters. One day the old father made himself ready for a journey, and calling to his three daughters straightly charged them to feed and water his favourite horse, even though they neglected everything else. He loved the horse so much that he would not suffer any stranger to come near it.

The Padishah went on his way, but when the eldest daughter brought the fodder into the stable the horse would not let her come near him. Then the middling daughter brought the forage, and he treated her likewise. Last of all the youngest daughter brought the forage, and when the horse saw her, he never budged an inch but let her feed him and then return to her sisters. The two elder sisters were content that the youngest should take care of the horse, so they troubled themselves about it no more.

The Padishah came home, and the first thing he asked was whether they had provided the horse with everything. "He wouldn't let us come near him," said the two elder sisters, "it was our youngest sister here who took care of him."

No sooner had the Padishah heard this than he gave his youngest daughter to the horse as a wife, but his two other daughters he gave to the sons of his Chief Mufti and his Grand Vizier, and they celebrated the three marriages at a great banquet, which lasted forty days. Then the youngest daughter moved

Tales of the Meddahs: Tales from the Turkish tradition

into the stable, but the two eldest dwelt in a splendid palace. In the daytime the youngest sister had only a horse for a husband and a stable for a dwelling; but in the night-time the stable became a garden of roses, the horse-husband a handsome hero, and they lived in a world of their own. Nobody knew of it but they two. They passed the day together as best they could, but eventide was the time of their impatient desires.

One day the Padishah held a tournament in the palace. Many gallant warriors entered the lists, but none strove so valiantly as the husbands of the Sultan's elder daughters.

"Only look now!" said the two elder daughters to their sister who dwelt in the stable. "Only look now! How our husbands overthrow all the other warriors with their lances. Our two lords are not so much lords as lions! Where is this horse-husband of yours?"

On hearing this from his wife, the horse-husband shivered all over, turned into a man, threw himself on horseback, told his wife not to betray him on any account, and in an instant appeared within the lists. He overthrew everyone with his lance, unhorsed his two brothers-in-law, and re-appeared in the stable again as if he had never left it.

The next day, when the sports began again, the two elder sisters mocked as before, but then the unknown hero appeared again, conquered and vanished. On the third day the horse-husband said to his wife, "If ever I should come to grief or you should need my help, take these three wisps of hair, burn them, and it will help you wherever you are."

With that he hastened to the games again and triumphed over his brothers-in-law. Everyone was amazed at his skill, the two elder sisters likewise, and again they said to their younger sister, "Look how these heroes excel in prowess! They are very different to your dirty horse-husband!"

The girl could not endure standing there with nothing to say for herself, so she told her sisters that the handsome hero was no other than her horse-husband. No sooner had she pointed at him than he vanished from before them as if he had never been. Then only did she call to mind her lord's

Tales of the Meddahs: Tales from the Turkish tradition

command to her not to betray her secret, and away she hurried off to the stable. But it was all in vain, as neither horse nor man came to her, and at midnight there was neither rose nor rose-garden.

"Alas!" wept the girl, "I have betrayed my lord, I have broken my word, what a crime is mine!"

She never closed an eye all that night but wept till morning. When the red dawn appeared, she went to her father the Padishah, complained to him that she had lost her horse-husband, and begged that she might go to the ends of the earth to seek him. In vain her father tried to keep her back, in vain he pointed out to her that her husband was now most probably among devils, and she would never be able to find him, but he could not turn her from her resolution. What could he do but let her go on her way?

With a great desire the damsel set out on her quest, she went on and on till her tender body was all weary, and at last she sank down exhausted at the foot of a great mountain. Then she called to mind the three hairs, and she took out one and set fire to it. Her lord and master was in her arms again, and they could not speak for joy.

"Did I not bid you tell no one of my secret?" cried the youth sorrowfully, "and now if my hag of a mother sees you, she will instantly tear you to pieces. This mountain is our dwelling-place. She will be here immediately, and woe to you if she sees you!"

The poor Sultan's daughter was terribly frightened and wept worse than ever at the thought of losing her lord again, after all her trouble in finding him. The heart of the devil's son was touched at her sorrow, and he struck her once, changed her into an apple, and put her on the shelf. The hag flew down from the mountain with a terrible racket and screeched out that she smelt the smell of a man, and her mouth watered for the taste of human flesh. In vain her son denied that there was any human flesh there, but she would not believe him one bit.

"If you will swear by the egg not to be offended, I'll show you what I've hidden," said her son. The hag swore, and her son gave the apple a tap, and

Tales of the Meddahs: Tales from the Turkish tradition

there before them stood the beautiful damsel. "Behold my wife!" said he to his mother. The old mother said never a word, for what was done could not be undone. "I'll give the bride something to do all the same," thought she.

They lived a couple of days together in peace and quiet, but the hag was only waiting for her son to leave the house. At last, one day the youth had work to do elsewhere, and scarcely had he put his foot out of doors when the hag said to the damsel, "Come, sweep and sweep not!" and with that she went out and said she should not be back till evening. The girl thought to herself again and again, "What am I to do now? What did she mean by 'sweep and sweep not'?" Then she thought of the hairs, and she took out and burned the second hair also. Immediately her lord stood before her and asked her what the matter was, and the girl told him of his mother's command to 'sweep and sweep not!' Then her lord explained to her that she was to sweep out the chamber, but not to sweep the antechamber.

The girl did as she was told, and when the hag came home in the evening she asked the girl whether she had accomplished her task. "Yes, little mother," replied the bride, "I have swept and I have not swept."

"You daughter of a dog," cried the old witch, "It's not your own wit that's saved you, it's my son's mouth that has told you this thing."

The next morning when the hag got up, she gave the damsel vases, and told her to fill them with tears. The moment the hag had gone the damsel placed the three vases before her, and wept and wept, but what could her few teardrops do to fill them? Then she took out and burned the third hair.

Again, her lord appeared before her, and explained to her that she must fill the three vases with water, and then put a pinch of salt in each vase. The girl did so, and when the hag came home in the evening and demanded an account of her work, the girl showed her the three vases full of tears.

"You daughter of a dog!" chided the old woman again. "That is not your work, but I'll do for you yet, and for my son too."

The next day she devised some other task for her to do; but her son guessed that his mother would vex the wench, so he hastened home to his bride.

226

Tales of the Meddahs: Tales from the Turkish tradition

There the poor thing was worrying herself about it all alone, for the third hair was now burnt, and she did not know how to set about doing the task laid upon her.

"Well, there is now nothing for it but to run away," said her lord, "for she won't rest now till she has done you a mischief." And with that he took his wife, and out into the wide world they went.

In the evening the hag came home and saw neither her son nor his bride. "They have flown, the dogs!" cried the hag, with a threatening voice, and she called to her sister, who was also a witch, to make ready and go in pursuit of her son and his bride. So, the witch jumped into a pitcher, snatched up a serpent for a whip, and went after them.

The demon-lover saw his aunt coming, and in an instant changed the girl into a bathing-house, and himself into a bath-man sitting down at the gate. The witch leaped from the pitcher, went to the bath-keeper, and asked him if he had not seen a young boy and girl pass by that way.

"I have only just warmed up my bath," said the youth, "there's nobody inside it. If you do not believe me, you can go and look for yourself."

The witch thought, "It's impossible to get a sensible word out of a fellow of this sort," so she jumped into her pitcher, flew back, and told her sister that she couldn't find them. The other hag asked her whether she had exchanged words with any one on the road. "Yes," replied the younger sister, "there was a bathhouse by the roadside, and I asked the owner of it about them, but he was either a fool or deaf, so I took no notice of him."

"It's you who were the fool," snarled her elder sister. "Did you not recognise him as my son, and in the bathhouse my daughter-in-law?" Then she called her second sister and sent her after the fugitives.

The devil's son saw his second aunt flying along in her pitcher. Then he gave his wife a tap and turned her into a spring, but he himself sat down beside it, and began to draw water out of it with a pitcher. The witch went up to him and asked him whether he had seen a girl and a boy pass by that way.

Tales of the Meddahs: Tales from the Turkish tradition

"There's drinkable water in this spring," replied he, with a vacant stare, "I am always drawing it." The witch thought she had to do with a fool, turned back, and told her sister that she had not met with them. Her sister asked her if she had not come across any one by the way. "Yes, indeed," replied she, "a half-witted fellow was drawing water from a spring, but I couldn't get a single sensible word out of him."

"That half-witted fellow was my son, the spring was his wife, and a pretty wiseacre you are!" screeched her sister. "I shall have to go myself, I see," and with that she jumped into her pitcher, snatched up a serpent to serve her as a whip, and off she went.

Meanwhile the youth looked back again and saw his mother coming after them. He gave the girl a tap and changed her into a tree, but he himself turned into a serpent, and coiled himself around the tree. The witch recognised them and drew near to the tree to break it to pieces; but when she saw the serpent coiled round it, she was afraid to kill her own son along with it, so she said to her son, "Son, son! Show me, at least, the girl's little finger, and then I'll leave you both in peace."

The son saw that he could not free himself from her any other way, and that she must have at least a little morsel of the damsel to nibble at. So, he showed her one of the girl's little fingers, and the old hag wrenched it off, and returned to her domains with it. Then the youth gave the girl a tap and himself another tap, put on human shape again, and away they went to the girl's father, the Padishah. The youth, since his talisman had been destroyed, remained a mortal man, but the diabolical part of him stayed at home with his witch-mother and her kindred. The Padishah rejoiced greatly in his children, gave them a wedding-banquet with a wave of his finger, and they inherited the realm after his death.

Tales of the Meddahs: Tales from the Turkish tradition

HOW THE FARMER LEARNED TO CURE HIS WIFE—A TURKISH ÆSOP

This story has been adapted from Told in the Coffee House by Cyrus Adler and Allan Ramsay, published in 1898 by MacMillan and Company, London. Allan Ramsay was a Scottish poet, playwright, publisher, librarian and wigmaker active in the early and mid-eighteenth century. Cyrus Adler adapted Ramsay's work in the nineteenth century, being an American educator, Jewish religious leader and scholar.

There once lived a farmer who understood the language of animals. He had obtained this knowledge on condition that he would never reveal its possession, and with the further provision that should he prove false to his oath the penalty would be certain death.

One day he chanced to listen to a conversation his ox and his horse were having. The ox had just come in from a weary and hard day's work in the rain.

"Oh," sighed the ox, looking over to the horse, "how fortunate you are to have been born a horse and not an ox. When the weather is bad you are kept in the stable, well fed, groomed every morning, and caressed every evening. Oh, that I was a horse!"

"What you say is true," replied the horse, "but you are very stupid to work so hard."

"You do not know what it is to be goaded with a spear and howled at, or you would not accuse me of being stupid to work so hard," replied the ox.

Tales of the Meddahs: Tales from the Turkish tradition

"Then why don't you feign sickness," continued the horse.

On the following day the ox determined to try this deceit, but he was stung with remorse when he saw the horse led out to take his place at the plough. In the evening, when the horse was brought to the stable very tired, the ox sympathized with him, and regretted his being the cause, but at the same time expressed astonishment at his working so hard.

"Ah, my friend, I had to work hard. I can't bear the whip. The thought of the hideous crack, crack, makes me shiver even now," answered the horse.

"But leaving that aside, my poor horned friend," proceeded the horse, "I am now most anxious for you. I heard the master say tonight that if you were not well in the morning, the butcher was to come and slaughter you."

"You need not worry about me, friend horse," said the ox, "as I much prefer the yoke to chewing the cud of self-reproach."

At this point the farmer left the animals and entered his home, smiling at his own wily craft in re-establishing, if not contentedness, at least resignation to their fate. Meeting his wife, she at once inquired as to the cause of his happy smile. He put her off, first with one excuse then with another, but to no avail; the more he protested, the stronger her inquisitiveness grew. Her unsatisfied curiosity at length made her ill. The endeavours of the numerous doctors brought to her assistance were as futile as the incantations of the sages from far and near, and as powerless to remove the spell as were the amulets, the charms, and the abracadabras conceived and written by holy men. The evil prompting gnawed her, and she visibly pined away. The poor farmer was distracted. Rather than see her die, he at last decided to tell her, and forfeit his own life to save hers. Deeply dejected, for no man quits this planet without a pang, he sat at the window gazing, as he thought, for the last time on these familiar surroundings. Of a sudden he noticed his favourite chanticleer, followed by his numerous harem, sadly strutting about, only allowing his favourites to eat the morsels he discovered, and ruthlessly driving the others away. To one he said, "I am not like our poor master, to

Tales of the Meddahs: Tales from the Turkish tradition

be ruled by one or a score of you. He, poor man, will die today for revealing his secret knowledge to save her life."

"What is the secret knowledge?" asked one of the hen wives, and the chanticleer flew at her and thrashed her mercilessly, saying at each vigorous blow, "That is the secret, and if our master only treated the mistress as I treat you, he would not need to give up his life today."

And as if maddened at the thought, he beat them all in turn. The master, seeing and appreciating the effect from the window, went to his wife and treated her in precisely the same manner. And this did what neither doctors, sages, nor holy men could do, for it quite cured her.

Tales of the Meddahs: Tales from the Turkish tradition

Tales of the Meddahs: Tales from the Turkish tradition

THE SILENT PRINCESS

This story has been adapted from Andrew Lang's version of the same tale that originally appeared in The Olive Fairy Book, published in 1907 by Longmans, Green And Co., London and New York. This tale was originally adapted by Andrew Lang from Türkische Volksmärchen aus Stambul, by Dr. Ignácz Kúnos. and published in 1905 by E. J. Brill of Leiden.

Once upon a time there lived in Turkey a pasha who had only one son, and so dearly did he love this boy that he let him spend the whole day amusing himself, instead of learning how to be useful like his friends.

Now the boy's favourite toy was a golden ball, and with this he would play from morning till night, without troubling anybody. One day, as he was sitting in the summerhouse in the garden, making his ball run all along the walls and catching it again, he noticed an old woman with an earthen pitcher coming to draw water from a well which stood in a corner of the garden. In a moment he had caught his ball and flung it straight at the pitcher, which fell to the ground in a thousand pieces. The old woman started with surprise but said nothing. She turned round to fetch another pitcher, and as soon as she had disappeared, the boy hurried out to pick up his ball.

Scarcely was he back in the summerhouse when he beheld the old woman a second time, approaching the well with the pitcher on her shoulder. She had just taken hold of the handle to lower it into the water, when the ball crashed into it again. The pitcher lay in fragments at her feet. Of course, she felt very angry, but for fear of the pasha she still held her peace and spent her last pence in buying a fresh pitcher. But when this also was broken by a blow

Tales of the Meddahs: Tales from the Turkish tradition

from the ball, her wrath burst forth, and shaking her fist towards the summerhouse where the boy was hiding, she cried, "I wish you may be punished by falling in love with the silent princess." And having said this she vanished.

For some time, the boy paid no heed to her words. Indeed, he forgot them altogether; but as years went by, and he began to think more about things, the remembrance of the old woman's wish came back to his mind.

"Who is the silent princess? And why should it be a punishment to fall in love with her?" he asked himself and received no answer. However, that did not prevent him from putting the question again and again, till at length he grew so weak and ill that he could eat nothing, and in the end was forced to lie in bed altogether. His father the pasha became so frightened by this strange disease, that he sent for every physician in the kingdom to cure him, but no one was able to find a remedy.

"How did your illness first begin, my son?" asked the pasha one day. "Perhaps, if we knew that, we should also know better what to do for you."

Then the youth told him what had happened all those years before, when he was a little boy, and what the old woman had said to him.

"Give me, I pray you," he cried, when his tale was finished, "give me, I pray you, leave to go into the world in search of the princess, and perhaps this evil state may cease." And, sore though his heart was to part from his only son, the pasha felt that the young man would certainly die if he remained at home any longer.

"Go, and peace be with you," he answered, and went out to call his trusted steward, whom he ordered to accompany his young master.

Their preparations were soon made, and early one morning the two set out. But neither old man nor young had the slightest idea where they were going, or what they were undertaking. First they lost their way in a dense forest, and from that they at length emerged in a wilderness where they wandered for six months, not seeing a living creature and finding scarcely anything to eat or drink, till they became nothing but skin and bone, while their garments

Tales of the Meddahs: Tales from the Turkish tradition

hung in tatters about them. They had forgotten all about the princess, and their only wish was to find themselves back in the palace again, when, one day, they discovered that they were standing on the shoulder of a mountain. The stones beneath them shone as brightly as diamonds, and both their hearts beat with joy at beholding a tiny old man approaching them. The sight awoke all manner of recollections, and the numb feeling that had taken possession of them fell away as if by magic, and it was with glad voices that they greeted the newcomer. "Where are we, my friend?" They asked and the old man told them that this was the mountain where the sultan's daughter sat, covered by seven veils, and the shining of the stones was only the reflection of her own brilliance.

On hearing this news all the dangers and difficulties of their past wandering vanished from their minds. "How can I reach her soonest?" asked the youth eagerly. But the old man only answered, "Have patience, my son, yet awhile. Another six months must go by before you arrive at the palace where she dwells with the rest of the women. And, even so, think well, when you can, as should you fail to make her speak, you will have to pay forfeit with your life, as others have done. Beware!"

But the prince only laughed at this counsel, just as all others had done.

After three months they found themselves on the top of another mountain, and the prince saw with surprise that its sides were coloured a beautiful red. Perched on some cliffs, not far off, was a small village, and the prince proposed to his friend that they should go and rest there. The villagers, on their part, welcomed them gladly, and gave them food to eat and beds to sleep on, and thankful indeed were the two travellers to repose their weary limbs.

The next morning, they asked their host if he could tell them whether they were still many days' journey from the princess, and whether he knew why the mountain was so much redder than other mountains.

Tales of the Meddahs: Tales from the Turkish tradition

"For three and a half more months you must still pursue your way," answered he, "and by that time you will find yourselves at the gate of the princess's palace. As for the colour of the mountain, that comes from the soft hue of her cheeks and mouth, which shines through the seven veils which cover her. But none have ever beheld her face, for she sits there, uttering no word, though one hears whispers of many having lost their lives for her sake."

The prince, however, would listen no further, and thanking the man for his kindness, he jumped up and, with the steward, set out to climb the mountain.

On and on and on they went, sleeping under the trees or in caves, and living upon berries and any fish they could catch in the rivers. But at length, when their clothes were nearly in rags and their legs so tired that they could hardly walk any further, they saw on the top of the next mountain a palace of yellow marble.

"There it is, at last," cried the prince; and fresh blood seemed to spring in his veins. But as he and his companion began to climb towards the top they paused in horror, for the ground was white with dead men's skulls. It was the prince who first recovered his voice, and he said to his friend, as carelessly as he could, "These must be the skulls of the men who tried to make the princess speak and failed. Well, if we fail too, our bones will strew the ground likewise."

"Oh, turn back now, my prince, while there is yet time," entreated his companion. "Your father gave you into my charge, but when we set out, I did not know that certain death lay before us."

"Take heart, O Lala, take heart!" answered the prince. "A man can only die once. And, besides, the princess will have to speak someday, you know."

They went on again, past skulls and dead men's bones in all degrees of whiteness. And by-and-by they reached another village, where they determined to rest for a little while, so that their wits might be fresh and bright for the task that lay before them. But this time, though the people were

Tales of the Meddahs: Tales from the Turkish tradition

kind and friendly, their faces were gloomy, and every now and then woeful cries would rend the air.

"Oh, my brother, have I lost you?"

"Oh, my son, shall I see you no more?"

And then, as the prince and his companion asked the meaning of these laments, which, indeed, was plain enough, the answer was given,"Ah, you also have come here to die! This town belongs to the father of the princess, and when any rash man seeks to move the princess to speech, he must first obtain leave of the sultan. If that is granted, he is then led into the presence of the princess. What happens afterwards, perhaps the sight of these bones may help you to guess."

The young man bowed his head in token of thanks and stood thoughtful for a short time. Then, turning to the Lala, he said, "Well, our destiny will soon be decided! Meanwhile we will find out all we can and do nothing rashly."

For two or three days they wandered about the bazaars, keeping their eyes and ears open, when, one morning, they met a man carrying a nightingale in a cage. The bird was singing so joyously that the prince stopped to listen, and at once offered to buy him from his owner.

"Oh, why cumber yourself with such a useless thing," cried the Lala in disgust, "have you not enough to occupy your hands and mind, without taking an extra burden?"

But the prince, who liked having his own way, paid no heed to him, and paying the high price asked by the man, he carried the bird back to the inn, and hung him up in his chamber. That evening, as he was sitting alone, trying to think of something that would make the princess talk, and failing altogether, the nightingale pecked open her cage door, which was lightly fastened by a stick, and, perching on his shoulder, murmured softly in his ear, "What makes you so sad, my prince?"

The young man started. In his native country birds did not talk, and, like many people, he was always rather afraid of what he did not understand. But

Tales of the Meddahs: Tales from the Turkish tradition

in a moment, he felt ashamed of his folly, and explained that he had travelled for more than a year, and over thousands of miles, to win the hand of the sultan's daughter. And now that he had reached his goal, he could think of no plan to force her to speak.

"Oh, do not trouble your head about that," replied the bird, "it is quite easy! Go this evening to the women's apartments, and take me with you, and when you enter the princess's private chamber hide me under the pedestal which supports the great golden candlestick. The princess herself will be wrapped so thickly in her seven veils that she can see nothing, neither can her face be seen by anyone. Then inquire after her health, but she will remain quite silent. Next say that you are sorry to have disturbed her, and that you will have a little talk with the pedestal of the candlestick. When you speak, I will answer."

The prince threw his mantle over the bird, and started for the palace, where he begged an audience of the sultan. This was soon granted to him, and leaving the nightingale hidden by the mantle, in a dark corner outside the door, he walked up to the throne on which his highness was sitting and bowed low before him.

"What is your request?" asked the sultan, looking closely at the young man, who was tall and handsome; but when he heard the tale, he shook his head pityingly.

"If you can make her speak, she shall be your wife," answered he, "but if not, did you mark the skulls that strewed the mountain side?"

"Someday a man is bound to break the spell, O Sultan," replied the youth boldly, "and why should not I be he as well as another? At any rate, my word is pledged, and I cannot draw back now."

"Well, go if you must," said the sultan. And he bade his attendants lead the way to the chamber of the princess, but to allow the young man to enter alone.

Catching up, unseen, his mantle and the cage as they passed into the dark corridor, for by this time night was coming on, the youth found himself

Tales of the Meddahs: Tales from the Turkish tradition

standing in a room bare except for a pile of silken cushions, and one tall golden candlestick. His heart beat high as he looked at the cushions, and knew that, shrouded within the shining veils that covered them, lay the much longed-for princess. Then, fearful that after all other eyes might be watching him, he hastily placed the nightingale under the open pedestal on which the candlestick was resting, and turning again he steadied his voice, and asked the princess to tell him of her well-being.

Not by even a movement of her hand did the princess show that she had heard, and the young man, who of course expected this. He went on to speak of his travels and of the strange countries he had passed through, but not a sound broke the silence.

"I see clearly that you are interested in none of these things," said he at last, "and as I have been forced to hold my peace for so many months, I feel that now I really must talk to somebody, so I shall go and address my conversation to the candlestick." And with that he crossed the room behind the princess, and cried, "O fairest of candlesticks, how are you?"

"Very well indeed, my lord," answered the nightingale, "but I wonder how many years have gone by since anyone has spoken with me. And now that you have come, rest, I pray you, awhile, and listen to my story."

"Willingly," replied the youth, curling himself up on the floor, for there was no cushion for him to sit on.

"Once upon a time," began the nightingale, "there lived a pasha whose daughter was the most beautiful maiden in the whole kingdom. Suitors she had in plenty, but she was not easy to please, and at length there were only three whom she felt she could even think of marrying. Not knowing which of the three she liked best, she took counsel with her father, who summoned the young men into his presence, and then told them that they must each of them learn some trade, and whichever of them proved the cleverest at the end of six months should become the husband of the princess.

"Though the three suitors may have been secretly disappointed, they could not help feeling that this test was quite fair, and left the palace together,

Tales of the Meddahs: Tales from the Turkish tradition

talking as they went of what handicrafts they might set themselves to follow. The day was hot, and when they reached a spring that gushed out of the side of the mountain, they stopped to drink and rest, and then one of them said, 'It will be best that we should each seek our fortunes alone, so let us put our rings under this stone, and go our separate ways. And the first one who returns here will take his ring, and the others will take theirs. Thus, we shall know whether we have all fulfilled the commands of the pasha, or if some accident has befallen any of us.'

"'Good,' replied the other two. And three rings were placed in a little hole, and carefully covered again by the stone.

"Then they parted, and for six months they knew nothing of each other, till, on the day appointed, they met at the spring. Right glad they all were, and eagerly they talked of what they had done, and how the time had been spent.

"'I think I shall win the princess,' said the eldest, with a laugh, 'for it is not everybody that is able to accomplish a whole year's journey in an hour!'

"'That is very clever, certainly,' answered his friend, 'but if you are to govern a kingdom it may be still more useful to have the power of seeing what is happening at a distance, and that is what I have learnt,' replied the second.

"'No, no, my dear comrades,' cried the third, 'your trades are all very well, but when the pasha hears that I can bring back the dead to life he will know which of us three is to be his son-in-law. But come, there only remain a few hours of the six months he granted us. It is time that we hastened back to the palace.'

"'Stop a moment,' said the second, 'it would be well to know what is going on in the palace.' And plucking some small leaves from a nearby tree, he muttered some words and made some signs, and laid them on his eyes. In an instant he turned pale and uttered a cry.

"'What is it? What is it?' exclaimed the others, and, with a shaking voice, he gasped, 'The princess is lying on her bed, and has barely a few minutes to live. Oh, can no one save her?'

240

Tales of the Meddahs: Tales from the Turkish tradition

"'I can,' answered the third, taking a small box from his turban, 'this ointment will cure any illness. But how to reach her in time?'

"'Give it to me,' said the first. And he wished himself by the bedside of the princess, which was surrounded by the sultan and his weeping courtiers. Clearly there was not a second to lose, for the princess had grown unconscious, and her face cold. Plunging his finger into the ointment he touched her eyes, mouth and ears with the paste, and with beating heart awaited the result.

"It was swifter than he supposed. As he looked the colour came back into her cheeks, and she smiled up at her father. The sultan, almost speechless with joy at this sudden change, embraced his daughter tenderly, and then turned to the young man to whom he owed her life, saying, 'Are you not one of those three whom I sent forth to learn a trade six months ago?'

The young man answered yes, and that the other two were even now on their way to the palace, so that the sultan might judge between them."

At this point in his story the nightingale stopped, and asked the prince which of the three he thought had the best right to the princess.

"The one who had learned how to prepare the ointment," replied he.

"But if it had not been for the man who could see what was happening at a distance, they would never have known that the princess was ill," said the nightingale. "I would give it to him." And the strife between them waxed hot, till, suddenly, the listening princess started up from her cushions and cried, "Oh, you fool! Can't you understand that if it had not been for him who had power to reach the palace in time the ointment itself would have been useless, for death would have claimed her? It is he and no other who ought to have the princess!"

At the first sound of the princess's voice, a slave, who was standing at the door, ran at full speed to tell the sultan of the miracle which had taken place, and the delighted father hastened to the spot. But by this time the princess saw that she had fallen into a trap which had been cunningly laid for her and would not utter another word. All she could be prevailed on to do was to

Tales of the Meddahs: Tales from the Turkish tradition

make signs to her father that the man who wished to be her husband must induce her to speak three times. And she smiled to herself beneath her seven veils as she thought of the impossibility of that.

When the sultan told the prince that though he had succeeded once, he would have twice to pass through the same test, the young man's face clouded over. It did not seem to him fair play, but he dared not object, so he only bowed low, and contrived to step back close to the spot where the nightingale was hidden. As it was now quite dark, he tucked unseen the little cage under his cloak and left the palace.

"Why are you so gloomy?" asked the nightingale, as soon as they were safely outside. "Everything has gone exactly right! Of course, the princess was very angry with herself for having spoken. And did you see that, at her first words, the veils that covered her began to rend? Take me back tomorrow evening and place me on the pillar by the lattice. Fear nothing, you have only to trust to me!"

The next evening, towards sunset, the prince left the cage behind him, and with the bird in the folds of his garment slipped into the palace and made his way straight to the princess's apartments. He was at once admitted by the slaves who guarded the door and took care to pass near the window so that the nightingale hopped unseen to the top of a pillar. Then he turned and bowed low to the princess, and asked her several questions; but, as before, she answered nothing, and, indeed, gave no sign that she heard. After a few minutes the young man bowed again, and crossing over to the window, he said, "Oh, pillar! It is no use speaking to the princess, she will not utter one word, and as I must talk to somebody, I have come to you. Tell me how you have been all this long while?"

"I thank you," replied a voice from the pillar, "I am feeling very well. And it is lucky for me that the princess is silent, or else you would not have wanted to speak to me. To reward you, I will relate to you an interesting tale that I lately overheard, and about which I should like to have your opinion."

"That will be charming," answered the prince, "so pray begin at once."

Tales of the Meddahs: Tales from the Turkish tradition

"Once upon a time," said the nightingale, "there lived a woman who was so beautiful that every man who saw her fell in love with her. But she was very hard to please, and refused to wed any of them, though she managed to keep friends with all. Years passed away in this manner, almost without her noticing them, and one by one the young men grew tired of waiting, and sought wives who may have been less handsome, but were also less proud, and at length only three of her former wooers remained - Baldschi, Jagdschi, and Firedschi. Still, she held herself apart, and thought herself better and lovelier than other women. Then on a certain evening, her eyes were opened at last to the truth. She was sitting before her mirror, combing her curls, when amongst her raven locks she found a long white hair!

"At this dreadful sight her heart gave a jump, and then stood still.

"'I am growing old,' she said to herself, 'and if I do not choose a husband soon, I shall never get one! I know that either of those men would gladly marry me tomorrow, but I cannot decide between them. I must invent some way to find out which of them is the best and lose no time about it.'

"So, instead of going to sleep, she thought all night long of different plans, and in the morning, she arose and dressed herself.

"'That will have to do,' she muttered as she pulled out the white hair which had cost her so much trouble. 'It is not very good, but I can think of nothing better, and, well, they are none of them clever, and I dare say they will easily fall into the trap.'

Then she called her slave and bade her let Jagdschi know that she would be ready to receive him in an hour's time. After that she went into the garden and dug a grave under a tree, by which she laid a white shroud.

"Jagdschi was delighted to get the gracious message, and, putting on his newest garments, he hastened to the lady's house, but great was his dismay at finding her stretched on her cushions, weeping bitterly.

"'What is the matter, O Fair One?' he asked, bowing low before her.

Tales of the Meddahs: Tales from the Turkish tradition

"'A terrible thing has happened,' said she, her voice choked with sobs. 'My father died two nights ago, and I buried him in my garden. But now I find that he was a wizard, and was not dead at all, for his grave is empty and he is wandering about somewhere in the world.'

"'That is evil news indeed,' answered Jagdschi, 'but can I do nothing to comfort you?'

"'There is one thing you can do,' replied she, 'and that is to wrap yourself in the shroud and lay yourself in the grave. If he should not return till after three hours have elapsed, he will have lost his power over me, and be forced to go and wander elsewhere.'

"Now Jagdschi was proud of the trust reposed in him, and wrapping himself in the shroud, he stretched himself at full length in the grave. After some time Baldschi arrived in his turn and found the lady groaning and lamenting. She told him that her father had been a wizard, and that in case, as was very likely, he should wish to leave his grave and come to work her evil, Baldschi was to take a stone and be ready to crush in his head, if he showed signs of moving.

"Baldschi, enchanted at being able to do his lady a service, picked up a stone, and seated himself by the side of the grave wherein lay Jagdschi.

"Meanwhile the hour arrived in which Firedschi was accustomed to pay his respects, and, as in the case of the other two, he discovered the lady overcome with grief. To him she said that a wizard who was an enemy of her father's had thrown the dead man out of his grave and had taken his place. "But," she added, "if you can bring the wizard into my presence, all his power will go from him, but if not, then I am lost."

"'Ah, lady, what is there that I would not do for you!' cried Firedschi, and running down to the grave, he seized the astonished Jagdschi by the waist, and flinging the body over his shoulder, he hastened with him into the house. At the first moment Baldschi was so surprised at this turn of affairs, for which the lady had not prepared him, that he sat still and did nothing. But by-and-by he sprang up and hurled the stone after the two flying figures,

244

Tales of the Meddahs: Tales from the Turkish tradition

hoping that it might kill them both. Fortunately, it touched neither, and soon all three were in the presence of the lady. Then Jagdschi, thinking that he had delivered her from the power of the wizard, slid off the back of Firedschi, and threw the shroud from him.'

"Tell me, my prince," said the nightingale, when he had finished his story, "which of the three men deserved to win the lady? I myself should choose Firedschi."

"No, no," answered the prince, who understood the wink the bird had given him, "it was Baldschi who took the most trouble, and it was certainly he who deserved the lady."

But the nightingale would not agree, and they began to quarrel, till a third voice broke in, "How can you talk such nonsense?" cried the princess, and as she spoke a sound of tearing was heard. "Why, you have never even thought of Jagdschi, who lay for three hours in the grave, with a stone held over his head! Of course, it was he whom the lady chose for her husband!"

It was not many minutes before the news reached the sultan, but even now he would not consent to the marriage till his daughter had spoken a third time. On hearing this, the young man took counsel with the nightingale how best to accomplish this, and the bird told him that as the princess, in her fury at having fallen into the snare laid for her, had ordered the pillar to be broken in pieces, he must be hidden in the folds of a curtain that hung by the door.

The following evening the prince entered the palace and walked boldly up to the princess's apartments. As he entered the nightingale flew from under his arm and perched himself on top of the door, where he was entirely concealed by the folds of the dark curtain. The young man talked as usual to the princess without obtaining a single word in reply, and at length he left her lying under the heap of shining veils, now rent in many places, and crossed the room towards the door, from which came a voice that gladly answered him.

For a while the two talked together: then the nightingale asked if the prince was fond of stories, as he had lately heard one which interested and

Tales of the Meddahs: Tales from the Turkish tradition

perplexed him greatly. In reply, the prince begged that he might hear it at once, and without further delay the nightingale began, "Once upon a time, a carpenter, a tailor, and a student set out together to see the world. After wandering about for some months, they grew tired of travelling, and resolved to stay and rest in a small town that took their fancy. So, they hired a little house, and looked about for work to do, returning at sunset to smoke their pipes and talk over the events of the day.

"One night in the middle of summer it was hotter than usual, and the carpenter found himself unable to sleep. Instead of tossing about on his cushions, making himself more uncomfortable than he was already, the man wisely got up and drank some coffee and lit his long pipe. Suddenly his eye fell on some pieces of wood in a corner and, being very clever with his fingers, he had soon set up a perfect statue of a girl about fourteen years old. This so pleased and quieted him that he grew quite drowsy and going back to bed fell fast asleep.

"But the carpenter was not the only person who lay awake that night. Thunder was in the air, and the tailor became so restless that he thought he would go downstairs and cool his feet in the little fountain outside the garden door. To reach the door he had to pass through the room where the carpenter had sat and smoked, and against the wall he beheld standing a beautiful girl. He stood speechless for an instant before he ventured to touch her hand, when, to his amazement, he found that she was fashioned out of wood.

"'Ah, I can make you more beautiful still,' said he. And fetching from a shelf a roll of yellow silk which he had bought that day from a merchant, he cut and draped and stitched, till at length a lovely robe clothed the slender figure. When this was finished, the restlessness had departed from him, and he went back to bed.

"As dawn approached the student arose and prepared to go to the mosque with the first ray of sunlight. But, when he saw the maiden standing there, he fell on his knees and lifted his hands in ecstasy.

246

Tales of the Meddahs: Tales from the Turkish tradition

"'Oh, you are fairer than the evening air, clad in the beauty of ten thousand stars,' he murmured to himself. 'Surely a form so rare was never meant to live without a soul.' And forthwith he prayed with all his might that life should be breathed into it.

"And his prayer was heard, and the beautiful statue became a living girl, and the three men all fell in love with her, and each desired to have her to wife.

"Now," said the nightingale, "to which of them did the maiden really belong? It seems to me that the carpenter had the best right to her."

"Oh, but the student would never have thought of praying that she might be given a soul had not the tailor drawn attention to her loveliness by the robe which he put upon her," answered the prince, who guessed what he was expected to say, and they soon set up quite a pretty quarrel. Suddenly the princess, furious that neither of them alluded to the part played by the student, quite forgot her vow of silence and cried loudly, "Idiots that you are! How could she belong to any one but the student? If it had not been for him, all that the others did would have gone for nothing! Of course, it was he who married the maiden!" And as she spoke the seven veils fell from her, and she stood up, the fairest princess that the world has ever seen.

"You have won me," she said smiling, holding out her hand to the prince.

And so, they were married, and after the wedding-feast was over they sent for the old woman whose pitcher the prince had broken so long ago, and she dwelt in the palace, and became nurse to their children, and lived happily till she died.

Tales of the Meddahs: Tales from the Turkish tradition

Tales of the Meddahs: Tales from the Turkish tradition

THE GOLDEN-HAIRED CHILDREN

This story has been adapted from Turkish Fairy Tales and Folk Tales by Dr. Ignácz Kúnos, published in 1901 by A. H. Bullen, London.

Once upon a time, in days long gone by, when my father was my father, and I was my father's son, when my father was my son, and I was my father's mother, once upon a time, I say, at the uttermost ends of the world, hard by the realm of demons, stood a great city.

In this same city there dwelt three poor damsels, the daughters of a poor woodcutter. From morn to eve, from evening to morning, they did nothing but sew and stitch, and when the embroideries were finished, one of them would go to the marketplace and sell them, and so purchase the things they needed to live upon.

Now it fell out, one day, that the Padishah of that city was angry with the people, and in his rage, he commanded that for three days and three nights nobody should light a candle in that city. What were these three poor sisters to do? They could not work in the dark. So, they covered their window with a large thick curtain, lit a tiny rushlight, and sat down to earn their daily bread.

On the third night of the prohibition, the Padishah took it into his head to go around the city himself to see whether everyone was keeping his commandment. He chanced to step in front of the house of the three poor damsels, and as the folds of the curtain did not quite cover the bottom of the window, he caught sight of the light within. The damsels, however, little

Tales of the Meddahs: Tales from the Turkish tradition

suspecting their danger, went on sewing and stitching and talking amongst themselves about their poor affairs.

"Oh," said the eldest, "if only the Padishah would wed me to his chief cook, what delicious dishes I should have every day. Yes, and I would embroider him a carpet so long that all his horses and all his men could find room upon it."

"As for me," said the middling damsel, "I should like to be wedded to the keeper of his wardrobe. What lovely, splendid raiment I should then have to put on. And then I would make the Padishah a tent so large, that all his horses and all his men should find shelter beneath it."

"Well," cried the youngest damsel, "I'll look at nobody but the Padishah himself, and if he would only take me to wife, I would bear him two little children with golden hair. One should be a boy and the other a girl, and a half-moon should shine on the forehead of the boy, and a bright star should sparkle on the temples of the girl."

The Padishah heard the discourse of the three damsels, and no sooner did the red dawn shine in the morning sky than he sent for all three to come to the palace. The eldest he gave to his head pantler, the second to his head chamberlain, but the youngest he took for himself.

And in truth it fared excellently well with the three damsels. The eldest got so many rich dishes to eat, that when it came to sewing the promised carpet, she could scarce move her needle for the sleepiness induced by her constant eating. Because of this lethargy they sent her back again to the woodcutter's hut. The second damsel, too, when they dressed her up in gold and silver raiment, would not deign to dirty her fingers by making tents, so they sent her back too, to keep her elder sister company.

After nine months and ten days the two elder sisters came sidling up to the palace to see if their poor younger sister would really be as good as her word and bring forth the two wondrous children. In the gates of the palace, they met an old woman, and they persuaded her with gifts and promises to meddle in the matter. Now this old woman was the devil's own daughter, so that

Tales of the Meddahs: Tales from the Turkish tradition

mischief and malice were her meat and drink. She now went and picked up two pups and took them with her to the pregnant woman's bed.

The Padishah's wife brought forth two little children like shining stars. One was a boy, the other a girl. On the boy's forehead was a half-moon and on the girl's a star, so that darkness was turned to light when they were nearby. Then the wicked old woman exchanged the children for the pups and told the Padishah that his wife had brought forth two pups. The Padishah almost had a seizure in the furiousness of his rage. He took his poor wife, buried her up to the waist in the ground, and commanded throughout the city that every passer-by should strike her on the head with a stone. But no sooner had the evil witch got hold of the two children, than she took them a long way outside the town, exposed them on the bank of a flowing stream, and returned to the palace, glad that she had done her work so well.

Now close to the water where the two children lay stood a hut where an aged couple lived. The old man had a she-goat which used to go out in the morning to graze, and come back in the evening to be milked, and that was how the poor people kept body and soul together. One day, however, the old woman was surprised to find that the goat did not give one drop of milk. She complained about it to the old man her husband and told him to follow the goat to see if perhaps there was anyone who stole the milk.

The next day the old man went after the goat, which went right up to the water's edge, and then disappeared behind a tree. And what do you think he saw? He saw a sight which would have delighted your eyes also, that being two golden-haired children lying in the grass. The goat went right up to them and offered them her teats to suck. Then she bleated to them a little, and so left them and went off to graze. And the old man was so delighted at the sight of the little starry things, that he almost lost his head for joy. He took the little ones, for Allah had not blessed him with children of his own, and he carried them to his hut and gave them to his wife. The woman was filled with a still greater joy at the children which Allah had given her, and took care of them, and brought them up. But now the little goat came bleating in

Tales of the Meddahs: Tales from the Turkish tradition

as if in sore distress, but the moment she saw the children, she went to them and suckled them, and then went out to graze again.

But time comes and goes. The two wondrous children grew up and scampered up hill and down dale, and the dark woods were bright with the radiance of their golden hair. They hunted the wild beasts, tended sheep, and helped the old people by word and deed. Time came and went till the children had grown up, and the old people had become very old indeed. The golden-haired ones grew in strength while the silver-haired ones grew in feebleness, till, at last, one morning they lay there dead, and the brother and sister were left all alone. Sorely did the poor little things weep and wail, but was ever woe mended by weeping? They buried their old parents, and the girl stayed at home with the little she-goat, while the lad went hunting, for finding food was now their great care and their little care too.

One day, while he was hunting wild beasts in the forest, the boy met his father, the Padishah, but he did not know it was his father, and neither did the father recognize his son. Yet the moment the Padishah beheld the wondrously beautiful child, he longed to clasp him to his breast, and commanded those about him to inquire of the child where he came from.

Then one of the courtiers went up to the youth, and said, "You have shot much game there, my Bey!"

"Allah also has created much," replied the youth, "and there is enough for you and for me also," and with that he left him like a blockhead.

But the Padishah went back to his palace and was sick at heart because of the boy, and when they asked what ailed him, he said that he had seen such a wondrously beautiful child in the forest, and that he loved him so that he could rest no more. The boy had the very golden hair and the same radiant forehead that his wife had promised him.

The evil old woman was very afraid at these words. She hurried to the stream, saw the house, peeped in, and there sat a lovely girl, like a moon fourteen days old. The girl treated the old woman courteously and asked her what she sought. The old woman did not wait to be asked twice. Indeed, her

Tales of the Meddahs: Tales from the Turkish tradition

foot was scarce across the threshold when she began to ask the girl with honey-sweet words whether she lived all alone.

"No, my mother," replied the girl. "I have a young brother. In the daytime he goes hunting, and in the evening he comes home."

"Don't you grow weary of being all alone here by yourself?" inquired the witch.

"If even I did," said the girl, "what can I do? I must fill up my time as best I may."

"Tell me now, my little diamond, do you dearly love this brother of yours?"

"Of course, I do."

"Well, then, my girl," said the witch, "I'll tell you something, but don't let it go any further! When your brother comes home this evening, fall to weeping and wailing, and keep it up with all of your strength. When he asks what ails you, do not answer him, and when he asks you again, again give him never a word. When, however, he asks you a third time, say that you are tired to death with staying at home here all by yourself, and that if he loves you, he will go to the garden of the Queen of the Peris, and bring you from there a branch. A lovelier branch you have never seen all your life long." The girl promised she would do this, and the old woman went away.

Towards evening the damsel burst forth weeping and wailing till both her eyes were as red as blood. The brother came home in the evening and was amazed to see his sister in such dire distress, yet he could not prevail upon her to tell him the cause of it. He promised her all the grass of the field and all the trees of the forest if she would only tell him what the matter was, and, to satisfy the desire of his sister's heart, the golden-haired youth set off next morning for the garden of the fairy queen. He went on and on, smoking his chibouk and drinking coffee, till he reached the boundaries of the fairy realm. He came to deserts where no caravan had ever gone. He came to mountains where no bird could ever fly. He came to valleys where no serpent can ever crawl. But his trust was in Allah, so he went on and on till he came to an immense desert which the eye of man had never seen, nor the foot of

253

Tales of the Meddahs: Tales from the Turkish tradition

man trodden. In the midst of it was a beautiful palace, and by the roadside sat the Mother of Devils, and the smell of her was pestilence in the air all about her.

The youth went straight up to the Mother of Devils, hugged her to his breast, kissed her all over, and said, "Good-day, little mother mine! I am your own true lad till death!" and he kissed her hand.

"A good day to you also, my little son!" replied the Mother of Devils. "If you had not called me your dear little mother, if you had not embraced me, and if your innocent mother had not been under the earth, I would have devoured you at once. But tell me now, my little son, where are you going?"

The poor youth said that he wanted a branch from the garden of the Queen of the Peris.

"Who put that word in your mouth, my little son?" asked the woman in amazement. "Hundreds and hundreds of talismans guard that garden, and hundreds of souls have perished there by reason of it."

Yet the youth did not hold back. "I can only die once," he thought.

"You go to salute your innocent, buried mother," said the old woman, and then she made the youth sit down beside her and taught him the way. "Set out on your quest at daybreak, and never stop till you see right in front of you a well and a forest. Draw forth your arrows in this forest and catch five to ten birds but catch them alive. Take these birds to the well, and when you have recited a prayer twice over, plunge the birds into the well and cry aloud for a key. A key will straightway be cast out of the well. Take it and go on your way. You will come presently to a large cavern. Open the door with your key, and, as soon as your foot is inside, stretch out your right hand into the blank darkness, grip fast of whatever your hand touches, drag the thing quickly out, and cast the key back into the well again. But never look behind you, or Allah have mercy on your soul!"

Next day, when the red dawn was in the sky, the youth went forth on his quest, caught the five to ten birds in the forest, got hold of the key, opened the door of the cavern. He stretched out his right hand, gripped hold of

Tales of the Meddahs: Tales from the Turkish tradition

something, and, without once looking behind him, dragged it all the way to his sister's hut, and never stopped till he got there. Only then did he cast his eyes upon what he had in his hand, and it was neither more nor less than a branch from the garden of the Queen of the Peris. But what a branch it was! It was full of little twigs, and the twigs were full of little leaves, and there was a little bird on every little leaf, and every little bird had a song of its own. Such music, such melody was there as would have brought even a dead man to life again. The whole hut was filled with joy.

Next day the youth again went forth to hunt, and, as he was pursuing the beasts of the forest, the Padishah saw him again. He exchanged a word or two with the youth, and then returned to his palace, but he was now sicker than ever, by reason of his love for his son.

Then the evil old woman strolled off to the hut again, and there she saw the damsel sitting with the magic branch in her hand. "Well, my girl!" said the old woman. "What did I tell you? But that's nothing at all. If your brother would only fetch you the mirror of the Queen of the Peris, Allah knows that you would cast that branch right away. Give him no peace till he gets it for you."

The witch had no sooner departed than the damsel began screaming and wailing so that her brother was at his wit's end how to comfort her. He said he would take the whole world on his shoulders to please her and went straight off to the Mother of Devils. He begged advice of her so earnestly that she had not the heart to deny his questions.

"You have made up your mind to go under the sod to your innocent, buried mother, I see," cried she, "for not by hundreds but by thousands have human souls perished in this quest of yours."

Then she instructed the youth where he should go and what he should do, and he set off on his way. He took an iron staff in his hand and tied iron sandals to his feet, and he went on and on till he came to two doors, as the Mother of Devils told him he would beforehand. One of these doors was open, the other was closed. He closed the open door and opened the closed

Tales of the Meddahs: Tales from the Turkish tradition

door, and there, straight before him, was another door. In front of this door was a lion and a sheep, and there was grass before the lion and flesh before the sheep. He took up the flesh and laid it before the lion, then he took up the grass and laid it before the sheep, and they let him enter unharmed. But now he came to a third door, and in front of it were two furnaces, and fire burned in the one and ashes smouldered in the other. He put out the flaming furnace, stirred up the cinders in the smouldering furnace till they blazed again, and then through the door he went into the garden of the Peris, and from the garden into the Peri palace. He snatched up the enchanted mirror and was hurrying away with it when a mighty voice cried out against him so that the earth and the heavens trembled.

"Burning furnace, seize him, seize him!" cried the voice, just as he came up to the furnace.

"I can't," answered the first furnace, "for he has put me out!" But the other furnace was grateful to him for kindling it into a blaze again, so it let him pass by too.

"Lion, lion, tear him to pieces!" cried the mighty voice from the depths of the palace, when the youth came up to the two beasts.

"Not I," answered the lion, "for he helped me to a good meal of flesh!"

Nor would the sheep hurt him either, because he had given it the grass.

"Open door! Do not let him out!" cried the voice from within the palace.

"Nay, but I will!" replied the door, "for had he not opened me I should still be closed!"

All told, the golden-haired youth was not very long in getting home to the great joy of his sister. She snatched at the mirror and instantly looked into it, and, Allah be praised, she saw the whole world in it. Then the damsel thought no more of the Peri's branch, for her eyes were glued to the mirror.

Once again, the youth went hunting, and again he caught the eye of the Padishah. But the sight of the youth this third time so touched the Padishah's

Tales of the Meddahs: Tales from the Turkish tradition

fatherly heart that his men carried him back to his palace half fainting. Then the witch guessed only too well how matters stood.

So, she arose and went to the damsel, and so filled her foolish little head with her tales that she persuaded her not to give her brother rest day and night till he had brought her the Queen of the Peris herself. "That'll make him break his hatchet anyhow!" thought the old woman. But the damsel rejoiced beforehand at the thought of having the Queen of the Peris also, and in her impatience could scarce wait for her brother to come home.

When her brother came home, she shed as many tears as if she were a cloud dripping rain. In vain her brother tried to prove to her how distant and how dangerous was the way she would have him go.

"I want the Queen of the Peris, and have her I must," cried the damsel.

The youth set out on his journey, went straight to the Mother of Devils, pressed her hand, kissed her lips, pressed her lips and kissed her hand, and said, "Oh, my mother! Help me in this my sore need!" The Mother of Devils was amazed at the valour of the man, and never ceased dissuading him from his purpose, for every human soul that goes on such a quest must needs perish.

"Die I may, little mother," cried the youth, "but I will not come back without her."

What could the Mother of Devils do but show him the way. "Go the same road," said she, "that led you to the branch, and then go on to where you found the mirror. You will come at last to a large desert, and beyond the desert you will see two roads, but look neither to the right hand nor yet to the left but go right on through the sooty darkness between them. When it begins to grow a little lighter, you will see a large cypress wood, and in this cypress wood a large tomb. In this tomb, turned to stone, are all those who ever desired the Queen of the Peris. Do not stop there but go right on to the palace of the Queen of the Peris and call out her name with the full strength of your lungs. What will happen to you after that not even I can tell you."

257

Tales of the Meddahs: Tales from the Turkish tradition

Next day the youth set out on his journey. He prayed by the wayside well, opened all the gates he came to, and, looking neither to the right hand nor to the left, went on straight before him through the sooty darkness. All at once it began to grow a little lighter, and a large cypress wood appeared right in front of him. The leaves of the trees were of a burning green, and their drooping crowns hid snow-white tomb, but they were not tombs, but stones as big as men. In fact, they were not stones at all, but men who had turned, who had stiffened, into stone. There was neither man, nor spirit, nor noise, nor breath of wind, and the youth froze with horror to his very marrow. Nevertheless, he plucked up his courage and went on his way. He looked straight before him all the time, and his eyes were almost blinded by a dazzling light. Was it the sun he saw? No, it was the palace of the Queen of the Peris! Then he rallied all the strength that was left in him and shouted the name of the Queen of the Peris with all his might, and the words had not yet died away upon his lips when his whole body up to his kneecap stiffened into stone. Again, he shouted with all his might, and he turned to stone up to his navel. Then he shouted for the last time with all his might and stiffened up to his throat first and then up to his head, till he became a tombstone like the rest.

But now the Queen of the Peris came into her garden, and she had silver sandals on her feet and a golden saucer in her hand, and she drew water from a diamond fountain, and when she watered the stone youth, life and motion came back to him.

"Well," said the Queen of the Peris, "It's not enough, then, that you have taken away my Peri branch and my magic mirror! It seems that you must venture here a third time! You shall share the fate of your innocent buried mother. Stone you shall become, and stone shall you remain. What brought you here? Speak!"

"I came for you," replied the youth very courageously.

"Well, as you have loved me so exceedingly, no harm shall befall you, and we will go away together."

258

Tales of the Meddahs: Tales from the Turkish tradition

Then the youth begged her to have compassion on all the men she had turned to stone and give them back their lives again. The Peri returned to her palace, packed up her baggage, which was small in weight but priceless in value, filled the little golden saucer with water, and sprinkled it on all the stones and the whole multitude of the stones became men. They all took horse, and as they quitted the Peri realm, the earth trembled beneath them and the sky was shaken as if the seven worlds and the seven heavens were mingled together, so that the youth would have died of fright if the Queen of the Peris had not been by his side. Never once did they look behind them, but galloped on and on till they came to the house of the youth's sister, and such was their joy and gladness at seeing each other again that room could scarce be found for the Queen of the Peris. But now the youth was in no great hurry to go hunting as before, for he had changed hearts with the lovely Queen of the Peris, and she was his and he was hers.

Now when the Queen of the Peris had heard the history of the children and their parents, and the fate of their innocent mother, she said one morning to the youth, "Go hunting in the forest, and you will meet the Padishah. The first thing he will do will be to invite you to the palace but beware lest you accept his invitation."

And so indeed it turned out. Scarcely had he taken a turn in the wood than the Padishah stood before him, and, one word leading to another, he invited the youth to his palace, but the youth would not go.

Early next morning the Peri awoke the children, clapped her hands together and called her Lala, and immediately a huge servant sprang up before them. "What do you command of me, my Sultana?" cried the Lala.

"Fetch me here my father's steed!" commanded the Peri.

The efrit vanished like a hurricane, and a moment afterwards, the steed stood before them, and the like of it was not to be found in the wide world.

The youth leaped upon the horse, and the splendid suite of the Padishah was already waiting for him at the roadside.

Tales of the Meddahs: Tales from the Turkish tradition

But I have forgotten the best of the story. The Peri charged the youth as he quitted her to take heed, while he was in the palace of the Padishah, to the neighing of his horse. At the first neighing he was to hurry back. The youth went to meet the Padishah on his diamond-bridled charger, and behind him came a gay and gallant retinue. He saluted the people on the right hand and on the left all the way to the palace, and there they welcomed him with a pomp the like of which was never known before. They ate and drank and made merry till the Padishah could scarce contain himself for joy, but then the steed neighed, the youth arose, and all their entreaties to him to stay could not turn him from his set purpose. He mounted his horse, invited the Padishah to be his guest on the following day, and returned home to the Peri and his own sister.

Meanwhile the Peri dug up the mother of the children, and so put her to rights again by her Peri arts that she became just as she was in the days of her first youth. But she spoke not a word about the mother to the children, nor a word about the children to the mother. On the following morning she rose up early and commanded that on the spot where the little hut stood a palace should rise, the like of which eye has never seen nor ear heard of, and there were as many precious stones heaped up there as were to be found in the whole kingdom. In the the garden that surrounded that palace there were multitudes of flowers, each one lovelier than the other, and on every flower, there was a singing bird, and every bird had feathers aglow with light, so that one could only look at it all open-mouthed and cry, "Oh! Oh!" And the palace itself was full of domestics, there were harem slaves, and captive youths, and dancers and singers, and players of stringed instruments, more than you can count, and words cannot tell of the splendour of the retinue which went forth to greet the Padishah as a guest.

"These children are not of mortal birth!" thought the Padishah to himself, when he beheld all these marvels, "or if they are of mortal birth a Peri must have had a hand in the matter."

They led the Padishah into the most splendid room of the palace, they brought him coffee and sherbet, and then the music spoke to him, and the

260

Tales of the Meddahs: Tales from the Turkish tradition

Padishah could have listened to the singing birds for ever and ever! Then rich meats on rare and precious dishes were set before him, and then the dancers and the jugglers diverted him till the evening.

At eventide the servants came and bowed before the Padishah and said, "My lord! Peace be with you! They await you in the harem!" So, he entered the harem, and there he saw before him the golden-haired youth, with a beautiful half-moon shining on his forehead, and his bride, the Peri-Queen, and his own consort, the Sultana, who had been buried in the earth, and by her side a golden-haired maiden with a star sparkling on her forehead. The Padishah stood there as if turned to stone, but his consort ran up to him and kissed the edge of his garment, and the Peri-Queen began to tell him the whole of her life and how everything had happened.

The Padishah was near to dying in the fulness of his joy. He could scarce believe his eyes, but he pressed his consort to his breast and embraced the two beauteous children, and the Queen of the Peris likewise. He forgave the sisters of the Sultana their offences, but the old witch was mercilessly destroyed by lingering tortures. But he and his consort and her son and the Queen of the Peris, and his daughter, and his daughter's bridegroom sat down to a great banquet and made merry. Forty days and forty nights they feasted, and the blessing of Allah was upon them.

Tales of the Meddahs: Tales from the Turkish tradition

Tales of the Meddahs: Tales from the Turkish tradition

THE LANGUAGE OF BIRDS

This story has been adapted from Told in the Coffee House by Cyrus Adler and Allan Ramsay, published in 1898 by MacMillan and Company, London. Allan Ramsay was a Scottish poet, playwright, publisher, librarian and wig-maker active in the early and mid-eighteenth century. Cyrus Adler adapted Ramsay's work in the nineteenth century, being an American educator, Jewish religious leader and scholar.

There once lived a Hodja who, it was said, understood the language of birds, but refused to impart his knowledge. One young man was very persistent in his desire to know the language of these sweet creatures, but the Hodja was inflexible.

In despair, the young man went to the woods at least to listen to the pleasant chirping of the birds. By degrees it conveyed to him a meaning, till, finally, he understood that the birds were telling him that his horse would die. On returning from the woods, he immediately sold his horse and went and told the Hodja.

"Oh Hodja, why will you not teach me the language of birds? Yesterday I went to the woods, and they warned me that my horse would die, thus affording me an opportunity of selling it and avoiding the loss."

The Hodja was silent but would not give way.

The following day the young man again went to the woods, and the chirping of the birds told him that his house would be burned. The young man hurried

Tales of the Meddahs: Tales from the Turkish tradition

away, sold his house, and again went to the Hodja and told him all that had happened, adding, "See, Hodja Effendi, you would not teach me the language of the birds, but I have saved my horse and my house by listening to them."

On the following day, the young man again went to the woods, and the birds chirped him the doleful tale, that on the following day he would die. In tears the young man went to the Hodja for advice.

"Oh Hodja Effendi! Alas! What am I to do? The birds have told me that tomorrow I must die."

"My son," answered the Hodja, "I knew this would come, and that is why I refused to teach you the language of birds. Had you borne the loss of your horse, your house would have been saved, and had your house been burned, your life would have been saved."

Tales of the Meddahs: Tales from the Turkish tradition

THE SWALLOW'S ADVICE

This story has been adapted from Told in the Coffee House by Cyrus Adler and Allan Ramsay, published in 1898 by MacMillan and Company, London. Allan Ramsay was a Scottish poet, playwright, publisher, librarian and wigmaker active in the early and mid-eighteenth century. Cyrus Adler adapted Ramsay's work in the nineteenth century, being an American educator, Jewish religious leader and scholar.

A man one day saw a swallow and caught it. The bird pleaded hard for liberty, saying, "If you will let me go, your gain will be great, for I will give you three counsels that will hereafter be of use to you."

The man listened to the bird and let it go. Flying to a tree close by it perched on a branch, and said, "Listen and give your ear to the three pieces of advice that will guide you. The first is, do not believe things that are incredible, the second is, do not attempt to stretch out your hand to a place you are unable to reach, and the third advice I give you is, do not pine after a thing that is past and gone. Take these my counsels and do not forget them."

The bird then tempted the man, saying, "Inside of me there is a large pearl of great value. It is both magnificent and splendid, and as large as the egg of a kite."

Now, hearing this, the man repented at having let the bird go, the colour of his face went to sadness, and he at once stretched out his hand to catch the swallow, but the latter said to the foolish man, "What! Have you already forgotten the advice I gave you, and the lie which I told you, have you

Tales of the Meddahs: Tales from the Turkish tradition

considered as true? I had fallen into your hands, yet you were unable to retain me, and now you are sorrowing for the past for which there is no remedy."

Such are those that worship idols and give the name of God to their own handiwork. They have left aside God Almighty and have forgotten the Great Bestower of all good gifts.

Tales of the Meddahs: Tales from the Turkish tradition

MAD MEHMED

This story has been adapted from Turkish Fairy Tales and Folk Tales by Dr. Ignácz Kúnos, published in 1901 by A. H. Bullen, London.

Once upon a time in the old old days when the camel was only a spy, when toads rose in the air on wings, and I myself rode in the air while I walked on the ground and went up hill and down dale at the same time, in those days, I say, there were two brothers who dwelt together.

All that they had inherited from their father were some oxen and other beasts, and a sick mother. One day the spirit of division seized upon the younger brother, and he went to his brother and said, "Look now, brother, at these two stables! One of them is as new as new can be, while the other is old and rotten. Let us drive our cattle here, and whatever goes into the new stable shall be mine, and all the rest shall be yours."

"Not so, Mehmed," said the elder brother, "let whatever goes into the old stable be yours!"

To this also the half-crazy Mehmed agreed. That same day they went and drove up their cattle, and all the cattle went into the new stable except a helpless old ox that was so blind that it mistook its way and went into the old stable instead. Mehmed said never a word. He took the blind old ox into the fields to graze early every morning, and late every evening he drove it back again. One day when he was on the road, the wind began to shake a big wayside tree so violently that its vast branches whined and whimpered again.

267

Tales of the Meddahs: Tales from the Turkish tradition

"Hi! Whimpering old dad!" said the fool to the tree, "Have you seen my elder brother?"

But the tree, as if it didn't hear, only went on whining. The fool flew into such a rage at this that he caught up his chopper and struck at the tree, when out of it gushed a whole stream of golden sequins. At this the fool rallied what little wits he had, hastened home, and asked his brother to lend him another ox, as he wanted to plough with a pair. He found a cart and some empty sacks. These he filled with earth and set out forthwith for his tree. There he emptied his sacks of their earth, filled them with sequins instead, and when he returned home in the evening, his brother well-nigh dropped down for amazement at the sight of the monstrous treasure.

They could think of nothing now but dividing it, so the younger brother went to their neighbour for a three-peck measure to measure it with. Now the neighbour was curious to know what such clodpoles could have to measure. So, he took and smeared the bottom of the measure with tar, and, sure enough, when the fool brought the measure back a short time afterwards, a sequin was sticking to the bottom of it. The neighbour immediately went and told it to another, who went and told it to a third, and so it was not long before everybody knew all about it.

Now the wiser brother did not know what might happen to them now that they had all this money, and he began to feel frightened. So, he snatched up his pick and shovel, dug a trench, buried the treasure, and made off as fast as his heels could carry him. On the way it occurred to the wise brother that he had done foolishly in not shutting the door of the hut behind him, so he sent off his younger brother to do it for him. The fool went back to the house, and he thought to himself, "Well, since I am here, I ought not to forget my old mother either." So, he filled a huge cauldron with water, boiled it, and soused his old mother in it so thoroughly that her poor old head was never likely to speak again. After that he propped the old woman against the wall with the broom, tore the door off its hinges, threw it over his shoulders, and went and rejoined his brother in the wood.

Tales of the Meddahs: Tales from the Turkish tradition

The elder brother looked at the door and listened to the sad case of his poor old mother, but scold and chide his younger brother as he might the latter grew more cock-a-hoop than ever, for he fancied he had done such a clever thing. He had brought the door away with him, he said, in order that no one might get into the house. The wise brother would have given anything to have got rid of the fool and began turning over in his mind how he might best manage it. He looked before him and behind him, and then he looked down the high-road, and there were three horsemen galloping along. The thought instantly occurred to the pair of them that these horsemen were on their track, so they scrambled up a tree forthwith, door and all. They were scarcely comfortably settled when the three horsemen drove up beneath the tree and encamped there. The dusk of evening had come on at the very nick of time, so that they could not see the two brothers in the tree.

Now the two brothers would have done very well indeed up in the tree had not one of them been a fool. Mehmed the fool began to practise pleasantries which disturbed the repose of the horsemen beneath the tree. Presently, however, came a crash and down on the heads of the three sleepers fell the great heavy door from the top of the tree.

"The end of the world has come, the end of the world has come!" cried they, and they rushed off in such a fright that no doubt they haven't ceased running to this very day. This finished the business so far as the elder brother was concerned. In the morning he arose and went on his way and left the foolish younger brother by himself.

Thus, poor silly Mehmed had to go forth into the wide world alone. He went on and on till he came to a village, by which time he was very hungry. There he stood in the gate of a mosque and got one or two paras from those who went in and out till he had enough to buy himself something to eat. At that moment a fat little man came out of the mosque, and casting his eyes on Mehmed, asked him if he would like to enter his service.

"I don't mind if I do," replied Mehmed, "but only on condition that neither of us is to get angry with the other for any cause whatever. If you are angry with me, I'll kill you, and if I get angry with you, then you may kill me also."

269

Tales of the Meddahs: Tales from the Turkish tradition

The fat man agreed to these terms, for there was a great lack of servants in that village.

In order to make short work of the fat little man the fool began by at once chasing all the hens and sheep off his master's premises. "Are you angry, master?" he then inquired of his lord. His master was amazed, but he only answered, "Angry? Not I! Why should I be?" At the same time, he entrusted nothing more to Mehmed, and let him sit in the house without anything to do.

His master had a wife and child, and Mehmed had to look after them. He liked to dandle the child up and down, but he knocked it about and hurt it, so clumsy was he, so he soon had to leave that off. But the wife began to be afraid that her turn would come next, sooner or later, so she persuaded her husband to run away from the fool one night. Mehmed overheard what they said, hid himself in their store-box, and when they opened it in the next village, out he popped.

After a while his master and his wife agreed together that they would go and sleep at night on the shores of a lake. They took Mehmed with them, and put his bed right on the water's edge, that he might tumble in when he went to sleep. However, the fool was not such a fool but that he made his master's wife jump into the lake instead of himself.

"Are you angry, master?" cried he.

"Angry indeed! How can I help being angry when I see my property wasted, and my wife and child killed, and myself a beggar, and all through you!"

Then the fool seized his master, put him in mind of their compact, and pitched him into the water.

Mehmed now found himself all alone, so he went forth into the wide world once more. He went on and on. He did nothing but drink sweet coffee, smoke chibouks, look about over his shoulder, and walk leisurely along at his ease. As he was knocking about, he chanced to light upon a five-para piece, which he speedily changed for some lebleb (roasted chickpeas), which he immediately fell to chewing, and, as he chewed, part of it fell into a wayside

Tales of the Meddahs: Tales from the Turkish tradition

spring, whereupon the fool began roaring loud enough to split his throat, shouting, "Give me back my lebleb, give me back my lebleb!"

At this frightful bawling a Jinn popped up his head, and he was so big that his head swept the sky, while his feet hid the earth. "What do you require?" asked the Jinn.

"I want my lebleb, I want my lebleb!" cried Mehmed.

The Jinn ducked down into the spring, and when he came up again, he held a little table in his hand. This little table he gave to the fool and said, "Whenever you are hungry you have only to say, 'Little table, give me something to eat', and when you have eaten your fill, say, 'Little table, I have now had enough.'"

So, Mehmed took the table and went with it into a village, and when he felt hungry, he said, "Little table, give me something to eat!" and immediately there stood before him so many beautiful, nice dishes that he couldn't make up his mind which to begin with. "Well," thought he, "I must let the poor people of the village see this wonder also," so he went and invited them all to a great banquet.

The villagers came one after another. They looked to the right, they looked to the left, but there was no sign of a fire, or any preparations for a meal. "No, but he would needs make fools of us!" thought they. But the young man brought out his table, set it in the midst, and cried, "Little table, give me something to eat!" and there before them stood all manner of delicious meats and drinks, and so much of it that when the guests had stuffed themselves to the very throat, there was enough left over to fill the servants.

Then the villagers made plans to see how they might manage to have a meal like this every day. "Come now!" said some of them, "let us steal a march upon Mehmed one day and lay hands upon his table, and then there will be an end to the fool's glory." And they did so.

What could the poor, empty-bellied fool do then? Why he went to the wayside spring and asked again, "I want my lebleb, I want my lebleb!" And he asked and asked so long that at last the Jinn popped up his head again out

Tales of the Meddahs: Tales from the Turkish tradition

of the spring and inquired what was the matter. "I want my lebleb, I want my lebleb!" cried the fool.

"But where's your little table?"

"They stole it."

The Jinn again popped down, and when he rose out of the spring again, he had a little mill in his hand. This he gave to the fool and said to him, "Grind it to the right and gold will flow out of it, grind it to the left and it will give you silver."

So, the youth took the mill home and ground it first to the right and then to the left, and huge treasures of gold and silver lay heaped about him on the floor. He grew to become such a rich man that his equal was not to be found in the village, nor in the town either.

But no sooner had the people of the village got to know all about the little mill than they laid their heads together and schemed and schemed till the mill also disappeared one fine morning from Mehmed's cottage. Then Mehmed ran off to the spring once more and cried, "I want my lebleb, I want my lebleb!"

"But where is your little table? Where is your little mill?" asked the Jinn.

"They have stolen them both from me," lamented the witless one, and he wept bitterly.

Again, the Jinn bobbed down, and this time he brought up two sticks with him. He gave them to the fool and impressed upon him very strongly on no account to say, 'Strike, strike, my little sticks!"

Mehmed took the sticks, and first he turned them to the right and then to the left but could make nothing of them. Then he thought he would just try the effect of saying, 'Strike, strike, my little sticks!" and no sooner were the words out of his mouth than the sticks fell upon him unmercifully and hit him on every part of the body that can feel till he was nothing but one big ache.

Tales of the Meddahs: Tales from the Turkish tradition

"Stop, stop, my little sticks!" cried he, and the two sticks were still. Then, for all his aches and pains, Mehmed rejoiced greatly that he had found out the mystery.

He had no sooner got home with the two sticks than he called together all the villagers, but he said nothing about what he meant to do. In less than a couple of hours everybody had assembled there and awaited the new show with great curiosity. Then Mehmed came with his two sticks and cried, "Strike, strike, my little sticks, strike, strike!" whereupon the two sticks gave the whole lot of them such a rub-a-dub-dubbing that it was as much as they could do to howl for mercy.

"Now," said Mehmed, who was getting his wits back again, "I'll have no mercy till you have given back to me my little table and my little mill."

The people of the village, all bruised and bleeding as they were, consented to everything, and hurried off for the little table and the little mill. Then Mehmed cried, "Stand still, my little sticks!" and there was peace and quiet as before.

Then the man took away the three gifts to his own village, and as he now had money, he grew more sensible, and there also he found his brother. He gave all the buried treasure to his brother, and each of them sought out a damsel to be a wife, and married, and lived each in a world of his own. And there was not a wiser man in that village than Mad Mehmed now that he had grown rich.

Tales of the Meddahs: Tales from the Turkish tradition

Tales of the Meddahs: Tales from the Turkish tradition

WE KNOW NOT WHAT THE DAWN MAY BRING FORTH

This story has been adapted from Told in the Coffee House by Cyrus Adler and Allan Ramsay, published in 1898 by MacMillan and Company, London. Allan Ramsay was a Scottish poet, playwright, publisher, librarian and wig-maker active in the early and mid-eighteenth century. Cyrus Adler adapted Ramsay's work in the nineteenth century, being an American educator, Jewish religious leader and scholar.

In the age of the Janissaries the Minister of War, in all haste, called the chief farrier of the Army and ordered him to have made immediately two hundred thousand horseshoes. The farrier was aghast and explained that to make such a quantity of horseshoes, both time and smiths would be required. The Minister replied, "It is the order of his Majesty that these two hundred thousand horseshoes be ready by tomorrow, and if not, your head will pay the penalty."

The poor farrier replied, that knowing now that he was doomed, he would be unable, through nervousness, to make even a fifth of the number. The Minister would not listen to reason, and left in anger, reiterating the order of his Majesty.

The farrier retired to his rooms deeply dejected. His wife, woman-like, endeavoured to encourage and comfort him, saying, "Cheer up, husband, drink your raki, eat your mézé, and be cheerful, for we know not what the dawn may bring forth."

Tales of the Meddahs: Tales from the Turkish tradition

"Ah!" said the farrier, "The dawn will not bring forth two hundred thousand horseshoes, and my head will pay the penalty."

Late that night there was a tremendous knocking at his door. The poor farrier thought that it was an inquiry as to how many horseshoes were already made, and trembling with fear went and opened the door. What was his surprise, when on opening the door and inquiring the object of the visit, he was greeted with, "Haste, farrier, let us have sixteen nails, for the Minister of War has been suddenly removed to Paradise by the hand of Allah."

The farrier gathered, not sixteen but forty nails of the best he had, and handing them to the messenger, said, "Nail him down well, friend, so that he will not get up again, for had this not happened, the nails would have been required to keep me in my coffin."

Tales of the Meddahs: Tales from the Turkish tradition

OLD MEN MADE YOUNG

This story has been adapted from Told in the Coffee House by Cyrus Adler and Allan Ramsay, published in 1898 by MacMillan and Company, London. Allan Ramsay was a Scottish poet, playwright, publisher, librarian and wig-maker active in the early and mid-eighteenth century. Cyrus Adler adapted Ramsay's work in the nineteenth century, being an American educator, Jewish religious leader and scholar.

In Psamatia, an ancient Armenian village situated near the Seven Towers, there lived a certain smith, whose custom it was, in contradiction to prescribed rules, to curse the devil and his works regularly five times a day instead of praying to God. He argued that it is the devil's fault that man had need to pray. The devil was angered at being thus persistently cursed, and decided to punish the smith, or at least prevent his causing further trouble.

Taking the form of a young man he went to the smith and engaged himself as an apprentice. After a time, the devil told the smith that he had a very poor and mean way of earning a living, and that he would show him how money was to be made. The smith asked what he, a young apprentice, could do. Thereupon the devil told him that he was endowed with a great gift. He had the power to make old men young again. Though incredulous, after continued assurance the smith allowed a sign to be put above his door, stating that aged people could here be restored to youth. This extraordinary sign attracted a great many, but the devil asked such high prices that most went away, preferring age to parting with so much money.

Tales of the Meddahs: Tales from the Turkish tradition

At last, one old man agreed to pay the sum demanded by the devil, whereupon he was promptly cast into the furnace, the master-smith blowing the bellows for a small remuneration. After a time of vigorous blowing the devil raked out a young man. The fame of the smith extended far and wide, and many were the aged that came to regain their youth. This lucrative business went on for some time, and at last the smith, thinking to himself that it was not a difficult thing to throw a man into the furnace and rake him out from the ashes restored to youth, decided to do away with his apprentice's services, but kept the sign above the door.

It happened that the captain of the Janissaries, who was a very aged man, came to him, and after bargaining for a much more modest sum than his apprentice would have asked, the smith thrust him into the furnace as the devil, his apprentice, used to do, and worked at the bellows. He afterwards raked in the fire for the young man, but he only raked out cinders and ashes. Great was his consternation, but what could he do?

The devil in the meantime went to the head of the Janissaries and the police and informed them of what had taken place. The poor smith was arrested, tried, and condemned to be bowstrung, as it was proved that the Janissary was last seen to enter his shop.

Just as the smith was about to be executed, the devil again appeared before him in the form of the discharged apprentice, and asked him if he wished to be saved? If so, he said that he could save him, but only on one condition - that he ceased from cursing the devil five times a day, snd instead should pray as other Muslims prayed. He agreed. Thereupon the apprentice called in a loud voice to those who were about to execute him, "What do you want with this man? He has not killed the Janissary. He is not dead, for I have just seen him entering his home." This was found to be true, and the smith was liberated, learning the truth of the proverb, 'Curse not even the devil.'

Tales of the Meddahs: Tales from the Turkish tradition

THE ROSE-BEAUTY

This story has been adapted from Turkish Fairy Tales and Folk Tales by Dr. Ignácz Kúnos, published in 1901 by A. H. Bullen, London.

Once upon a time in the old old days when straws were sieves, and the camel a chapman, and the mouse a barber, and the cuckoo a tailor, and the donkey ran errands, and the tortoise baked bread, and I was only fifteen years old, but my father rocked my cradle, and there was a miller in the land who had a black cat - in those olden times, I say, there was a King who had three daughters, and the first daughter was forty, and the second was thirty, and the third was twenty. One day the youngest daughter wrote this letter to her father:

"My lord Father! My eldest sister is forty and my second sister is thirty, and still you have given neither of them a husband. I have no desire to grow grey in waiting for a husband."

The King read the letter, sent for his three daughters, and addressed them in these words, "Look now! Let each one of you shoot an arrow from a bow and seek her sweetheart wherever her arrow falls!"

So, the three damsels took their bows. The eldest damsel's arrow fell into the palace of the Vizier's son, so the Vizier's son took her to wife. The second girl's arrow flew into the palace of the Chief Mufti's son, so they gave her to him. The third damsel also fired her arrow, and it stuck in the hut of a poor young labourer.

Tales of the Meddahs: Tales from the Turkish tradition

"That won't do, that won't do!" They all cried. So, she fired again, and again the arrow stuck in the hut. She aimed a third time, and a third time the arrow stuck in the hut of the poor young labourer. Then the King was angry and cried to the damsel, "Look now, you slut! You have got your deserts. Your sisters waited patiently, and therefore they have got their hearts' desires. You were the youngest of all, yet it was you who wrote me that saucy letter, hence your punishment. Out of my sight, you slave-girl, to this husband of yours, and you shall have nought but what he can give you!" So, the poor damsel departed to the hut of the labourer, and they gave her to him as his wife.

They lived together for a time, and on the tenth day of the ninth month the time came that she should bear a child, and her husband, the labourer, hurried away for the midwife. While the husband was away his wife had neither a bed to lie down upon nor a fire to warm herself by, though grinding winter was upon them. All at once the walls of the poor hut opened here and there, and three beautiful damsels of the Peri race stepped into it. One stood at the damsel's head, another at her feet, the third by her side, and they all seemed to know their business well. In a moment everything in the poor hut was in order, the princess lay on a beautiful soft couch, and before she could blink her eyes a pretty little new-born baby girl was lying by her side.

When everything was finished the three Peris were about to leave, but first of all they approached the bed one by one, and the first said, "Rosa is your daughter's name, and she shall weep pearls instead of tears!"

The second Peri approached the bed and said, "Rosa is your daughter's name, and the rose shall blossom when she smiles!"

And the third Peri wound up with these words, "Rosa is your daughter's name, and sweet verdure in her footsteps spring!"

As she finished speaking all three disappeared.

Now all this time the husband was seeking a midwife but could not find one anywhere. What could he do but go home? But when he got back, he was amazed to find everything in the poor hut in beautiful order, and his wife

Tales of the Meddahs: Tales from the Turkish tradition

lying on a splendid bed. Then she told him the story of the three Peris, and there was no more spirit left in him, so astounded was he. But the little girl grew more and more lovely from hour into day, and from day to week, so that there was not another like her in the whole world. Whoever looked upon her lost his heart at once, and pearls fell from her eyes when she wept, roses burst into bloom when she smiled, and a bright riband of fresh green verdure followed her footsteps. Whosoever saw her had no more spirit left in him, and the fame of lovely Rosa went from mouth to mouth.

At last, the King of that land also heard of the damsel, and instantly made up his mind that she and nobody else should be his son's consort. He sent for his son and told him that there was a damsel in the town of so rare a beauty that pearls fell from her eyes when she wept, roses burst into bloom when she smiled, and the earth grew fresh and green beneath her footsteps, and with that he bade him up and woo her.

Now the Peris had for a long time shown the King's son the beautiful Rose-damsel in his dreams, and the sweet fire of love already burned within him, but he was ashamed to let his father see this, so he hung back a little. At this his father became more and more pressing, urging him to go and woo her at once, and he commanded the chief dame of the palace to accompany his son to the labourer's hut. They entered the hut, said on what errand they came, and claimed the damsel for the King's son in the name of Allah. The poor folks rejoiced at their good luck, promised the girl, and began to make ready.

Now this palace dame's daughter was also a beauty, and not unlike Rosa. The palace dame was terribly distressed that the King's son should take to wife a poor labourer's daughter, instead of her own child, so she made up her mind to deceive them and put her own daughter in Rosa's place. On the day of the banquet, she made the poor girl eat many salted meats, and then brought a pitcher of water and a large basket, got into the bridal coach with Rosa and her own daughter, and set out for the palace. As they were on the long road the damsel grew thirsty and asked the palace dame for some water.

"Not till you have given me one of your eyes," said the palace dame.

Tales of the Meddahs: Tales from the Turkish tradition

What could the poor damsel do? She was dying with thirst. So, she cut out one of her eyes and gave it the palace dame in exchange for a drink of water.

They went on and on, further and further, and the damsel again became thirsty and asked for another drink of water. "You shall have it if you give me your other eye," said the palace dame. And the poor damsel was so tormented with thirst that she gave the other eye for a drink of water.

The old dame took the two eyes, pitched the sightless damsel into the big basket, and left her all alone on the top of a mountain. She put the beautiful bridal robe upon her own daughter, brought her to the King's son, and gave her to him with the words, "Behold your wife!"

They made a great banquet, and when they had brought the damsel to her bridegroom and taken off her veil, he saw that the damsel who now stood before him was not the damsel of his dreams. As, however, she resembled her a little he said nothing about it to anybody. They lay down to rest, and when they rose up again early next morning the King's son was quite sure that he had been deceived, for the damsel of his dreams had wept pearls, smiled roses, and sweet green herbs had grown up in her footsteps, but this girl had neither roses nor pearls nor green herbs to show for herself. The youth felt there was some trickery at work here. This was not the girl he had meant to have.

"How am I to find it all out?" He thought to himself, but not a word did he say to anyone.

While all these things were going on in the palace, poor Rosa was weeping on the mountain top, and so many pearls fell from her by dint of her sore weeping that there was scarce room to hold them all in the big basket. A mud-carrier happened to be passing by who was carting mud away, and hearing the weeping of the damsel was terribly afraid, and cried, "Who are you? A Jinn or a Peri?"

"I am neither a Jinn nor yet a Peri," replied the damsel, "but the remains of a living child of man."

Tales of the Meddahs: Tales from the Turkish tradition

The mud-raker took courage, opened the basket. He saw there a poor sightless damsel who was sobbing, and her tears fell from her in showers of pearls. He took the damsel by the hand and led her to his hut, and as the old man had nobody about him, he adopted the damsel as if she were his own child and took care of her. But the poor girl did nothing but weep for her two eyes, and the old man had all he could do to pick up the pearls, and whenever they were in want of money, he would take a pearl and sell it, and they lived on whatever he got for it.

Time passed, and there was mirth in the palace, and misery in the hut of the mud-raker. Now it chanced one day as fair Rosa was sitting in the hut, that something made her smile, and immediately a rose bloomed. Then the damsel said to her foster-father, the mud-raker, "Take this rose, papa, and take it to the palace of the King's son, and cry aloud that you have roses for sale that are not to be matched in the wide world. But if the dame of the palace comes out, see that you do not give her the rose for money, but say that you will sell it for a human eye."

The man took the rose and stood in front of the palace, and began to cry aloud, "A rose for sale, a rose for sale, the like of which is nowhere to be found." Now it was not the season for roses, so when the dame of the palace heard the man crying about a rose for sale, she thought to herself, "I'll put it in my daughter's hair, and then the King's son will think that she is his true bride." She called the poor man to her, and asked him what he would sell the rose for?

"For nothing," replied the man, "for no money told down, but I'll give it you for a human eye." Then the dame of the palace brought forth one of fair Rosa's eyes and gave it for the rose. Then she took it to her daughter, plaited it in her hair, and when the King's son saw the rose, he thought of the Peri of his dreams, but could not understand where she had gone. Nevertheless, he now fancied he was about to find out, so he said nothing to anyone.

Meanwhile, the old man went home with the eye and gave it to the damsel, fair Rosa. Then she fitted it in its right place, sighed from her heart in prayer to Allah, who can do all things. She could see right well again with her one

Tales of the Meddahs: Tales from the Turkish tradition

eye, and the poor girl was so pleased that she could not help smiling, and immediately another rose sprang forth. This also she gave to her father that he might walk in front of the palace and give it for another human eye. The old man took the rose, and scarcely had he begun crying before the palace when the old dame again heard him.

"He has just come at the nick of time," thought she. "The King's son has begun to love my rose-bedizened daughter. If I can only get this rose also, he will love her still better, and this serving-wench will go out of his mind altogether."

So, she called the mud-raker to her and asked for the rose, but again he would not take money for it, though he was willing to let her have it in exchange for a human eye. Then the old woman gave him the second eye, and the old man hastened home with it and gave it to the damsel. Rosa immediately put it in its proper place, prayed to Allah, and was so rejoiced when her two bright eyes sparkled with living light that she smiled for a whole day, and roses bloomed on every side of her. Henceforth she was lovelier than ever.

One day beautiful Rosa went for a walk, and as she smiled continually as she walked along, roses bloomed around her, and the ground grew fresh and green beneath her feet. The palace dame saw her and was terrified. What will become of me, she thought, if my treatment of this damsel comes to be known? She knew where the poor mud-scraper lived, so she went all alone to his dwelling, and terrified him by telling him that he had an evil witch in his house. The poor man had never seen a witch, so he was terrified to death, and asked the palace dame what he had better do.

"Find out, first of all, what her talisman is," advised the palace dame, "and then I'll come and do the rest."

The first thing the old man did when the damsel came home was to ask her how she, a mere child of man, had come to have such magic power. The damsel, suspecting no ill, said that she had got her talisman from the three Peris, and that pearls, roses, and fresh sweet verdure would accompany her so long as her talisman was alive.

Tales of the Meddahs: Tales from the Turkish tradition

"What then is your talisman?" asked the old man.

"A little deer on the hilltop. If it dies, then I'll also die," she answered.

The next day the palace dame came to the mud-raker's hut in the utmost misery, heard about the damsel's talisman from the mud-scraper, and hastened home with great joy. She told her daughter that on the top of the neighbouring hill was a little deer which she should ask her husband to get for her. That very same day the Sultana told her husband of the little deer on the top of the hill, and begged and implored him to get her its heart to eat. After a few days the Prince's men caught the little deer and killed it and took out its heart and gave it to the Sultana. At the same instant when they killed the little fawn fair Rosa died. The mud-raker sorrowed over her till he could sorrow no more, and then took her body and buried her.

Now in the heart of the little fawn there was a little red coral eye which nobody took any notice of. When the Sultana ate the heart, the little red coral eye fell out and rolled down the steps as if it wanted to hide itself.

Time went on, and in not more than nine months and ten days the Prince's consort was brought to bed of a little daughter, who wept pearls when she cried, dropped roses when she smiled, and sweet green herbs sprang up in her footsteps.

When the Prince saw it, he mused and mused over it. The little girl was the very image of fair Rosa, and not a bit like the mother who had borne her. His sleep offered him no rest, till one night fair Rosa appeared to him in his dreams and spoke these words to him, "Oh, my prince! Oh, my betrothed! My soul is beneath your palace steps, my body is in the tomb, your little girl is my little girl, my talisman is the little coral eye."

The Prince had no sooner awakened than he went to the staircase and searched about, and there was the little coral eye. He picked it up, took it into his chamber, and laid it on the table. Meanwhile, the little girl entered the room, saw the red coral, and scarcely had she laid hold of it than she vanished as if she had never been. The three Peris had carried off the child

Tales of the Meddahs: Tales from the Turkish tradition

and taken her to her mother's tomb, and scarcely had she placed the coral eye in the dead woman's mouth than she awoke up to a new life.

But the King's son was not easy in his mind. He went to the cemetery, had the tomb opened, and there in her coffin lay the Rose-beauty of his dreams, with her little girl in her arms and the coral talisman in her mouth. They arose from the tomb and embraced him, and pearls fell from the eyes of both of them as they wept, and roses from their mouths as they smiled, and sweet green herbs grew up in their footsteps.

The palace dame and her daughter paid for their crimes, but beautiful Rosa and her father and her mother, the Sultan's daughter, were all re-united, and for forty days and forty nights they held high revel amidst the beating of drums and the tinkling of cymbals.

Tales of the Meddahs: Tales from the Turkish tradition

THE BRIBE

This story has been adapted from Told in the Coffee House by Cyrus Adler and Allan Ramsay, published in 1898 by MacMillan and Company, London. Allan Ramsay was a Scottish poet, playwright, publisher, librarian and wig-maker active in the early and mid-eighteenth century. Cyrus Adler adapted Ramsay's work in the nineteenth century, being an American educator, Jewish religious leader and scholar.

There once lived in Istanbul a man and wife who were so well mated that though married for a number of years their life was one of ideal harmony. This troubled the devil very much. He had destroyed the peace of home after home. He had successfully created, between husband and wife, father and son and brothers, the chasm of envy wide and deep, so wide that the bridge of life could not span the gap. In this one little home alone did he fail in spite of his greatest endeavour. One day the devil was talking to an old woman, when the man who had thus far baffled him passed by. The devil groaned at the thought of his repeated failures. Turning to the old woman he said, "I will give you as a reward a pair of yellow slippers if you make that man quarrel with his wife."

The old woman was delighted, and at once began to scheme and work for the coveted slippers. At an hour when she was sure to find the lady alone, she went and solicited alms, weeping and bemoaning her sad fate at being a lonely old woman whose husband was long since dead. She appealed to the lady for such compassion as matched the happiness that the wife and husband enjoyed together. The lady was very generous to the old woman,

Tales of the Meddahs: Tales from the Turkish tradition

each day giving her something, so much so, that the thought that her good husband might think her extravagant often gave her some uneasiness.

One day the old woman called at the shop of her benefactress's husband and planted the first evil seed by calling out, "Ah, if men only knew where the money they work for from morning till night goes or knew what their wives did when they were away, some homes would not be so happy."

The evil woman then went her way, and the good shopman wondered why she had said these words to him. A passing thought suggested that it was strange that of late his wife had asked him several times for a few extra piasters. The next day, the old woman as usual solicited alms of her victim. In the fulness of her hypocrisy she embraced the young lady before departing, taking care to leave the imprint of her blackened hand on her dupe's back. The old woman then went to the shop again, looked at her victim's husband, and said, "Oh, how blind men are! They only look in a woman's face for truth and loyalty. They forget to look at the back where the stamp of the lover's hand is to be seen."

As before, the old woman disappeared. But the mind of the shopman was troubled, and his heart was heavy. In this oppressed state he went to his home, and an opportunity offering he looked at his wife's back and was aghast to see there the impression of a hand. He got up and left his home, a broken-hearted man.

The devil was deeply impressed at the signal success of the old woman and hastened to redeem his promise. He took a long pole, tied the pair of slippers at the end, and hurried off to the old woman. Arriving at her house he called out to her to open the window. When she did this, he thrust in the pair of yellow slippers, begging her to take them, but not to come near him, for they were hard-earned slippers, he said. She had succeeded where he had failed, and he was afraid of her and was anxious to keep out of her way.

Tales of the Meddahs: Tales from the Turkish tradition

THE THREE ORANGE-PERIS

This story has been adapted from Turkish Fairy Tales and Folk Tales by Dr. Ignácz Kúnos, published in 1901 by A. H. Bullen, London.

In the olden times, when there were sieves in straws and lies in everything, in the olden times when there was abundance, and men ate and drank the whole day and yet lay down hungry, in those olden, olden times there was once a Padishah whose days were joyless, for he had never a son to bless himself with.

One day he was relaxing with his Vizier, and when they had drunk their coffee and smoked their chibouks, they went out for a walk, and went on and on till they came to a great valley. Here they sat down to rest a while, and as they were looking about them to the right hand and to the left, the valley was suddenly shaken as if by an earthquake, a whip cracked, and a dervish, a green-robed, yellow-slippered, white-bearded dervish, suddenly stood before them. The Padishah and the Vizier were so frightened that they dared not budge, but when the dervish approached them and addressed them with the words, 'Selamun aleykyum," they took heart a bit, and replied courteously, "Ve aleykyum selam."

"What is your errand here, my lord Padishah?" asked the dervish.

"If you know that I am a Padishah, you also know my errand," replied the Padishah.

Tales of the Meddahs: Tales from the Turkish tradition

Then the dervish took from his bosom an apple, gave it to the Padishah, and said these words, "Give half of this to your Sultana, and eat the other half yourself," and with these words he disappeared.

Then the Padishah went home, gave half the apple to his consort, and ate the other half himself, and in exactly nine months and ten days there was a little prince in the harem. The Padishah was beside himself for joy. He scattered sequins among the poor, restored to freedom his slaves, and the banquet he gave to his friends had neither beginning nor end.

Swiftly flies the time in fairy tales, and the child had reached his fourteenth summer even though his parents still cared for him as a child. One day he said to his father, "My lord father Padishah, make me now a little marble palace, and let there be two springs under it, and let one of them run with honey, and the other with butter!"

Dearly did the Padishah love his little son, because he was his only child, so he made him the marble palace with the springs inside it as his son desired. The King's son sat in the marble palace, and while he was looking at the springs that bubbled forth both butter and honey, he saw an old woman with a pitcher in her hand, and she would have liked to fill it from the spring. Then the King's son caught up a stone and flung it at the old woman's pitcher and broke it into pieces. The old woman said nothing, and she went away.

But the next day she was there again with her pitcher, and again she made as if she would fill it, and a second time the King's son cast a stone at her and broke her pitcher. The old woman went away without speaking a word. She came on the third day also, and it fared with her pitcher then as on the first two days. Then the old woman spoke. "Oh, youth!" cried she, "'tis the will of Allah that you should fall in love with the three Orange-peris," and with that she quitted him.

From then on, the heart of the King's son was consumed by a hidden fire. He began to grow pale and wither away. When the Padishah saw that his son was ill, he sent for the wise men and the leeches, but they could find no remedy for the disease. One day the King's son said to his father, "Oh, my

Tales of the Meddahs: Tales from the Turkish tradition

dear little daddy Shah! These wise men of yours cannot cure me of my disease, and all their labours are in vain. I have fallen in love with the three Oranges, and never shall I be better till I find them."

"Oh, my dear little son!" groaned the Padishah. "You are all that I have in the wide world. If you leave me, in whom can I rejoice?"

Then the King's son slowly withered away, and his days were like a heavy sleep. His father saw that it would be better to let him go forth on his way and find, if he might, the three Oranges that would be the balsam of his soul. "Perhaps he may return again," thought the Padishah.

The King's son arose one day and took with him things that were light to carry, but heavy in the scales of value, and pursued his way over mountains and valleys, rising up and lying down again for many days. At last, in the midst of a vast plain, in front of the high road, he came upon her Satanic Majesty the Mother of Devils, as huge as a minaret. One of her legs was on one mountain, and the other leg on another mountain. She was chewing gum, her mouth being full of it, so that you could hear her half-an-hour's journey off. Her breath was a hurricane, and her arms were yards and yards long.

"Good-day, little mother!" cried the youth, and he embraced the broad waist of the Mother of Devils.

"Good-day, little sonny!" she replied. "If you had not spoken to me so politely, I should have gobbled you up." Then she asked him where he came from and where he was going.

"Alas, dear little mother," sighed the youth, 'such a terrible misfortune has befallen me that I can neither tell you nor answer your question."

"No, come, out with it, my son," urged the Mother of Devils.

"Well then, my sweet little mother," cried the youth, and he sighed worse than before, "I have fallen violently in love with the three Oranges. If only I might find my way to them."

"Hush!" cried the Mother of Devils, "It is not lawful to even think of that name, much less pronounce it. I and my sons are its guardians, yet even we

291

Tales of the Meddahs: Tales from the Turkish tradition

don't know the way to it. Forty sons have I, and they go up and down the earth more than I do. Perhaps they may tell you something of the matter."

When it began to grow dusk towards evening, before the devil-sons had come home, the old woman gave the King's son a tap, and turned him into a pitcher of water. And she did it not a moment too soon, for immediately afterwards the forty sons of the Mother of Devils knocked at the door and cried, "Mother, we smell man's flesh!"

"Nonsense!" cried the Mother of Devils. "What, I should like to know, have the sons of men to do here? It seems to me you had better all clean your teeth." She gave the forty sons forty wooden stakes to clean their teeth with, and out of one's tooth fell an arm, and out of another's a thigh, and out of another's an arm, till they had all cleaned their teeth. Then they sat them down to eat and drink, and in the middle of the meal their mother said to them, "If you had a man for your brother, what would you do with him?"

"Do?" they replied. "Why, love him like a brother, of course!"

Then the Mother of Devils tapped the water-jar, and the King's son stood there again. "Here is your brother!" cried she to her forty sons.

The devils thanked the King's son for his company with great joy, invited their new brother to sit down, and asked their mother why she had not told them about him before, as then they might all have eaten their meal together.

"No, my sons," cried she. "He does not live on the same sort of meat as you. Fowls, mutton, and such-like is what he feeds on."

At this one of them jumped up, went out, fetched a sheep, slew it, and laid it before the new brother.

"Oh, what a child you are!" cried the Mother of Devils. "Do you not know that you must first cook it for him?"

Then they skinned the sheep, made a fire, roasted it, and placed it before him. The King's son ate a piece, and after satisfying his hunger, left the rest of it. "Why, that's nothing!" cried the devils, and they urged him again and

Tales of the Meddahs: Tales from the Turkish tradition

again to eat more. "No, my sons," cried their mother, "men never eat more than that."

"Let us see then what this sheep-meat is like," said one of the forty brothers. So, they fell upon it and devoured the whole lot in a couple of mouthfuls.

Now when they all rose up early in the morning, the Mother of Devils said to her sons, "Our new brother has a great trouble."

"What is it?" cried they, "for we would help him."

"He has fallen in love with the three Oranges!"

"Well," replied the devils, "we do not know the location of the three Oranges ourselves, but perhaps our aunt may know."

"Then lead this youth to her," said their mother, "and tell her that he is my son and worthy of all honour. Let her also receive him as a son and ease him of his trouble." Then the devils took the youth to their aunt and told her on what errand he had come.

Now this Aunt of the Devils had sixty sons, and as she did not know the location of the three Oranges, she had to wait till they came home. But lest any harm should happen to her new son, she gave him a tap and turned him into a piece of crockery.

"We smell man's flesh, mother," cried the devils, as they crossed the threshold.

"Perhaps you have eaten man's flesh, and the remains are still within your teeth," said their mother. Then she gave them great logs of wood that they might pick their teeth clean, and so be able to swallow down something else. But in the midst of the meal the woman gave the piece of crockery a tap, and when the sixty devils saw their little human brother, they rejoiced at the sight, made him sit down at table, and bade him fall to if there was anything there that he took a fancy to.

Tales of the Meddahs: Tales from the Turkish tradition

"My sons," said the Aunt of the Devils to her sixty sons when they all rose up early on the morrow, "this lad here has fallen in love with the three Oranges, can you show him the way there?"

"We do not know the way," replied the devils, "but perhaps our old great-aunt may know something about it."

"Then take the youth there," said their mother, "and bid her hold him in high honour. He is my son, let him be hers also and help him out of his distress." Then they took him off to their Great-Aunt and told her the whole business. "Alas, I do not know, my sons!" said the old, old Great-Aunt, "but if you wait till the evening, when my ninety sons come home, I will ask them."

Then the sixty devils departed and left the King's son there, and when it grew dusk the Great-Aunt of the Devils gave the youth a tap, turned him into a broom, and placed him in the doorway. Shortly afterwards the ninety devils came home, and they also smelt the smell of man, and took the pieces of man's flesh out of their teeth. In the middle of their meal their mother asked them how they would treat a human brother if they had one. When they had sworn upon eggs that they would not hurt so much as his little finger, their mother gave the broom a tap, and the King's son stood before them.

The devil brothers treated him courteously, inquired after his health, and served him so heartily with eatables that they scarcely gave him time to breathe. In the midst of the meal their mother asked them whether they knew where the three Oranges were, for their new brother had fallen in love with them. Then the least of the ninety devils leaped up with a shout of joy and said that he knew.

"Then if you know," said his mother, 'see that you take this son of ours there, that he may satisfy his heart's desire."

On arising next morning, the devil-son took the King's son with him, and the pair of them went merrily along the road together. They went on, and on, and on, and at last the little devil said these words, "My brother, we shall soon come to a large garden, and in the fountain, there are the three Oranges.

Tales of the Meddahs: Tales from the Turkish tradition

When I say to you, 'shut your eye, open your eye!" lay hold of what you see."

They went on a little way further till they came to the garden, and the moment the devil saw the fountain he said to the King's son, 'shut your eye and open your eye!"

He did so and saw the three Oranges bobbing up and down on the surface of the water where it came bubbling out of the spring, and he snatched up one of them and popped it in his pocket. Again, the devil called to him, "Open your eye and shut your eye!" He did so, and snatched up the second orange, and so it was with the third.

"Now take care," said the devil, "that you do not cut open these oranges in any place where there is no water, or it will go ill with you." The King's son promised, and so they parted, one went to the right, and the other to the left.

The King's son went on, and on, and on. He went a long way, and he went a short way, he went across mountains and through valleys. At last, he came to a sandy desert, and there he remembered the oranges, and drawing one out, he cut it open. Scarcely had he cut into it when a damsel, lovely as a Peri, popped out of it before him. The moon when it is fourteen days old is not more dazzling.

"For Allah's sake, give me a drop of water!" cried the damsel, and because there was no trace of water anywhere, she vanished from the face of the earth. The King's son grieved sorely, but there was no help for it, the thing was done.

Again, he went on his way, and when he had gone a little further, he thought to himself, "I may as well cut open one more orange." So, he drew out the second orange, and scarcely had he cut into it than there popped down before him a still more lovely damsel, who begged piteously for water, but as the King's son had none to give her, she also vanished.

"Well, I'll take better care of the third," cried he, and continued his journey. He went on and on till he came to a large spring, drank out of it, and then thought to himself, "Well, now I'll cut open the third orange."

Tales of the Meddahs: Tales from the Turkish tradition

He drew it out and cut it, and immediately a damsel even lovelier than the other two stood before him. As soon as she called for water, he led her to the spring and let her drink, and the damsel did not disappear, but remained there as large as life.

The damsel was mother-naked, and as he could not take her to town like that, he bade her climb up a large tree that stood beside the spring, while he went into the town to buy her raiment and a carriage.

While the King's son had gone away, a servant came to the spring to draw water, and saw the reflection of the damsel in the watery mirror. "Why, I am quite beautiful," said she to herself, "and ever so much lovelier than my mistress, so, she ought to fetch water for me, not I for her." With that she broke the pitcher in two, went home, and when her mistress asked where the pitcher of water was, she replied, "I am much more beautiful than you, so you must fetch water for me, not I for you."

Her mistress took up a mirror, held it before her, and said, "I think you must have taken leave of your senses. Look at this mirror!"

The slave girl looked into the mirror and saw that she was as plain as ever. Without another word she took up the pitcher, went again to the spring, and seeing the damsel's face in the mirror, again fancied that it was hers.

"I'm right, after all," she cried. "I'm ever so much more beautiful than my mistress." She broke the pitcher to pieces again and went home. Again, her mistress asked her why she had not drawn water.

"Because I am ever so much more beautiful than you, so you must draw water for me," replied she.

"You are downright crazy," replied her mistress, drew out a mirror, and showed it to her, and when the slave-girl saw her face in it, she took up another pitcher and went to the fountain for the third time. The damsel's face again appeared in the water, but just as she was about to break the pitcher, the damsel called to her from the tree, "Break not your pitchers, 'tis my face you see in the water, and you will see yours there also."

Tales of the Meddahs: Tales from the Turkish tradition

The slave girl looked up, and when she saw the wondrously beautiful shape of the damsel in the tree, she climbed up beside her and spoke coaxing words to her, "Oh, my little golden damsel, you will get the cramp from crouching there so long. Come, rest your head!" And with that she laid the damsel's head on her breast, felt in her bosom, drew out a needle, pricked the damsel with it in the skull, and in an instant the Orange-Damsel was changed into a bird, and pr-r-r-r, she was gone, leaving the slave girl all alone in the tree.

Now when the King's son came back with his fine coach and beautiful raiment, looked up into the tree, and saw the plain face, he asked the girl what had happened to her.

"A nice question!" replied the slave girl. "Why, you did leave me here all day, and go away, and so of course the sun has tanned and dried my skin."

What could the poor King's son do? He made the damsel sit in the coach and took her straight home to his father's house.

In the palace of the Padishah, they were all waiting, full of eagerness, to behold the Peri-Bride, and when they saw the plain-faced damsel they said to the King's son, "However could you lose your heart to such a plain maid?"

"She is not a plain maid," said the King's son. "I left her at the top of a tree, and she was roasted there by the rays of the sun. If only you let her rest a bit, she'll soon return to her full beauty again." And with that he led her into her chamber and waited for her to return to her natural beauty again.

Now there was a beautiful garden in the palace and one day the Orange-Bird came flying on to a tree there and called down to the gardener.

"What do you want with me?" asked the gardener.

"What is the King's son doing?" inquired the bird.

"He is doing no harm that I know of," replied the gardener.

"And what about his plain-faced bride?"

"Oh, she's there too, sitting with him as usual."

Tales of the Meddahs: Tales from the Turkish tradition

Then the little bird sang these words:

"She may sit by his side,

But she shall not abide,

For all her fair showing

The thorns are a-growing.

As I hop on this tree,

It will wither "neath me."

And with that it flew away. The next day it came again and inquired once more about the King's son and his consort and repeated what it said before. The third day it did in like manner, and as many trees as it hopped upon withered right away beneath it.

One day the King's son felt weary of his strange bride, so he went out into the garden for a walk. Then his eye fell on the withered trees, and he called the gardener and said to him, "What is this, gardener? Why do you not take better care of your trees? Do you not see that they are all withering away?"

Then the gardener replied that it was of but little use for him to take care of the trees, for a few days ago a little bird had been there, and asked what the King's son and his consort were doing and had said that though she might be sitting there, she should not sit for ever, but that thorns would grow, and every tree it lit upon should wither.

The King's son commanded the gardener to smear the trees with birdlime, and if the bird then lit upon it, to bring it to him. So, the gardener smeared the trees with birdlime, and when the bird came there next day he caught it, and brought it to the King's son, who put it in a cage. Now no sooner did the slave woman look upon the bird than she knew at once that it was the damsel. So, she pretended to be very ill, sent for the chief medicine-man, and by dint

Tales of the Meddahs: Tales from the Turkish tradition

of rich gifts persuaded him to say to the King's son that his consort would never get well unless he fed her with such and such birds.

The King's son saw that his consort was very sick, he sent for the doctor, went with him to see the sick woman, and asked him how she was to be cured. The doctor said she could only be cured if they gave her such and such birds to eat.

"Why, only this very day have I caught one of such birds," said the King's son, and they brought the bird, killed it, and fed the sick lady with the flesh. In an instant the plain-faced slave damsel arose from her bed. But one of the bird's dazzling feathers fell accidentally to the ground and slipped between the planks, so that nobody noticed it.

Time went on, and the King's son was still waiting and waiting for his consort to turn back to beauty. Now there was an old woman in the palace who used to teach the dwellers in the harem to read and write. One day as she was going down-stairs she saw something gleaming between the planks of the floor, and going towards it, perceived that it was a bird's feather that sparkled like a diamond. She took it home and thrust it behind a rafter. The next day she went to the palace, and while she was away the bird's feather leaped down from the rafter, shivered a little, and the next moment turned into a most lovely damsel. She tidied the room, cooked the meal, set everything in order, and then leaped back upon the rafter and became a feather again. When the old woman came home, she was amazed at what she saw. She thought, "somebody must have done all this," so she went up and down, backwards and forwards through the house, but she could see nobody.

Early next morning she again went to the palace, and the feather leaped down again in like manner, and did all the household work. When the old woman came home, she perceived the house all nice and clean, and everything in order. "I really must find out the secret of this," thought she, so next morning she made as if she were going away as usual, and left the door ajar, but went and hid herself in a corner. All at once she saw that there was a damsel in the room, who tidied the room and cooked the meal,

Tales of the Meddahs: Tales from the Turkish tradition

whereupon the old woman dashed out, seized hold of her, and asked her who she was and from where she came. Then the damsel told the old woman of her sad fate, and how she had been twice killed by the slave girl and had come there in the shape of a feather.

"Distress yourself no more, my lass," said the old woman. "I'll put your business to rights, and this very day, too." And with that she went straight to the King's son and invited him to come and see her that evening. The King's son was now so sick to death of his strange bride that he was glad of any excuse to escape from his own house, so the evening found him punctually at the old woman's. They sat down to supper, and when the coffee followed the meats, the damsel entered with the cups, and when the King's son saw her, he almost fainted. "No, but, mother," said the King's son, when he had come to himself a little, "who is that damsel?"

"Your wife," replied the old woman.

"How did you get that fair creature?" inquired the King's son. "Will you give her to me?"

"How can I give her to you, seeing that she was your own once upon a time," said the old woman, and with that the old woman took the damsel by the hand, led her to the King's son, and laid her on his breast. "Take better care of the Orange-Peri another time," said she.

The King's son now nearly fainted in real earnest, but it was from sheer joy. He took the damsel to his palace, put to death the plain-faced slave-girl, and then held high festival with the Peri for forty days and forty nights. They had the desire of their hearts, and may Allah satisfy your desires likewise.

Tales of the Meddahs: Tales from the Turkish tradition

HOW THE DEVIL LOST HIS WAGER

This story has been adapted from Told in the Coffee House by Cyrus Adler and Allan Ramsay, published in 1898 by MacMillan and Company, London. Allan Ramsay was a Scottish poet, playwright, publisher, librarian and wig-maker active in the early and mid-eighteenth century. Cyrus Adler adapted Ramsay's work in the nineteenth century, being an American educator, Jewish religious leader and scholar.

A peasant, ploughing his field, was panting with fatigue, when the devil appeared before him and said, "Oh, poor man! You complain of your lot, and with justice, for your labour is not that of a man, but is as heavy as that of a beast of burden. Now I have made a wager that I shall find a contented man, so give me the handle of your plough and the goad of your oxen, that I may do the work for you."

The peasant consenting, the devil touched the oxen and in one turn of the plough all the furrows of the field were opened up and the work finished.

"Is it well done?" asked the devil.

"Yes," replied the man, "but seed is very dear this year."

In answer to this, the devil shook his long tail in the air, and little seeds began to fall like hail from the sky. "I hope," said the devil, "that I have gained my wager."

"Bah," answered the peasant, "what's the good of that? These seeds might be lost. You do not take into consideration frost, blighting winds, drought, damp, storms, diseases of plants, and other things. How can I judge as yet?"

Tales of the Meddahs: Tales from the Turkish tradition

"Behold," said the devil, "in this box are both sun and rain, take it and use it as you please."

The peasant did so and to very good purpose, for his corn soon ripened and up to that time he had never seen so good a harvest. But the corn of his neighbours had also prospered from the rain and sun.

At harvest time the devil came and saw that the man was looking with envious eyes at his neighbour's fields where the corn was as good as his own.

"Have you been able to obtain what you desired?" asked the devil.

"Alas!" answered the man, "All the barns will break down under the weight of the sheaves. The grain will be sold at a low price. This fine harvest will make me sit on ashes."

While he was speaking, the devil had taken an ear of corn from the ground and was crushing it in his hand, and as soon as he blew on the grains, they all turned into pure gold. The peasant took up one and examined it attentively on all sides, and then in a despairing tone cried out, "Oh, my God! I must spend money to melt all these and send them to the mint."

The devil wrung his hands in despair. He had lost his wager. He could do everything, but he could not make a contented man.

Tales of the Meddahs: Tales from the Turkish tradition

THE STAG-PRINCE

This story has been adapted from Turkish Fairy Tales and Folk Tales by Dr. Ignácz Kúnos, published in 1901 by A. H. Bullen, London.

Once upon a time, when the servants of Allah were many, there lived a Padishah who had one son and one daughter. The Padishah grew old, his time came, and he died. His son ruled in his stead, and he had not ruled very long before he had squandered away his whole inheritance.

One day he said to his sister, "Little sister, all our money is spent. If people were to hear that we had nothing left they would drive us out of doors, and we should never be able to look our fellow men in the face again. Far better, therefore, if we depart and take up our abode elsewhere."

So, they tied together the little they had left, and then the brother and sister quitted their father's palace in the night-time and wandered forth into the wide world. They went on and on till they came to a vast sandy desert, where they were like to have fallen to the ground for the burning heat. The youth felt that he could go not a step further, when he saw on the ground a little puddle of water.

"Little sister!" said he, "I will not go a step further till I have drunk this water."

"Nay, dear brother!" replied the girl, "who can tell whether it really be water or filth? If we have held up so long, surely, we can hold up a little longer. We are bound to find water soon."

Tales of the Meddahs: Tales from the Turkish tradition

"I tell you," replied her brother, "that I'll not go another step further till I have drunk up this puddle, though I die for it." With that he knelt down, sucked up every drop of the dirty water, and instantly became a stag.

The little sister wept bitterly at this mischance, but there was nothing for it but to go on as they were. They went on and on, up hills and down dales, right across the sandy waste till they came to a full spring beneath a large tree, and there they sat them and rested.

"Listen now, little sister," said the stag. "You must mount up into that tree, while I go to see if I can find something to eat."

The girl climbed up into the tree, and the stag went about his business, ran up hill and down dale, caught a hare, brought it back, and he and his sister ate it together, and so they lived from day to day and from week to week.

Now the horses of the Padishah of that country were wont to be watered at the spring beneath the large tree. One evening the horsemen led their horses up to it as usual, but just as the horses were on the point of drinking, they caught sight of the reflection of the damsel in the watery mirror and reared back. The horsemen fancied that perhaps the water was not quite pure, so they drew off the trough and filled it afresh, but again the horses reared backwards and would not drink of it. The horsemen did not know what to make of it, so they went and told the Padishah.

"Perhaps the water is muddy," said the Padishah.

"No," replied the horsemen, "we emptied the trough once and filled it full again with fresh water, and yet the horses would not drink of it."

"Go again," said their master, "and look well about you. Perhaps there is someone near the spring of whom they are afraid."

The horsemen returned, and, looking all about the spring, and finally cast their eyes upon the large tree, on the top of which they perceived the damsel. They immediately went back and told the Padishah. The Padishah took the trouble to go and look for himself, and raising his eyes he too saw in the tree a damsel as lovely as the moon when she is fourteen days old, and he

Tales of the Meddahs: Tales from the Turkish tradition

absolutely could not take his eyes off her. "Are you a spirit or a peri?" said the Padishah to the damsel.

"I am neither a spirit nor a peri, but a mortal as you are," replied the damsel.

In vain the Padishah begged her to come down from the tree. In vain he implored her, but nothing he could say would make her come down. Then the Padishah grew angry. He commanded his men to cut down the tree. The men brought their axes and started hewing at the tree. They hewed away at the vast tree, they hewed and hewed until only a little strip of solid trunk remained to be cut through. Then, at eventide, when it began to grow dark, they left off their work, which they proposed to finish the next day.

Scarcely had they departed when the stag came running out of the forest, looked at the tree, and asked the little sister what had happened. The girl told him that she would not descend from the tree, so the Padishah's men had tried to cut it down.

"You did well," replied the stag, "and take care you do not come down in future, whatever they may say." With that he went to the tree, licked it with his tongue, and immediately the tree grew bigger around the hewed trunk than before.

The next day, when the stag had again departed about his business, the Padishah's men came and saw that the tree was larger and harder around the trunk than ever. Again, they set to work hewing at the tree, and hewed and hewed till they had cut half through it, but by that time evening fell upon them again, and again they put off the rest of the work till the morrow and went home.

But all their labour was lost, for the stag came again, licked the gap in the tree with his tongue, and immediately it grew thicker and harder than ever.

Early next morning, when the stag had only just departed, the Padishah and his woodcutters again came to the tree, and when they saw that the trunk of the tree had filled up again larger and firmer than ever, they determined to try some other means. So, they went home again and sent for a famous old witch, told her of the damsel in the tree, and promised her a rich reward if she would, by subtlety, make the damsel come down. The old witch willingly took the matter in hand, and bringing with her an iron tripod, a cauldron, and sundry raw meats, placed them by the side of the spring. She placed the tripod on the ground, and the kettle on the top of it but upside down, drew water from the spring and poured it not into the kettle, but on the ground beside it, and with that she kept her eyes closed as if she were blind.

The damsel fancied she really was blind and called to her from the tree. "No, my dear elder sister! You have placed the kettle on the tripod upside down and are pouring all the water on the ground."

"Oh, my sweet little damsel," cried the old woman, "that is because I have no eyes to see with. I have brought some dirty linen with me, and if you do love Allah, you will come down and put the kettle right, and help me to wash the things."

Then the damsel thought of the words of the little stag, and she did not come down.

The next day the old witch came again, stumbled about the tree, laid a fire, and brought forth a heap of meal in order to sift it, but instead of meal she put ashes into the sieve.

"Poor silly old granny!" cried the damsel compassionately, and then she called down from the tree to the old woman and told her that she was sifting ashes instead of meal.

"Oh, my dear damsel," cried the old woman, weeping. "I am blind, I cannot see. Come down and help me a little in my affliction."

Now the little stag had strictly charged her that very morning not to come down from the tree whatever might be said to her, and she obeyed the words of her brother.

On the third day the old witch again came beneath the tree. This time she brought a sheep with her, and brought out a knife to flay it with, and began to jag and skin it from behind instead of cutting its throat. The poor little

Tales of the Meddahs: Tales from the Turkish tradition

sheep bleated piteously, and the damsel in the tree, unable to endure the sight of the beast's sufferings, came down from the tree to put the poor thing out of its misery. Then the Padishah, who was concealed close to the tree, rushed out and carried the damsel off to his palace.

The damsel pleased the Padishah so mightily that he wanted to be married to her without more ado, but the damsel would not consent till they had brought her brother, the little stag, to her. Until she saw him, she said, she could have not a moment's rest. Then the Padishah sent men out into the forest, who caught the stag and brought him to his sister. After that he never left his sister's side. They lay down together, and together they rose up. Even when the Padishah and the damsel were wedded, the little stag was never far away from them, and in the evening when he found out where they were, he would softly stroke each of them all over with one of his front feet before going to sleep beside them, saying, "This little foot is for my sister. That little foot is for my brother."

But time, as men count it, passes quickly to its fulfilment, more quickly still passes the time of fairy tales, but quickest of all flies the time of true love. Yet our little people would have lived on happily if there had not been a female slave in the palace. Jealousy devoured her at the thought that the Padishah had taken to his bosom the ragged damsel from the tree-top rather than herself, and she watched for an opportunity of revenge.

Now there was a beautiful garden in the palace, with a fountain in the midst of it, and there the Sultan's damsel used to walk about. One day, with a golden saucer in her hand and a silver sandal on her foot, she went towards the great fountain, and the slave followed after her and pushed her in. There was a big fish in the basin, and it immediately swallowed up the Sultan's pet damsel. Then the slave returned to the palace, put on the damsel's golden raiment, and sat down in her place.

In the evening the Padishah came and asked the damsel what she had done to her face that it was so much altered. "I have walked too much in the garden, and so the sun has tanned my face," replied the girl. The Padishah believed her and sat down beside her, but the little stag came also, and when

307

Tales of the Meddahs: Tales from the Turkish tradition

he began to stroke them both down with his forefoot he recognised the slave-girl. He said, "This little foot is for my sister. This little foot is for my brother."

Then it became the one wish of the slave-girl's heart to be rid of the little stag as quickly as possible, lest it should betray her. After a little thought she made herself sick, and sent for the doctors, and gave them much money to say to the Padishah that the only thing that could save her was the heart of the little stag to eat. The doctors went and told the Padishah that the sick woman must swallow the heart of the little stag, or there was no hope for her. Then the Padishah went to the slave-girl whom he fancied to be his pet damsel, and asked her if it did not go against her to eat the heart of her own brother?

"What can I do?" sighed the impostor, "if I die, what will become of my poor little pet? If he be cut up, I shall live, while he will be spared the torments of those poor beasts that grow old and sick." Then the Padishah gave orders that a butcher's knife should be whetted, and a fire lighted, and a cauldron of water put over the fire.

The poor little stag saw all the bustling about and ran down into the garden to the fountain, and called out three times to his sister, "The knife is on the stone. The water's on the boil. Hurry, little sister, hurry!"

And three times she answered back to him from the fish's maw, "Here am I in the fish's belly. In my hand I hold a golden saucer. On my foot is a silver sandal. In my arms a little Padishah!" For the Sultan's pet damsel had brought forth a little son while she lay in the fish's belly.

Now the Padishah was intent on catching the little stag when it ran down into the garden to the fountain, and, coming up softly behind it, heard every word of what the brother and sister were saying to each other. He quietly ordered all the water to be drained off the basin of the fountain, drew up the fish, cut open its belly, and what do you think he saw? In the belly of the fish was his wife, with a golden saucer in her hand, and a silver sandal on her foot, and a little son in her arms. Then the Padishah embraced his wife,

Tales of the Meddahs: Tales from the Turkish tradition

and kissed his son, and brought them both to the palace, and heard the tale of it all to the very end.

But the little stag found something in the fish's blood, and when he had swallowed it, he became a man again. Then he rushed to his sister, and they embraced and wept with joy over each other's happiness.

But the Padishah sent for his slave girl and asked her which she would like the best; four good steeds or four good swords. The slave-girl replied, "Let the swords be for the throats of my enemies but give me the four steeds that I may take my pleasure on horseback." Then they tied the slave-girl to the tails of four good steeds and sent her out for a ride; and the four steeds tore the girl into little bits and scattered them abroad.

But the Padishah and his wife lived happily together, and the king's son who had been a stag lived with them. They gave a great banquet, which lasted four days and four nights, and they attained their desires, and may you, O my readers, attain your desires likewise.

Tales of the Meddahs: Tales from the Turkish tradition

Tales of the Meddahs: Tales from the Turkish tradition

THE EFFECTS OF RAKI

This story has been adapted from Told in the Coffee House by Cyrus Adler and Allan Ramsay, published in 1898 by MacMillan and Company, London. Allan Ramsay was a Scottish poet, playwright, publisher, librarian and wig-maker active in the early and mid-eighteenth century. Cyrus Adler adapted Ramsay's work in the nineteenth century, being an American educator, Jewish religious leader and scholar.

Bekri Mustafe, who lived during the reign of Sultan Selim, was a celebrated toper, and perhaps at that time the only Muslim drunkard in Turkey. Consequently, he was often the subject of conversation in circles both high and low. It happened that his Majesty the Sultan had occasion to speak to Bekri one day, and he asked him what pleasure he found in drinking so much raki, and why he disobeyed the laws of the Prophet. Bekri replied that raki was a boon to man, that it made the deaf to hear, the blind to see, the lame to walk, and the poor rich, and that he, Bekri, when drunk, could hear, see, and walk like two Bekris. The Sultan, to verify the truth of this statement, sent his servants into the highways to bring four men, the one blind, the other deaf, the third lame, and the fourth poor. Directly these were brought, his Majesty ordered raki to be served to them in company with Bekri.

They had not been drinking long when, to the glory of Bekri, the deaf man said, "I hear the sound of great rumbling."

And the blind man replied, "I can see him. It is an enemy who seeks our destruction."

Tales of the Meddahs: Tales from the Turkish tradition

The lame man asked where he was, saying, "show him to me, and I will quickly despatch him."

And the poor man called out, "Don't be afraid to kill him. I've got his blood money in my pocket."

Just then a funeral happened to pass by the Palace buildings, and Bekri got up and ordered the solemn procession to stop. Removing the lid of the coffin, he whispered a few words into the ear of the dead man, and then putting his ear to the dead man's mouth, vented an exclamation of surprise. He then ordered the funeral to proceed and returned to the Palace.

The Sultan asked him what he had said to the dead man, and what the dead man replied.

"I simply asked him where he was going and from what he had died, and he replied he was going to Paradise, and that he had died from drinking raki without a mézé."

Whereupon the Sultan understanding what he wanted, ordered that the mézé should be immediately served.

Tales of the Meddahs: Tales from the Turkish tradition

HISTORICAL NOTES

This section contains some brief biographical notes about the original collectors and their books featured in this collection. These notes have been adapted from those primarily on Wikipedia along with other supporting sources and notes.

Andrew Lang

Andrew Lang FBA was a Scottish poet, novelist, literary critic, and contributor to the field of anthropology. He is best known as a collector of folk and fairy tales. The Andrew Lang lectures at the University of St Andrews are named after him.

Lang was born on 31st March 1844 in Selkirk. He was the eldest of the eight children born to John Lang, the town clerk, and his wife Jane Plenderleath Sellar, who was the daughter of Patrick Sellar, factor to the first duke of Sutherland. On 17th April 1875, he married Leonora Blanche Alleyne, youngest daughter of C. T. Alleyne of Clifton and Barbados. She was (or should have been) variously credited as author, collaborator, or translator of Lang's Colour / Rainbow Fairy Books, which he edited.

He was educated at Selkirk Grammar School, Loretto School, and the Edinburgh Academy, as well as the University of St Andrews and Balliol College, Oxford, where he took a first class in the final classical schools in 1868, becoming a fellow and subsequently honorary fellow of Merton College. He soon made a reputation as one of the most able and versatile

Tales of the Meddahs: Tales from the Turkish tradition

writers of the day as a journalist, poet, critic, and historian. In 1906, he was elected FBA.

He died of angina pectoris on 20th July 1912 at the Tor-na-Coille Hotel in Banchory, survived by his wife. He was buried in the cathedral precincts at St Andrews, where a monument can be visited in the south-east corner of the 19th century section.

Lang is now chiefly known for his publications on folklore, mythology, and religion. The earliest of his publications is *Custom and Myth* (1884). In *Myth, Ritual and Religion* (1887) he explained the "irrational" elements of mythology as survivals from more primitive forms. Lang's *Making of Religion* was heavily influenced by the 18th century idea of the "noble savage", in it, he maintained the existence of high spiritual ideas among so-called 'savage" races, drawing parallels with the contemporary interest in occult phenomena in England.

His *Blue Fairy Book* (1889) was a beautifully produced and illustrated edition of fairy tales that has become a classic. This was followed by many other collections of fairy tales, collectively known as *Andrew Lang's Fairy Books*. In the preface of the *Lilac Fairy Book* he credits his wife with translating and transcribing most of the stories in the collections.

Lang was one of the founders of "psychical research" and his other writings on anthropology include *The Book of Dreams and Ghosts* (1897), *Magic and Religion* (1901) and *The Secret of the Totem* (1905). He served as President of the Society for Psychical Research in 1911.

He collaborated with S. H. Butcher in a prose translation (1879) of Homer's *Odyssey*, and with E. Myers and Walter Leaf in a prose version (1883) of the *Iliad*, both still noted for their archaic but attractive style.

Lang's writings on Scottish history are characterised by a scholarly care for detail, a piquant literary style, and a gift for disentangling complicated questions. *The Mystery of Mary Stuart* (1901) was a consideration of the fresh light thrown on Mary, Queen of Scots, by the Lennox manuscripts in

Tales of the Meddahs: Tales from the Turkish tradition

the University Library, Cambridge, approving of her and criticising her accusers.

Lang was active as a journalist in various ways, ranging from sparkling "leaders" for the Daily News to miscellaneous articles for the Morning Post, and for many years he was literary editor of Longman's Magazine.

Allan Ramsay

At the time of compiling these notes I have yet to find out anything significant about Allan Ramsay, who worked alongside Cyrus Adler, whose brief biography is next in this section. All that I do know is that our Allan Ramsay was married to Winifred, and that he is not related to the Scottish Ramsay family, with father and son, both named Allan, playing substantial roles in the Scottish Enlightenment of the eighteenth century, the father being a poet and the son an artist.

Hopefully one day soon I'll be able to add more notes here…

Cyrus Adler

Adler was born in Van Buren, Arkansas on September 13, 1863, but in the next year his parents removed to Philadelphia, Pennsylvania, and soon he attended the public schools there, and in 1879 he entered the University of Pennsylvania, where he graduated in 1883. He afterwards pursued Oriental studies at Johns Hopkins University, was appointed university scholar there in 1884, and was fellow in Semitic languages from 1885 to 1887, when he gained the first American Ph.D. in Semitics from the University, where he was appointed instructor in Semitic languages and promoted to be associate professor in 1890. He taught Semitic languages at Johns Hopkins from 1884 to 1893.

In 1877 he was appointed assistant curator of the section of Oriental antiquities in the United States National Museum and had charge of an exhibit of biblical archaeology at the centennial exposition of the Ohio

Tales of the Meddahs: Tales from the Turkish tradition

valley in 1888. He was a commissioner for the world's Columbian exposition to the Orient in 1890, and he passed sixteen months in Turkey, Syria, Egypt, Tunis, Algiers, and Morocco securing exhibits. For a number of years, he was employed by the Smithsonian Institution at Washington, with a focus on archaeology and Semitics, serving as the Librarian from December 1, 1892, to 1905. In 1895, after years of searching, he located the Jefferson Bible and purchased it for the Smithsonian Institution from the great-granddaughter of Thomas Jefferson.

He was made lecturer on biblical archaeology in the Jewish Theological Seminary in New York, president of the American Jewish Historical Society, U.S. delegate to a conference on an international catalogue of scientific literature in 1898, and honorary assistant curator of historic archaeology and custodian of historic religions in the U.S. national museum.

In 1900, he was elected as a member of the American Philosophical Society.

He was also a founder of the Jewish Welfare Board. He was president of Dropsie College for Hebrew and Cognate Learning from 1908 to 1940 and Chancellor of the Jewish Theological Seminary of America. In addition, he was a founding member of the Oriental Club of Philadelphia. He was involved in the creation of various Jewish organizations including the Jewish Publication Society, the American Jewish Historical Society, the American Jewish Committee (also its president in 1929–1940), and the United Synagogue of America. Adler served a variety of organizations by holding various offices. For example, he was on the board of trustees at the American Jewish Publication Society and Gratz College, served as vice-president of the Anthropological Society of Washington, and as member of council of the Philosophical Society of Washington.

Adler was a bachelor much of his life, marrying Racie Friedenwald of Baltimore in 1905, when he was 42. They had one child, a daughter Sarah. From 1911 until 1916, Adler was Parnas (president) of Congregation Mikveh Israel of Philadelphia. He died in Philadelphia, and his papers are held by the Center for Advanced Judaic Studies at the University of Pennsylvania.

Tales of the Meddahs: Tales from the Turkish tradition

Adler was an editor of the Jewish Encyclopaedia and in collaboration with Allen Ramsay wrote *Tales Told in a Coffee House* (1898). He was part of the committee that translated the Jewish Publication Society version of the Hebrew Bible published in 1917. At the end of World War I, he participated in the Paris Peace Conference in 1919.

He was also a contributor to the New International Encyclopaedia. His many scholarly writings include articles on comparative religion, Assyriology, and Semitic philology. He edited the *American Jewish Year Book* from 1899 to 1905 and the *Jewish Quarterly Review* from 1910 to 1940. He also contributed to the *Journal of the American Oriental Society*, the *Proceedings of the American Philological Association*, the *Andover Review*, *Hebraica*, *Johns Hopkins University Circular* and numerous reviews.

Dr. Ignácz Kúnos

Ignácz Kúnos was born as Ignácz Lusztig on 22nd September 1860, in Hajdúsámson in Hungary. He was a Hungarian linguist, Turkologist, folklorist, and a correspondent member of the Hungarian Academy of Sciences. At his time, he was one of the most recognised scholars of Turkish folk literature and Turkish dialectology.

Kúnos attended the Reformed College in Debrecen, then studied linguistics at the Budapest University between 1879 and 1882. With the financial support of the Hungarian Academy of Sciences and the Budapest Jewish community he spent five years in Constantinople studying Turkish language and culture. In 1890 he was appointed at the Budapest University as professor of Turkish philology. Between 1899-1919 he was the director of the newly organized Oriental College of Commerce in Budapest. From 1919 until 1922 he held the same post at the Oriental Institute integrated into the Budapest University of Economics, and then from 1922 he taught Turkish linguistics at the university. In the summer of 1925 and 1926, invited by the Turkish government, he was a professor at the Ankara and Istanbul

Tales of the Meddahs: Tales from the Turkish tradition

Universities, and in 1925 he organized the Department of Folkloristics at Istanbul University. He died during the soviet siege of Budapest in 1945.

At the beginning of his career, he mainly focused on the dialectology, phonological and morphological matters of the Hungarian language as well as the ones of the Mordvinic languages. Being a pupil of Ármin Vámbéry, his interest was directed towards Turkish language and philology. From 1885 until 1890, during his stay in Constantinople, he traveled to Rumelia, Anatolia, Syria, Palestine and Egypt. During his trip he observed and studied the characteristics of the Turkish dialects, ethnography, folk poetry and folk customs of Turkish and other local peoples. One significant achievement was that he collected an impressive amount of folk tales and anecdotes that were published in Hungarian as well as many other European languages. As a recognition of his scientific contributions, he was elected a correspondent member of the Hungarian Academy of Sciences, but he also was a vice-president of the International Society for the Investigation of Central and Eastern Asia.

Epiphanius Wilson, A.M.

Epiphanius Wilson was born in Liverpool in 1845. After ordination as an Episcopal minister, Wilson became a missionary to Labrador, Newfoundland.

Afterward, he was a professor of classics at Queens College, Windsor, Nova Scotia, and la-er, rector of St. Mark's Church, Mount Kisco, New York.

After leaving St. Mark's, he was literary editor of *The Churchman* for many years. He was foreign edi-or for the *Literary Digest* between 1904 and 1914, translating extracts from Spanish, Italian, French and German newspapers, and was one of the editors of the *Library of Modern Eloquence.*

Tales of the Meddahs: Tales from the Turkish tradition

ORIGINAL FICTION BY CLIVE GILSON

- Songs of Bliss
- Out of the Walled Garden
- The Mechanic's Curse
- The Insomniac Booth
- A Solitude of Stars

AS EDITOR – *FIRESIDE TALES – Part 1, Europe*

- Tales From the Land of Dragons
- Tales From the Land of The Brave
- Tales From the Land of Saints And Scholars
- Tales From the Land of Hope And Glory
- Tales From Lands of Snow and Ice
- Tales From the Viking Isles
- Tales From the Forest Lands
- Tales From the Old Norse
- More Tales About Saints and Scholars
- More Tales About Hope and Glory
- More Tales About Snow and Ice
- Tales From the Land of Rabbits
- Tales Told by Bulls and Wolves
- Tales of Fire and Bronze
- Tales From the Land of the Strigoi
- Tales Told by the Wind Mother
- Tales from Gallia
- Tales from Germania

Tales of the Meddahs: Tales from the Turkish tradition

EDITOR – *FIRESIDE TALES – Part 2, North America*

- Okaraxta - Tales from The Great Plains
- Tibik-Kìzis – Tales from The Great Lakes & Canada
- Jóhonaa'éí –Tales from America's Southwest
- Qugaaĝix̂ - First Nation Tales from Alaska & The Arctic
- Karahkwa - First Nation Tales from America's Eastern States
- Pot-Likker - Folklore, Fairy Tales, and Settler Stories from America

EDITOR – *FIRESIDE TALES – Part 3, Africa*

- Arokin Tales – Folklore & Fairy Tales from West Africa
- Hadithi Tales – Folklore & Fairy Tales from East Africa
- Inkathaso Tales – Folklore & Fairy Tales from Southern Africa
- Tarubadur Tales – Folklore & Fairy Tales from North Africa
- Elephant And Frog – Folklore from Central Africa

Tales of the Meddahs: Tales from the Turkish tradition

ABOUT THE EDITOR

I was born in 1962 into a predominantly sporting household – Dad being a good senior amateur and lower league professional footballer, as well as running his own businesses in partnership with mum, herself an accomplished and medal winning dancer.

I obtained a degree in History from Leeds University before wandering rather haphazardly into the emerging world of information technology in the late nineteen-eighties.

A little like my sporting father, I followed a succession of amateur writing paths alongside my career in technology, including working as a freelance journalist and book reviewer, my one claim to fame being a by-line in a national newspaper, The Sunday People.

I also spent 10 years treading the boards, appearing all over the south of the UK in pantos and plays, in village halls and occasionally on the stage of a professional theatre or two.

Following the sporting theme, and a while after I hung up my own boots, I worked on live TV broadcasts for the BBC, ITV, TVNZ, and EuroSport as a rugby 'stato', covering Heineken Cups, Six Nations, World Sevens and World Cups in the late '90's. You can find out more at: www.clivegilson.com

Printed in the USA
CPSIA information can be obtained
at www.ICGtesting.com
LVHW091334261023
761971LV00009B/181/J